RIVER

Esther Kinsky grew up by the river Rhine and lived in London for twelve years. She is the author of three volumes of poetry and two novels (*Summer Resort* and *Banatsko*) and has translated many notable English (John Clare, Henry David Thoreau, Lewis Grassic Gibbon) and Polish (Miron Białoszewski, Zygmunt Haupt, Ida Fink, Olga Tokarczuk) authors into German. *River* won the Adelbert von Chamisso Prize 2016, the Franz Hessel Prize 2014, the Kranichsteiner Literature Prize 2015 and the SWR Prize for the best fiction book 2015, and was longlisted for the German Book Prize 2014.

Iain Galbraith was born and grew up on the west coast of Scotland and now lives in Germany. He is a poet and translator (Natascha Wodin, Alfred Kolleritsch, W. G. Sebald, Jan Wagner) and has received several prizes for his work, including, most recently, the Popescu European Poetry Translation Prize (2015) and the Schlegel-Tieck Prize (2016).

'*River* is an unusual and stealthy sort of book in that it's the opposite of what it appears to be – which is a rather apt dissimulation, as it turns out. Yes, it rifles through both the rich and rank materials of the world, turning over its trinkets and its tat, in a manner that is initially quite familiar – however, this curious inventory demonstrates an eye for the grotesque and does not hold the world aloft, or in place. Here, details blur boundaries rather than reaffirming them, positing a worldview that is haunted and uncanny. Shifting through unremarkable terrain we encounter the departed, the exiled, the underneath, the other side. We are on firm ground, always; yet whether that ground is here or there, now or then, is, increasingly, a distinction that is difficult and perhaps irrelevant to make. Sea or sky, boy or girl, east or west, king or vagrant, silt or gold; by turns grubby, theatrical, and exquisite, we are closer to the realm of Bakhtin's carnival than we are to the well-trod paths of psychogeography. Kinsky's *River* does indeed force us to stop in our tracks and take in the opposite side.'
—— Claire-Louise Bennett, author of *Pond*

'Esther Kinsky's novel outlasts everything that has recently been published in the German language with patient stamina. It is full of culture without being erudite, and full of knowledge without being smart-alecky. *River* is a democratic book, witty, wise and touchingly beautiful.'
—— Katharina Teutsch, *Frankfurter Allgemeine Zeitung*

'Written in a style that is both precise and dream-like, *River* is a great book about the obliteration of landscape.'
—— Christine Lecerf, *Le Monde*

'An extraordinary book and a major writer.'
—— Nelly Kapriélan, *Les Inrockuptibles*

Fitzcarraldo Editions

RIVER

ESTHER KINSKY

Translated by

IAIN GALBRAITH

For the blind child

CONTENTS

'Your eye, the wanderer, sees more.'
— Charles Olson, 'A Discrete Gloss'

I. KING

Some time before I left London I happened upon the King. I saw him in the evening, in the turquoise twilight. He was standing at the park entrance gazing east, where a deep, blue haze was already ascending, while behind him the sky was still aglow. Moving out of the shadow of the bushes by the gate he took a series of short soft-footed steps to the edge of the green, above which, at this time of the day, the many ravens of the park flew in restless circles.

The King stretched out his hands and the ravens gathered around him. Several settled on his arms, shoulders and hands, briefly flapping their wings, lifting again and flying a short distance, then returning. Perhaps each bird wanted to touch him at least once, or perhaps they had no choice. Thus encircled by birds, he began to make gentle swinging and circling movements with his arms, as if they were haunted by a memory of wings.

The King wore a magnificent headdress of stiff, brocaded cloths, held together by a clasp adorned with feathers. The gold thread of the brocade and the clasp itself still gleamed in the declining light. He was attired in a short robe, with gold-embroidered edgings shimmering around his neck and wrists. The robe, which hung to his thighs, was bluey-green and fashioned from a taut, heavy fabric with a woven feather pattern. His long black legs protruded beneath the cloth. They were naked, and on his bare, wizened-looking feet, whose wrinkles contrasted oddly with his youthfully slim and sinewy knees and calves, he wore wedge-heeled sandals. The King was very tall and stood upright among these birds, and as he let his arms circle and swing his neck remained straight and steady, as if he kept a whole world in his headdress. His profile stood out against the western sky, and all I can say about it is that it was regal, conversant with grandeur, but also used to desolation. He was a king turned melancholy in his majesty, far from his country, where his subjects probably thought of him as missing or deposed. Nothing about his figure was connected to the surrounding landscape: to the towering age-old trees, the late roses of a mild winter, the surprising emptiness of the marshland opening up beyond the steep downward slope at the edge of the park, as if this was where the town abruptly ended. In his stark solitude he had emerged as a king at the edge of a park that the great city had more or less forgotten, and these birds with their sooty flutter and fading croaks were his sole allies.

The park was empty at this hour. The observant Jewish women and children who walked here during the afternoon had long since gone home, as had the Hasidic boys, whom I sometimes espied at lunchtime nervously giggling and smoking behind the bushes. Their sidelocks trembled when they were cold, and, as I saw from the length of the red glow that briefly appeared in front of each mouth in turn, they drew far too hurriedly on the cigarette they were passing round, while a hubbub of voices and children's singing carried in waves from the windows of their school beyond the park hedge, rising and falling in the wind. The rose trees, with the exception of those still sporting yellowish-pink blossoms in this frostless, misty-white winter, carried dark red rose hips. By the time of day when the King put in his appearance, the rose hips hung drably in the dusk.

At the foot of the slope, behind the trees, flowed the river Lea. In wintertime its water glittered between the bare branches. Behind it stretched the marshland and meadows, which, as evening fell, resembled the enormous palm of a hand full of ever thickening twilight, across which the occasional brightly lit train snaked on its north-easterly journey along the raised embankment.

It was quite still in the early evening when I walked back through the streets from the park to my flat. Now and again an observant Jew would come hurrying by, giving me a wide berth as he passed; more rarely still I would see children; they were always rushing along to prayers, a meeting, a meal, or some other duty. They often had rustling plastic bags of shopping dangling from their hands, especially loaves, which stood out visibly through the thin polythene. On Saturdays and holidays, when windows were open in warmer weather, the sing-song of blessings could be heard on the street. There was the clatter of china, children's voices, small groups of the pious passing to and fro between temple and home. In the evenings the men stood in the glow of the street lamps laughing, their faces relaxed, the feast behind them.

Back in my flat I stood at the bay window in the front room and watched the day turning to night. The shops on the other side of the street were brightly lit. Greengrocer Katz packed delivery boxes until late in the evening, orders for prudent housewives and their families: grapes, bananas, biscuits, soft drinks in various colours. Once a week, in the morning, Greengrocer Katz took delivery of these soft drinks. The orange, pink and yellow plastic bottles were manhandled out of a lorry on pallets and shouldered by assistants to be carried to a storeroom at the back of the shop.

Next door to Greengrocer Katz was a pool club, which stayed open until the early hours. Men, always black, could be discerned in the dim, smoke-filled

17

interior, often pacing with a thoughtful stoop around the pool tables, or leaning over them, intently focussed. Big cars halted in front of the café; men came and went, often accompanied by beautiful, strikingly-dressed women. There were fights. Once there was a gunshot; the police appeared, followed by an ambulance, and the flickering blue of its light filled my room.

After many years I had excised myself from the life I had led in town, just as one might cut a figure out of a landscape or group photo. Abashed by the harm I had wreaked on the picture left behind, and unsure where the cut-out might end up next, I lived a provisional existence. I did so in a place where I knew none of my neighbours, where the street names, views, smells and faces were all unfamiliar to me, in a cheaply appointed flat where, for a while, I would be able to lay my life aside. My furniture and packing cases stood about in the cold rooms in a random jumble, apparently committed to oblivion, just as undecided as I was, and uncertain whether a serviceable domestic order of any kind could ever be re-established. We, the objects and I, had left our old house one blue and early morning with the August moon still visible against the bright haze of a late summer's sky, and we were now loafing about in East London, all our prospects wintery. Tirelessly, we played out the farewell scenes we hadn't had. With a slowness that seemed like eternity, imaginary cheeks and hands brushed, teardrops welled in the corners of eyes, interminable trembling of every book's, picture's or piece of furniture's lower lip, throats choking on speech at every turn; a slow-motion valediction, turning to a scar before the ending had even come, every second of it as long as a day, and all movement heavy going, an unspeakable crunching as through frozen snow.

When I slept I dreamed of the dead: my father, my grandparents, people I had known. In a small room accessed by several steps from the main flat, and just long enough for me to stretch out and sleep on the floor when I felt like it, I spent hours trying to memorise every detail I saw in the yard, the garden, and the section of the street that was visible between two houses. I got to know the light too. From April until August I read what the big sycamore wrote on the one-windowed brick wall of a neighbouring house at the bottom of the garden. It was late summer, it was autumn, then it was winter. Spring came, a west wind, shadows of leaves scribbling notes to the station, where a few metres beyond the garden on the tracks below a train came to a halt every quarter-hour. Or, more seldom, a north wind, with the last leaves flickering unquietly across the whole wall in the sharp light; by midday the shadow of the treetop was as clearly defined on the wall as the map of some unknown town. Winter, after a stormy autumn, was unusually windless, and the bare tree appeared on the wall as a barely perceptible shadow in the uniformly milky light; it wrote messages that were hard to decipher, as if sent from far away, but which, because of the peaceful justice shown by this light towards all things that lacked shadows, were not sad.

I lay awake at night, listening to the new noises around me. The trains beyond the garden stopped with a long-grinding groan and a sigh. In time, I learned that the groaning sounds came from the trains on their way from the city centre, which, shooting out of a tunnel just before the station, seemed taken aback by the proximity of the platform and ground to a halt, whereas the commuter trains bound for the centre sighed and softly squeaked. Somebody on crutches that creaked like old

19

bedsprings hobbled about on the narrow path between the garden and the railway embankment, which fell away to the platforms and tracks. The man on crutches sometimes sang, a sound that was quiet and dark; the contours of his head could be made out in the lamplight, looming above the fence. He was doing business, and his customers came and went, the wind bringing scraps of their conversation. Sometimes he was forced to make a run for it, and the metallic wheezing of his spring-borne crutches would recede amid the flurry of thumping feet of those who had taken flight with him.

Foxes were mating on the flat gravel-strewn roof of an annexe. They let out yearning barks and cries, and the chippings scattered in all directions under their darting, scrabbling paws, some flying against the window of my room. Once I went to the window to look. Motionless in the lamplight, the foxes stared right at me. From that moment onwards I thought of the man on crutches as fox-like.

I spent my days walking in the area, enjoying the sight of the pale Hasidic children in their islands of sheltered piety, on their way to school, or running messages to the shops, and remembered the little girl in West End Lane whom I had often encountered on afternoons years before, with her calf-length, dark-blue skirt usually askew, her thick glasses and fine hair. She was always alone, pushing her small but forceful determination in front of her fearful, short-sighted eyes like a wedge before which the pedestrians approaching on the pavement would part to let her pass. Here, the children went in groups, white-skinned and fearful of strangers, keenly devoted to their own world; maybe this was a good life, secluded from the things that were going on outside their streets. Shortly after arriving in the area I happened upon Springfield Park. It was a cloudy day, and not many people were about. A group of gaily dressed African women were toing and froing between the viewing-bench niches along the cropped hedge, apparently looking for something. They called aloud to one another, glancing here and there, staring down at the ground as if attempting to rediscover a track they had followed into the park and subsequently lost. A flock of crows rose into the air, their beating wings creating a commotion; after a semi-circle over the grass, they settled again on the other side of the lawn, watchful of the rose bushes, the African women, me.

There were also houses in the distance across the marshes, but it was as if they belonged to a different country. The rose beds, the rare exotic trees, the extensive glazing of the sleepy café, the trimmed hedges around the benches, all of these signified a town, contrasting with the land that stretched out at the foot of the slope: flatlands on thin ground over water, already a part of the Thames Estuary area.

The river Lea, here dividing the town from open terrain, does not have a long journey. Rising among the low hills to the northwest of London, it flows through smiling countryside before reaching the frayed urban edgelands and snaking through endless suburbs. It then casts an arm around the old, untameably streetwise, commercial centre of London, and finally, eight miles southeast of Springfield Park, and as one of several solicitous tributaries from the north and west that deposit their sand and gravel at the city's feet, flows into a Thames that is already bound for the sea. On its way, constantly brushing with the city and with the tales told along its banks, the Lea branches, forms new little arms that reach into the meadowland and boggy thickets, hides for a couple of miles at a time behind different names, but after squirming in indecision and unravelling into its muddy delta, it has no choice but to flow between the factories and expressways of Leamouth into the Thames, which it reaches just upstream of the sea-monster-like gates of the flood barrier and the large sugar factory, which, for riverboats, marks the mouth of the city.

The Lea is a small river, populated by swans. White, still and aloof, almost imperceptibly hostile to spectators, they sail through the dwindling light. That autumn, however, I noticed how many of them were intent on becoming wild. They chased each other across the water, flying a couple of metres above the surface, uttering helpless, sullen cries, their underwing plumage dirty and ruffled, their stretched out necks and focussed heads fiercely thirsting for adventure. A few moments later they would be floating along on the surface again, each and every one of them Crown property, sometimes coveted by migrant Gypsies, who, so people said, loved them for their gamey, somewhat bitter flavour.

Now that I had discovered the park and the marshes, the paths I followed led me there almost every day. I generally walked downstream, a little bit further each time, sticking to the river as if clutching a rope while balancing on a narrow footbridge. On its back the river carried the sky, the trees along its banks, the withered cob-like blooms of water plants, black squiggles of birds against the clouds. Between the empty lands to the east of the river and the estates and factories along the other bank, I rediscovered bits and pieces of my childhood, found snippets cut from other landscapes and group photographs, unexpectedly come here to roost. I stumbled on them between willows under a tall sky, in reflections of impoverished housing estates on the town side of the river, amongst a scatter of cows on a meadow, in the contours of old brick buildings – factories, offices, former warehouses – against an exceptionally red-orange sunset, along the raised railway embankment where forlorn-looking, quaintly clattering trains receded into the distance, or when watching roaming gangs of children lighting fires and burning odds and ends, fighting each other close to the flames, and unresponsive when a mother, standing between lines of flapping washing, held one hand up to shelter her eyes as she called them in.

I saw the King when I returned from my walks. Leaving the river behind me, I would climb the slope and there he would be at the top, on the grass plateau, or still on his way from the shadows by the entrance, like a sentinel. Without wanting or knowing it and certainly without noticing me returning from the river, he marked for me the moment of transition between a landscape abandoned to all kinds of wildness, and the city.

I did not come across the King in any other place, and had trouble imagining him in a flat in the dark red-brick building opposite the park entrance, or in one of the newer, rough-and-ready terraces along my short walk from the park to the loud main road I had to cross. I felt relieved never to have seen him emerging from one of the dark alleyways between the old blocks of flats, or returning to the pale cone of lamplight in the doorway of one of the box-like houses.

II. HORSE SHOE POINT

At the foot of Springfield Park was a small village of houseboats on the river Lea. Surrounded by swans, the boats had presumably long since become one with the mud and rushes, their taste for cruising the river lost in days gone by, their anchors inextricably snarled in the roots of the bushes along the bank. As long as it was not too cold in the evenings the inhabitants sat on deck, clattering with plates and cutlery, while cats arched their backs between pots of geraniums. With all pretence to mobility forfeit, this theatre of sedentariness was, for the time being, the city's parting word. On the other side of the river was an alder carr, a semi-wild place where mist would gather on colder days. This whole grove could have become the Erl-King's enchanted realm had not park employees, unschooled in wildness, tried their hand at deforestation. They had wanted to get the better of this place between marsh and alder grove: they had tried to turn it into a picnic spot, but had evidently reconsidered. Table and bench stood athwart wild growth on a levelled triangle of grass, hemmed in by mounds of earth that were now overgrown with weeds. The felled trees in the alder carr lay where they had fallen. The glade was a product of senseless decimation, and was already thick with saplings. Despite the celandine and wild green of the anemones and violets surrounding the abandoned tree trunks and orphaned stumps, it remained a scene of devastation, for a moment awakening a similar unease in me to that aroused by the little aisles cut through the woods of my childhood, where the raw stumps of felled trees jutting out of the low undergrowth, those cleanly sawn seats, spelled only the absence of any gathering, and my grandfather, in his tone of voice reserved for warnings, would say: Hush now – for these are the seats of the Invisible!

It was a small piece of land, more suited to short forays than proper walks. Further into the grove the ground became boggy, and a pool would gather there after rainy days. Nobody strayed here, and in spite of the swathes slashed through the trees, the grove had something unruly about it, indeed the very attempts to tame it had made its impenetrability plain for all to see, so that walkers tended to avoid it and stick to the marked-out paths that pushed into the marshes before petering out. Young Jewish couples took their Saturday afternoon walk along these ways; phlegmatic dog-owners trudged along the levelled paths with panting terriers, turning on their tracks as soon as the gravel gave way to grass.

I discovered the little wood on a map, and also its name: Horse Shoe Point. It was practically an islet, or holm, a limb of marshland that caused the river to curve in a gentle loop around its mysterious island shape. I visited the alder grove every day. Late summer soon slipped into autumn: I sat on the tree stumps, stroking their bark, the encrusted furrows on a watery gloss. I heard curlews, lapwings, bitterns, melancholy calls from throats not at all in mourning, and saw my grandmother standing at the window again, emitting these calls, imagining she could beguile the birds, and that the sadness of her heart gave her the facility of imitating cries from throats that were in fact perfectly serene and wholly innocent of their heart-rending sound. Thus nature touches a human life – its dispassionate heartbeat tipping the balance of a sorrow we call heartfelt. Under a pale sun and in the whitish, shadowless light peculiar to this place and these seasons, I took to following tracks which, time and again, led me back through the alder grove. This partly mutilated wetland wood with its childhood flowers and wild birds secretly appealing to my memory was my gateway to the lower reaches, to the path downstream that gradually taught me, during the final months of my stay, to find my own names for a city I had already spent many years labouring to decipher – names only walking and looking could force me to extract and reassemble from a web of trickling memories, a debris of stored images and sounds, a tissue of tangled words.

One day, when I was sitting on one of the alder stumps, I remembered my old camera. That same day, back in my temporary dwelling, I started opening my moving-boxes for the first time, sifting the contents of at least a dozen cases before I discovered the camera. I found myself trying out the old, simple hand movements: inserting the instant film, closing the back, the special firm yank for extracting the protective foil and picture. Then the counting of seconds as the photograph developed, how to peel off the foil.

In the alder grove I began to photograph things that were irreconcilable with my previous life in London, things I had stumbled across in the Lea Valley, scenes I wanted to keep, chance aspects, things that had unexpectedly entered my field of focus. Was what I found in these photos there by magic or accident? The camera casing was so light it was difficult to imagine it containing much in the way of optics; its mechanics were so primitive that the whole device looked like a crude fake, like fairground flimflam, or some gadget for over-eager kids who were perfectly happy just to 'do pretend' and brandish it about with a repertoire of adult gestures. Whenever I activated the release it felt to me like a hoax of some kind, and yet I still pulled the photograph out of the machine and kept it in my hand for the number of seconds prescribed for the relevant weather conditions, if it was cold slipping it into the inside pocket of my jacket. And whenever I did so I felt the same astonishment when I saw what the eye, lens and lighting – along with the reaction of chemicals with light and air – had conspired to produce. Each time the same thought entered my mind: the secret of this rather unsightly plastic box was probably that its pictures had less to do with the things seen than with the person seeing them. What came to light when the developer foil was peeled from the black-and-white photo with its countless shades of grey was a memory I did not even know I had. The pictures showed something that lay behind the things the lens had focussed on, things which, for an imperceptible moment in time, the shutter release must have brushed aside. The images belonged to a past I could not even be sure was my own, touching on something whose name I must have forgotten, or possibly never knew. There was something unquestionably familiar about these landscape scenes which, apart from the odd passer-by, were generally empty. Something waved to me, whispering: Do you remember? You do remember, don't you? from some remote depth within the white-edged surface of the photograph. And right beside it the world of the negative: nocturnal, putting a strange face on things, casting into doubt what belonged to which side, whether it was here or there, right or left.

Sometimes, on my way home in cold weather, I would remember a picture I had inserted into my jacket pocket to develop. It was difficult, then, to separate the foil from the photo; the former would remove strips of surface coating with it, leaving a wounded landscape. A rent would gape in the middle of the grey, fuzzy scenery of the traduced and fragmentary reminiscence, and through this cleft broke a formless world of dull colouring, unmasking the black-and-white surface as a flimsy disguise for a wild variegation that was wholly unconnected to memory. These shattered images scared me sometimes, as if they were evidence of a trauma. They had nothing to do with my walks along the no-man's-edge of the river Lea, but I returned to them again and again, as if their unmasking of the degenerative process of imaging might provide a clue to unravelling the secret of the relationship between picture-taking and memory. At the same time, it was only the undamaged pictures that I arranged on my house-moving boxes and pieces of furniture, looking at them with such frequency and so intensively that they eventually turned into a story.

My days always followed the same route: downstream and back. I returned with photographs and small found objects such as feathers and stones, or the seed pods of withered flowers. Little by little the fluvial landscape took over my flat, something Greengrocer Katz or the black pool players, occasionally and unintentionally glancing through my window, would never have guessed. The river itself would probably have been astonished.

III. RHINE

What were my memories of rivers, now that I lived on an island whose thoughts were turned seawards, where rivers looked shallow and pretty, noticeable only when they frayed into flats, or cut deep channels as they flowed out to sea? Sometimes I dreamed of rivers I had known, rivers that cleaved their way through plains and towns, rivers kept at bay by flood defences, or which rippled through the bright countryside. I remembered ferries and bridges and endless searching in unfamiliar terrain for ways to cross a foreign river. I spent my younger years by a river that appeared to me in dreams when I ran a fever.

The river of my childhood was the Rhine. The chugging of barges echoed from the gentle wooded and wine-growing slopes at the northern edge of the Siebengebirge. In a west wind the trains on the opposite bank sounded so close that the tracks could have passed through our garden, and the air smelled salty and fishy as if the sea were not far away. From the garret window you looked west; trams, barely visible through the pale standing corn in summer, passed along the bottom of a field; behind that came the factories, then the poplars along the riverbank. And in the blue beyond, a range of low hills was visible under the horizon across the river. That was where the sun set in winter.

The river rearranged the landscape by night: darkness was a hollow body where the sounds of the world were different from those of day. The barges resounded from the hills behind the small town; the dry gasping sough of a gravel chute, barely perceptible by day, hung in the sky. I lay awake in bed and the river felt nearer and larger than before, challenging daylight rules, and under the dome of the night sky I could never be sure what world I would wake to the following morning.

As children we often went down to the river. We stood on the breakwaters, and the bow waves of barges almost washed over our feet. We waved as they glided past, their decks full of flapping washing, bicycles and barking dogs, and sometimes there would be somebody waving back from that restless, transient land between two riverbanks. We learned how to skim flat stones, watching them skip several times across the surface. Our fingertips remembered the feel of different kinds of pebbles, the rounded edges of river-washed shards of glass, shiny clumps of fool's gold which, always on the lookout for something precious, we would carry home. We stood on the stony shore with Grandfather, who taught us to tell the time by the church-tower clock face on the opposite bank. We got to know the two species of inland gulls that hung about the jetties and ferry piers, screeching as if by the sea. My grandfather could foretell the weather by the smell of the river.

The river meant dislocation, confusion and unpredictability in a world that craved order. On its back it bore a travelling, unimaginable life form in the shape of barges we never saw at anchor, plying up and down between far-flung places. Barges with black coal, dull-red basalt, light-grey grit – moving hillocks rolling by. The yearly floods washed away any sense of order. The water rose slowly, sloshing over the breakwaters, sand-rooted willows, footpaths, and climbed the railway embankment. It clawed at things that seemed fixed and inviolable: benches, trees, little pavilions in places where the riverside was levelled, grassed and looked after. For every object it took, the river deposited something else it had torn away further upstream: unfamiliar filth, dark matter for which we had no name. When the water fell, it left behind a strip of foul-smelling devastation which, depending on the height of the flood, could stretch up the embankment to the tracks themselves.

The trains on our side of the Rhine were mostly freight. The tracks ran along raised embankments parallel to the riverside footpath and divided the town from the world of the river. Life in the small towns and villages went round and round in circles, at each turn straightening up, smoothing out, obliteratingever more of whatever had been there before our childhood: wasteland, the faded names of businesses on house fronts, debris and empty spaces, the backyard world of lopsided and lean-to sheds by and by converted into lawns bounded by thuya hedges. The last-remaining domain of disorder was an unsettling factory site with burnt smells, chalk and stone dust, and murky barracks for foreign workers on a piece of sodden grass between factory and railway embankment. The hinterland was connected to the river-world by damp, mouldy-smelling subways; there were always pools of water in the middle of these paths; we bet on who was going to have the loudest echo when we screamed, and held our hands over our ears whenever a train thundered over our heads. Nettles grew along the riverside and emitted a sour acidic fragrance during rainy summers; the slopes of the rail embankment were out of bounds, and the smell of nettles in the summer rain suggested something illicit to me ever after. Rubbish amassed between the stones and willows along the riverbank, and sometimes dead fish would wash up for days on end; we were forbidden to touch them, even with the toes of our shoes. Breakwaters pushed into the river from the reinforced banks. Willow growth, small sandy bays and pebble banks lay below the footpath. Bulky flotsam, left hanging in the willow branches by receding floods, stayed where it was till it fell apart; rusty frames, their original function impossible to guess at, stuck out of the shallow water by the bank. But what distinguished this untidy strip of land from the towns was not merely its disarray and the fortuity of found objects, it was also the motion of the river itself, its one-way flow towards a north that always seemed brighter, where the land levelled to a plain and there was not a hill to be seen, only the silhouettes of larger buildings against the white background of the sky. The barges gliding downstream towards this brighter patch of sky had an easy job, while those struggling against the flow looked heavier, blacker and uncertain as they pushed their way towards darker parts of the country. Upstream, where the valley abruptly narrowed, and the river still seemed to have no inkling of the sea, stood some blackish-brown stumps, a colour reminiscent of charred rock: the remains of a bridge that once had straddled this bridgeless section of the river, where only ferries now ran. The ruined pillars were a memory of *war*, a word that weighed heavily on our childhood. I wanted nothing to do with them, and kept my eyes hidden whenever I thought the stumps were near, only uncovering them when my father called 'now'.

My father was very attached to the river, and would travel by ferry whenever the opportunity arose. He knew all the ferrymen, and while we children huddled in the lee of the bulwarks, he liked to stand in the wind beside them, his hands in his pockets like them, talking about the weather. One of the ferrymen had artificial hands of dark brown leather because a grenade had torn both his hands off in the war. We stared at his leather hands, knowing it was bad manners, and our skin crawled, not just because of his creepy hands, but because we had

34

stared despite it being against the rules. When the ferry put out, the second ferryman, who was responsible for tying and untying the mooring lines, holding a thick hawser in one hand, took a mighty leap across the ever-widening gap of black water between quay and ferry. The ramp thudded into place, and we hung onto the railing, giddy with gazing into the boiling water below, at passing boats, or the pitching landscape. Reaching the middle of the river the ferry turned, a troublemaker for barges plying up and down; we saw the Siebengebirge to the south, first one bank then the other, the sky in the bright north, lost our bearings, forgot where we were going, and were surprised by the loud bang as the ramp went down, and by finding ourselves on the other side, as if in a foreign land.

In autumn there were days of fog that called the truth of everyday experience into question. The rules of direction were cancelled, upstream and downstream ceased to exist, there was no this side facing that side. The opposite bank had disappeared, no ferries crossed, the barges' foghorns sounded muffled while the boats gliding past were barely more than shadows; or else nothing was visible at all, and nothing in this thick, whitish grey moved, only the waves, small and shy, rolling over pebbles, resounding as if in an enclosed space, a cloud chamber perhaps, in which, unbeknownst to those standing on the riverbank, some experiment had been set up – the unveiling of a new world. Were the fog now to lift on a different landscape, the scene behind the curtain would have shifted to reveal the sea in a subtle, rarefied light, where usually, prior to the fall of the curtain, the town's first high-rise buildings had stood.

Back at home Grandmother sat at the sewing machine singing the song of the prince and princess who could not meet because the water was too deep. Their love, as celebrated in the song, ended badly. In fact my grandmother didn't hail from the Rhine at all; she had grown up beside a different, smaller river of icy swirls and eddies, which, so she told us, nonetheless flowed with a sweetness eclipsing all the Rhine had to offer through a land of placid water meadows and friendly towns. It was only when the snow thawed and the ice broke up that the gentle river became a raging torrent, and to prove it she would sometimes open a red, linen-bound album containing nothing but photographs of a river in full spate – the so-called *hundred-year flood*. Over pages of punched-out prints with serrated edges we were able to view various stages of a bridge's collapse under the pressure of water and ice. First we saw walls of snow by the roadsides, ice on the river, a snow-bound countryside, then ice floes – yellowed with age on the glossy paper – collecting against the bridge pillars, water foaming, ever wilder, higher in every picture, reaching the parapet of the bridge and washing into gardens along the riverside slopes, small figures balancing bales of hay and sacks on their heads between last patches of snow and mud-dark earth, then the pillars buckling, the bridge caving in, folding into the river, stumps sticking out of the water, part of the balustrade lying at an angle to a tree on the riverbank. This image of the devastated crossing between the two banks, this glaring wildness of a river that my grandmother, with a girlishness befitting of her world of ballads and fairy tales, had walked or cycled over daily, became a regular feature of my bad dreams.

In primary school we had to learn sayings about Father Rhine, none of which had anything to do with the river I had walked along in the years before starting school. These sayings left an unpleasant aftertaste, which became much bitterer one day when the bow wave of a huge barge dragged a child in my class off the end of a breakwater. The Rhine had revealed Himself to be a nasty character. For days it seemed the river had taken our tongue and weighed so heavily in our clothes we could barely move. Rumours circulated, there was whispering and gossip of bloated corpses and little white coffins, until several days later the child's body was discovered in riverside scrub some distance downstream.

The Rhine was the first border I ever knew, and it was constantly present. It taught us what was here and what was there. 'Our' side, with its villagey ways in relentless decline, its factories, shacks and freight trains, stood opposite the other side where the sun set. That side, remote and blurry, a hazy land of melting shapes and washed colours, provided a background to many of our family photographs. My father never tired of taking pictures of us children, whether by the river or on a ferry, sometimes with the wind ruffling our hair, sometimes standing in sparse snow before a riverside tree, behind us a black jetty, seagulls in the sky. Before our time, photographs taken by the river had sealed and attested certain festive occasions; behind the starched newlyweds – with or without parents, bridesmaids and best men – black barges or white pleasure steamers slid through the picture. One sepia portrait shows a pair of dark-suited brothers with black hats and walking sticks, their arms thrown around each other's shoulders in a conciliatory gesture for the group photo; they are standing directly in front of the river on an uneven shore of Rhine gravel. Who, after funeral or wedding, would have asked them to stand there? In all likelihood the travelling photographer, of whom my grandfather spoke with admiration, and to whom, in his anecdotes, and in contrast to the various other dodgy characters who filled his stories – travelling salesmen from foreign parts, fairground hands, spoon-hawkers, tinkers and scissors grinders – he gave no name. He was simply the photographer, wandering from one place to the next along the river, his camera and tripod on a little pushcart. People sent for him when a wedding was due, and hoped he would be there when funerals occurred. If they were lucky and he was there in time, he would photograph the deceased straight away, all laid out in his white shirt before being lifted to his coffin. A picture of one such ancestor, evidently lifeless in the slanting light while his relatives, headless dark figures – praying? weeping? staring? hoping for a picture of themselves while still alive? – thronged together in the background, was inserted loosely between the pages of an album. The photo remained unmounted and, oddly, would frequently change places; one never knew where it would turn up next. Suddenly there it would be, between two pages, half obscuring a different picture; it always sent a cold shiver down our spines, as if it were something forbidden. I would picture the photographer against the landscape of my childhood: the astonishing spectacle he must have presented as half of him disappeared under the black cloth he had spread over his camera in order to work wonders that would survive the people he had photographed; the way he would direct his instrument equally dispassionately at corpses and at the living, at funeral goers and at revelling wedding guests, providing souvenirs to people he did not know, while he himself would find it increasingly difficult to prevent the repetitive details of strangers' lives from invading his own memories, which perhaps were solely of the river.

Pitted against the fickle autonomy of the river was

a sparer landscape of orderliness and seeming legibility, which, as a child, I tried to get the hang of but could not understand. This consisted of names and numbers reminiscent of royalty – Roswitha, Monika and Michael I, II and III – on pitching boats and ferries moored at precarious jetties, also timetables and route maps, signs with variously interpretable symbols rammed into riverbeds along navigable channels, pennants and flags at the sterns of barges and ferries, combinations of numbers and letters on the sides of boats that could mean anything or nothing, huge kilometre markers, black on whitewashed surfaces, or white on black rock faces, purporting to measure the length of flowing water and establish an order of things which in reality everything eluded. Trying to learn and use these numbers and symbols was a game that was over as soon as I started to search for a meaningful connection between the words and signs. Unable to find the story that linked them, I tired of looking and turned my back on the Rhine.

A few years later, I would spend the better part of school days hanging about on my own by the river, cycling back and forth along the bank, sitting for hours on embankments that were reinforced with black, tar-covered boulders, searching for the same letters and symbols: names of ships, kilometre markers, registration numbers of barges. I was only interested now in what was going downstream towards the brightness where you would eventually come to the sea. For a while I kept a little notebook where I jotted down everything I could decipher on the barges passing downstream, as if, given time, I would be able to find a pattern. What I later remembered were columns of symbols divided into weekly blocks, which, on the squared paper, looked like the verses of a poem: ciphers of movement, of an elsewhere.

IV. WALKING

My strolls by the river Lea were slow and haphazard. I looked and listened and sought after memories. I took pictures and peeled back the memories layer by layer. My oldest memories lay at the top. I saw myself during my initial months here, roaming the London streets, listening to a new country. I was surrounded by roaring and humming. Every morning and every evening bluish birds drew the same single circle above the chimney cowls, then disappeared. The night rasped against thin, reverberating window panes; voices tumbled down the chimney into the ash pan, and in the evening, between two dark chunks of wall, illuminated trains passed across the sky.

Hoping to acquire the composure of the native, I took to walking. I learned the smells of a city so enormous it would take more than a lifetime to roam it. I committed the smells of bricks, river, and scrubby wasteland grass to memory; I learned the fragrance of rain and dust, pigeon feathers, waterlogged wood and pink hawthorn bushes, the aromas of the countless dishes cooked by foreigners, distinguishing them by degrees of sweetness, bitterness and spice. I visited markets, saw pink, grey and brownish fish twitching in the morning light, though supposed to be long dead. By evening there were heads, fins, scales and fishtails in the gutters, which ran with the water used for cleaning. The fishmongers were exhausted and trod on the remains without a thought. The meat of dressed sheep and goat hanging from heavy hooks in front of the red awnings of butchers' stands had darkened by the end of the day. Rejected cuts hacked from butchered animals collected in large plastic tubs under layers of fat and grease. The fowl, too, swinging on finer hooks in the fresh sea breeze, had turned pale and grey, and the complexion of the poulterers in the early evening light seemed to match the sallow skin of the plucked birds. The coloured flags decorating carts of cheap eggs and quietly rotting fruit had lost their thrill. Fruit leftovers, handled too often and gone soft, were at a discount to the last customers of the day: the poor, shyly emerging from the shadows, holding out small coins they had long held clenched in their fists. The tradesmen picked the coins from the sour sweat of their outstretched palms before tipping the goods into their open plastic bags.

With a cheap little camera I took photos I later felt ashamed of. When I looked at them, it felt almost indecent to keep in my room these fragments of other people's existence, images of a fleeting gesture, a wandering gaze, skulking figures, snippets of the lives of strangers who knew nothing of the persistence in my possession, for the time being, of a fragment of their life. Two black women in brightly coloured trainers and striped jackets turned up in several pictures. They are seen choosing some fish that look golden under the red glow of the awning, but will be yellow and dull at home in their kitchen. They linger over a display of white lace presided over by a yawning saleswoman in a brown anorak. In one picture a hand reaches indecisively towards a pale-looking banana plant, its fingers wrinkled with cold craning like timid necks; the blurred stripy pattern of the sleeve shows the hand belongs to one of the two women. On one occasion, a young man with dark locks came up to me in a fury and held his hand in front of my camera lens, waving his other hand about in the air. No no, he said loudly, no no. I moved on, and it was only later that I realized he had been frightened. Following this experience I resolved to photograph only inanimate subjects. I mostly took pictures by the canal, a dirty unused waterway linking the east and west of the city. At the weekend anglers sat on the narrow concrete path that went along just above the surface of the water; next to them were thermos flasks, picnic baskets and plastic boxes with square compartments for differently coloured worms. The tiny worms seethed and slithered, seeking shelter underneath or close to one another, all hurrying to be at the centre of their own warm pile of kindred beings. The anglers sat motionless on their folding chairs and waited for a fish to bite. Then they pulled their catch out of the water, always white-bellied fish with silvery backs that quickly dulled in the air; the fish thrashed about on the swinging line and choked on the worm that had brought them such misery. But the anglers only rejoiced in their catch for an instant, before taking the fish in their hands, removing the hook and throwing it back in the water. The fish, mortally wounded or scared to death, would soon be seen floating motionless on the surface, their eyes and mouths wide open and red, tossing on tiny waves whipped up by the wind and surrounded by a little wreath of foam.

On the other side of the canal stood empty factories, warehouses and other gloomy buildings, their windows shattered or blinded by grime. Stacks of boxes, silhouettes of immobilized machines and defunct lamps were visible through the dark glass, and the brickwork, almost up to the lower windows, was saturated with patches of damp. The shapely turrets of magnificent old train stations and the glittering sheen of bustling financial and trading institutions were visible through gaps between the buildings.

There was not much to see on the photographs.

Twisted grates with jagged shards of smashed window panes, a sharp shadow across one picture, broken off plaster with older layers of paint showing underneath. Signs corroded by the air, shreds of letters a passer-by might turn into words, whether guessed or made up. Nothing spelled out; everything left to luck. Black burn marks on rough boards nailed across windows. Bullet holes from random gunfights. Dents left by points and blades on battered bits of metal, whose last flakes of green and red paint were peeling; rust, like a blaze eating its way from the edges to the heart of a piece of paper, gets to all things in the end. Long strung-out buildings divided into rows of austere square fronts reflect in the water, gold light falls on the cracks in a disused concrete bridge in the distance, clumps of green gushing out of the bigger, gaping clefts on a fine day in February.

Away from the canal I visited pubs where they had live music to tempt people in from the surrounding streets. In a pub called the Rosemary Branch, three men played accordion, fiddle and trumpet, while a red-headed woman sang in a polka-dot dress. The songs were ones everybody knew, without perhaps being able to remember where or when they had heard them. Taciturn men with beards stared into mugs of dark beer; women squealed and kicked high-heeled legs in the air as their spirits rose and their companions gave them a tickle or a pinch. People went up to the bar and ordered drinks they had never tried before, which always tasted different from what they had imagined. The food smelled rancid, but it had quite a few takers all the same, especially the tickled women in high spirits. Stylishly-dressed male couples snuggled up close and passed notes with musical requests to the band.

One evening in the Rosemary Branch a man in a dark coat sat down at my table. He had a tremulous voice, crooked teeth and a shaggy black goatee beard. He introduced himself as a former circus rider, and claimed that in better days he had been world-famous. Those delicious days of world renown, he said over and over again, licking his lips each time, his clumsy attempt to pronounce the words betraying his foreignness. Since I could think of nothing to say, he slipped off his coat with practiced elegance, revealing the gold-sequined leotard he was wearing underneath. In some places the shiny spangles had fallen off, and a somewhat threadbare yellowy-green fabric showed through. Do believe me! he said, and I nodded. His arms appeared to be covered with tattoos, although I could not make them out in the dim light. Without prompting he told me that these arms had once been toned and beautiful. They had been massaged with oil before every performance; they gleamed, reflecting the myriad lights of the big top as he rode around the ring. His arms turned his act into a highlight, he assured me, and in all the great cities of the world audiences had lain at his feet. May I presume... he said suddenly, in German; it was obvious he hadn't spoken the language for a while. I nodded and stood him an insipid wine. As I was preparing to leave, he rose to his feet like a gentleman. He ran his hand over his head, smoothing his pomaded hair; a tuft stayed between his fingers, and one or two hairs fluttered down to land in the last of his wine. Excuse me, he whispered.

My meeting with the equestrian artiste, an unsolicited wave from my country of origin, had unsettled me. I walked through the dark streets, asking myself what if anything linked me to this circus rider, I who had not set foot in a circus since my childhood. It was a summer's evening, and a last streak of twilight hung over the city. There was a strong wind, and I struggled to ward off the rubbish that kept blowing into my face, the rustling detritus of a day's street trading. One or two late salesmen, loitering in dark entrances to buildings, held out what was left of their goods, and, because I showed no interest, yelled curses after me.

V. PINHOLE CAMERA

My flat was not far from Abney Park Cemetery. Had I leaned out of the bay window in my front room I would have been able to see the cemetery gate whose defiant grandeur stood out from everything else in the area, even from the cemetery behind it. On a walk some years earlier, I had taken a detour through the cemetery. It was springtime, and there were small clumps of yellow and white blooming daffodils everywhere. Although I had not been alone at the time and was given all kinds of explanations about the history of the graves, the cemetery had seemed like a deep forest to me, a dank and musty island, half-wild, drifting in the river of the city. At the time I should not have been surprised to stumble out through one of the two gates into a London that was wholly different from the one I had previously entered from. Now that I was so near to this forest full of graves, I rarely visited it. It was autumn. Poisonous flowers blossomed in the shade of the tall trees and brushwood; the leaves rustled after a dry summer, but had retained their tired green instead of turning yellow. The cemetery seemed like an incongruous counter to the wilderness beyond the river Lea, which lay in the opposite direction. The cemetery belonged to the city; it was a small outgrowth from it, not an island in a river. There was no surprise for me to look forward to on leaving the gate at the other end of the cemetery; in fact, that way led towards my old London life, whose familiarity I wished to slough off. I confined myself to short tours between the graves, trees, flowers and undergrowth. I avoided little groups of drug dealers and their customers, and the dreamy visitors sitting on graves in the few patches of sunlight.

One day, in the middle of the cemetery, I came across a young girl and her boyfriend in a clearing. She had a pale, drained face, and was looking up with a timid, rapt expression at her companion, a large black man sitting very upright on a tree trunk or gravestone. He was staring into the bushes, but his gaze was so earnest and lofty that he seemed to be looking over the tops of the trees, into some uncharted yonder. The girl reminded me of a sepulchral angel, its face worn by wind and weather; her skin was like porous stone, and her features had a certain flatness, as if they had been sandpapered to erase severity. But she had lovely long red hair, and I secretly called her Sonja because she reminded me of a character in Chekhov. A few days later I saw Sonja in the cemetery by herself; she was sitting in a different part of the clearing, where she had set up a pinhole camera to take a picture. I asked her about the camera, which she had balanced with some difficulty on a tree trunk, and she explained its simple construction. On windless days the pictures can look like delicate sketches, she said. And sometimes they show angels.

Sonja was a firm believer in the pinhole camera. She showed me all kinds of wondrous phenomena made possible by the device: the reproduction of images; bringing to light the invisible. She went on to explain how leaves also acted as a kind of pinhole camera; the spots of light observable under foliage on a sunny day were countless tiny suns. Countless tiny suns, she repeated. It was a chilly, whitish-grey day, and I thought of the three suns seen by members of an expedition to the ice-wastes of the North Pole four centuries ago.

I would sometimes meet Sonja on the street, or in the second-hand clothes shop a few houses away from my flat. The shop was managed by a thin-lipped Croat, who professed to be running the place on behalf of a Bosnian charity. It was chock-a-block with stuff: clothes, suitcases, toys, shoes. I ran into Sonja a couple of times there trying on shoes. She didn't like them, or they didn't fit her, and on one of these occasions the thin-lipped man went to the back of the shop and reappeared with a large rubbish bag full of shoes, which he proceeded to empty onto the floor in front of Sonja. At last she found one that suited and fitted her, whooping with joy at how lovely it was as she rummaged in the shoe-heap; its other half was nowhere to be found. Sonja left the shop without purchasing anything. The Croat calmly picked up the dumped shoes, including the single one, and put them back in the bag.

To avoid having to search my house-moving boxes for crockery I bought some tea glasses from the Croat, and a metal teapot tarnished by constant scrubbing during its years of service in some canteen or cheap roadside café. The Croat stood behind his makeshift shop counter, where some pieces of jewellery were displayed. This was a motley jumble of brooches and rings, which the donors may have overlooked on lapels or in pockets as they hurried to stuff the clothes into bags. The Croat gave me the odd bit of advice as I studied the jewellery. This brooch was very becoming, or that ring showed off my hand very nicely, but I was not persuaded.

Sonja worked in a small grocer's next to the charity for Bosnian refugees. I sometimes met her there. On one occasion I wanted to tell her about my instant pictures, indeed I had even prepared a little talk in my head about the relationship between these pictures and memory, but the talk went awry, my words sounded muddled, and she regarded me with disbelief. I mistrust memory, she said. The next time we met, she mentioned that she had started work on a photographic study. She mumbled an attempt to explain the study to me. You know, she said, beauty, light, reality, that sort of thing. A kind of law. Her voice became ever quieter, and I could barely understand what she was saying, but when I gave her a quizzical look, she shrugged her shoulders. A kind of law, she repeated, craning her face so far forward that it almost came up against my own. What is actually beautiful in what we see? she asked so suddenly and loudly that the few other customers in the shop turned to look. Following this conversation I stayed away from the shop, but a few weeks later Sonja came to see me. She was pregnant. Her features had become sharper; the weather-worn stone angel was no more, while her red hair, plaited into a braid, hung down in front of her shoulder. She lowered her eyes and soft bluish eyelids; she was no longer Sonja but a pre-Raphaelite vignette. That day at the grocer's she had handed in her notice; she intended to move to a houseboat on the Lea. As a farewell gift she had brought me two photographs she had taken with her pinhole camera. On one of them I recognized a view of the garden behind where I lived: the flat gravel-strewn roof, the sycamore, the window of my small room, where I had so often stood. For a moment I was taken aback; I felt watched, and caught at trying to memorize things. The window of the little room looked empty, however; there was no sign of any figure.

The other picture showed Sonja's clearing at Abney Park Cemetery: the trees, grass, half-overgrown gravestones, the deserted tree stump where she had sat with her friend. It really did look like a drawing.

An angel! she said, pointing to a thin, apparently hovering white shape in the bottom corner of the picture of the clearing. It was a blot of the kind that had occasionally appeared in the photos I took with my old instant camera: white shadows, caused by light penetrating the primitive casing.

Thank you, I said. It's very beautiful.

Sonja, who since her metamorphosis may have been called Gabriella, took her leave. She walked slowly and ponderously, not towards the Abney Park Cemetery, but in the other direction. I began to imagine her in Springfield Park, where, who knows, she might cross paths with the King, but then I saw her turning down the lane that ran along between my back garden and the embankment above the train station. The moment she vanished I was no longer certain I would recognize her if I saw her again in a different place.

I gave the two pinhole photographs a place in my flat. And there they stood, one at either end of the series I had taken of the Lea, like two distant relatives from a branch of the family thought to have withered away.

VI. WALTHAMSTOW MARSHES

From the foot of the bridge across the Lea I had a view of the open country of the Marshes, a landscape I was only just beginning to understand. I had lived in an urban environment for such a long time that, notwithstanding the hundreds of miles I had wandered over the years under the delusion of belonging – along canals, through parks and the more out-of-the-way London streets, I was going to have to rediscover old habits of finding my own way through open country, judging distances, directions and the course of my route according to bearings I would have to find and set myself. I crossed the river and made for the alder grove, leaving the between-zone where I had deposited the accoutrements of my previous life behind me. Before me lay an expanse that reached to the horizon under a vast sky, a terrain undescribed enough for me to apply my own names to it.

The Walthamstow Marshes are not big, just as the lands of a childhood are not big, but I thought of their borders as drawn by heaven and history long ago – railway embankments, thorn bushes and marshland; on this map, the industrial parks and reservoirs to the east and north were still white spots. For a time the Marshes became the heart-healing training ground for my later walks downriver, indeed for the whole of this leave-taking of London life: the ineptly cut-out image of an increasingly arbitrary seeming northwest London street that was remoter from the Marshes now than the messy riverbank of my childhood. Between autumn and spring, the area between the mutilated alder wood, the railway lines, and the rough path along the Lea, was where I began my daily walks south, working my way downstream towards where the Lea flowed into the Thames.

The poles on this first stage of my walk were the alder grove in the north and, to the south, a sparse willow copse beyond the forking railway embankments and in sight of a blue-white synthetic dome, which, viewed from the willow grove in the right light, could seem like an extension of the sky, or an opening into some sudden fabulous vastness, an illusion dispelled only as one approached it.

Behind the alder grove and weed-covered mound, the latter a vestige of the attempt to transform Horse Shoe Point, an area of brush and thickets grew along the raised railway embankment. Here were dry, thin grass-blades, bramble hedges with pale, shrivelled berries, willow bushes, rose briars, scattered hawthorns, and all so faded their colours could only have been drained by last year's 'summer of the century', or by the wind, and this autumn's still white sky. Even the rose hips on the long thorny branches of the briar roses were not red or orange, but brown and black. Beaten tracks threaded between the bushes; they were evidently in use, trodden frequently enough not to be overgrown. In their forlornness these paths, dotted here and there with heaps of rags, had something mysterious about them; in fact the whole hinterland area of the path along the river was so far from any real use value that I could not make head nor tail of it. Only once did I see someone, a lone man galloping through the rough terrain on an old BMX bike, who emerged so abruptly from behind a wall of thorn bushes that I received quite a shock. He soon came to a standstill behind a bush some distance away, appearing to watch me. I went on my way. On turning again I no longer saw him. The railway line that crossed the Lea on an old brickwork bridge forked halfway between the river and another railway embankment at the edge of the Marshes. One of the tracks ran further east towards the Thames Estuary, the other northeast to Essex and Suffolk. The triangle enclosed by the three embankments, reached by a subway between brambles, resembled an island, and was just as colourless as the area crossed before entering the subway; here, however, in spite of the frequent train traffic, everything lay under a canopy of intense silence. The undergrowth was not as rampant, and the grass was taller, rustling softly, with only a single, barely noticeable path traversing the triangle. The ground was uneven, with shallow depressions concealed under the grass. These were small sinkholes of the kind found in the Karst, where the earth above unfathomable underground chambers had collapsed, forming a landscape that was barely detectable from a distance, and which only at close proximity, on the brink of such a sinkhole, revealed its inverted hilliness: a landscape negative corresponding to its positive counterpart in distant hills. The sinkholes of the Karst were less familiar to me than the gravel pits of the Rhineland. These were surrounded by cone-shaped heaps of quarried sand and gravel; there was a continual rattling and sighing of gravel chutes, under whose conveyor arms ever new heaps would grow. Gravel pits made barren terrain, and green groundwater shimmered on the pit bottom – overshadowed by stories of drowned people and children who had disappeared while playing, buried alive in dark holes that could suddenly gape in the yellowish walls of the pits.

The trains on the Marshes did not glide past with the gentle swoosh of modern locomotives; the angular carriages of blue and yellow with their old-fashioned rounded roofs clattered slowly along the ancient track system, a noise which, with so many trains passing through, hung almost constantly over the landscape, a sound suggesting a cut-out garland of dull hammer blows on dry wood, such was the shuddering clatter of these short trains along the edges of the triangular island, and sometimes the wind whipped up one of these garlands, blowing it to and fro above the quiet tract of land.

I knew the line that headed northeast out of Liverpool Street Station. Standing there between the railway embankments, I remembered the feeling of astonishment I always had when the train put the yards, buildings, roofs, and scrap heaps of Hackney and Bethnal Green behind it and plunged into open countryside. This almost always took place in the early morning, and emerging from what passed for night in the brightly lit city we would suddenly find ourselves immersed, on the other side of the Lea, in a grey or pink-streaked morning light, in which the few unidentifiable objects and buildings appeared to be weightless. It felt strange to be standing in the very landscape whose sudden transition from town to country, seen from a train window, had seemed so unreal to me, and even stranger to think of passengers looking out of passing trains and seeing me standing here now. Somebody peering out of a train window on their way to the airport or the Thames Estuary and astounded by the abrupt change of scenery, momentarily anxious perhaps that she had boarded the wrong train, was probably watching me now, registering me as one of the disconcerting features of the landscape, a nameless item of the incomprehensible and sparse Walthamstow Marsh furniture.

I liked being on the island. It brought memories not only of the gravel pits, but also of a different hollow, which had long lain hidden under brambles and thorns, where a rumour, spread to scare children off, had said that it was home to snakes. The thorns, snakes and bristly inaccessibility of this overgrown hollow had made it seem menacing and unmentionable, as if it had no place in an area such as ours, where life was getting better by the day and one little wilderness after another disappeared under new houses. One summer, the hollow, bordering on a narrow field, in fact the only field left in our sprawling suburban corner of the world, was cleared of bushes, the pit underneath it levelled, and the steep slope planted with grass and shrubs. Men worked there day in, day out in the hot sun, and we neighbourhood children lay in the knee-high oats, staring down into the pit at the men's sweaty backs and arms as they drank beer or pissed against an elder bush near the flat pit entrance. Sometimes a blond-haired woman on a horse rode up the apple-tree lined path to the pit. She trotted over to the building site to inspect the progress of the work; the men joked with her, and her laugh was loud and pointed. Then the stables behind the apple trees were repaired, and in the autumn they opened a new riding school, where the horses went round and round in the pit and little girls with black riding hats sat with their backs straight as ramrods, learning how to walk, trot and do tricks. As long as it stayed warm and dry, there would be two or three of us lying in the stubble watching the girls learning to ride and wishing we could be one of them. One day, a girl joined us. She came and went, staying on a weekly basis with her grandparents at the station master's cottage next to a disused station. Her name was Elvira, and my grandmother called her the wild girl; when we sat at our kitchen table drinking juice, I noticed my grandmother stealthily inspecting her hair for lice. After the riding lesson we stumbled home across the field. Elvira swung to and fro for a while on our garden gate, and I waited for her to start telling one of her amazing stories about her father who'd *done a bunk* to Munich, as she put it, and who sent her photos of his fabulous wealth. But instead she said: I wouldn't go riding there; they shot some people in that pit.

The island was sheltered from the wind and quite still. I occasionally saw a fox. There may well have been snakes there, too, and in the silence between trains I heard larks in the sky, lapwings in the distance, crows on the other side of the tracks, the strangled squawking of swans attempting to fly. I took pictures of all I saw. The mesh of bramble stalks, the puddles in the subways, the stiff pylons along the embankment against a background of reeds leaning skew to the wind. All the pictures were bathed in mellow light greys, their contours so soft it was like looking at things through a very thin veil. And in each photograph there was something I had not seen when looking through the view-finder: a pair of track workers with a pickaxe on the embankment. A heron. A bicycle in the grass. My own shadow.

VII. RIVER THAMES

Back in my flat I began to prepare myself for the uncertain months ahead. I tentatively opened my house-moving boxes to search for winter things – a warmer duvet, a pullover, gloves for walks in the cold mist I was anticipating; summer was still holding on, although the persistently mild nights were drawing in. Reluctantly opening boxes, my mind focussed on winter, I chanced on a box of old family photographs. My father had been the photographer of the family, lord over the dark-brown battered leather camera case, a buff wallet with his light meter, and his black tripod. He took pictures of his wife and children, landscapes and places of interest, and was especially keen on details of the Italian Renaissance. In these first weeks of protracted leave-taking I often dreamed of my father. He was usually standing in a bright strip of light, waving to me in the shadows. It was always winter in these dreams; he was wearing a thick, fur-lined coat, his shoulders hunched against the cold, and he smiled crookedly, like anyone with a cigarette in his mouth. His camera hung from his neck, dangling down in its open case, and in these dreams, and even from a distance, I could feel under the tips of my fingers the slightly roughened surface of the inside of the case. Still half asleep, the first thing I remembered on waking up were his gestures while taking pictures. The way he would hold up the light meter in his outstretched left hand, with the case flap open, studying it continuously with his far-sighted eyes as if it might tell his fortune. The way he balanced the tripod, and how he got in behind his view-finder, the part of his face that was not obscured by the camera puckered with tension. Taking one photo after another out of the box,

I realized for the first time that I was seeing all this – my mother, my siblings and myself, as well as bridges, squares, Alpine peaks, the pale light of northern Italy in springtime, Renaissance palaces in Florence, the angels of Fra Angelico – through my father's eyes. These tiny segments of the world showed the decisions he had taken behind his camera's view-finder, and he too must have viewed them with astonishment sometimes, since they would have reminded him of things to which the scenes depicted held the sole remaining clue, a clue only he was capable of finding.

The old colour photographs had taken on a greenish or reddish tinge, or a bluish paleness, which placed their subjects at an indefinable distance that had no basis in time or place. These paler photographs in particular suggested to me memories my father might have in his realm of the dead, and the thought of that endeared them to me.

I was astounded how many of these pictures had been taken on or beside a river. Some with my siblings and me, two or three of us standing together, sometimes with my mother, or my mother on her own, on bridges; grey, yellow-sandstone or white bridges, red-brick bridges, wooden bridges. We stood on waterside promenades, leaning against a parapet, on the deck of a boat, clinging firmly to the railings. Sometimes there were famous buildings in the background, sometimes only sky and water, in a winter or green landscape. These shy-looking children who always looked cold and thin-skinned, their teeth chattering, and the brittle, tense woman, who always seemed to have some wretched pain to contend with, just seemed to be standing there and to have no appreciable relation to all these background scenes, as if they had been added later for no particular reason, mounted together on a piece of paper. For a moment I entertained the notion that my father – a man who, the moment he crossed a border, would throw himself with relish into any home-grown culture he encountered, which was sure to embarrass my mother – had used his photographs to cast a momentary veil of foreignness over us. Perhaps because we were foreigners to him, or perhaps it was because, in these different places, he wanted us to assume the mantle of foreignness he refused to accept for himself. I immediately abandoned the idea; it seemed so unfair to my father who was now all alone in the winter light of my dreams, waving to me.

One picture showed me on Westminster Bridge in London, leaning over the parapet and looking down at the water, the wind blowing my hair across my face. I knew it was me because of the coat; more than standing on Westminster Bridge in the wind, I remembered its blue-green material and smooth buttons, and I knew that in that picture I was eleven years old. It was my first time in London. It was May, the wind cold; there are clouds in the picture, and between them tiny shreds of blue, and in one corner a part of the river reflecting a veiled sky and hint of azure. I remembered the boat trip on the Thames, which had probably taken place on the same day. It was a smallish boat with wooden benches, unlike the Rhine pleasure boats on which our grandparents sometimes took us on unappreciated day trips that sailed past dark rocks and the alarming stumps of ruined castles. Ah, River Thames, my father said, as the boat put out, and he tried to strike up a conversation with the boat-master. The Thames ferry rolled, the water felt close and rubbish floated on the murky waves. My father explained that the river was tidal, and named the bridges as we passed under them. I have never forgotten those dripping, uncannily echoing shadows between the great bridge piles, nor emerging into the light after each bridge as if we had entered a different river or a different city. The boat-master pointed out the sights to us that were visible from the river; my father repeated the names several times, chewing on them until his pronunciation began to approximate the boat-master's. We sailed past docks, past endless warehouses, past the green slopes of Greenwich Park. I remembered the cold sun on my face, the rolling of the boat, the roughness of the boat-master. The smell of salt water and decay, the blinding white of the seagulls as the sunlight broke through the clouds. In my memories London, on the day of our trip, was a deserted city. Deserted on the river, deserted on the bridges, deserted on the riverbanks, deserted around the Tower, where we disembarked on our return from Greenwich. An enormous city, presenting to the river an empty face. Was it because of the cold wind? Because of the abandoned docks, so forlorn and off-putting? Later on we had a meal in a deserted pub with large, floor-length windows and a view onto a kind of short promenade, which was divided from the river by a head-high wall. The wind, trapped between promenade wall and windows, gathered the rubbish into small swirling droves. A sweetish, burnt smell of unknown foods hung over us as we ate. Faded cakes were displayed behind glass at the counter. As we ate, the waitress stood in silence at the window, wringing her apron. Are you German, she asked indifferently as she cleared away the plates, East or West? My father was at a loss for an answer. He said nothing.

I set down the box of photographs beside the window in the little room and did not open it again for a while. But whenever I stood there looking out into the garden or at the big brick wall, I remembered more about the holiday. A baker's shop in a little town on the Thames. The river was gentle and narrow there, with a tree-lined path along it. Women pushed prams into a bleak May wind, and a long rowing boat passed, with a determined uniformity of coordinated movement that I found unappealing; my father smiled and told me he had been a rower like that too, on the Rhine, as a boy. The town was getting ready for a fair, and children in brown school uniforms were exchanging blows behind a merry-go-round which was just being set up. At a baker's, where looking over the counter I saw women in a kind of sales pit on a lower level serving customers through a small, low street window, I bought a gooseberry turnover, which, dressed in its strange name, sounded almost exotic to me. We sat in the car and devoured our cakes while my parents argued about whether or not to go on to Oxford. I remembered the Thames of the villages to the west of London, around Hampton Court and Henley, a river small by comparison, like the one my grandmother had spoken of with such tenderness, with meadows and little grey stone bridges that recalled the one in her old red album. And an endless walk along the Thames from Pimlico to Earls Court, then me among crowds of people in Earls Court Road in the twilight, sent out alone with a little money in my hand to buy something, while my parents took a rest in our guesthouse where everything smelled of turmeric and fenugreek – to me the English names of these oriental spices were like lovers in a fairy tale whose story would surely end more happily than that of the prince and princess unable to meet because the water was too deep. And I remembered bustling groups of observant Jews in black garments hurrying down a sloping street with their arms swinging, holding firmly onto their hats in the wind, laughing light-heartedly when they met one another in passing, kings in black, with somewhere to go in a hurry under the cloudy London sky. Shortly after leaving the city on our way to Dover, we took a wrong turning and ended up standing by a pier that jutted out into the broad grey estuary. On the opposite shore were cranes, dockyards and ships, bigger than anything I had ever seen. We ate sour-smelling chips wrapped in newspaper while seagulls screamed over our heads, flying so close that they cast shadows although the sky was overcast and the day quite dull. The dark shapes of ships, factory chimneys and stacked containers seemed to hover in the air. It was low tide; a number of unrecognizable objects protruded from the murky water near the shore, betraying, at least to us stray tourists soon to leave the island behind us, nothing of any function they may once have had. It must have been on this return trip to the continent that, stranded, and led by my father who had no real desire to return home, we spent the night in a small town at the edge of the delta. Although it had been a sunless day, a spread of pink tinted the water in the evening. Through this pink haze glided gigantic ships; at the same time the opposite shore of the estuary was barely visible, a faint line that could have been water or sky. Another river joined the Thames here, and together they flowed into the sea, the eastern horizon faltering grey-green as the night came in. As darkness fell, lights in different colours sprang up in the distance, garlands and festoons of sparkling fairy lights in estuary towns, gifts of glittery ear- and nose-rings for the river before it lost itself in the sea.

My father visited me in London only once. He picked me up from the radio station where I was then working. It was a very large, old building, and I often lost my way there. The corridors, dark offices and tiny studios plunged me into confusion, though less so than the recordings of my own voice reading short reports from distant lands. Most of these were about political unrest or disasters. On the day my father picked me up I had wounded my finger, not for the first time, while cutting the tape of my recording, and I knew that traces of blood would be on the tape. I handed it in nonetheless, and decided never to come back again. My father was waiting for me in the foyer. He was sitting in a high-backed chair facing away from the door I came through; I immediately recognized the patch of yellowy-grey hair sticking up above his chair, and I found both his smallness in the chair and his yellowish tint simultaneously dismaying and funny. We walked to the Thames and crossed the river on the constantly swaying Hungerford Bridge. The old Hungerford Bridge, a ramshackle walkway along the steel girders of the railway bridge, was for a long time my favourite. There was so much sky over the city to the east, and the sheltering shadow of the railway bridge, with its trains passing to and from Charing Cross, was a comfort to me when I heard ghosts of the inter-war years whispering in the alcoves of Hungerford Bridge – *inter-war* being a word I had first heard on this bridge. I attempted to explain this preference to my father, but he could not understand what I meant. It's openness I like, he said. We walked as far as Westminster Bridge. It was winter; my father was wearing his fur-lined coat, one he had had for many years. We did not find much to say to each other, just as we hadn't on similar walks along the Rhine when I was a child. We stood for a while at the parapet of Westminster Bridge and looked down at the water, then we took a bus home.

My father died the following summer. A chance job

offer had landed me temporary work in a basement office of the Jewish Refugee Committee. The office was situated in a dark building on a permanently busy thoroughfare near the big north London train stations. My task was to translate Russian and Serbo-Croatian letters and deal with enquiries concerning the whereabouts of German Jewish refugees who had come to England in the 1930s. Heirs were sought for the worldly goods of those who had died lonely deaths. People who had composed themselves for death recalled relatives who had boarded a train somewhere between Breslau and Aachen more than fifty years ago, hoping to find safety in England: roughly remembered names of people from the smaller or larger German towns of long ago inserted into perfectly phrased, polite enquiry-English. After my few hours of work there every day I left the crepuscular cellar and its files for the muggy summer smog and noise of the Euston Road, but I always took the names of the missing with me. I reeled miles of microfilm through the reader, copies of files, letters, documents. I collated names, dates and addresses, became embroiled in stories of strangers whose lives were not the focus of enquiry, and was taken up for days with cases I thought I could solve on the basis of a few details, chasing a single name across a dozen addresses in variously sized towns, whose names often incorporated those of the rivers that ran through them. The tracks always broke off: a date of death was noted, or the journey continued to a different country.

It was the hottest June of the century, and the day on which my father died was the hottest day of that June. On the way home from the office I had to cross Hammersmith Bridge on foot because it was closed for bus traffic. It was so hot the soles of my shoes kept sticking to the melting tarmac. The Thames ran softly, flowing browny-green under the bridge. Some rowers were training, and their cox, shouting commands through his megaphone, was audible above the afternoon hubbub. From above, the obedient, diligent, fervent rowers looked like wind-up toys. The river around them glared so brightly in the sun it hurt my eyes. It was a different Thames from the one I knew.

VIII. CRATERS

During my first autumn in London I learned the word *equinoctial gale*. The spring and autumn storms were the force that tore at the equality of day and night, throwing the equinox out of kilter. For nights on end I lay awake and listened to the storm, to the mauled voices outside, to the groaning of the house, the whole city a surging tumult around me. Getting used to the wind was a demanding ritual, an integral part of settling in a city whose foreignness it took me some time to acknowledge.

Initially I lived in a small terraced house. There were similar houses on either side of the street; a century old now, they had learned in their increasing decrepitude to hang on to each other. On blustery days the wind blew through the chinks and cracks. Whatever the wind or weather, I'd hear the rag-and-bone man pass outside with his squeaking cart, yelling his patter, on the look-out for anything worry or grief could play into his hands. There is a lot of dying in a big city, and it is not uncommon for the deceased to leave behind a heap of rags or a suitcase full of junk. Almost everyone desires prosperity, and invests their hopes in worldly goods. The hopes may crumble, but some still find it hard to part from their accumulated belongings, stowed away and forgotten until they die, when their surviving relatives, all hope of a windfall inheritance abandoned, throw them, sometimes in exchange for a pittance, onto the rag-merchant's cart. The mascot of the rag-and-bone-man's guild was the three-legged dog, who happily hobbled and stumbled along beside the cart, avoided unfriendly kicks with remarkable skill, knew his manners, and was as silent as a true heraldic beast, ignoring battle-ready street cats and trotting on regardless, the cart's robotic companion.

Again and again during those wind-buffeted weeks, I picked up my battered suitcase with the intention of setting off on a journey. On each occasion, however, I turned back. Barely had I set foot outside the front door when the journey seemed too burdensome, and I reminded myself of my desire to settle down, which, owing to the draughtiness of my home, had become less urgent. Not far from the city lay the sea, which I would have to cross; the coasts that stood in my way had little to offer. Few things were sadder than an eagerly anticipated coastline that turns out to be dismal: blurred outlines, the inconclusive discontinuance of the flat land, charmless villages where the only thing happening is washing flapping in the wind, and silt-bound, sea-filled boats. After a while I learned to roam without thoughts of travel or a suitcase in my hand; I made a home for myself by walking, and casting my eyes with ever increasing dedication upon the unremarkable things that lay unheeded by the wayside, things lost and not found, things left behind, unclaimed, thrown aside, going to rack and ruin, beyond retrieval or recognition. I was fond of faded typefaces on scraps of paper, tufts of hair and fragments of buttons, broken writing utensils, buckles and clasps and tinny pieces of jewellery, old gym-shorts and foreign coins. I did not remove anything, but examined my findings where they lay, sometimes making a quick sketch in a notebook or noting down striking features: gym-shorts, blue, red nametape, Ben Jacobs, U5b. Fur purse, white, shape of an animal ear, contained 36p. Was it a sheep's ear? A goat's ear? Could it have been a leaving present in a distant land, given by a shepherd or owner of a large herd to someone who was leaving and going abroad, unaware that he would lose his little purse not far from my street while blowing his nose, or engaged in a fight, or fleeing from some sinister figure? Sometimes there were even small pieces of furniture left by the side of the road; I could have done with them myself, but I feared that fate would enter my flat with the object, taking hold, making itself at home. At first it would sit quietly in its corner, but soon enough it would get cocky, tapping its feet, finally insisting on smoking and gossip.

Treading ever tighter circles around the radiant amusements and nightlife of the inner city, I finally dared enter, letting the light of its pleasure centres fall on my hands and dusty shoes, breathing in aromas that welled onto the streets from its restaurants. A delirious mindlessness, from which I felt utterly remote, held sway over everything. The people, dressed brightly and far too thinly even for this season's rare, milder evenings, laughed with disturbing vehemence and without cessation, friends and complete strangers throwing themselves into each other's naked arms. On every side, under the laughter, were light slapping and sucking sounds as bare flesh embraced or released bare flesh, the whispering of skin brushing skin, the rustling of hair entangling in hair. In every doorway and at every wide-open window of a pub, people drank and drank and drank; they laughed and drank, stretching their arms out towards each other, as snippets and strings of music tumbled from doors and windows, flickering in the glare of flashing advertisements between the drinking, craving crowds, among whom the lonely paced this way and that, gradually losing hope, their hands grasping nothing over and over again, their naked arms covered in gooseflesh and their laughter bloodless and bland. Here and there, too, were scenes of flaring violence as claims and entitlements to certain bodily parts clashed, as people felt cheated of drinks, caresses, laughter, perhaps even love or money, and suddenly duller, harder sounds filled the air as fists, noses, elbows and the sides of hands collided. But for all the acrimony and fiery exuberance of its amusement quarter, the city presented itself each and every morning in its mellowest and most conciliatory dawn colours.

At any moment, however, this gentleness could reveal itself as deceptive. Explosions rent the air; there was virtually a season of almost daily bomb warnings, during which the traffic stood still, train and underground stations were evacuated, people – the locals unruffled, the foreigners panic-stricken – forced to stand for hours in the wind and rain and wait in vain for the predicted detonation. The boundaries between ill luck, mishap and attack were fluid. People would suddenly appear in droves, as if they had been on standby somewhere, waiting for a deafening blast in order to scramble and converge with all possible haste on the presumed scene of devastation. They pressed forward to the tattered edge of the freshly torn crater and stared with curiosity into its depths. Sirens were heard in the distance and the rhythmical gallop of the approaching mounted police, whose first action on arrival was to push the onlookers back from the edge and form a protective cordon around the crater. Without a murmur the onlookers turned their attention to the scattered debris and desisted from any attempt to look into the crater. Meanwhile, a number of uninjured people had emerged from the depths to be greeted as heroes. Their faces were black with dirt and dust, but their eyes shone brightly. The injured were counted and photographed, as were the unscathed, who were then allowed home with their instant photographs. A second detachment of mounted police had now arrived, and their horses snorted and whinnied and stood tethered to sundry bits of metal sticking up from the rubble, while the officers took up position. The onlookers scattered, each finding a little souvenir to his or her taste. The sun sank in the sky, its red rays playing on the glassy tops of modern stations in the distance and reflected in a window pane that had miraculously survived in one piece, still in its frame in a block of debris. The wreckage was cordoned off, and police officers turned a blind eye as the last onlookers left, their souvenirs barely disguised under jackets or in their bags. As soon as the public was out of sight the police officers, almost without exception, reached for small thermos flasks of tea, from which they proceeded to drink in the evening light.

I shuddered at the thought of how the force of the explosion would continue to resonate for weeks in the souvenirs people had picked up and taken away, and I avoided these gaping craters until they showed the first signs of scarring, when the sharp jags around their edges grew softer and first stalks of grass appeared, when the few undamaged objects remaining had succumbed to weather and vandalism, when rain and wind had smoothed the edges of the broken glass, the saline odour of the ruptured earth had evaporated, the hoof and foot prints were obliterated, the police warning signs had weathered under the assaults of the pugnacious sea wind. Following the initial excitement, the craters went unheeded for months. Everywhere I went in town I came across more or less overgrown, replanted or provisionally redeveloped scabbed-over wounds of this kind; at the same time it was in the nature of the local population to make nothing of such matters. I observed to my astonishment how quickly and literally grass could grow over a thing, and how that thing, even in the testimony of witnesses of the harm it had done, could become something else, something harmless.

When I thought I was alone, I would scrape with the toe of my shoe at the thin layer of soil that had settled over the rubble, and unobtrusively bend over to have a look. My finds did not amount to very much, however. I contented myself with a fragment of a cheap teacup or with a crumpled photograph. It was only reluctantly that I took the few small photographs I had found on such occasions home with me; I was averse to the idea of having such evidence of great destruction amongst the little I owned. I deposited the photos in a box, onto which, as a child, I had stuck some thin, fragile mussels gathered from the riverbank. All that was left of the mussels were tiny broken stumps that had coalesced with the layer of glue. I seldom removed the photographs to look at them, and when I did, it was less out of curiosity than with a sense of obligation, as if I owed the people in the pictures my attention. They showed people who meant nothing to me, and did not appeal to me. A group of pushy, fawning children, a middle-aged couple with discontent written all over their faces, and a man in hiker's garb with a black-and-white spotted dog. My hope had been that destiny was playing a game with these found objects, and that one day their meaning would be revealed. But I was wrong. When I looked at the finds, nothing at all sprang to mind.

On one occasion I encountered the circus rider beside one of the craters. He too was skulking about somewhat furtively. At first, our glances barely met, and quickly returned to the ground again. But the sun soon set and we said good evening. Have you found anything nice? I asked, to break the embarrassed silence that had fallen as we had said hello. He responded negatively. Found objects were no longer of value to him, he claimed. He raised his hat in an old-fashioned, courteous manner, and I saw he was almost wholly bald. Only a few isolated tufts of hair sprouted from his scalp. We left the overgrown disaster scene and walked along the river together. It had grown dark, and the city lights reflected in the water. I asked him if he had fond memories of his riding days, thinking to be consolatory, but he batted my enquiry away with an impatient gesture of his hand: it's nothing but a swindle, he riposted, the audiences are blinded by the sparkle of brass-sequinned leotards and strong, oiled arms. They cheer mere chimeras. He hissed the words through his teeth; it sounded as if he were practising how to pronounce a specific sound. We came to a bridge, and went our separate ways. It all felt autumnal, and the air smelled sour. Away from the river people thronged the streets, and lights gleamed and flickered wherever one looked.

IX. TABERNACLES

Each morning the thin-lipped Croat would stand in front
of his shop, squint into the whitish light, and smoke. He
had little to do until the afternoon or early evening,
and might just as well wait until lunchtime to open, but
when the children passed on their way to school in the
morning there he was, standing at the open door to his
treasure trove, taking his time over a flowery mug of
coffee, the same old tracks by Neil Young and Grateful
Dead always audible out on the street. I wondered
whether he lived in his shop, making his bed on a pile of
second-hand coats every evening, with sheets that had
served their time long ago in genteel households, and as
blankets the somewhat fusty cashmere shawls of ladies
who had travelled extensively or received exotic pres-
ents. Perhaps Neil Young and Grateful Dead were put
to bed then too, replaced by the quiet murmur of Balkan
folk music. Pinned to a small part of the wall behind the
counter were postcards of Mediterranean landscapes:
blue, pink, pine-green and rock-grey. Serbo-Croatian
greetings ran across the landscapes, to which greetings
in Italian or Greek would have seemed no less ger-
mane. Sometimes he received phone calls from fellow
countrymen, in which case, pressing the receiver to his
ear, he would take himself out of the way and disappear
among the trousers, which were the garments hanging
nearest to the counter, muttering in Croatian, or Serbo-
Croatian, whichever of the two he called his language.
I once tried to get him to talk about former Yugoslavia,
dropping the names of a few places I knew. It was meant
to be harmless, an attempt at conversation after a day of
silence, but he narrowed his eyes and gave me a lopsided smile, taking a drag from his cigarette and shrugging

his shoulders. Very bad thing, he said after a while, with a concerned expression on his face, tapping his foot to the music, 'Everybody knows this is nowhere' jangling from the loudspeaker of his cassette recorder.

In the morning light the smoking Croat would greet everyone in the neighbourhood. He was even companionable with the observant Jews who came by, on occasion making as if to stroke the heads of boys with kippahs and side-locks. He showed the same friendliness to everyone, even to the Rastafarians, who wandered round the block like pillars of fire. In the afternoons he drank tea with a Pakistani who ran an internet café, where after classes boys in white kaftans and skullcaps from a local school tussled with each other for places at computer seats. Afterwards he would stand on the other side of the street, squinting into the light, occasionally throwing a glance over at his little shop. You couldn't say he was overly interested in business, however. He would hand over clothes or toys for a trifle; whole families would buy their winter clothes there, leaving only a modest banknote for the lot, a symbolic offering for the families of Bosnian war victims. Yet the Croat's shop never seemed to get any emptier, and sacks of second-hand goods, ready to be unpacked, piled up in his back room. Sometimes, passing his shop, I would peek in and see him standing amidst his goods, his hands gripping the edges of his counter top, the Mediterranean postcards mere shadows at his back, staring wide-eyed into the street to the sound of some unbearably incongruous Neil Young song, a crestfallen captain who can no longer hide his ineptitude as a seafarer.

The observant Jews of the area were preparing for the Feast of Tabernacles and carrying materials for their improvised booths through the streets. On patios,

balconies and in the narrow yards of Victorian houses, they used wattle, bundles of twigs and straw mats to
build these hut-like tabernacles, where the stars could
shine in their soup, as someone once told me as a child.
Both festive and absurd at the same time, the image of
plates of night-coloured soup with tiny shining stars in
them had remained in my mind ever since, a dish that
could only be eaten on early autumnal evenings when
the air was damp and smoky and dark winter apples still
hung on the trees.

In Greengrocer Katz's window was a display of lu-
lavs, the festive bunches of palm and willow fronds, and
beside them lay gorgeous, lemon-shaped etrogs. Orders
in packed boxes were stacked up inside, and children
came to ask for old fruit crates to build more humble tabernacles with: the important thing was to have one. On
the first morning of the holiday there had been something of a dispute when an itinerant trader of the ritual
bunches came too close to Greengrocer Katz's shop and
had already succeeded in selling lulav bunches and
etrogs to two pious Jews with children in tow. The Croat
had sauntered across the street and was inspecting the
travelling salesman's etrogs, which were of great interest to him as a southern European, when Greengrocer
Katz came out of his shop in person, evidently with the
intention of sending the pedlar on his way. The lulav
salesman was a shy man, and much too embarrassed to
decline the assistance offered by the Croat not only in
allocating him a new pitch outside the pool club, but in
actually joining him in carrying his few delicate goods
to their new location.

During the entire week of the Feast of Tabernacles
the light was white and sunless; it was bright, but with
no shadows. It did not rain and the wind was gentle;

everything looked as peaceful as an old painting. The trees along my street slowly lost their leaves. On the poplar-bordered piece of no-man's-land I passed every day, clumps of white asters pushed up between the paving stones. Behind the locked gate with its rusty chains and padlocks, a cloud of sweet fragrance rose out of the soft yellow leaf-hearts covering the ground. Wading through poplar leaves in a place that was usually out of bounds – the ownerless wilderness behind our garden – had been part of my childhood, its smells forevermore linked to a furtive world of secret activities, the need for whose concealment eludes a child's grasp. Walking through the streets, I heard plates clattering, voices, and table prayers spoken in the festively decorated gardens and backyards of the pious. I was glad it was not raining in their dishes, and sorry that the thin blanket of motionless clouds meant no star could shine in the children's soup. There was something about this festival I especially liked, with its rehearsed atmosphere of provisional arrangements and make-believe fragility of dwellings. It was the opposite of homelessness. It was not even the annual restaging of an interim period of wandering; the homeland of their customs and the Word was so large, they could invite all the heavens to reflect in their food.

X. LEYTON MARSH

During my first weeks by the Lea I only went as far as the willow copse. I passed close to the alder grove, walked across the island, returned along the riverbank path, through the passage under the railway line. It was always damp under the brickwork archway; puddles stayed there for weeks, and my steps on the unpaved path echoed bleakly from the walls. I waited until a train passed; the bridge and ground trembled slightly; the chunking and banging sounds on the old track bed became ever softer, a rhythm that reminded me of the sounds of trains travelling through my childhood nights, when the directions of all noises reversed in the dark.

Beyond the underpass was the open path along the river. The swans were sometimes demure, sometimes strident, and the sky rested on the water below the reflection of the small, cheap-looking housing units on the opposite bank, where there was never anyone to be seen.

Only rarely did I meet someone else walking along the Lea. Once or twice I saw an angler surreptitiously fishing between two bushes, glancing up nervously, seemingly not a local, but knowledgeable enough to realize he couldn't brazenly fish here. Perhaps he was fishing because of hunger, perhaps he just longed to cast a line or stand in the water, gazing at the reflection of the sky in the quietly flowing river. Or perhaps he was one of the notorious swan catchers who were rumoured to sit under bridges on autumn evenings, roasting swans on open fires, accompanied by the distant wailing of their victims' fellow creatures.

A stretch of the path passed between the river and a marsh area of high reeds, where there was always a sound of wind, or the noises of animals, especially birds. Walkways cut through the reeds, almost certainly a product of the same craving for order as the clearing of the alder grove and, like there, intended as a defence against wilderness rather than for its protection. Sometimes I saw a woman roaming the walkways with her dog, her long, grey hair in a plait, her clothes a wintry, reedy colour. Her dog wanted to hunt, and trembled, its whimpering suppressed, until she signalled permission with a movement of her hand. As soon as she raised her hand it threw itself into the marsh; there was a commotion between the reed stalks, and the dog brought back some small prey. Barely a step outside the city and already driven by hunger to hunt.

In the distance I could see the willow copse where the marsh ended with a pond. Beyond, a path branched off into open countryside, on either side of which were typical growths of the English margins – hazel, hawthorn, elm. There were cows grazing around the pond; they looked up, innocent, unburdened by the knowledge that they, together with the clandestine hunters, had been appointed as guardians of this interstitial wilderness.

I pondered, scrutinized and photographed the willow copse from all sides, from a distance as well as from close up, and I could find no name for whatever it was that I found so lovely. On photographs it seemed to me like a boundary marker, although it took me some time to work out what the boundary divided. It was very quiet here; the noise of trains was like a faraway thud of small wooden beads being strung on a thread, only to dissolve in the air. Looking across the wind-combed reeds the railway embankment seemed to have retreated into the distance, while the island was altogether hidden. Instead, a small building that could not be seen from the island had come into view near the tracks, a brick shed with a large, indecipherable graffito on its rear wall. This was probably where the lines forked and the points were set, and the shed would be where the track workers and navvies who checked the rails and sleepers for damage and removed any run over animals kept their equipment. When it rained, maybe they sat by the open door of the shed and drank tea out of thermos flasks, gazing towards the island, purposely putting off their return to the city.

Nowhere between Springfield Park and the mouth of the river Lea was the sky as vast as it was here. Elsewhere, if the sky seemed a uniform whitish-grey, you knew that here there would be distinct clouds; if the wind elsewhere were gentle, here it would be boisterous. And here, too, the clouds constantly changed their shape and stratification; they were sea clouds, drifting in from or towards the Thames Estuary, and it was here, above this strip of land, that they would turn about. Between the willow copse and the railway embankment a corridor had opened, a strip of land that did not succumb to use, an undesignated, vulnerable patch in the city through which something had entered that undermined the ruthlessness of all regimes. Under a bigger sky than anybody with an orderly life could possibly need, this place lay under the aegis of the willow copse, which, in an unusually clear light under gaily coloured autumn clouds scurrying east, I suddenly recognized as the epitome of the boundaries common to every childhood: a sparse grove inconspicuously dividing two worlds one must inevitably choose between.

One day I caught sight of several children dancing about next to the willow bushes. Smoke hung between the branches; the children had lit a fire, were fanning its flames, throwing things onto it, taking running jumps over it. I could hear their wild and raucous laughter, their yells, even the thumps they gave each other in their playful attempts to knock each other down while jumping. Their wildness knew no bounds, they bent the branches of the low bushes down so far that they caught fire, then let them bounce back again, scattering sparks. One of them emptied the contents of a plastic bag into the flames and they hooted with laughter as smoke began to rise in big thick billows. The crackling became louder too, but then the flames faded and all that was left were thick fumes spiralling upward slowly and reeking of burning plastic. As if responding to a command, the children were suddenly silent, picking their bicycles out of the grass and cycling over to the river and across the small bridge to the other side.

Pressing further that day for the first time I reached the domed synthetic roof, under which lay a deserted ice skating rink, and Lea Bridge Road, which crossed the river and cut the marshes in two. On the other side of the river was a funfair. The stalls, roundabouts, dodgems and somersault swings were set up on a large area of parkland, behind which a row of high plane trees divided the green area from some older, sombre-looking blocks of flats. Perhaps the fire-setting children, along with the throng that had quickly formed around them on the other side of the river, had come back to homes here, or perhaps they were among those moving about at the edge of the funfair, trying to climb into the dodgems behind the backs of the fairground workers. The funfair had not yet properly started, and someone was installing and testing fairy lights on a lime green shooting gallery; against the late afternoon light their flickering looked poor and desolate. The only music was from the caravans, where the fairground people were having an early evening meal. Perhaps the women were sitting at folding tables donning their make-up in their dressing gowns, while surly men sat around with toothpicks sticking out of their mouths. It was the last funfair of the season, but nobody here was well off.

It was getting dark, and that evening my way home took me up a street behind a housing estate and past disused factories. The road sloped upwards and from the top the marshes were visible between the chimneys and small towers of defunct works. The sky was low and hazy; not a star could be seen, only a couple of flickering lights to the southeast where the empty terrain stretched towards the horizon, but these too were drowned out as soon as the jarring blast of fanfares and sudden onset of musical entertainment heralded in the flashing, twinkling, beaming lightshows of the funfair attractions.

On the following day I inspected the remains of the children's bonfire. It wasn't large, smaller than the flames and smoke had suggested. The branches of the nearby bushes were singed. Among the ashes, which still stank of burnt plastic, was a charred doll. Its hair had melted to a clump of blackness and its arms and legs were ebonized stumps, but the sleepy blue eyes were unharmed and stared from its soot-covered face into the sky. It was a very ordinary doll, pulled off the shelf of some budget supermarket by a tired mother or grandmother on her way home from work on the eve of a child's birthday. She was just one doll among the many variously positioned dolls on a shelf, but this little woman in her sequin gown and long eyelashes, who had sneaked a wink at the mother or grandmother and taken her straight back to childhood, obviously had to be the one. Nobody could have foreseen her ending this way, neither the cashier at the budget supermarket nor the mother or grandmother, nor the birthday girl with her brothers and girlfriends. And yet, who does not recall those tiny and entirely reckless sacrificial altars of childhood, after which nothing will ever be the same again?

XI. ST LAWRENCE RIVER

My pile of moving-boxes had turned into a rugged landscape. Looking for things I had not expected to need, or whose existence I wanted to reassure myself of, I had moved the boxes around and opened their flaps; others had torn under the weight on top of them; the whole fabric of my collected worldly possessions had unravelled, boxes toppling, crashing down, splitting open, and objects unexpectedly gaining my attention. One victim of the shifting, sliding tectonics of my cardboard world was my box of maps, which was gradually buckling under the weight of two book boxes. Attempting to straighten the pile I pulled it out. Its floor immediately gave way and flapped open, and my entire collection of purchased, found and inherited maps fluttered to the floor: maps of countries I had forgotten, or which now seemed impossibly far away, or no longer even existed. Gathering the maps together I slotted them into the gaps between the boxes and set off for the river.

In Springfield Park I saw three elderly women sitting on a bench. From the tops of their heads down to their thick shoelaces, they were decked out in black, and there was something awkward about the way they were dressed up: they looked out of place here. They were speaking in a language I did not understand. When I came back from my walk they were still there, three female ravens waiting for a stage call, and who knows what had enticed them to the Springfield Park stage; perhaps it had been the promise of an appearance by the King. They nodded to me cordially, as if they now viewed me as an acquaintance. Then – I had already turned my back to go – a word came flying from their raven's beaks – Mississauga. No doubt the word had become Mississauga during its flight into my ear and had sounded quite different at the beginning of its trajectory, but now it was Mississauga, as on the freeway signs in the dazzling early summer light in Ontario a quarter, a third, half a lifetime ago? Almost still a child I had found myself, together with my son of a few weeks, in a big American sedan, a road-cruiser as people in Germany would have called it. The woman in whose house I was going to live had picked me up at the airport. She spoke a language I could not quite make out. Later I understood that in her mouth a German dialect unfamiliar to me and English were engaged in an unceasing struggle, now paralysing, then again racing at each other, and only occasionally, whether out of inattention or a generous mood, permitting a recognizable word in one or the other language, such as *formula* or *Boxboitl*, to leap from her tongue. Her six-year-old daughter sat in the front seat. After two sons who, under the rough buffets of their betterment-craving parents, had grown up into soft-hearted rascals, this little blonde-plaited late arrival was expected finally to drag the immigrant cart out of the mud. From time to time the girl interrupted her mother by reciting patriotic school verse; again and again she turned to the back seat in the course of her declamation, her vague child's gaze roving to the rear window, to the shimmering surface of the expressway flowing away behind us. She waved her hand in an exaggeratedly adult gesture of dismissiveness, and said through the gaps in her teeth: *The olden days they lie behind us.*

Too young, too confused, too dizzy from the flight and the sight of the ice floes, water, more water, islands and hard-to-distinguish barren land, to bid farewell to the *olden days* as cast-off ballast, I clung to my child and to the name Mississauga on the signs high above the roadway. Where had I arrived? Was I stranded, had I exiled myself? Toronto, Ontario, Mississauga, names unfamiliar and beautiful. Once I had swum through the river of these names, then – I thought of the ice floes I had seen from the airplane window and this estuary, which was in itself like a sea – then *the olden days, the olden lands* would be washed away, forgotten, forfeit, deposited in another space, another dimension.

I had not thought of Toronto for a long time, and not until this Mississauga – twisted by the wind and by the distant shrieks of a rare flock of seagulls above the river Lea houseboats – wafted over to me through the East London evening from the ravens' bench, did it come to mind again. Back in the flat I pulled the maps from the criss-cross of crevices into which they had slotted so nicely and unfolded the map of eastern Canada. Under my finger I felt the still, pale blue of the cold estuary, the countless small elevations of the islands, white and pale green in the river; they rubbed against my fingertip, pressing into the grooves and rings of my receptive skin.

This map was the first map I had owned, the almost untouched goodbye present from my map-obsessed father, which, weeping, he had placed in the baby basket at the airport. I had never seen my father weep before, and at first took it to be a trick, a clumsy actor's turn to pass time at the airport, or a game with a nod and a wink for my child, or for me, a little bit of clowning, which was supposed to say: you should be a map-reader too. But then came the tears which didn't seem to go with any antics or ham theatricals, and I turned away a little embarrassed, relieved that the flight was being called.

I had spread out the map only once before, on the

floor of the sparsely furnished dark room on the lower ground floor of the wooden house on Roxborough St West, a room with a kitchenette and a little bathroom. In a moment of armistice in the mouth of the landlady the word *gahdenruhm* tumbled from her lips, and with her chin she indicated the wire mesh door, secured with a hook, which gave onto the narrow dustbin passage between this house and the next, and from there out to the street between the meagre front gardens. Meanwhile the six-year-old was turning pirouettes and singing a Canadian homeland song in French; her pigtails spun and once struck me quite painfully on my bare arm.

I spread out the map when Aunt Liesl wanted to explain to me where she had lived on the St Lawrence River. She spoke a kind of Austrian sprinkled with English. She too had a room in the landlady's big house, under the roof, and every morning, while it was still dark, she came down the creaking stairs in her clumpy black shoes and made her way to the Hungarian Bakery where, under the name Ershinanie, she talked and laughed in a language I did not understand. Folding the map up again it became clear to me that the raven women had reminded me of Aunt Liesl. Was it because of her shoes? Because of the defenceless blonde layer on her grey locks, because of the made-up narrow mouth, the pale, blue-tinged face of the heart-disease sufferer? On this one occasion Aunt Liesl's elderly, manicured hand had gone up and down the river on the map – by the great St Lawrence River, she said again and again. I thought I could feel the little islands on the map arching their backs under her pointed fingertip, the ice floes further up in the estuary producing a faint buzz as they brushed against the grooves in the skin of Aunt Liesl's fingers.

In the evenings Aunt Liesl came back with a white linen bag with bread that had been left over in the bakery, dark rye bread with a shiny hard crust, crescent-shaped *kifli* that had started to turn dry, cardboard boxes with slices of strudel. She gave the landlady some of it, sometimes also gave me something; once she invited me to eat cake with her. The window in her room was open; I saw into the tops of trees, which seemed much higher than trees in Europe, full of birds with calls I did not know. On the walls there were photographic prints, calendar pictures of sunsets shining on wide plains and smooth water surfaces. We ate the strudel from the cardboard box and drank ginger beer, while outside in the tall trees the birds warbled and trilled their shrill melodies, a communication about a landscape of treetops and roofs of which, in my basement room, I had been entirely ignorant. Aunt Liesl took down an old shoebox from the wardrobe; a specimen illustration of the black shoes she wore when she went to the bakery was still stuck to its cardboard. She laid photos on the low table, black and white pictures, colour photos with a blue cast, on which a greenish pallor coated the faces of those pictured. As if she had a hand of cards, she dealt out the photos into several small piles, making brief comments as she did so: one pile was for her husband, who 'had made off over the river to the States', a broad-shouldered fellow with a tentative smile and a straw hat. I wondered how to picture this 'making off over the river', with or without a straw hat: swimming? in a boat? riding on the back of a giant fish? perhaps on an old-fashioned ferry, on which he had signed on as a ticket seller, only to disappear unobserved into the embankment bushes of the 'States'? I had no idea what the riverbanks of the Saint Lawrence River might be like. Were they forested or built on, were they covered in undergrowth, lined by overhanging flood-plain trees, meadowland, or did one busy settlement follow another?

The other piles were for Aunt Liesl's sister, who liked to pose in traditional costumes, for landscape and, as Aunt Liesl said, for the olden days. In the olden days Aunt Liesl had lived by a very little river – that was the Raab, she said, as if the little river didn't exist anymore, which had bubbled and gently glided through the olden days, and occasionally, when swollen by floodwater, caused unpleasantness. That, too, was pictured: the foaming Raab and battered wooden bridge being examined by a concerned young Aunt Liesl with her soldierly husband. My son began to cry; Aunt Liesl took him in her arm and rocked him jerkily by the window, as if she wanted to thrust him out into the twittering, whirring and trilling, perhaps give him a bath in these alien strains. I followed her instructions and picked up one photo at a time, noticing how on every picture of the St Lawrence River ships were to be seen in the background, big black barges, huge tankers, floating cranes, little white pleasure boats with waving passengers at the railings, the opposite shore very far away.

I grew up by the Rhine, I said in passing, once I had looked at the photos. My child had become quite still from the jerky rocking; she put him back in the carrycot, which was gradually becoming too small for the baby. I'll take you down to the St Lawrence River sometime, she said.

It was a very hot summer in Toronto. On the walls of the houses water trickled from the buzzing *dehumidifiers*, a word on everyone's lips that I had never heard before. I carried my son to Ramsden Park: we lay in the shade, I stared at the treetops, listened to the noise of children in the paddling pool. Other young women with children came and joined us. Their conversations usually revolved around quantities: how big was the baby, how heavy, how much weight had it put on – these questions were ticked off as if on a list. The women were all young, poor and unemployed, a couple even younger than I was; girls with small pigtails wearing cut-off jeans and their ex-boyfriends' cheap T-shirts who played with their babies as if with dolls, were always hungry, rolled joints, laughed a lot and imagined futures in which they made good as hairdressers or receptionists. Sandy, a girl with red hair, was somewhat older; she had a pram for her little daughter and talked about her weekend job in a motel in the west of the city. Towards Mississauga, she said, and waved her hand in the direction of the park exit. Her boyfriend was working night shifts in a factory; they wanted to get out of the city. Sandy considered the pram to be a good investment, because it made it easier to steal food in the Chinese supermarkets of the neighbourhood, stuffing it under a blanket around the child and into the basket. Out of the remainder of the tiny inheritance with which I had come to Toronto, I bought a dark blue pram which was on offer in Bargain Hunter under the somewhat old-fashioned term *baby carriage*, as well as a record player and a second-hand portable typewriter, because my landlady had found me a small job, which consisted of translating business letters for a wholesaler of expensive porcelain. The landlady was proud of her success and swore that in a few years I could rise to be the porcelain dealer's personal assistant. Once a week my father called. The phone hung on the wall in the landlady's hallway, and she left the kitchen door open and listened without embarrassment, sometimes hearing me crying or saying to my father: Don't cry, I'm fine, after which she gave me tips on how to save money on transatlantic phone calls, which I was supposed to pass on to my father. Sometimes she invited me to watch TV in the kitchen with her family. The television was on very loud, to drown out the buzzing dehumidifier. I sat between the kitchen table and refrigerator and saw the heads of the three family members outlined against the screen. The fat father came home at the weekends from a building site in Rochester in the States. He sat on his chair in his undershirt and stared into space more than at the screen. The family ate liver with cucumber salad and huge, dry, boiled potatoes. From time to time the little girl turned around to me, pigtails swinging, and smiled, a little bit of friendliness for the stranger in the cheap seat. I soon sneaked away. When my son slept, I lay on the bed in the dark and quietly listened to the Neil Young records I had brought with me from Germany, or listened to the racoons that were busy at the refuse bins.

I took lessons from Sandy at the Chinese supermarket around the corner. When I stole a basket of pale green summer apples by myself for the first time, the shop owner came running after me, shouting; a bevy of black-pigtailed Chinese children stood in a row in front of the fruit display and flailed their arms, but the man quickly gave up, in order not to leave his shop unattended. Outside, after days of stifling heat a terrific thunderstorm was in the offing. A gust of wind caught hold of a dress just picked up from the cleaners, which had been lying spread out still in its cellophane wrapping across the back seat of a convertible, and deposited it, rustling, on top of my pram full of the early apples. The woman in the car had not noticed the flight of the dress and, with squealing tyres, turned into Avenue Road, while the puffed-out plastic covering slowly subsided. It was a dark blue summer dress with little white flowers and a white collar, a sleeveless chiffon item, which the owner will have seen herself in at a garden or a cocktail party. Now it hung on the door of my cellar room and the cellophane sheath from the laundry swelled listlessly in the flurries of wind which burst through the mesh door. The next moment a deafening rainfall descended. Shortly afterwards the air was full of the sirens of the fire engines fighting water, fire and storm damage.

I plaited my hair into little braids, cut myself a fringe in front of my pocket mirror and put on the dress. I didn't have a large mirror, just looked down at myself and felt as I had once done in the clothes my grandmother had sewn for us for dressing-up games from her worn-out or moth-eaten things.

The summer lay heavy and motionless over the city, a kind of animal, its sighs slow and laborious. The air was so close that I sometimes thought I wouldn't be able to breathe any more. Sandy and I took the underground to the lake and walked with our prams through Budapest Park, a green space and promenade with a view of the lake and with little wooden buildings where you could sit in the shade. Like all wooden arbours in public parks they smelled of urine and moss; from the lake came the warm fug of water, oil, tar and sewage, and seagulls hovered indolently on the small currents of air above the dully-reflective surface of the water. Sandy explained that the lake was really a river; she described it as a huge river bulge, which grew thinner again towards the northeast and drained into the sea. Anyway, she said, with a sweeping gesture, anyway, all these lakes here are just river bulges, huge broadenings of rivers that absorbed too much water to be able to conduct it to the sea, so they gave birth to one river bulge after another, in which the quantities of water lay sloshing around, behaving like little oceans and waiting to be allowed to move seawards. Sandy grew more and more excited, as if these expanses of water were something close to her heart. She outlined the shapes of the lakes in the air, called birds and fishes by names I had never heard before, rose to her feet as if she wanted to turn directly towards the lake with her exposition, and before my eyes there appeared the picture of a land mass, one half of which was still dreamily attached to the Flood and, with its regular breath, alternately tended towards ocean and mainland. All water wants to reach the sea, she said finally, and sat down again. Lake Ontario itself was like a sea: the various marine birds, the harbour smell, the big tankers and barges shadowy in the haze were reminiscent of something oceanic. There was never an outline of an opposite shore.

Once Sandy and I took the ferry to Toronto Island. It was a very hot day in September, with the leaves hanging tiredly from the trees, and the days were already noticeably shorter than in summer. It was a Sunday or a holiday, the ferries shuttling ceaselessly back and forth, and on the expanses of grass and on the picnic tables big Chinese families had spread out countless bowls, plates and dishes. I pushed my baby carriage along the paths beside Sandy and felt like a child with a doll's pram, while we talked about our childhoods, of standing by the river and of looking seawards, and of the barges passing by: two monologues, in which the St Lawrence River further north, freed from its bulges, the fabulous stretch of water inhabited by countless islands that I had seen from the airplane, trumped the Rhine, which, described from the great distance of this other continent, appeared so small and slight that my childhood by its banks suddenly seemed weightless and fleeting. We sat

98

on the bank of the river disguised as a lake and ate our meagre picnic, threw stones into the water and looked at the dark violet cloud front that was pushing closer. Wind came up, and the lake began to throw up waves like the wake of a huge ship. Thunder rumbled; the families hastily gathered up their picnic spreads and formed into small troops trotting to the ferry landing stage, their plastic rain capes billowing out as they went: white, blue and pink flightless birds, whose wings, overwhelmed by the rain, were soon sticking to their bodies. We got going, but had to seek shelter from the sudden furious rainfall in a small pavilion, through whose windows we saw the city skyline disappearing behind veils of water and waves breaking onto the lawns and paths. The small ferries stopped running; now and then a ship's siren slid between the drumming of the rain and the thunder. Our children in their pillows looked anxious; we laughed to give them courage and sang 'Helpless' to them, because that was the only song we both knew by heart. Finally the thunder ceased and the rain eased.

With this thunderstorm the autumn came. I lost touch with Sandy after I moved into a flat on the first floor of another house belonging to my landlady, where from the kitchen I looked out at a winter-bare tree and a bit of garden which no one looked after. My son sat on a blanket on the floor and played with coloured spoons and a rag doll, while I learned Russian and read him the short lessons I was working my way through. I pushed the pram through the snow to the Hungarian Bakery and chatted to Aunt Liesl behind the counter. Sometimes she dropped by and brought leftover bread and dry cake in her bag. She sat down in the only easy chair I owned, an old dark red piece, from which the yellowish foam rubber was trying to escape through tears and burst seams. On my son's first birthday she brought him a red fire engine with six little firemen who had painted-on moustaches and stood stiffly in their little recesses, their palms, in soldierly fashion, flat on their painted-on trouser seams.

Not until the following spring did I see Sandy again. She now occasionally worked in a shop called Mother Earth, where she sold soya bean sprouts, molasses and brick-heavy loaves. Her hair was no longer red but pitch black and hung down her back in long thick pigtails. In the morning sun of May days we pushed our children to the play park, where they played glumly in the sandbox among intrusive grey squirrels. A bold grey side of nature, completely dedicated to the refuse of the city, made its presence felt everywhere: the fat squirrels, the racoons, the crows, even the flocks of gulls, which in the morning swung over the flatter parts of the city – they were all grey.

Sandy told me that in reality she was First Nation. I had never heard the phrase before. She whispered the word 'Indian' as if she didn't want to say it out loud. She told me she had dyed her hair red the previous summer. On the way to the play park we came past the employment office, in front of which clusters of men gathered in the mornings. The Indians were a head taller than all the rest and stood quietly at the side without talking; they remained impassive when Sandy attempted to greet them with gestures and incomprehensible words.

One day, said Sandy, they were going to leave the city and settle in a forest. She described the advantages of life in her *compound*, a word that sounded military and didn't call to mind the wild life she was describing. She disappeared, the summer spread out its damp, warm blankets over the city again, and in the hot nights

I sat with my son on the steps of the front veranda until we were so tired that we could sleep. That summer the district around Bernard was a quarter of sects and runaways, who lived in and wore out the old wooden houses, pending the day when the Great Improvement would sweep them out with a few strokes of the broom. Hare Krishna followers had settled into a shut-down church at the corner; they pushed through the streets in small orange groups, and pale, pasty-faced women in long dirty skirts took their shaven-headed children to the play park. The houses were divided into cheap bedsits in which young couples lived; sometimes a whole floor was taken over as a communal flat. The marijuana clouds hung thick and motionless in the humid air, the sounds of boisterous cocaine parties spilled out of the windows of the communal apartments, bottles smashed, police cars drove slowly, softly and aimlessly along the lit-up streets as in American movies. Across the street a girl in a yellow dress played guitar at night and sang in a shrill voice; from time to time she came over, and with the air of a clumsy actor trying to play an uncle, gave my son a friendly tickle under the chin. She claimed to have a child, too, said she was going to live in the country soon. Just this one more summer here, then: nature, *there's nothing like nature*, she said again and again. I never saw her during the day, only at night, sometimes wandering down the street arm in arm with a young man; they strolled, stopped here and there, began conversations. Everywhere the sleepless sat on the veranda steps and stared at the variations on the late-night film which, evening after evening, played out in the neighbourhood. Hardly a week passed without a house burning down. One night the church of the Hare Krishnas went up in flames. The sirens of the police cars and fire engines wailed for hours. At the corner of my street a fire engine skidded and crashed into a lamppost. The fire engines in Toronto looked like big toy cars. The firemen, holding onto iron handles, stood on running boards alongside the vehicle, their immobile faces under their helmets staring ahead towards their fate. Fortunately none of them came to harm when the engine went out of control at the street corner; they were skilful and practiced at jumping off before the vehicle came to a halt in order swiftly to take up position at a fire. Now they stood around looking a little awkward until the engine had been manoeuvred onto the road again. The impact had not been very violent, and the firemen all leapt onto their running boards again and raced off. The extinguished street lamp leant crookedly into the front garden of the corner house.

One morning Sandy appeared in a big, old road-cruising saloon to pick me and my son up for an outing to the country. We drove past the airport, under the signs for Mississauga. Again and again along the way the city already seemed to be crumbling away into rows of one-storey shops, car dealerships and workshops with gaps between them, only to catch and hold its breath again with yet another suburb. At some point, wasteland and scrub started to appear between the rows of shops, which meanwhile looked more like stands intended to hide a great emptiness. Finally open country spread out, huge fields, young straggly copses.

Sandy's compound was in some sparse woodland not far from a small town that was surrounded by its own little ring of low sheds and shops. There was a gleam of bright water between the trees, and on one side a high dark fence ran through the wood, behind which lay who knew what. The living quarters were tent-like huts, which Sandy called our wigwams: ragged tarpaulins, cardboard boxes and pieces of corrugated iron were tied to bound branches and scrap wood, also patchwork roofs, through whose cracks one might have seen the stars, had the tops of the tall trees not arched over them. Discarded objects stood around between the wigwams, shabby finds, donations, remnants of a life before the forest: an old cooker, a settee, a sunshade. In a little hollow away from the compound packing refuse piled up, which animals had torn, scratched and bitten: milk cartons, corn flake packets, chocolate wrappers, beer cans, and disposable plates with traces of bloody pieces of meat.

At midday Sandy went to the river to fish, and the children slept in the shade. We sat on an old lump of concrete by the riverbank. Sandy talked without stopping about the new life in the woods and by the river, about how they would behave like Indians once more, live on berries, mushrooms and fish and read the stars. The children woke up crying. Sandy didn't catch a single fish and asked me to collect brushwood with her, which was supposed to drive away the mosquitoes in the evening.

The evening was beautiful. A breeze blew from the river. It was peaceful, the waves lapped softly, the treetops stirred in the wind, and now and then individual stars in the sky could be seen through the foliage. Sandy lit a fire, giving the appearance of really having mastered the tricks of life in the wilds; the flames rose and crackled cheerfully. A man with a moustache played the guitar and sang: *Look at mother nature on the run in the nineteen seventies.* Everyone could sing along to that, producing an oppressive kind of cosiness from which I would gladly have fled.

I shared the sleeping bag I had brought with me

with my son and was unable to fall asleep. There was a musty smell in the wigwam; the man with the moustache and his friends muttered and hummed by the fire. Now scraps of music drifted through the wood from the distance, accordion and harmony singing, which were louder than the rustling and the whispering of the wilderness. The *Donner Swaben*, said Sandy in explanation in the darkness. They're on the other side of the fence.

The next morning the sky was milky white. It was very warm: the birds trilled lethargically in the treetops, flies gathered in vibrating swarms around each crumb on the floor. Sandy showed me a spot where you could look over the fence from an easily climbed tree. Big trailers, decked out like little family homes on wheels, stood on bright green grass. A swimming pool glimmered turquoise a little distance away. In front of a long hut two women in floral aprons were laying a table. The sound of church bells rang from the open windows of the hut. The whole park, apparently completely enclosed by the tall fence, seemed as if bathed in a dazzling light, although the sky above the woods was overcast. Everyone wants a paradise that the angel is not allowed to enter, said Sandy.

It was only later I came to realize that these were not Donner Swaben but Donauschwaben, or Danube Swabians, who in this seclusion may have hoped to create the impression for themselves that the river at the bottom of their neat and tidy settlement was the Danube, which had somehow managed to lose its way and was now flowing under this North American sky, which was so much higher than any in Europe.

Later in the day we drove back into town. We stopped at a lopsided shop at the edge of the city, where Sandy's boyfriend conducted a few small business deals. My son whimpered from the heat on the sticky imitation leather seat. *Leatherette* it was called here, a word that seemed absurdly delicate in the face of these seats. As consolation for their artificiality things are given a pet name.

Sandy's boyfriend gave us all sugary drinks and pushed a bundle of banknotes over to her for household shopping. Flies gathered around the little pools of spilled liquid beside the glasses. Sandy's boyfriend was expecting a customer. We set off again. On the car radio there was news every quarter of an hour about a mysterious virus which someone had brought in from Africa. The woman responsible had collapsed and died at the airport. The passengers on her flight were requested to report to quarantine; the possible symptoms of the sickness were listed. Hours after the first report the hospitals of the city were already crowded with patients who had fallen ill with one or more of the symptoms described. Sandy gave a brief raucous laugh each time the identical report was broadcast, while we slowly drove down the heat-flickering streets of the inner city and, after the cloudy day, there was a red evening sun in the rearview mirror.

In late summer Aunt Liesl was knocked down by a fire engine and died of her injuries two weeks later. I heard it from my landlady when she collected the rent. The funeral was a couple of days later, in Kingston, where Aunt Liesl had bought a plot. The landlady generously offered to take me to the funeral with her. In the days leading up to the burial I was haunted by the image of the silent embarrassed firemen standing around the body of the casualty. Had it been a call-out for water damage or a fire? Had Aunt Liesl been lying in a thunderstorm puddle, in still-pouring rain, or on the hot asphalt, in the dark, in the light of a street lamp?

On the day of the funeral there was a cool wind
blowing, already autumnal, bitter. The light here was
different from Toronto; it seemed sharper to me, the
shadows more pointed. Soon it would be autumn again.
We stood by the grave under swiftly moving clouds,
a little group without tears. The priest launched into a
hymn that no one could sing. After the funeral I went
walking by the river with my son. I'll take you to the St
Lawrence River one day, Aunt Liesl had said. The sun
shone down obliquely from the west, there was a greenish blue above the clouds. I looked downriver towards
the northeast and felt a little nearer to Europe until I
remembered the ice floes, which I had seen from the
plane when I arrived. My son didn't say a word, as if he
took no interest in the names of things but, laughing,
threw stones into the water, and at the sight of the big
ships spread out his arms. A steamer pitched and rolled
past, a sign on its railing advertising: *St Lawrence River
Gateway to North America*. For a moment I was confused
and dismayed. Where did this river lead? Out to sea, or
into the land? I looked at the water, and couldn't make
out which way it was flowing. The waves were colliding
and parting, flowing this way and that, and I was overcome by a sudden fear, catching all reason unawares,
that my child and I were at the mercy of a region in
which we would never be able to rely on anything, not
even that a river flowed to the sea.

A couple of weeks later the two soft-hearted rascal
sons of the landlady drove me to the airport. As a farewell present they awkwardly accepted my three Neil
Young LPs; they probably had them already. It was a rare
humid autumn day, a reminder of the summer. The air
over the road to the airport was full of dust, the sun squat-
ted heavy and red under the sign saying 'Mississauga',

which stretched over the carriageway. I thought I recognized the lopsided shop in which Sandy's boyfriend conducted business, and I looked for a road-cruising saloon in which Sandy and her child might sail by. At the airport I squeezed the rascals' hands; their soft faces twisted into friendly expressions and, meaning well, they pinched my son's cheek. He cried. I quickly took him in my arm, and before I entered the terminal building threw three handfuls of dusty dusk over my left shoulder for both of us. That, Sandy had once said, is what the Indians do before crossing a river.

XII. WASH HOUSE

After my first few weeks in London I began to look for a job. There were job advertisements aplenty. Londoners were avid newspaper readers and newspaper salesmen were everywhere, raucously yelling their headlines and attempting to drown one another out, which was hardly necessary, since all day long a constant stream of passers-by, in exchange for a silver coin, tore the fresh print from their hands. The waste bins overflowed with newspapers people had stuffed into them in passing, and when it was blustery freak gusts snatched up pages from every street corner, blowing them in waves through the streets, where they got caught in hedges and trees and, when the wind had nowhere else to go, covered cars and even small buildings.

The abundance of adverts got me nowhere, however; I had interviews, gave presentations, showed myself willing, auditioned, and sent portfolios demonstrating my abilities, but couldn't find anyone to employ me. I regretted never having learned something practical, something that might have impressed people, like being able to fold pastel-coloured cloth napkins at record speed into little military-looking caps of the kind one saw arranged in piles in the countless Indian restaurants, many of which emblazoned the names of famous battles, admirals and viceroys or their wives. Even as a practiced transmuter of napkins, however, I would have been no match for the waiters in these restaurants, who at all times of the day or night could be observed through windows folding, with staggering dexterity, the used napkins of guests who had only just left the establishment back into caps with perfectly spotless peaks and points for incoming guests. I had spent years pushing words across from one language into another, a mysterious task resembling a never-ending board game and a skill London did not need. I was not even sure I missed it much; to me it belonged to the tarnished lustre of yesteryear, far beyond the line I had drawn in the waters of the English Channel. But that distant lustre would do nothing – as some people put it rather bluntly – to put any food in my mouth, and so I traipsed around the shops, offices and public amenities always on the lookout for a vacancy I could fill with any of the few skills I had casually acquired.

Every day I passed a public wash house in my neighbourhood, a magnificent redbrick building with gables, bay windows and turrets, built at the beginning of the century when water became fashionable. Ancient blue washing machines stood in the main hall, and only graduates of a school for laundresses could operate them. The laundresses here were all big women and wasted no time in grabbing the washing from customers' hands and bundling it onto an old-fashioned weighing scales. Dangling from most of the machines in the mangle corner were handwritten cardboard 'Out of Order' labels, not unlike the scribbled name labels of the working-class children evacuated to the countryside during the war. The washerwomen tacitly permitted well-behaved homeless people to sleep between the faulty mangles. The homeless stayed put in their places for days on end, sleeping, eating and drinking quietly between the reluctant mangles, their benefactresses occasionally slipping them a ticket for the swimming pool, separated from the laundry hall by a glass door. It was a lovely old swimming bath with tiled walls and a domed roof whose skylights were gradually succumbing to moss. The fitments – such as taps, towel hooks, ladders and the benches against the walls – were relicts of what people called the old days, when the baths were built, and had gathered so much patina over the years that, especially through the slightly misted panes of the glass door, they had come to glimmer with a sumptuous sheen.

There were tub rooms, too, which were probably used secretly by the homeless people. These rooms were as good as condemned and nobody bothered to scrub them or eradicate the multifarious vermin that came and went there. The day was nigh when the enamelled sheet-metal tubs in the cabins would be wrenched from their anchoring and their pipes and drains sawn through; greenish limescale would flake from pipe ends to the stone floor, and the dismantled taps would clatter and clang in the tubs. Compared to the laundry hall the bathing cabins upstairs were deserted and desolate. Now and again a lean and elderly man with waving hair would turn up and buy a bathing ticket from the washerwomen. He would climb the steps with his creaking, pointy knees, but instead of bathing would indulge in his childlike art of playing tunes on the metal baths, tunes he had kept since boyhood. In order to perform these little pieces, which wafted down to the laundry hall as if from another country, he would bring with him an assortment of small, tried and tested memorabilia – broken toys, a battered pen-case, a dented gun made of shining tin – with which to set the edges of the bathtub vibrating.

On one or two occasions, unbeknownst to the washerwomen, I slunk up the stairs and had a look around, finding nothing but a rusty hairgrip, in which I fancied I had discovered the sole remaining witness of past family bath days: there would have been a strict order of bathing, with the father as the dirtiest of all entering the tub first, while the little giggling girls who stepped into the lukewarm, murky water last had little more to rinse away than a streak of jam behind one ear and a bit of dirt under their nails, and after a couple of minutes were climbing back out of the tub shivering and darkened by the dirt of their father's working week.

All the same, I would have liked to work down in the laundry hall. The laundry women did not talk over-much to the customers. Their movements too were carefully weighted and gauged, accompanied by the chirping, sighing, juddering and humming noises of machines and appliances, and all of it under a bright light, and in the fresh wind that arose between the swinging doors at both ends of the hall. Everything was in constant motion: customer, bundle, scales, pick-up ticket, machine. And now and then there were terse exchanges with the homeless people and white-haired tubbers, the washerwomen's whispers and bright bursts of laughter. Hanging about among the customers sub-missively queuing to get rid of their fusty-smelling bundles of washing, I attempted to memorize the washer women's routine, taking special note of the gestures and facial expressions with which they went about their daily business, intending to practise them as soon as I got home. Who knows, maybe I could use them, maybe I'd have some opportunity to show them off one day, for example at the end of a leaving party for a laundress who was getting married and going to live in the coun-try, with a spread on the ironing boards, a bunch of carnations and a pink cream cake to see her off. There would be paper plates of leftover cake being greedily eyed by the homeless, and cups with the sediment of sweet elderberry bubbly standing around on the wash-ing machines, and while the washerwomen sat around exhausted by cake and wine, I would seize my moment to show them what I had learnt. But of course that never happened, and I prowled around observing everything until eventually they saw me as a candidate for the mangle corner. Oh no, no – shaking my head I pointed to the cheap camera hanging around my neck, thereby identifying myself as a foreigner or even a tourist and garnering looks of blank incomprehension. Thus ended my foolhardy dream of becoming a washerwoman in a beautiful Victorian public baths and wash house, and although I set out to search anew, my wash house failure had left me with little appetite for a respectable London job.

It was not long afterwards, on one of my walks, that I once again bumped into the circus rider, whom I thought I had lost sight of forever. Slumped on a bench overgrown by thorn bushes next to the canal, he was so absorbed in himself that I thought I might creep past unnoticed. I had barely come level with the bench, however, when he suddenly flung a stick across the path, which almost tripped me up and gave me quite a shock. I'm so ill, he said without waiting, momentarily covering his face with his hands. The black sleeve of his coat slipped up his arm revealing red blotches on his forearm that had obliterated all trace of his tattoos. I told him about my hunt for a job, and as he listened a tired smile, almost like a sneer, played about his lips. It's always the same, always the same, he said at last. Allow me to recommend the Great World Radio Show. Bent forward, his arms propped on his knees and his gaze fixed on the evergreen weeds pushing up between the shattered paving stones of the former towpath, he gave a mumbling description, as much to himself as to me, of the vast, tireless, sleepless work of the International Radio programme, which, all day and all night, broadcast its programmes in every language to the whole world. He set out a vision of an entire universe of voices, local registers, tones emitted by countless throats, a web of languages weaving endlessly behind a façade of broken splendour, spinning its threads around everything and everyone in the rooms and studios of the radio station.

Following my setback in the wash house, the prospect of working in crepuscular chambers immersed in clouds of incessant and incomprehensible babble seemed appealing. One would, I imagined, be a voice, invisible and incognito; one would enter that International Radio World, where audibility was all, and later leave, a pale, bleary-eyed spectre of one's previous self, threading one's way through congested traffic, transported home to sleep it off until one's next performance. Even if, in my rashness, I spoke aloud in the street, nobody would recognize me or put a name to me, because the International Radio Show was not made for this country.

XIII. THEATRE

The window in the brick wall that I could see from my
little room was now lit up every night. Through the milk
glass window I could make out two shadowy figures in
the white light, heads slightly bowed, wearing bonnets or
bonnet-like heads of hair, busy hands, unrecognizable
objects. They bent down, handed things to each other,
their deft arms reaching this way and that, up and down
and to and fro. I pictured them preparing food. Since
there were no restaurants nearby they would probably
be selling home-cooked food, with their dishes passed
in buckets, baskets and boxes from back door to driver
then transported who-knows-where. Or maybe they
were just kitchen dogsbodies, peeling, dicing, coring,
grating, jointing and mincing what others would roast,
boil and bake, a small contribution to the huge amount
of food devoured in the city every day and then forgotten. The silhouettes were busy until the early hours of
the morning, their movements brisk, their hands occasionally flicking back and forth in front of their faces, as
if gesticulating during a lively discussion. One evening
I watched one of the figures stretch forward and suddenly raise a large knife: for several seconds the knife
hovered between their faces while nothing else in the lit
window moved. Then the hand sank with the knife, and
shortly afterwards they were both at work again.

Despite the incident with the knife these little nightly
shadow performances appeared benign, and I saw myself, placed in the backyard circle, as their only audience
member. Down among the fallen leaves, which now
covered the whole garden, the foxes contributed their
rustling sounds to these silent window shows. The neighbouring back gardens, into which the leafless bushes

115

and trees now permitted an interrupted gaze, looked mysterious in the light of the back lane's sole street lamp. What by day had looked like several collapsed huts and an agglomeration of building junk, looked by night like a stage area crowded with theatrical debris, waiting to be flooded with proper lighting while the shadow play ran as a kind of support act.

It was on a night like this that a house in my street, just a few hundred yards away from where I was lying in my little room, burnt to the ground without my even noticing. The house stood opposite the fenced-in, poplar-bordered piece of waste ground; it was narrow and old, and to judge by the many doorbells at the entrance, it had been divided into at least a dozen different living and sleeping units, where several people had burned to death in the night.

When I went to my front-room window the following morning to present my secret compliments to Greengrocer Katz from behind the curtain, I saw the boys from the Islamic school, which was a few houses away from my flat, standing in a group in the street. It was a fine morning with an almost wintery light, and the boys wore dark, quilted anoraks with their white kaftans and skullcaps. In their confusion they were jostling one another, helpless, tussling and constantly yelling. Their school stood only a couple of houses away from the scene of the fire, and the whole block had been closed off. There was a policeman guarding a blue-and-white taped police line that was stretched across the street; another directed traffic back to the main road. Responding to the pedestrians' queries the policemen pointed assertively towards the lane behind the gardens, where they could avoid the restricted block. As he did every morning, Greengrocer Katz unlocked the metal

shutter in front of his shop windows and sent it clattering up, while the Croat, excited, paced from one side of
the street to the other and back with his cup of coffee
in his hand, attempting to start up conversations with
passers-by and policemen. Somebody turned up to lead
the schoolboys away down the road somewhere, a helicopter circled above, a delivery van arrived with goods
for Greengrocer Katz, who was expecting to take large
orders that day, and after a brief exchange of words with
the police, the driver was allowed to park his vehicle.

It was not until midday that I heard what had happened. Leaving the house to go for my walk, I saw police
tape and the last police cars in front of the scene of the
fire. The Croat was standing on his own in front of his
shop, glancing about him edgily. Out of respect for the
casualties he had decided not to switch on his music. The
event had conferred upon him a new significance; with
the smell of burning he had sensed the new role he could
play as an explainer of this misfortune to the clueless. He
came up to me and described what had happened, and,
when I told him I had heard nothing during the night,
threw me a mistrustful glance from between half-closed
lids. He painted his remotely accrued knowledge of the
case in colours that betrayed how lurid they must have
become during the course of the morning. He spoke of
arson, acts of vengeance, the residents' relatives who
had stood in front of the house tearing their hair in the
flame-lit night.

While the gesticulating Croat attempted to paint a
picture of the fire in the air, Greengrocer Katz's shop
assistant was toiling with countless packages of brightly
coloured drinks, which the van driver had set down on
the pavement. Mr Katz himself stood inside the shop,
packing boxes, weighing oranges and bananas, apples

and pears, and scribbling on his order sheets. He was a serious man, imperturbable and pious. The Tzitzit of his prayer shawl stuck out under his shirt, keeping him from erring ways.

I took the prescribed detour along the back lane. There were tall weeds at the door of the house where the shadow theatre took place, as if nobody had used it for months, and the windows along the lane were hidden behind metal shutters.

When I came back from my walk the police cordon was gone. A single officer had remained to guard the burnt-out house. In the front garden under the soot-enwreathed caverns of windows lay broken glass together with various objects the residents, surprised by the fire, had attempted to save, but which had been soaked by the extinguishing water and trodden into the soil by the firemen's boots: pieces of clothing, a fleecy blanket, a brightly coloured plastic toy. Already two or three thin bouquets of flowers had appeared on the garden wall: pale carnations or freesias, short stems with tired-looking heads packed in cellophane, such as one finds at the checkout of any supermarket. At the first news of such an incident there were always people in a hurry to bring these little flower bouquets to the scene, even when the accident had no direct bearing on their own lives, as a kind of sacrificial gift of gratitude that they had been spared. The poplar leaves on the fenced-in piece of empty wasteland opposite had turned completely dry and were strewn with flakes of ash.

The causes of the fire were quite different from those the Croat had put about. It had been a case of spontaneous combustion, it was later agreed; fires igniting by themselves had often been reported, so it was said, as if there were sparks lying dormant under the floorboards, between the rafters, or in other forgotten corners of the houses of this city, that were merely biding their time to flare up and start a fire. The victims were foreigners, three men sleeping in a small room that was just big enough for a triple bunk bed, who did not even speak the language in which people must have tried to wake them and alert them to the danger. They will almost certainly have been exhausted, desperate for sleep and the opportunity to visit places other than their small room, and though it may briefly have torn them from their dreams, they will have put the noise out of their minds.

For weeks afterwards a yellow police notice stood in front of the house asking the public to come forward with anything that was known of the three victims of the fire. Their names, nationality, place of work. Anything. One day, after one of the few stormy nights of that winter, it was gone. Standing at the fence of the patch of wasteland, where the weather had long dispersed the last ash flakes, I hoped the wind, which, fortunately, usually blew from the west, would carry some partly burnt snippets with the victims' names all the way to the places they had called home.

The light on the day after the fire, at any rate, was unforgettable and not in any way English; it was light-blue and silver, as if a momentary off-centre spin of the Earth had let it stream in from the Bug and Vistula Rivers in deepest Middle Europe.

XIV. HACKNEY MARSHES

Walthamstow Marshes ended at the ice-skating rink, whose curved roof, from a distance, always seemed so deceptively sky-coloured. A small bridge across the river led to an empty park lined with plane trees, North Millfields, a fairground and playing field for the wind, which, before heading on, took a deep breath here, flattening the rough grass, blowing the fallen plane leaves this way and that. In the background were old blocks of flats, a stillness sprawling between houses, smooth-barked tree trunks and over the grass, life's pale shadows prowling around the houses at noon, stiff washing hanging from the balconies: a hushed interval between marshland and city.

At the foot of North Millfields the river curled around a boatshed and a small protuberance with some baffled birds and washed-up rubbish before disappearing under a bridge. The road that divided the marshland in two here was one of the old arteries between the town and far-away places, fringes, and countryside. Here, sore-footed travellers bound for the city from villages, distant towns and other shores had time to ponder turning back or, bent over the parapets, gaze at their reflections in the water, or, racked by indecision, to search upstream and down. Fugitives from the city who were oppressed by its grinding noise and were at last able to survey the open expanses beyond its reach might let their hands wander to their hearts and back to the steadying parapet.

There was a distinct sense of permeability about this crossing place of waterway and thoroughfare: a tidal pull washing the hidden gills of a great urban fish beached on seemingly dry land. Here, currents of difference streamed in and out of the city; the fairground people with stalls on North Millfields came and went; it was a place where for centuries people had chosen between town and country, the Thames and the sea, factories and rural suburbs. For as long as the city had existed, waves of migration to and from the city had crossed the plains that stretched between its eastern edgelands and the Channel coastline's islets and inlets, its estuarial spits and spurs, flowing water increasingly covering its surfaces the nearer it came to the sea.

Beyond the bridge the river Lea forked into the old straightened navigation canal to the west and, further east, a smaller river whose banks were bordered with patches of wilderness. Between them the broad meadowland of Hackney Marshes was draped on cool mornings with a thin blanket of mist, above which loomed the mysterious uprights of goalposts and, in the distance, electricity pylons. I would invariably follow one arm of the Lea downstream to Hackney Wick, where the two rejoined, choosing the other arm for my northbound return. The first stretch along the canal, before the playing fields, was complicated terrain: it was not exactly wild, but nor was it tame, path and water passing between a brick wall and the thick unruly scrub along the opposite bank. Here swans and crows held sway over an assortment of inscrutable buildings and a lumber of cumbersome jetsam, bridges that were none, staircases to nowhere, windowless blocks, fences among the tall weeds, rubbish – blown across from the town side where the buildings, behind the briars, came almost to the water's edge – entangled in branches and thick weeds, new estates before which swans rested motionless on the surface: a quiet detour that belonged nowhere, outside the city yet debarred from the wilderness behind the wall. In this stillness I was beset by unease. I was reminded of paths through similar spaces of pointlessly disturbed wilderness that were gradually succumbing to weeds and neglect, alien to beauty of any kind. There had been such prematurely tarmacked paths to nowhere in my childhood too: pending the erection of housing between the river and the village, along the railway embankments, through dank subways, and in the trembling shadows cast by pointy trees, fringed by rampant undergrowth, places for the furtive activities of strangers, which one wanted to forget straight away. There were weed-infested work-tracks around gravel pits in sight of the crater's edge, between the lean remains of sand and gravel piles. Such paths were harbingers of landscape upheavals, which sometimes were no more than rumours, forerunners of the dream of the Great Straightening of the World.

Round a bend the view opened up. To the west were the purpose-built dwellings of a district that was not much loved: council flats and cheap housing, the high-rise blocks and prefab family homes of an era when shoddiness was the order of the day and prosperity was inconceivable. They had been built on land cleared of war debris, the clayey ground of the old brickworks, where bricks had once been fired for the sprawling city. The hasty cobbling together of housing in an effort to remove all trace of what lay underneath had been a major feature of my childhood in a region where prosperity became desirable and attainable earlier than it did in London. Buildings were constantly demolished, sites excavated and levelled, and the signs of a past that had gone awry were overlaid with impenetrable crusts. Disintegrating brickwork, in whose nooks and crannies the hair of former residents who had turned to snow still hung in rustling spider webs, was buried under the pale-grey, post-war pressed stone, permitted its return to the earth under new roads. Day after day, and before our very eyes, strips of wilderness fell victim to the building frenzy: an enclosure of briars behind rusty gates where flowerless woody roses ran wild, where the branches of unpruned fruit trees interlaced, and once green benches, thick with rampant weeds, would have crumbled to dust at the touch of a human hand, gardens whose unremembered owners had fled their own names. Here in London the reasons for erasing traces of the past may have been different from those in the country of my childhood, but the unhappiness that inhabited the drab chasms between the houses looked remarkably similar in both.

Refuse floated on the water; occasional fragments of speech, cries of children playing or arguing hung in the air above the river, streaks of sound, shreds of goings-on behind and between the houses, whose still, dark reflections in the water blocked any notion of the barges that had once left here loaded up with bricks for destinations upstream or downstream. London's bricks had been made elsewhere for some time, and working barges were a thing of the past. The water here now was no more than a boundary between land that had been built up and land that had not, between the housing estates of Homerton and the broad meadowlands of Hackney Playing Fields that lay open to the east of the path, at the far side of which were the woodlands and bushes that marked the course of the navigation canal's wilder sister. I took a photo of the reflection of the housing blocks in the water and as I was peeling the film off, the picture fell in the river. The swans at the edge of the reflected buildings craned their necks but did not move. I broke a twig off the little hawthorn tree which, together with a few other

124

puny bushes, formed a thin border to Hackney Playing Fields, bent down over the edge of the grassy bank and fished the picture out of the water. It curled in my hand and a dull film covered its surface. In return for the hawthorn's broken twig I placed the photograph in the fork of one of its branches, and there it remained for weeks, a tiny discarded mirror of a section of the opposite side of the river, until sometime towards the end of the winter, it disappeared after a bout of hefty storms.

The Hackney Playing Fields consisted of a single enormous expanse of grass. Goalposts stood in various places across it, and when there was no mist, they looked like flimsy toys lost in an ocean of green, or something somebody had forgotten to remove that could easily be blown over in a wind, or something a storm had actually deposited there, something to be picked up and put down at will, which a group of children counting to three together could heave from one place to another without doing themselves any damage.

The days grew shorter, winter was on its way; dawn was laggard and broke later. It was only at the weekends now that sparse groups of footballers came to train, fathers bringing their children, small knots of players who looked lost in this vast space. Restive youths on bikes hung about at the edges, casually letting their bicycles fall in the grass as they joined in little games or hunted for items people had left in the changing rooms. On cooler, misty Sunday mornings the shivering voices of footballers in a mixture of languages threaded the cold air with imploring commands that were impossible to ascribe to individual callers, a soundtrack banner trailing over the capacious sports field, edging blindly across a picture of tiny figures on an immense field in the morning mist, without necessarily belonging to it.

On weekdays the playing fields were mostly empty, and the grass, ever paler as winter approached, blew this way and that, flattened by gusts of wind. Sometimes a raptor hovered overhead, a denizen of the city scanning its territory for prey; long weaned from the real wilderness, its attentions were focused on the small, recklessly scurrying creatures of its liminal habitat. As I walked further into the stillness the air began to vibrate with the soft buzzing of the pylons at the edge of the sports field, the indecipherable language of motionless giants that hovered airily in the pale light of early winter and only from a distance brought to mind shapes I remembered from the dreary hinterland of the Rhine valley, where the pylons lined up in orderly fashion in the fields, their legs apart, hollow-chested armies through which the wind whistled, the light entangling in their struts.

Viewed from the Playing Fields, the function of the grey nondescript blocks of buildings along the path was apparent: changing rooms, rooms for small events, a shelter for sudden changes of weather. The image imposed itself on my mind of teams decked in two colours rushing across the field with heads ducked under a downpour and flashes of lightning, then thronging together under the heavy concrete overhang of the roof, breathless and dripping, flushed with their pumping hearts.

Hidden in the middle of the large Hackney Marshes Playing Fields, as in the depths of the instant pictures I had taken with my bulky camera, were memories I was only gradually learning to read: the steady drone of an invisible plane above the white cloud cover, chirring pylons lisping messages from the air, the wispy rustling of pale winter grass in the wind, and between it all a stillness that masked the proximity of the city. I thought of the sports ground of my childhood, so far away from here and foreign, a scrap of memory bubbling up in my mind between the words 'playing fields' and *sportplatz*, between barely perceptible traces of marking lime on the grass and the chalk marks and circles I had known on lawns, sand and basalt. The sports ground of my childhood, a small flat area between a midden and the vineyards, was surfaced with the spongy volcanic gravel of the region and bounded by a flat-roofed sports hall with adjoining flat for the *turnwart*, the gymnastics supervisor. *Turnwart* – what a word, redolent of the reek of summer rubbish, the smell of linoleum from the gym, the odour of sweat, which, an invisible flag, is the marker of any sports facility. The gymnastics supervisor had two daughters with blond pigtails who were always dressed in tracksuit bottoms and permanently ready to perform any exercise that would show their mettle, turning cartwheels or somersaults, doing flips over the rickety balustrades at the sports hall entrance, pigtails and gym shoes flying; the latter, presumably white under their coating of reddish gravel dust, were probably scrubbed and washed by the *turnwart*'s wife before sports days, then laid on window ledges to dry in the sun. Geraniums, called pelargoniums in those days, blossomed in front of the *turnwart*'s windows. When the door of the sports hall was open the smells of linoleum, rubber and leather leapt at me like an animal escaping from a cage, a raw sharp gym smell that went for my throat. This gymnastics supervisor, to whom his daughters reported at a blast of his whistle, was something of a grumpy type who permitted or forbade children to play around the goalposts as he saw fit (goalposts that were just as flimsy and susceptible to the wind as those on Hackney Playing Fields), and who would occasionally

127

go out with a large cudgel to hunt the rats that collected at the rubbish tip. He killed them whenever he caught up with them and put down poison for the rest, later gathering the cadavers of the rats and cats that had succumbed and burning them in a stinking fire. The bonfire ground was a dark patch between the sports fields and the rubbish tip, bounded by thin brown scrub that always looked singed, a strip of land set aside by tacit agreement and used not only for burning the cadavers of poisoned animals, but also for celebrations and feast days, when the gymnastics supervisor was also in charge. There were occasions in summer and winter when the supervisor would gather wood and set it upright along with other inflammable junk he had lugged unceremoniously from the rubbish heap, exciting expectations of a crackling fire whose blaze would be seen from far away. While he was building the fire his daughters bustled about him eagerly, dragging over rotten or splintered material that somebody had pronounced unfit for use but which they, learning from their father the tricks of how to set up a grand yet obedient bonfire, had deftly and dauntlessly salvaged from among the other rubbish on the heap. The gym supervisor was so skilled at making fires he might just as well have been hailed as a fire supervisor, at least on days like these, when the size and intensity of the fire were the important things, and the celebratory nature of the occasion required procurement of additional resources. In late autumn, following their torchlight procession through air that was moist from rain and heavy with the soot of coal fires, the schoolchildren were urged, as a rat-scaring sacrifice, to throw the lanterns they had so painstakingly constructed and protected from wind, weather, and the strangeness of the November evening into the *turnwart*'s fire; the children

128

grew fractious, for walking through this very evening they had only just lost their hearts to these lanterns, in which all their manual awkwardness had been transformed into comforting brightness and gaiety. Their teachers' digs in the ribs or cuffs on the backs of heads over the clumsiness of their work, the ridicule poured over their misfortune by others whose own fingers too were smeared with glue, and whose equally frightened eyes glinted above their derisive mouths, and who hoped their jibes would ward off taunts against their own misshapen efforts – all of this had dissolved in the dainty curls of smoke from their candles. Although their precious creations were born of such hardship, they wept in vain at having to give them up, for the *turnwart*'s daughters were everywhere; it was as if they had multiplied in the brilliance of the fire, their pigtails making long and lightsome shadows as they cajoled the children, rebuked them, pushed them and pulled them, pressing them to surrender their lanterns.

Having lost so much the children stayed away from the bonfire ground for a while; the smell of burning hung in the air as winter approached, and the shadowy ghosts of pigtails were all about. It could take half a winter to recover from such a fire, from the faces of the grownups, parents, teachers, the *turnwart* and his daughters, all of whom were in cahoots with the fire, jerking, grinning and bawling in time with its crackling flames.

Summer saw the spread of fires other than those built by the gymnastics supervisor and occasionally, when the supervisor had not exercised due care and attention, as it was put, a spark would leap unseen from one of the small incinerations of dead animals to the rubbish dump, starting a smouldering fire, sending brownish fumes in all directions just a few feet above the ground, as if the smoke were viscid and heavy. The fire brigade arrived, the sports ground was cordoned off, the gym was shut, the pigtails of the inquisitively peeping supervisor's daughters dangled between the pelargoniums. The supervisor of gym and fires stood accused of carelessness and neglect. Sullen, shamefaced and at a loss, he stood aside while the firemen were extinguishing the fire. Meekly disgruntled, he turned his back on the bonfire ground during the weeks that followed, an absence gypsies were quick to make use of, arriving overnight with their shaggy ponies and going about their lives surrounded by the protective quadrangle of their caravans. On our way to school we saw the new children searching for kindling among the elder and willow scrub on the other side of the sports ground, and the supervisor's daughters came running to check on them, representing their much-maligned father. Women in headscarves and long skirts stood in front of the caravans surveying the rubbish dump, their eyes sheltered by their hands. From the outside, the only signs of the small fires glowing in the square bounded by the caravans were ringlets of smoke coiling upwards into a pale, cloudy sky. The days were sunless and without shadow; the newcomers kept themselves to themselves, searching furtively in the rubbish dump for metal and other hardware, although with little hope, for these were the days of the scrap kings, who harvested their tacitly and mutually defined kingdoms regularly and thoroughly. The gypsy children joined us for a few days at school, then they were gone, leaving nothing behind them on the bonfire ground but a black crater at the centre of the singed brown, where their fires had burnt deeper into the ground than those of the *turnwart*.

One spring a rumour went around that the gymnastics

supervisor's wife had run out on him. The pelargoniums hung their heads and the pigtailed girls skulked
in their unscrubbed gym shoes. In the lee of the jilted
turnwart's rumoured addiction to drink standards fell
into decline. The sports ground turned into a play-
ground where small groups of rambling children played
football and got up to whatever they felt like. A man with
a penchant for dropping his trousers whenever the boys
passed on their way home from football would loiter on
the path through the rampant thorn bushes that were
no longer kept in check by burning animal corpses. In
the end, all of it – supervisor, sports hall, pigtailed girls,
sports ground, rubbish heap, occasional gypsy camps,
the fires and dropped trousers – was abruptly terminat-
ed by yet another grand levelling scheme that saw the
bank of scrub steamrollered, the fire crater and rubbish
pit filled, and everything else bulldozed until all that
remained was a raw dark plain as flat as the high full
moon in winter. By the following spring uniform rows
of dazzling-white, private, box-like homes stood on
either side of freshly tarmacked streets, and all that had
been was buried under them, becoming the past.

Winter light, white, milky, tempering all that was
sharp and hard, mingled with the weekday stillness,
spreading a blanket across the empty Hackney Marshes.
The clattering of trains on the embankments that ran
through the meadows and reed beds beyond Lea Bridge
Road reached my ears in quiet waves, muffled swathes of
sounds that had detached themselves along the route and
which now fluttered freely, soaring in the sky together
with the occasionally stuttering hum of a small plane,
invisible above the clouds, high over the hawthorn with
the spoiled photo. This was what the planes sounded
like when we hid in gravel-pit caves, which were out

of bounds to us children; we hunkered down with our knees drawn up to our chins, silent, entirely motionless, waiting for someone to find us, half hoping that the person who came looking would be more frightened of the caves collapsing than we were. For a short while beneath the sluggish vibrating drone of the invisible plane in the blue sky – a slanting, wave-edged segment of which ran across the cave mouth – we imagined ourselves unfound for an undefined Forever.

I took a picture of the little hawthorn tree back with me to my flat: past the railway embankments, the alder grove, the Springfield Park ravens awaiting the return of the King. In the little improvised café two waitresses were heaving a potted plant into the glass porch. Watching them was a Jewish woman with a bevy of small children. The children were well-behaved and asked questions, perhaps about the plant. I heard the woman say: Hadassah. Hadassah, Hadassah, cried the little girls. I knew the word, but had forgotten what it meant. The few scraps of Ivrit I knew lay tied up in a bundle beyond the range of my memory. And this although I had once been of the opinion that the tongue and throat were better suited to this harsh and tender language than to any other.

XV. NAHAL HA YARKON

After my father's death I travelled to Israel for the first time. I took his suitcase, which I had chosen from among the things he had left behind, and stuffed it full of the useless things one packs when it is not clear what the journey is for or when one will return. I had no place to go and no particular plan and, for the first time, no fear of flying either. For some time before the plane landed, dawn had shown its hand as a red streak on the horizon, but when we got down and left the plane it was still dark. I let myself be pushed and shoved by the crowd of passengers, and I pushed and shoved back; rudeness was everywhere in the large arrivals hall, as if the mask of politeness had slid from the faces of passengers who, in the plane, had been so careful not to tread on one another's feet; it was as if they were steeling themselves for something. There was a military presence too, and I saw weapons flashing even before I collected my luggage. My old suitcase caused a stir; a few people gathered around me, including two or three armed soldiers. Aha, a refugee's case, somebody expertly determined, giving it a light tap with the toe of his shoe as if expecting a reaction from the suitcase that might confirm his hypothesis, but the suitcase didn't move, and the officers remained on the alert, following me at a distance. I pretended not to care, but the truth was that I enjoyed the furore this heirloom from my father had caused on my arrival in Israel, and the promptness with which its special nature had been recognized impressed me.

I stepped outside; the day had begun. The fragrance, the heat, the early brightness all belonged to a different continent. On the way to Tel Aviv I saw blue morning light over the industrial zone which, as in most cities, characterized the outskirts of the town: a soft glow over a landscape where empty space and barrenness existed side by side with bustling life. The sky still had some of its morning red, but as was typical in hot countries, the air in the distance had begun to shimmer.

For a few days I stayed in various lodgings in town, always in narrow box-like rooms with views into the chasms of streets still under construction, until I eventually found accommodation in a housing block. My flat was a modest affair, an almost empty space, suspended among a host of unfamiliar noises that surged though the walls by day and by night. The mornings arrived early and suddenly – voices, shouts, the unremitting noise of grinding machines that might be occupied with demolishing or building. The scaffolding swayed in the desert wind, the workers yelled whenever they needed to communicate. The silky blue of the morning light grew dull and whitish in the rising heat. On windy days it dazzled. The shade was deceptive, consisting only of dark silhouettes that offered no coolness. I crept through the parched parks past a slender trickle of a stream, sometimes walking as far as the beach with its compounded blinding glare of water and sky.

The heat consumed my energy and cramped my ability to think. After walking through town it was often an effort to get back to the block where I lived; I dragged myself into the lift, opening my flat door with trembling fingers. It wasn't unusual for me to get out on the wrong floor and end up in front of a stranger's door, futilely attempting to poke my key into the lock, until someone opened from within, their features contorted with an anticipation that crumbled into disappointment as soon as they saw my face. Aware that disappointment can often lead to fury, I quickly stepped back before the person could push me away, apologizing for the distress I had caused.

Darkness fell quickly, and the streets grew stiller. The blunt colours of flickering televisions reflected in the balcony doors and open windows. Men stood on the balconies smoking, speaking in a rough tongue broken by short, hoarse, sometimes chuckling, sometimes bellowing torrents of laughter, a language of which I understood no more than a few words. Later at night, a groaning and whimpering set in that penetrated the thin walls of my flat and left me baffled. It bore no relation to the brash, bustling days, the clattering of cutlery at mealtimes, the deep-voiced laughter of the women and the chuckling conversation of the men, not to the rats in the lift nor the clacking of steps along the echoing corridors.

So I lay awake at night and tried to make sense of it all. Of this country, its noises, the heat, light and shadows, the smells of burnt rubber and sewage, of mint, coffee and dust, the whimpering at night. I did not get far. I passed my mind's eye over people I had seen during the day, trying to link their faces with the noises I heard at night. In the morning I was increasingly overt in my observation of passers-by and residents of the housing block; I studied the corners of their mouths and eyes, searched for the tracks or salty residue of tears, and listened to the rawness and hoarseness of the men's voices, but then the language itself was hoarse and rough and foreign, and I reached no conclusion on the matter.

One day I became acquainted with one of my neighbours. Mi was an unshapely, fat woman, whose voice was as hoarse as those of the men I'd heard talking on their balconies in the evenings, and she had a similarly chortling and bellowing manner of laughing. She smoked all the time. Her handling of her lighter, cigarettes and packet had something robotic about it. Her small, cushion-like hands expedited the movements deliberately and economically, neatly and nimbly, as if independently of her large and lumbering body. Her tiny black eyes in her puffy face were in constant motion, searching incessantly for a purchase they never found. She spoke almost without interruption. Like me, she had spent part of her childhood on the Rhine, ten years before my own childhood and on the opposite bank of the river. Perhaps that was what brought us together; at any rate we seemed to be the only two people in this country who had these place names in common, names we occasionally recited to each other. Whenever Mi told me about those years, I saw her as an awkward girl with dark hair standing on the riverbank and gazing across at the opposite bank, gazing at my side of the river and the small town where I would grow up. On one occasion, she showed me some photos of herself as a child. Here I am standing by the Rhine, she said. They were blurred photos that looked cut off, although the smooth white edging went all around the photo. I saw a girl with plaits wearing a pleated skirt and a pullover, her face a blank spot in which only her spectacles were visible. The child stood at the left edge of the photograph, seen from the side with her face turned towards the beholder, her arms half raised as if she were stretching them out, perhaps to someone who did not make it into the picture, who was too slow for the impatient photographer. The photograph had evidently been taken out of doors, in a place that could be anywhere; the background was dark, a wall of a house or perhaps the pile of a bridge, but with no sign of the river. I didn't know what to say, for I was no longer interested in the Rhine, but only in the fact that this child, who had once been Mi, would have to stand there forever with empty arms. Mi seemed disappointed by my silence.

Mi had three sons and a slim husband whose shyness had given him a stoop and whom Mi had brought back from a later visit *back there* – meaning the Rhineland. He was employed as a caretaker at some institution Mi never named, and he generally had a grin on his face of which I could make no more sense than I could of the whimpering at night.

Soon each day saw me sitting in Mi's kitchen. Back at my own abode my things lay around deserted and would have been covered with dust if I hadn't handled them every day, picking them up, weighing them in my hand, only just hesitating, in a state of desire I could not admit to myself, to throw everything hastily into my suitcase, to close the lid, and, taking it up in my hand, to sally forth – only: where to? At night I lay in bed half asleep and heard my own voice mumbling: where to, where to...

In Mi's kitchen I drank vapid lemon tea, which her husband brewed by the litre every morning in large pots and pails. The lemon tea reminded me of my childhood; I thought of the pale, rainy summers and their putrid smells, the worm-infested apples lying at the edges of the roads, and the fermenting heaps of cut grass in hidden corners of bare gardens. In thousands of half-finished, garbled and largely meaningless sentences Mi told me the story of the many branches of her family who had lived in countless lands, followed countless trades, received honours, endured abuse and died excruciating deaths. Mi's voice was louder than mine; her laughter rolled in throaty waves through the tiny kitchen, flushing out all possibility of my telling her of my own family. I know, said Mi, as soon as I started to confirm or contradict what she was saying with some detail of my own life, but... And she held up her hand as if to warn me, winking ambiguously. *Mind you*, she would then say, for she was always using this little English phrase, *mind you*, in my family... The stories she told were sad, indeed awful, but they all ended in a hiatus, cut short by Mi's silence. Her great aunt, a splendid woman, a princess of the Orient, whom fate had removed to a cold and foreign land, glided – accompanied by sleigh-bells and pursued by a jeering mob – into the darkness of a yawn that swallowed up the rest of her story; a consumptive uncle, a valiant tailor in a distant land who, right in the middle of his flight with an unwieldy suitcase, chased across scree and wasteland, fell into a hole in her sentence and disappeared; she shut her mouth and he was never seen again. Her grandmother, kind-hearted and surrounded by the fragrance of cinnamon and cloves, wept over a great misfortune into her steaming soup and, a moment later, came undone in the fog of the story. Ah well, Mi would then say dismissively, not that I ever knew why.

Mi was very ill and often told me, interrupting her story with short barks of laughter, how one of her breasts had been affected by cancer, and that after it was removed, a strand of twenty-seven malignant lymph nodes was pulled from her armpit – like a string of pearls, she said repeatedly, like a string of pearls. As she said so, I had the feeling of something slipping through my fingertips, which, because of the heat, were particularly sensitive. She stroked her small, somewhat weak-minded son's head and pulled him onto her lap. Come on, my little cripple, she said and pressed him to her breast; the child grimaced and wept at the same time. Holding her reluctant son on her lap, she told me of her childhood on the Rhine and in other countries. The sun always shone in her gardens, and she was a girl

with pigtails. She travelled with her mother throughout Europe, following her father who went from town
to town celebrating scientific triumphs, covering his
tracks so his wife and daughter would not catch up with
him. She shook her head ponderously from side to side,
showing me how her pigtails bounced when she skipped
and went on the swings in the twilit summers or walked
through the streets, trying to track down her father.
Only her hair, which had become ever thinner and barely covered her balder patches, did not move, permitting
not even the most distant imitation of a girl's pigtails
fluttering through the streets of the Rhineland; strands
hugged her forehead and covered her ears, or at the back
fell to her nape, where they were gathered to a tiny stub.

Once I found Mi asleep. She had laid her head on her
arms. Her scalp was visible between her sparse strands
of hair, which was moist with sweat and stuck to her
head. Her hair was a dull black, here and there turning
grey. Her small pale ears stood out from her round head.
She was so motionless as she lay there that I thought she
was dead. I laid my hand on her shoulder, where her vest
strap cut into her skin. Her shoulder felt like a warm
piece of meat. Under my hand Mi was an alien bundle
of life, and I was horrified to notice how empty I felt. I
went back to my flat and sat on the bed for a long time,
thinking about the emptiness, attributing it to the pur-
poselessness of my life in this place. Prescribing myself
a change of walks I put on, against the sun, a long light
dress that had been fashionable some years earlier, and
set off towards the sea.

The wind twisted my dress around my legs, a hin-
drance it took me a while to get used to. Several of the
beaches were crowded, and I had no choice but to pick
my way between the prostrate bodies whose smells,

together with a buzzing profusion of voices, cries, screams, complaints, taunts, sighs and gasps, befuddled my mind, while at the same time I had to be careful to dodge flying beach balls. I took in the people, their arms, shoulders, the backs of their necks, lips and noses, and casually, running my hand quickly and furtively over my face, asked myself in what way, if any, I was similar to them. I thought of my father, stopped where I was and shut my eyes, trying to recall his facial features, his figure. I looked up and down the rows of people, and for a moment it seemed as if all the people who were lying there looked like him, although my father had despised lying on beaches of any kind all his life. I discovered peculiarities in these strangers' faces that suddenly seemed to me to have been cut out of his own; from some distance I saw a man whose figure, size and bearing looked so similar to his that I was startled, but when I approached, any semblance of similarity dissolved and I found myself facing a small dark-skinned man who was so unfamiliar that I was taken aback and felt ashamed, not only for approaching the man so closely in my delusion, but also because I sensed that in my search for similarities I had lost any clear picture of my father's face and figure.

The heat was such that I needed almost all day to walk along the beach and back, or, as it seemed to me, to march along it, to pace it out, for my way of walking had a strangely military feel to it. Between the busier sections of the beach were some screened off areas where pious women could bathe and feel protected from lustful eyes and chance contact with the warm, titillating skin of strangers. Behind the high screens they took off the magnificent wigs they wore when outside under everybody's gaze, like queens with crowns. Towards the south the beach frazzled to a no-man's-land overgrown with scrub, run through with trickling drains, and lined with dark ruins of mysterious origin interspersed with large boulders and weeds. This is where Arab families and groups of women and children sat, the boys playing football across thin rivulets while the women, wearing long black robes, their heads held high, walked far out into the waves laughing and splashing one another.

On the way back I noticed a crowd of people standing around the high chair of a lifeguard who was looking intently through a telescope and watching something out on the calm water that I thought I could just make out as a tiny dot near the horizon. There was great excitement and anxiety and a dark look in people's eyes as two vigorous musclemen leapt into a speedboat and put out over the evening ripples with their engine roaring and their keel slapping the sea. A swimmer had ventured out too far and the lifeguard had seen the danger he was in, or maybe his disregard for it, through his telescope – perhaps the swimmer was so distracted that he hadn't noticed how far he was from the coast. Were he to turn about now and lose heart at the sight of the great expanse of water between himself and the beach, the sight of the approaching motorboat and his rescuers might give him hope. He could be returned to dry land where he belonged. The sight of the swimmer gave me a feeling of sadness, for as I caught a glimpse of that tiny dot so close to the horizon, a distinct and palpable memory of my father arose in my mind.

Mi became the owner of a wheelchair that her husband had managed to get hold of, a ramshackle contraption he had probably spotted and bagged on some rust-flecked patch of waste ground. Mi was too heavy and too weak to get out on her own, she told me; her legs could no longer support her bloated body. The wheels were straightened and the seat mended, and then, with loud cries of encouragement, the family heaved her in, cheering and clapping when at last she was wedged in between the armrests. I heard them boisterously taking her down in the lift, and even thought I could distinguish their hooting voices in the sea of noise washing around the housing blocks towards evening.

On the following day Mi was exhausted; she wheezed as she spoke and frequently coughed, but as it got cooler in the late afternoon she asked to go out for a walk again. Out in the fresh air! she called, but her family had lost all interest in pushing her wheelchair. I offered to accompany her, and, as on the previous day, there was a great deal of heaving and shoving until finally, with her cushion-like hands flat on her armrests, Mi sat in her new vehicle and smiled contentedly. The wheelchair seemed amazingly light to me, as if her body, brimming over all edges and borders, were made of something almost weightless, a sponge constantly swelling under her skin.

When we got out the front door, we caused quite a stir. Neighbours who had not seen her for a while came over to say hello to Mi, inspecting her wheelchair, tapping her armrests, testing her tyres with the toes of their shoes, patting Mi's shoulder appreciatively. Mi waved her hand as graciously as a queen, at the same time impatiently bucking in her seat: she wanted to get going. To the river! she cried out to my astonishment at the first crossing we came to. I had seen no sign of a river in town, and feared for a moment that Mi might be in a muddle. Without a moment's hesitation, however, she directed me through the late-afternoon town, through little residential streets and well-frequented thoroughfares where the stink of exhaust fumes mixed with sweet and spicy aromas from kitchens and side-street gardens. Walking along I felt light-hearted for the first time since my arrival in Tel Aviv, happy even; the evening was lovely, the houses, the bushes arching over the wall, the people standing on the balconies smoking and calling to one another, the way we glided through this blue light, I light of foot, Mi so sure of her goal, and after a few hundred metres our trip had something entirely natural about it. Eventually we came to a park that had suffered very badly from the summer heat and aridity, through which flowed a feeble, foul-smelling stream. I had taken this trickle with its livid reeds for something channelling sewage to the sea. Mi, giggling hoarsely, slapped her thighs in glee at my astonishment. You thought I was going to take you to the Rhine, didn't you? Her question was drowned in a gurgle of laughing and coughing. The famous Yarkon River, she said in a pretend American accent, when she could breathe again. We followed the course of the stinking stream down to its mouth at the shore, a barren miniature delta against the background of an old power station that was already floodlit for the night. Mi lectured me about the river's past splendour, but I was unable to hear very much because when she spoke, continually interrupted by her fits of coughing, she stretched her head out a little way in front, as if sending her words out ahead to announce her arrival before she came wheeling through. I started pushing Mi away from the river and its desolate estuary and keeping the power station at our backs, until Mi demanded I halt for a view of the sea. It was very peaceful. The gentle sough of the waves was mild and Mediterranean, and in a blue-lit bar in a shack nearby, the nightlife was getting off to a slow start with someone playing a pop song for a few seconds, then silence, then again. I sat down on a small wall separating the shore from the rough road.

I told Mi about the incident of a few days before with the swimmer. As always she gave a hoarse laugh, but out here in the dark her voice sounded different, younger, calmer. That happens here all the time, she said. Some people call it immigrants' fever. A person who almost feels at home here swims out; he looks at the blindingly glittery sea, and suddenly he is overcome by such a powerful longing for all he has left behind that, looking back at the coast behind him, he convinces himself that the distance to the land he has left – in reality a far away coast, an indescribably distant prospect – is shorter than the return to the shore of his new homeland. And healthier for his heart.

Mi pulled a misshapen cigarette out of a fold in her tracksuit bottoms and lit it. We smoked slowly, taking turns, the sharp smell of burnt hay sticking in my throat and burning my eyes, while the gradual onset of dizziness was more pleasant than expected.

The way back was heavy-going; I felt exhausted, and Mi seemed heavier than before, swaying to and fro, her head frequently dropping onto her chest, so that I worried she might slip off her wheelchair. She did not want to return through the park and led me through the streets, unsure of the right direction, making wrong decisions at crossroads. All the pavements seemed uneven to me, and riddled with cracks. Despite the southern night and smell of the sea there were times when it felt like a suburb of Warsaw, and I lost any sense of direction. Starting up from my delusion as if from some feverish dream, I would see where I was and long for familiar streets, noises and smells. It was deep in the night before we reached our block of flats, and I was surprised by the stillness that had settled, which was untroubled by sighs and whimpers. In the lift Mi was suddenly wide awake and stared at the dirty narrow mirror on the wall, in which we were both visible. My face was above hers; in the bleak light I would not have recognized myself or her. Mi said nothing, but I could see her wide-open eyes in the mirror.

I was about to push her into the dark hallway of her flat, where her family were clearly fast asleep, when she clutched my arm. You don't need to stay here, she said. Nobody here has been waiting for you.

XVI. FIREWORKS

The beginning of November was a time of big fireworks displays, although we didn't see much of them here. In an area largely inhabited by observant Jews and immigrants people tended to have little use for local or national traditions; the waves of noise made by bangers and firecrackers seldom broke on our shores, leaving the pious unperturbed, and on the rare occasions anything was heard, elicited little more from the Croat than a slight quivering at the corner of his mouth. It was late autumn, the days bathed in a grey light, and the seasonal storms had not yet arrived.

While searching for a job during my first London autumn I was given plenty of opportunity to learn how to avoid the little wars fought out with bangers, firecrackers and rockets launched from the cover of street corners in preparation for Guy Fawkes Day. Embattled by fireworks and storms I had taken the advice of the circus rider and applied to the radio station, which promised security and a roof over my head. The radio station was housed in an enormous, palace-like building in the centre of town; it stood on a kind of island surrounded by surging traffic, towering above the confusion of the streets. By day variously coloured flags could be seen fluttering over its cornices; by night the building was floodlit in white, making the pillars and arches appear even grander. The steps from the street to the main entrance were so high that at first I had difficulty climbing them. When I reached the top of the steps I turned before entering the building and looked back. The roads flowed together below me; everything looked small. The milky-white autumn light over the town now seemed willing to commit the storms of recent weeks to oblivion.

All comers could enquire at the porter's lodge and be met by a Great Radio Show assistant, who would lead the candidate to his or her exam. The way from the entrance portal to the Examination Room passed though long, broad corridors and via imposing flights of stairs under high vaulted ceilings. By contrast, the Examination Room itself was an almost alarmingly small cubbyhole, where a wall-mounted loudspeaker transmitted instructions on whether to whisper, murmur, scream, screech or purr forth an arbitrary selection of words and phrases into a battered microphone. Following a short test I was told that my main duty would be in the Murmuration Room, my subsidiary duty in the Purring Room. I was issued with a number, red cap, which was part of the announcer's garb, and small whistle on which I was to blow a certain signal were I to get lost among the rambling corridors and flights of stairs. The assistant showed me to the Murmuration Room. In long rows of desks, which reminded me of old telephone switchboards, sat countless red-capped announcers wearing headphones over their ears and speaking into microphones protruding at mouth-height from the boards in front of them. Everyone in the room was speaking into a microphone in his or her own language; there were all sorts of people in each row, and the whole hall-like room was filled with an indescribable muttering and rustling from which individual words would briefly pop up, only to sink again in the ocean of sounds. In contrast to the Purring Room, where specific tasks were assigned, the murmurers were permitted to read out their own texts ad libitum, albeit without interruption, for that was what people liked about the murmuring programme: listeners throughout the world, so it was said, would sit entranced beside their radio sets listening to the rise and fall of the voices, trying to catch words in their own language, or to give meaning to sequences of words, and perhaps even to recognize the voices of people they knew.

My subsidiary duty in the Purring Room was concerned solely with broadcasting the so-called Happy News, a programme nothing like as popular as other broadcasts; in fact a rumour flared up at the time that the entire Purr-Programme was on the hit list, as they put it. Between the Purring News were longish musical breaks with international performances of cheerfully contemplative songs. In the meantime the announcers had time to compose themselves and rehearse more news, which came fluttering onto their desks incessantly in the form of sloppily scribbled or typed pieces of paper.

Thus one worked one's way from shift to shift, relaxing in the Relaxation Room, taking refreshments in the Refreshments Room. On leaving the building one had to hand in one's cap, whistle and number. Returning meant going through the whole process again from scratch: application, examination, allocation. In time you might be shown to a familiar desk, whereas at the beginning you were simply hustled from one programme to the next. The longer you had been an announcer, the smaller, more cramped, and higher up were the places of work, and the fewer the announcers in one room, until eventually you were on your own and could even stockpile tapes of your own voice for later use.

Although many advanced, a considerable number did not leave the building for weeks or even months, possibly for fear of losing a familiar work place, or because they were discontented with their wonted lives outside the radio station, or because of the genuine attachment they felt to their respective programme or their desk, or to trifling things like their red cap, the whistle or even their number. It was said of some individuals that they had spent years of their lives in the building, seeing neither daylight nor darkness, dwelling only in the gentle arms of their programmes, which they worked on with hundreds of others. They purred joyful tidings, screamed the war reports, screeched news of great human tragedies and whispered things that were unutterable, and every now and then, unheeded in the crepuscular light, would murmur the long, laborious and often sad stories of their own lives into the microphones of the Murmuration Room.

I never stayed there longer than a day, and on stepping outside the main entrance was always amazed at how quickly so much time had passed. From the landing in front of the main entrance I saw the crumbling façades of the upper floors of the palatial buildings on the opposite side of the street – where pigeon droppings had corroded the cornices, ledges and mouldings – and the most recent traces of collisions on the road. Determined never to return, I set off on my long journey home, always on foot, each step liberating me from the clinging web of voices.

Shortly after my appointment I was on my way home from the radio station when, for the very last time, I encountered the circus rider. Breathing heavily he stepped out of a doorway, as if he had been waiting for me to pass. His fever-bright eyes shone, and he carried an old flower-patterned camp bed in one hand, which he proudly held up for me to see; this was the bed, he told me, on which he hoped to end his days. Where on earth did he get hold of such a thing, which in our shared country of origin would surely have languished for decades on some rubbish tip or landfill, rusting and falling apart? Suddenly anxious he might be hoping to find a place for himself and his camp bed in my flat, I hurried onward, but he stayed on my heels for longer than I had expected, and I heard him behind me, shooting volleys of words at the back of my neck. Perhaps it was his way of trying to get me to slow my pace. Scurrying along at my back he gave a wheezing, broken account of the great fireworks display, and of how he had stood at the edge of the expectant crowd, whose excited gaze had been directed at the sky ever since the light had begun to fail and the town's jagged outlines at the foot of the hill had stood out sharply against the greenish sky. Shortly afterwards, the first rockets had shot vertically into the sky, whizzing and sizzling, their white plumes dissolving in the darkness, and at last all the other fireworks had started up, burgeoning into grandiose, colourful shapes and images. The crowd had cheered every explosion, and even when there had been nothing to see in the black sky but a gaily coloured spray of descending sparks, the crowd had cried ah and oh and swayed to and fro until it died away. As for him, he had merely stood on the sidelines and watched, but it had reminded him of happy days when he had occupied centre stage himself, galloping around while the audience applauded under a blaze of sparkling lights. And thus absorbed for a few moments in the happy voices of the fireworks spectators, he had been able to forget his fate, as he called it. I managed to throw him off my track by taking a sudden sidestep into the path that led to a narrow footbridge across the Thames, where at this time of the day there would be such a throng of people that the circus rider would be incapable of forcing his way through.

I for my part had glimpsed only a pale reflection of the fireworks; from my flat window I had seen nothing but occasional, haphazard trails of sparks criss-crossing the tiny section of sky above the railway embankment and between two disused factories. I was relieved to have survived the firework war; I would no longer have to seek shelter in the radio station, at least for the time being.

XVII. STOLLER'S

On the corner of the main road, its façade facing the cemetery, stood an old building housing a store and flats. Its name, Stoller's Kosher Egg Stores, stood in yellowy-white letters across the dark brick front of the building. In the evening, from the upper deck of a passing bus, passengers could look into the floor above the lettering, where old-fashioned standing lamps and furniture were stacked higgledy-piggledy in front of the window, a gallimaufry of objects waving from a bygone age, a greeting issued via has-been post-war accessories whose total redundancy was not yet a matter of unanimous agreement to those on the other side of these windows. In the store downstairs were 'pre-packaged goods': stridently labelled canned foods from America and Israel, biscuits, candles, plastic plates and cutlery for celebrations and households that lacked the space to keep separate cutlery, their wrapping shielding everything from unclean hands. There were egg-slicers too, of the kind I remembered from my childhood, and other objects for preparing foods served half a lifetime ago. Perhaps there were people here who still gathered of an evening to eat pumpernickel and cream cheese and salmon with egg slices of unerringly identical thickness. The woman at the checkout was wearing a dark-brown backcombed wig. Her hairdo was so big it resembled a ceremonial headdress. Mrs Stoller usually sat quietly on her stool, turning the pages of a little book in Hebrew script, an edificatory work, or guide to virtue and modest behaviour. Whenever her shrill, counter telephone rang, she lifted the receiver to her ear and as quick as a wink let loose a torrent of words, as if she had guessed who would be at the other end as soon as it rang. She spoke loudly, as one might expect for a call between continents, and talked about family visits, arrival and departure times, flight numbers. For her pious family, always on the move between London, Jerusalem, Baltimore and New York and probably other places too, Mrs Stoller pulled all the travel strings. I tried to overlook her quietly disapproving suggestion that her store was not the right place for me. Browsing the shelves in a manner that was all too obviously driven by curiosity, I purchased things that to her eyes must have been the wrong things for me, or else it was me who was wrong for the things I had purchased. Even if her eyes were generally on her book, she had sat at this counter for long enough, and had seen enough heads and legs above and below the advertising banner stuck across the window and door, to know that I did not belong with the grey fish-balls in aspic, or the oversweet borscht with 'Tastes like Bubbe's' on its label. There were not many customers. If another woman came into the shop they would mumble things to each other that were not meant for my ears. As soon as I approached the till she snapped her book shut, which was enclosed in a sumptuous-looking silvery metallic jacket embellished with coloured stones. The metallic cover was reminiscent of an icon cover. Mrs Stoller would stand when the customer paid, operating her electric calculator with one hand while resting her other on her precious book. She wasn't tall, and when you got close you could tell her beautifully coiffed luxuriously dark-haired wig was a red herring: Mrs Stoller was old; the backs of her hands were covered with brown flecks; her hands even trembled a little.

On one occasion two young men came into the store. They hurried up and down the short aisles between the shelves searching, their long black coats swishing against the edges of the racks and somehow managing miraculously not to knock down the small pyramids of stacked tins. The men pressed Mrs Stoller with questions; eventually they found what they were looking for. Arriving at the counter they attempted to haggle, and complained, taking turns to address her in a harsh, staccato Yiddish, but Mrs Stoller was unrelenting, with her eyes lowered and her hand placed firmly on her splendidly jacketed little book. As money changed hands both the men and Mrs Stoller were careful not to touch each other.

I only ever bought knick-knacks there, and, as Mrs Stoller had doubtless correctly guessed, did so out of a curiosity that embarrassed me. I had no need whatsoever of the articles in her store, which vaguely reminded me of my childhood, an era of belief in preserved foods and hygiene and of the silly gaudiness of useless objects standing around on pale Formica tops. Mrs Stoller would never have thought of the packets of pumpernickel, toothpicks, and yahrzeit candles I bought from her as souvenirs, as mementoes of my expeditions to a foreign world which, like all experiences of the unfamiliar, called forth lost memories. I placed these souvenirs on my house-moving boxes beside the instant pictures and the stones and pieces of wood that I had brought back from walks by the river Lea. At the least opportune moment of my life I had turned into a collector, never returning with empty hands to the flat where the barely decipherable archive of my homelessness grew.

The entrance to Stoller's Kosher Egg Stores' storage room was beside the little front extension where the Croat kept his shop. A narrow passageway between two houses crossed a backyard, which, if I craned my neck enough, I could see into from my little room's window, in fact right into the Stoller's storage room. This, the storeroom itself, as well as the yard and a bit of the pavement, was where Stoller's factotum worked, a man of about forty with a beautiful face that was continually twisted by a faintly pained expression. I had once heard the Croat call him 'Jackie', which from his mouth had sounded like 'Sheckie'. Jackie was not in the attire of the pious; he wore only a kippah and work clothes, under which no tzitzit were visible, and his main job consisted of moving and stacking goods and waiting for their delivery. Jackie was one of the Croat's closer street cronies, although he always kept a certain distance and I never saw him eating or drinking with the Croat. They stood at least a pace apart on the pavement, gazing at the same point in the white afternoon sky, raising a hand to greet someone across the street, or tapping their feet to the beat of the song on the Croat's cassette recorder. Sometimes they talked, but the Croat was always the one with the expressive gestures, and Jackie nodded appreciatively with his pained smile.

The lord over the Stoller kingdom between store and backyard was a stocky man in shirtsleeves and black kippah who delivered goods several times a week in his big car. Jackie stood at the ready whenever he came, abandoning all gazing, foot-tapping or smiling at the expressive Croat and setting to work immediately, while Prince Stoller's two young sons gambolled around him, pulling at his pullover and begging for brightly coloured drinks.

Jackie carried in the cartons one by one, slowly and carefully, at the same time placating the little boys, and, finally, with one or two motions of his arm, wiped the boot of the car.

156

On several occasions the deliveries were brought in a big lorry, bringing Jackie a whole day's work. On big delivery days he was given a hand truck, and I wondered where the contents of all these cases disappeared to, since they were certainly not sold under Mrs Stoller's watchful eyes to the few customers who came into the store. In the afternoon after school the Stoller children appeared and climbed onto the loading deck, playing hide-and-seek with Jackie behind the remaining cases, who carefully and deliberately cleared their hideouts away. The Croat stood at the edge of the pavement smoking, looking up at the loading deck and giving advice. Hey, Sheckie! he would call again and again, do it this way and do it that way! Hey Sheckie, not much left to do now! And he offered his help, undoubtedly eager to make inroads into the kingdom of the Stollers' storage room, which had always been out of bounds to him, but it was not to be.

Apart from the Croat, Jackie was the only person in the street who greeted people. He greeted men cordially, women furtively, with a slightly lopsided mouth, which mirrored his sad smile. From the loading deck of the lorry on big delivery days he could offer a greeting that was almost magisterial, with one hand slightly raised and his eyes gazing into the distance. From up there he would certainly be able to see the sepulchral monuments beyond the walls of Abney Park Cemetery, and it may have been from this view that his gestures derived their angelic aspect on the back of the lorry.

Looking out of my window I once saw Jackie pick something up off the street and put it down on the low wall that bordered the front garden under my window, something lost that he wanted to be found again instead of him taking it home, for it was unlikely that his flat

– which I imagined as a sort of sublet with relatives of some degree or other, board and lodging in exchange for a helping hand and errands – would have room for found objects. As soon as he was out of sight I went down to see what he had left there. It was a slightly underexposed black-and-white photograph of a bridge over a river. In the middle ground, on the embankment at the river's edge, a woman could be seen sitting on a rug in the shade of the bridge; in front of her at the water's edge, their feet perhaps covered by the closest waves, stood two children, white and blurred.

I took the photo and placed it on the removal boxes with the other things, even though I hadn't found it myself. It seemed out of place there, was somehow different from the other objects, and had no inclination to consort with them or make friends, not even with the trifles from Stoller's shop. I kept it nonetheless, giving it a place of its own and fancying it was something that Jackie, the handyman, however far away he was from the scene depicted, wished to stay linked with in somebody's memory.

XVIII. OLD RIVER LEA

Peevish swans kept watch over the tame, navigable arm of the Lea just beyond the weir, where the river forked and the wild Lea branched off. Ill-tempered guardians, gone into decline and close to neglect in their tired swan-white, which for all its grubbiness gleamed in this perennially umbrous corner between weir and bridge. Wardens on a hiding to nothing, between seedy patches of green, factory sites, an old power station, the quiet rustling of the filter beds and the muted hissing of the small weir, keepers of secrets of layers of the past, of barges plying goods upstream and down, of down-and-out tow-men and sweating draught horses, suburb loiterers, brick workers at the townward rear of the works by the canal: these old, tired swans persevered at the behest of an absent royalty, the sole remnant of which was revealed in the swaying and gliding of their small whiteness on the still surface of the water.

The sky above the swans was full of crows. They sat on the telegraph wires, wandered from riverbank to riverbank, perching in trees, flocking around little titbits that some passer-by had thrown away or lost, scraps blown this way by the wind, a legacy of the small number of walkers and cyclists who used the towpath. On pale winter's days the gathering crows were restless clouds that threw no shadow, but filled the air with rasping and rushing and clapping of wings, passing over like a forever unredeemed promise of rain.

The wild or so-called Old River Lea pushed through the brick-and-concrete filter beds; for more than two hundred years it had provided water to the north-eastern reaches of the city, which spilled over into the marshland here, drawn to the sea, stretching all its watery fingers towards the great estuary. The filter beds themselves lay hidden behind a wall in a rarely accessible, verdant enclosure. Once I found the gate open and strayed into its sheltered wilderness of herons and blue tits, wilted rose hip-bearing briars, elder bushes with wrinkled berries, rowans and head-high fern fronds. It had been a mild winter's day, calm and bright; a man sat smoking among the withered bushes. He noticed me with a start, and I was no less alarmed; his bicycle lay in the yellowing winter grass, which was dry and rustled; later he would pick it up and cycle away, and the spot where he had been would resemble the deserted lair of some wild animal that had passed through.

I returned on the path that looped around the filter beds and led back to the river between open terrain and the electricity pylons standing by as ever like lost, harmless giants frozen to the flat land, slender, immobile and delicate, their six arms splayed out to no conceivable purpose underlining their defencelessness, or their perplexity over the question of which way they should go next. The more familiar I became with this flat world in the milky winter light, the more I thought of the pylons as parts of the landscape that by some strange quirk of nature had surged out of the ground featherless, hairless and leafless in time immemorial, honest custodians of this intermediate realm between firm ground and a deceptive alluvial flood plain that was underwashed by countless waters; they were fine-boned guardians of the void uttering nothing but their spidery buzz and hum, a rarefied, highly-pitched song that was only audible in pauses between clattering trains, and which attempted again and again to subvert the city beyond the Lea whenever it drew a deep breath to roar.

From the marsh meadows the path took an unexpected

162

turn to a tree-lined section of the riverbank: first came spindly poplars, then willows, and alders, a comforting boscage of many-armed trees, grey concentrations of willow, trees that had toppled, now half in the flowing water, deciduous bushes between the trunks, the guttural calls of hidden birds. The river was shallow here and leisurely, and, as I walked, put me in mind of an oxbow by the Rhine on which my father once took us rowing in an old wooden boat. It was a damp, grey day, and was certainly not in summer, for there was barely a soul to be seen along the riverbank. My father was silent and quite absorbed in thought after an incident of some kind had caused him to remove us from the house with barely concealed haste and bring us to this quiet backwater of the river, where, from an acquaintance, he had borrowed a rowing boat which had to be dragged out of a dank shed. I had never seen my father row, and as he went through the motions he seemed familiar with every aspect. He told us where to sit and put out onto the dark water under the surprised gaze of his boat-hiring friend, so that we bobbed on the little waves made by his oars. In my memory we glided up and down the stagnant backwater for hours; the oars, entering the water with soothing regularity, resurfaced with thin bands of water which dissolved into drops that pattered back onto the surface as the oars lifted; low branches of tangled willow bushes flowed past, the gravel-covered banks, the little bay of white sand where we played in summer, and to see these things from the water seemed quite unreal: the unruly thickets and the tameness of our beach, which in the present grey forlornness could just as easily have been part of some enchanted wilderness. During the whole outing my sister had been firmly clutching a small plastic net of chocolate coins wrapped in gold foil, which someone had given us earlier that day, and as we clambered out of the boat onto the jetty, her hand was so stiff with cold that the little bag slipped from her grasp, fell into the water and vanished. The unexpected turn the path had taken in a landscape facing away from town, the tangle of willow bushes and open view of roots, the remoteness of the familiar and the disconcerting discovery of a hidden view of things – all of this had raised my memory of that earlier view of unruly bushes leaning into the water, a revelation which, at the time, I had found almost disturbing.

It was a fine walk along the Old River Lea, leaning on the crook of the river's wilder arm, safe and open to miracles; it was all too exotic in its seemingly lovely seclusion, for in fact it was an illusion, and one that could be undone by a single glance at the well-kempt green of the bank beyond the trees on the other side. And yet so long as one's gaze did not stray as far as that garish green between the trees opposite, a green that could only belong to some newly instated, clipped and cropped functional zone, one might imagine oneself in an outland that could only be called untame, secluded from all utility and predictability.

On one occasion I came upon a small animal skin on miry ground between two tree trunks. It looked as if it had been stretched flat; you could see where the four legs poked out, the place for its head, as if the animal had simply slipped out of it. The pelt was cleanly shed, with not a trace of blood, a sallow shape on the dark ground, or rather fallow: an animal colour, a word conjuring the romantic notion that flowing water cutting through a fugitive's tracks will leave the pursuer's dogs standing baffled on a riverbank.

Had animals hunted it, pinned it down, torn out the

viscera and left the hide? Or had someone crept up on it, killed and slaughtered it, removing the skin so skilfully that not a trace of flesh or guts was left? I knew as little of hunting lore as I did of predatory animals. What had become of what had been inside the skin? The eyes, teeth, gristly parts of the nose? The bones? The pelt was like a blaze, a way-mark, indicating the true nature of the path: wild terrain with rules of its own. Mores unlike those found on streets or squares, and whose writ, just a few hundred yards away in the shadow of flyover stilts and under a fog of traffic noise, had no more authority than the end of a wilderness petering out along the fence of a caravan park.

December in London offered no prospect of frost or snow. Calm, milky days were the rule, occasionally interrupted by short spells of boisterous gusts that sent purply-brown clouds scudding across the sky, and dark grey shadows flitting across the marshes. Glary coronas of sunlight edged the clouds, lending them a keenness of outline that was as extraordinary as it was short-lived. This was pre-winter, a season I'd taken years to get used to, which, during months when the usual equinoctial storms had failed to appear, seemed to creep by without storm or bluster. Whether by day or by night, any sign of a change in weather during these autumn weeks got me listening for that peculiarly high tone that would presage the approach of a storm between the lower layers of cloud, before it pitched into the tops of trees and filled the streets. Over the years these storms, so out of keeping with the country's semblance of composure, had grown on me, and now I was missing them. One December evening, however, a late autumn storm hurtled through like a long delayed express train, whose tense anticipation by trees, roofs, and loose junk on the streets had charged the air for whole days and nights. For a few days prior to the storm, objects, people, voices, and noises had collided in a series of unforeseeable calamities, and yet the concomitant jangling, clattering, crashing and splintering did not provide the slightest relief, until one late evening a highly pitched hum heralded the arrival of a storm which, with an unsettling roar, immediately unleashed itself on the treetops. Warm blasts of air plunged between the houses, tore at the trees and whipped their spoils through the streets. The air tasted of autumn and, at the same time, long-forgotten early springs; the almost putrid sweetness of the last few leaves ripped off by the storm created for a moment the delusion of a February's earthy aroma. The storm wreaked havoc along the Old River Lea, strewing branches over the ground, overturning trees, pulling up roots, damming the river with bulky tops of felled trees. Work on the green slope on the opposite bank had come to a standstill; everything seemed paralysed by the wind's reversal of all order, by the devastation in the wilderness. Birds of prey circled above the terrain. Rooks had gathered in silence beneath a pylon, a parliament in waiting. The storm had abated; distinctions between light and shadow were sharper than they had been for some time; rays of sunlight fell white around the clouds, which, in formations suggestive of a sophisticated game, let dark shadows skim across the landscape. Very rarely, as if from far away, an oddly clear sound entered the stillness: a helicopter, the clattering of trains on the embankment beyond Lea Bridge Road, the siren of a fire engine. The impression was that of scraps of sound that had loosed themselves from their respective sources during the storm and now hung aimlessly in the sky, without a beginning or end, directionless.

Forced to detour through the undergrowth because of the debris on the path, I stumbled across an animal trap between the trees; my foot bumped against an old piece of metal jammed between the layers of leaves and roots, and it gave a dry snap. I remember as a child people would point to certain men as poachers, men in flat caps and overalls stealing through the back gardens at first light with the meagre haul they had taken from the few woods left in our suburban area, where wildness of any kind gave people the shivers and we were taught to steer clear of it. Once my grandfather showed me a trap a poacher had set in a woodland thicket. I remembered a kind of iron clamp among the dry leaves, and the word my grandfather used for it: swan's-neck, such a strange word to use in a forest far from the river and the habitat of swans.

Continuing my walk I saw a fox between the sparse bushes just before the road pillars became visible between the trees. It was standing on the very edge of town, motionless, reddish-grey, its pricked up ears yellowy, waiting for something, fearless, and took to its heels only when my Polaroid clicked.

The path returned in a semi-circle to the towpath along the canal. On the other side was the city. Here and there, displayed on balconies, the paraphernalia of the season: a twinkling Christmas tree, probably of the kind that could be put up like an umbrella with all its decorations already attached. Behind the pillars of the intertwining carriageways, smoke curled into the sky above the caravans, of which it was difficult to say at first whether they intended to be part of the street scene or the area along the old river. Where did these semi-sedentary people belong, with their horse-drawn coaches exchanged for modern caravans, their horses for the battered cars on jacks that stood between the caravans? Was this their place, with their backs to a north-south axis of upstream and downstream, and above their heads and the roofs of their caravans the to and fro of the traffic flowing from east to west and west to east between the estuary region and the city? The caravans shone white in the brief phases of clear sunlight. They formed an island, unsure of which river they were in.

I had forgotten the photo in my pocket. Back in my flat, when I pulled off the negative foil, the picture showed the typical gaps where the layers of photographic colouring had come out and bled into a void. It showed branches of trees, bushes, a bit of the river. No sign of a fox.

It was during that winter that I chanced upon a picture in a second-hand bookshop, or it could have been a barrow or stall in Whitechapel, or in Bethnal Green. It was a poorly reproduced photograph, probably taken some hundred years earlier or more, showing waggons with shaggy thickset ponies and pipe-smoking women in headscarves and long skirts, one of whom, her hand shielding her eyes, was gazing into an invisible distance. Behind the little group you could see tents and covered wagons on a meadow, and in the background the billowing contours of riverside woods. The inscription under the photograph read: Gypsies on Hackney Marsh.

XIX. ODER

Whenever the word 'river' came to mind, I imagined panoramas, views, images from childhood – the post-cards memory had sent me. I ran these views and images by countless rivers, holding them up to each river land-scape as if to interrogate it for something specific. For distinct shades of blue both in the sky and in the sky's reflection on both sides of the river? For its capacity to make magic with mist, its seaward promise and pledge of a greater brightness? The comparative allure of its unknown opposite bank? I could not have said myself what it was.

We carry our hearts around with us in the wrong place: such thoughts came to mind beside every river I visited, and especially so by the Oder. Kleist had grown up by the Oder. Although, two hundred years earlier, he must have seen a different river – wider, with a broader sweep, its banks with their vast wetlands more bewil-dering – his eye may nonetheless have discerned the two shades of blue above rivers, the blue of this side and the blue of that side, conjuring at every river's edge the thought of the heart's being in the wrong place.

One autumn afternoon I stood by the Oder look-ing across to Słubice. On the previous day mist had obscured the far side of the river; its grey shrouds had solidified in a sudden early frost, leaving thick layers of rime on the bare trees. The mist had altered everything, for a short late autumn's day robbing the landscape of all similarity with the area where, many years earlier, I had crossed over to Poland for the first time. But now the mist had cleared, and unable to face the dreariness of its banks, the river ducked under the ugly bridge, stretch-ing out its arms this way and that, throwing up islands, deceptive little mounds of dry land, which the river, at the slightest sign of high water, could swallow again at a single gulp. The air shimmered in the brightness over the empty country to the south. I imagined the ice that on colder days would form a single blue expanse from one bank of the river to the other, softer and cracking where it met the rushes and willow clumps at the edges, with dead birds staring up at the sky, rigid under the frozen surface, just as I had seen them on a December's day in the Oderbruch. On one of the little islands that had appeared where the river branched between Frankfurt and Słubice stood two figures in pullovers of different shades of red. They were busy doing something with sticks, shifting between the willows and the water, smoke rising near them from what must have been a fire. Perhaps they were engaged in some kind of fishing known only to locals, poking around for prey that they would spear and then roast over the flames. The red of their pullovers stood out against the dull colours of the winter reeds, against the shimmering white sky, the grey flow of the river. In their two shades of red they were acting out a mime that chance observers might interpret at will. It was a game, a riddle in moving pictures, a piece of river theatre. Suddenly they were gone, swallowed up, eradicated from the landscape. All that was left were little clouds of smoke hanging motionless in the air above the little island. After a while, standing on the bridge, I saw a police boat heading towards the place where the two red figures had been. People on the riverbank waved to them: over there, there! That's where they disappeared.

Inland gulls with large beaks gathered on a small landing stage beside the bridge. Between crumbling older houses and new buildings in Słubice's sole shopping street, dogs went about their business while the shop owners loitered, mere extras in an urban wasteland that made its living from passing travellers and depended on a sluggish stream of chance shoppers, coffee drinkers and cigarette dealers, while going to wrack behind the scenes. For all its through traffic, constant din of vehicles, people in transit, none of whom intended to stop, and despite the constant trickle of decaying masonry, the place had come to a complete standstill; it was like one big theatre backdrop, a prop left by the side of a road which could be blown away in the next storm, or carried away in a flood.

Eventually the police boat departed, the riverbank spectators went on their way, the red pullovers were still missing. The evening came, the Kleist House on the far bank faded into the twilight, the headlamps of lorries on the bypass pushed their white beams through an evening full of the autumnal aromas of river and smoke.

Which place is wrong for the heart, which is right?

Every river is a border; that was one of the lessons of my childhood. It informs our view of what is other, forcing us to stop in our tracks and take in the opposite side. The river is dynamic, a bustling stage, in contrast with which the otherland opposite is integral to the fixed picture, a background painting which impresses itself on our memory. What if the river, beyond its capacity as a border created solely by its own course, is also a border between countries? Could its flow, the incessant press of its water towards an estuary, be more powerful than its significance as a line fixed to determine belonging? Does the water carry something away with it, leaving the stateliness of state-borders diminished and apparently subject to depreciation? Isn't it saying that what we really belong to is the gaze toward the other side?

171

Although I had set my heart and hopes on Poland, I had not attached much significance to the idea of the Oder as a border river when I crossed it on my first journey east. I had no idea of river landscapes, and the sound of very few town names had reached my ears. If, at the time, barely out of my childhood as I was, I had any notion of a river other than the Rhine, then it was the Vistula at Warsaw, which to me had the quality of true easterliness. I wanted to be far into the foreign place before taking proper account of it. Thus one early morning found me sitting on the train to Warsaw; the struts on the Oder bridge were black against a sky full of rain; I could barely make out the river. I was sharing an apartment with an old lady who was on her way back to Warsaw to die. Her daughter had travelled with us as far as Berlin Zoo; they sat whispering together on the lower bunk, the daughter combing and braiding her mother's long white hair. Then it was time for the daughter to leave; she stood on the platform waving as the train pulled out in the thickening September light. The old lady remained silent; contours of the passing landscape showed, emerging from the darkness in various tones of grey. The train stopped for a while in a station with no name sign; no doors opened or closed. Crossing the bridge the metallic throb of the wheels echoed as if in a hollow body; it was so still and empty it seemed any settlements on either side of the border must have withdrawn to the terra firma of a more unequivocal Here. Only when we had crossed the Oder did the elderly lady draw herself up and declare: Now we are in Poland. Her tone of voice was one of relief, a homecomer's tone of voice, as befits any place worth its name.

Some distance beyond the Oder the train stopped in Rzepin, a small town surrounded by pine forests. It was drizzling. I listened to the guards exchanging words in Polish; then silence, birds, the low squeak of a bicycle. Back then, travelling to Poland for the first time, these things would have sunk more deeply into my memory than the short journey across the river on the railway bridge, as if the subsequent passage through forest and occasional strips of clearing were the real border crossing and point of entry to the foreign land.

Shortly before Poznań, a watery September sun broke through the clouds. I was now sitting on the edge of the old lady's bunk holding her hand and looking out of the window at a landscape under a quite different light, softer than any I had known. The sky was of a blue I had never seen: further, brighter, curving towards a different horizon. I thought of my father's skill with blue, of the way he had often claimed an ability to determine the longitude of a place by its shade of blue. I wished I could put him to the test again with a snippet of this sky. I had put the West behind me, its light and landscapes, its fragments of disconnected scenes rushing past which would have no place under this sky. Where did we leave the West? It could only have been on the other bank, before our unspectacular crossing of the dawn-grey river, not among the drizzly pines of Rzepin.

It was a Sunday. Somewhere between fields and sparse little woods a woman in a tight dress and high heels was hurrying down a rough track towards a village and looming church spire, while a boy teetered along behind her on a bicycle that was much too large. Two children in red pullovers stood facing each other beside a brook throwing something back and forth; for the few moments when I was able to observe them through the train window they seemed to prosecute this game with an almost disconcerting serenity. In the field behind the brook a fire gave off clouds of smoke. On a deserted station platform the wind created by a passing train blew autumn leaves into a corner. The old lady asked me about my childhood in Germany, about my family, and why I was travelling to Poland. I replied in my modest Polish, and she told me about her own childhood in eastern Poland, on the far side of the Bug, a river that seemed to me as distant and steeped in legend as the fabled river that flowed out of Paradise. She told me of the turmoil following the First World War when she and her sister had stayed behind on their family estate. Their parents had gone west, to Warsaw, and having received no news the worried, marooned girls wanted to go after them. Aided by a governess, who had gone unpaid for some time, the two girls of about twelve or thirteen, whose dresses had grown too short over the summer, had leafed through fashion journals for patterns, and, lacking any money for clothes, transformed hangings and curtains into dresses that seemed to them western enough to wear on their way into town. They had walked along dusty farm tracks, or sometimes by the Bug itself, eventually finding a bridge and continuing their journey on the plodding trains of the post-war provinces, finally arriving in Warsaw. You always end up in Warsaw, she said, exhausted now, leaning back on her pillow, regardless of whether your sun is rising there or setting.

It was only later, in woodland near the mouth of the Varta, where for the first time in my life I had heard a golden oriole, that I learned how to look at the Oder. The bird's song, a shibboleth with roots in who-knows-what fairy tale, immune to fake or fudge, had blended as well with the blue sky east of the Oder as the softly lisping names of the local towns and villages; to me – even without at that time recognizing in its call that of Bobrowski's

174

beloved bird – it had seemed like a key to this river landscape, a place in which I might well ask my heart what place I was carrying it in. From the branching fork of the Varta mouth to the Szczecin Lagoon, the Oder drew a border line up and down the country, writing a Here and a There in the sandy earth. Under it, however, countless watery question marks and intertwining letters tugged in both directions, east and west, a water-script of histories granted continuity through the river, under it, beyond it, its tributaries and ramifications annotating the landscape, reversing its sides with befuddling mirror images of the sky and its blues of Here and There.

As I travelled up and down the bordering Oder, the river invariably seemed hushed, its abandoned riverbank idylls unsure whether they belonged to the water or the land, so deeply were questions of the heart's belonging inscribed beneath their leaves, scrub and crumbling stone. Crumblings of stone that had outworn its use in the derelict walls of old Küstrin, at the mouth of the Varta rows of poplars whispering to listening swans concealed in the reeds, timeless trees of sorrow that fringed every river in Europe. A winter harbour with endless rows of vacant fixtures jutting from the water like the towers of some sunken industrial complex, a mazy forest of spars in Szczecin marina, the edges of small riverside towns fraying quietly into unconvinced rusticity. Bridge stumps, pollarded willows, water meadows, the view from the opposite bank of the hulking concrete architecture of a promenade made for desolation, the loneliness of water level signs and kilometre markers, the river's gradual approach to the sea, legible in light and skies; then undecided, devoid of traffic, until widening to the sea it lets the broad, wandering landscape of the lagoon play border and succumbs to a final frenzy of activity in Szczecin. I had only seen Szczecin in winter, when the Oder was alien and severe, a changed river that had left the countryside behind it and turned its face to the sea. The winter's cold brought everything to a standstill. The snow fell diagonally, cross-hatching the widely visible sign *Port Szszecin*, reducing derricks and masts to blurred shapes. Ships frozen fast in the ice, the clanking of loose scaffolding in the wind, the grating of icy pennants on the frost-flowered windows of ferries, seagulls strutting on the river ice with its covering of snow. The opposite bank an unobtrusively inhabited strip of wilderness, more huts than houses between bare trees; slender poplars, stiff Heliades with hearts of frozen amber, joined the persistently skew-armed cranes in the background in writing something on the low, snow-filled sky, a winter dispatch to the sea. Szczecin was one of the iciest cities I had ever come across, where I imagined coal-dust covered heaps and lumps of snow lining the streets even in summer in the gloomy quarters full of old tenement blocks behind the seaward defences.

I once drove downstream from Słubice, to the north. It was a windy, changeable day in a mild winter, the western sky mottled with purple and brownish rags of cloud, with strips of bright turquoise in between. I remembered a little ferry that shuttled unhurriedly between two apparently deserted riverbanks; the villages it served lay some distance away, their faces averted from the river for fear of floods and desirous of less vulnerable ground. The riverbank consisted of willow thickets, marshes, and water meadows. However, the two access ramps – the eastern one right in front of my feet, the other small and indistinct on the western side beyond a surface so smooth and tame-looking that even its whirlpools masqueraded as benevolent waves – lay ferryless in the pale sunshine, which appeared through the clouds just as I arrived. Moss and weeds filled the concrete cracks of the eastern ramp; the ferry sign had rust holes and stood at a skewed angle to the river.

I looked around for the pub that had stood off the riverside road not very far away from the landing stage. A derelict building crouched down among the rampant willows, its windows boarded with rotten slats, its roof caved in. The landing ramp and pub may have been victims of flooding; in recent years there had been floods that had transformed this entire landscape beneath its two shades of blue into a single gigantic lake where furniture, uprooted trees and dead animals floated, and, it was said, whole roofs of houses too, with the occupants, unused to gradients as they were in these parts, clinging on in hope of rescue. The border river had become a border lake, making the land on both sides vanish without distinction.

I continued my journey north-east, following the bumpy road along the Oder riverbank, sometimes driving near to the river, sometimes further away. After some time I came to a large fallen tree blocking the road. It must have lain there making the road impassable for a long time because there was already a small bush growing behind the tree trunk, and saplings had broken through the tarmac and formed a new little landscape of fissures and bulges. As I turned the car I noticed two figures on a patch of grass. They had their backs to me and looked like two children, the way they were sitting there, eleven or twelve years old maybe, still in love with wildness. They both wore red pullovers and torn jeans, hunkering down over a pile of brushwood from which first rings of smoke curled skyward. They slowly turned to face me, a boy and a girl, or perhaps two girls, or two boys, or not children at all? Dark-faced, uninquisitive, both young and old, belonging to nothing but this background of river.

XX. WIND

The wind was a lesson every newcomer to the city had to learn. There were storms that would suddenly well up at night, filling the air with a cacophony of rattling, rending, clashing and clanking as all manner of objects began to detach themselves, lurching to and fro in the gusts, then tearing from their moorings completely, trundling down the streets, until eventually the paths of the wind crossed and its booty snagged and snarled, and all the plastic bottles, letterbox lids, exercise books, satellite dishes, window handles, cigarette lighters, items of washing and clothes pegs, photographs and carelessly hidden burglar's tools came to a halt and collapsed in a heap at a bend in the road or on the pavement. Then there were the long storms, which announced their approach with a high-pitched howl caused by the friction of differently fast and differently coloured layers of cloud, storms which would tail off as night fell only to start afresh at the first sign of dawn, as if they were determined their effect on the world should be witnessed. Among the most extraordinary phenomena were the tornados, which could touch down briefly and turn whole areas of town topsy-turvy, assailing rows of houses and leaving their upturned roofs thrashing about in clouds of dust, while the storm itself lifted and made a clean getaway.

To begin with I found all these different winds hard to handle. Perplexed and inexperienced as I was, I saw how adept these locals were, in their calm and collected manner, at flattening themselves against walls, dodging under gusts, finding quiet nooks to sidle through, or moving along in the famously sheltered eye of the storm, so that in contrast to those lacking in such experience, they were never caught in the bluster or buffeted off course. Ducking while walking, weaselling in and out of danger or side-stepping at just the right moment seemed skills they must have been born to, or which featured in some highly sophisticated school curriculum. The victims of storms were invariably outsiders. Those who went missing, blown away by strong gusts and scattered abroad, tended to be strangers unfamiliar with such vitally important skills and without the means to acquire them. While people in other countries would defy or avoid storms by withdrawing into barricaded flats and houses and listening for the rise and fall of the howling wind, people here adroitly harnessed the wind to expedite their own affairs, keeping themselves in trim, or confirming their sense of belonging, faithful to the indigenous principles of discretion, elegance and sangfroid even in the face of uprooted trees, falling balconies and roofs rent asunder. Such savoir faire in dealing with storms had its treacherous side, too, as foreigners, fearfully following events from their windows and seeing what appeared to be everyone hurrying with accustomed agility and ease through the streets, misinterpreted the wind's baying howls and high-pitched warning whistles and imagined the objects hurtling through the air to be lightweight mock-ups or joke articles. Thus the heedless foreigner would venture out, only to find himself suddenly treated as the storm's hapless football. He was no longer lord of his feet or destination; the wind pushed him down streets and alleyways he did not know and whose acquaintance he had never formed any intention of making, through places that put the fear of God into him, where people grabbed at and did with such a helpless individual as they saw fit, until finally, and probably to his own relief, a prodigious blast of wind picked him off his feet and whirled him aloft, brushing the tops of trees and barely clearing the roofs and their countless chimneys. Above a suburb somewhere the gust would run out of steam and set the highjacked traveller down. Such landings were seldom soft; dazed, the wind's victim remained supine on the grey street. Passers-by gathered around him and naturally recognized him as a newcomer, for it was only such-like persons who were transported so unexpectedly to their streets. Sometimes the locals, with pointed kindliness, would help the sky-rider to his feet and dust him down, uttering words of encouragement and escorting him to a crossroads, only to release him to the clutches of the next gust, which, to the hilarity of those left behind, who had sought the shelter of some wind-free corner, plucked him off his feet and spirited him away yet again. Or else they disregarded him and left him lying, and groups of children would arrive with sticks, which they proceeded to bore into the material of his jacket and trousers; small dogs nuzzled his ears, salivating onto his neck and even occasionally raising a leg over his hunched shoulders. The children soon lost interest in their find, whistling their dogs to heel and going on their way. Eventually the wind would tire itself out, and the person it had brought could pick himself up at last, shake off his daze and set off on the long trek back to his place of residence.

One windy day I was out looking for some useful article that might give me a sense of order and settledness and encourage me to lead my life in a more organized fashion, an object that might lure me away from living in hope of some beneficial, fortuitous event, to embrace instead the equanimity inhabited by those whose lives are shielded by habit and convention. I had already learned one or two tricks in my dealings with wind and weather, and had acquired the ability to dodge the gusts like any local, keeping my head down and my elbows bent in front of me. Adopting this posture I made my way through streets where dark-skinned traders under lean-tos and shacks, in derelict shops and on pavements were selling anything with a semblance of practicality, all spread out on cloths on the ground out of the wind. The sellers stood next to their wares as always, and the customers, wind-wise and without haste, pressed past, stopping to enquire about the use of things, pondering the purchase of even the smallest articles with such dedication and at such great length that the hearts of even the most hardened street-traders must have beat faster. But none of the various winds was good for business; the potential buyers moved on with a shrug of their shoulders, and the trader's heart, its hope thus cheated, stood still for a moment in disappointment.

Brilliant light alternated with the murkiest clouds, and shreds of turquoise blue and white sped across the sky. A cloudbank of dark purple nosed forward, and sometimes the air smelled so strongly of sea that you could almost hear the screaming gulls; at other times you could smell the putrescence that lay about in corners and fed the pigeons whose droppings had eaten into window ledges and frames, and even into the old, granite paving slabs. The wind changed into a storm. The street sellers shouldered their wares and left, or withdrew into the depths of their makeshift shops. In next to no time the storm had snatched from the unwary whatever they had not removed to safety, smashing it against the walls of houses and blowing it down alleys where all the rubbish collected. The pigeons squeezed into the dilapidated gables, and the cats vanished behind squeaking doors. It was a perfidious wind, jumping out behind your back, skulking in corners. I took shelter in the dark entrance of an abandoned garage under the overhead railway, where a few other stragglers had already crammed into the corners. The storm of a century raged outside, which after a couple of hours suddenly gave way to a profound silence. When I left my bolt-hole, the world looked different. The evening sky gleamed a bright green; standing out against it were the black shapes of havocked roofs, buckled lampposts and shredded trees, battered vehicles buried under the branches and heaps of rubbish the storm had driven before it and swept into the corners. Between the rows of houses everything was perfectly still.

I wanted to go home, but in this suddenly upside-down world, it was not easy to find the way. The streets seemed displaced and the points of the compass jumbled. I fairly strode along; since my arrival in London I had never felt as happy-go-lucky and fleet of foot as I did now, in this higgledy-piggledy and temporarily deserted landscape after the storm. The first creatures to make themselves noticed were the cats. They slunk from the safety of their hiding places, suspiciously circling wonted territories in which lay fallen trees and tumbled chimney pots, and crushed cars that blocked their accustomed views. The cats moved slowly, shiftily inspecting alien bits and pieces the wind had heaped on their patch, darting puzzled glances at the locked doors of houses where they presumably lived. Shortly afterwards crows entered the sky, the first doors and windows opened and people stuck their heads out, but stillness persisted, as if everyone first had to find their voices, blown into some out-of-the-way corner by the storm.

I was on a street that sloped slightly uphill in a north-westerly direction. Beyond the crest of the hill the sky was aglow in an early evening turquoise. The many chimneys of the little houses along the crest stood out blackly against the light, some of them with the jagged appearance of broken teeth. Fire-engine sirens could now be heard here and there. Further down the slope people exchanged words of encouragement. In front of a largely unscathed front garden somebody was righting a dented car that the storm had turned on its side. He raised his hand in a brief greeting and said something I didn't understand. Struggling, he succeeded in opening the car door and sat down behind the steering wheel; he started the stuttering engine and clapped his hands for joy. Dogs barked. A cat prowled around a small tower of bins that had been deposited by the storm and was now blocking its door. Responding to a faint cry for help, I dragged a bulky ash branch from a front garden, and an elderly lady in her shattered bay window, a cold headdress of electric curlers still crowning her head, its electric lead hung around her shoulders like a slender braid, graced me with a toothless smile. Now that the severe weather had passed, a blanket of benevolence had descended on the town, and the composure of those who had escaped in one piece was heard in their every enquiry and every gesture. There was an uninterrupted view south over the enormous city from the crest of the hill. The sun was sinking between two banks of cloud. Slanting in from the west, a mellow reddish-orange suffused the town at the foot of the green slope, and here and there a reflection of sunlight flashed in one of the intact windows. The town itself lay in a bed of deep blue, threaded by a Thames chastened to a luminous bright green. The city's apparently undamaged landmarks stood out as sharply-defined silhouettes against an auspicious evening sky. From here I could see where the streets ran, and I knew where my own house stood. Further down individual figures were crossing the slope. A stooping man with a rucksack. A woman picked one of the scattered sticks from the ground and threw it for her dog. The dog bounded after the flying stick, its barking remote, a cry unbound that slit the sky above the tranquil panorama and let the evening in.

XXI. FOLKLORE

The part of the street that included my temporary home
set out its array of small shops, storerooms and crumbling terraced housing like a protective barrier around
the domestic enclave of those observant Jews who led
regulated lives according to complex laws, with little
shops in neighbouring streets catering to their every
need. These pious people needed a fishmonger for herring and salmon, they needed a hatter, a clothes shop
with a permanent stock of women's and girl's clothes
with modest skirt and sleeve lengths, and they needed a
wig maker. There were also shops for decorations, ritual objects and devotional books. On Thursdays the fish
shop and Greengrocer Katz were busier than on other
days. From six in the evening, when the fishmonger's
metal shutters were already half down and the goyish,
rather dim-witted assistant in wellies was hosing down
the tiled floor and sluicing scales and fins down the
drain, women would bend down with their carrier bags
in front of the neon-lit opening of the half-closed shop
bargaining with the wellies, pacing to and fro for fish
cuttings and scraps for Friday. Now and then the freck-
led hand of the fishmonger would proffer a wrapped
package through the opening, receiving whatever coins
the first taker was prepared to submit in return. The
scrap-seekers would often go away with their hands
empty but for jangling small coin, while the shutters rattled to the ground, neon light glimmered through cracks
and the spray water from the hosepipe trickled onto the
street until the door behind was locked.

In winter the hatter shut his shop at five; customers
did not come after dark. The hatter was a tall thin man
who wore a medium-sized fur hat over his kippah, not

as magnificent as the ones worn by the highly devout in their shiny kaftans, but nonetheless a traditional fur hat resting atop his smallish head like a crown. He switched off the light in the window – the ladies' hats on display would have to make do with street lighting – and locked the shop door and shutters with keys on a big jangly bunch. The hatter had a gentle, almost other-worldly face. I would have been frightened to speak to him without good reason and ashamed if mere curiosity had led me to enter his shop, which looked long and thin and very dark at the back. By daylight, behind the hats in the shop window, you could make out the passage-like premises in whose depths the hatter spent his days. When not serving customers he sat at a small table, with his head bent over something. Was he reading bills? Studying hat designs, fabric samples, a devotional book? It was only rarely that he came to the window to look out, and not at the busy street, but beyond it to the other side, where the tops of the cemetery trees towered above the wall. When he did, his pale face with side-locks but uncrowned by fur appeared between the hats in the upper part of the shop window. Only rarely did I see customers enter or leave his shop; perhaps the hatter made hats to order, visiting his customers at home, where, having measured the head in question, he presented illustrations of his designs, or described them in such lively terms that the customer was able to select one. After locking his shop door the hatter set off in a northerly direction, clearing his way through the closing-time crowds that were pushing along the pavements to the bus stops, his fur-crowned head sailing above the heads of the pedestrians and disappearing into the evening.

Women were forever standing in front of the wig

maker's shop chatting and laughing, complimenting one another on their wigs or discussing the relative merits of whatever was on display in the window. The wig maker herself was a middle-aged woman of business-minded motherliness, who took leave of her young sheitel-wearing customers with an embrace at the door. I was constantly astounded by the sight of her extravagant head of somewhat jaded matt-blonde curls, whose bonnet-like superposition put me in mind of Mrs Stoller's coiffure. Most of the young women wore simple wigs and shoulder-length, preferably dark-blonde hair with an unassuming fringe and centre parting, while their own black curls, revealed only at home, languished underneath. Wealthier-looking women adorned themselves with more lavish hairpieces of golden blonde, which had probably been made not by the local wig maker, but rather in Cape Town or Baltimore, in places where a girl would be married away to Stamford Hill where, under a vast northerly sky full of wondrous clouds that harbingered the proximity of a cold sea, she would stand at the side of the husband chosen for her.

That winter an Eastern European grocery that had nothing to do with the life of the pious opened a few yards away from Stoller's emporium. Their plastic bags and cartons were labelled in Russian, Ukrainian and Polish; everything was pre-packaged, as it was at Stoller's, only nothing was kosher. They had borscht, poppy seed strudel and vodka, as they did at Stoller's, but also ham and sausages and boxes of chocolates decorated with blurry reproductions of famous paintings. The shop had appeared overnight in this little row of empty premises between two road junctions, without as much as a flyer or a poster to announce it. The goods were displayed on wobbly warehouse shelving

189

and crude trestle tables; weak neon lamps flickered constantly, making the daylight appear darker than it really was and, when darkness fell, spreading a cold, bleak light. The customers – almost exclusively the Russian, Ukrainian and Polish speaking occupants of furnished rooms in run-down houses with shared kitchens on the big through roads – stood in this light doing their shopping, fingering well-known foods with delight written on their faces, and with curiosity over less familiar goods. Men came from building sites and bought vodka and sausage; women came from their jobs as cleaners and waitresses and bought chocolate and powdered soups. They chatted, exchanged news and views, reminded each other of customs, names, aromas, discussed homeland dishes, and left with their ready-made foods for home. The packaging of the soup flakes, cakes and tins of fish sported the names of dull provincial towns, where the contents of these purportedly nostalgia-kindling and insipidly colourful packets and cartons had probably been shovelled, spooned or tipped from enormous sacks of unknown provenance. I called in at the shop quite often, even though I rarely found much to buy, but I liked to look at these things and touch them, things I knew from Eastern Europe and which always gave me a little pang of surrogate homesickness, a sort of second-hand homesickness of the kind you might feel for a place that – if you closed one eye to so-called reality – could easily have been your home. Sometimes I ran into the Croat there, who would shut his shop early in order to chat to the girls at the till. His thin lips twisted into a crooked smile as soon as he noticed me, winking at me conspiratorially for some reason as he tried to engage the girls in talk of homey things; he said a few words in Croatian and was visibly pleased when they understood him, or when he understood, or thought he understood, what they were saying. He wanted to teach them words in his language and kept on repeating certain names of things, adopting an expression of patience and cocking his head to one side, or waving his hands like a conductor as he got the girls to repeat. They laughed, mostly, but one young woman with a long pigtail and austere-looking spectacles did him the favour of repeating his words with a straight face and in a Polish accent. At lunchtime, if there were no customers in the shop, the girls would sing Ukrainian and Polish songs in their clear voices, swaying their hips as if at a village fair.

In December, though it was not cold, it was some time before I came across the King of Springfield Park in his magnificent half-length robe. On some evenings the ravens collected in the place where he would usually stand and gather them around him. The birds always seemed fidgety then, I noticed; they made no sound, only scuttling about a little, and yet as a flock they seemed to undulate, like a single shuddering body. One evening in the last light, coming up the slope to the crest of the park, I saw several African women in festive robes. They were wandering along the paths and edges of the trees, all repeating an identical cry consisting of several staccato syllables, at the same time breaking off sticks and beating the bushes. For a moment I thought they were looking for the King, supposing him among the hedges or bushes, a runaway king refusing to perform his appointed tasks. As if responding to a call, however, they all abruptly threw away their sticks, wrapped their arms around each other and walked up the lawn in a row, laughing, a group of carefree, relieved schoolgirls, as they suddenly appeared, young people in festive costumes, with stiff cloth wound into their heavy headdresses, whose gold-threaded patterns glinted in the last light of the setting sun.

Then, one day, I saw the King again. It was a cold afternoon; sharp gusts of wind tore at the leaves and I was making my way home earlier than usual. The King stood in the shelter of the big hedge at the entrance; his dark, naked legs had a bluish look. It was still bright, and the sun was thin behind banks of cloud, an inhospitable kind of light in which the King appeared down-at-heel; he was cocooned in a local kind of resignation, a gloomy melancholy that did not sit well with his royalty. The material of his robe looked threadbare, his headdress askew, his legs trembled a little, and I noticed his eye-balls were jaundiced, though I refrained from looking him in the eye. The hour of the King had not yet come, and the ravens were still pecking here and there on the lawn and in the flowerbeds between the last roses. Two observant Jews hurried by with flying coat-tails, talking loudly and laughing in the late light on their way through the park towards the housing estate where the sing-song of table blessings could be heard fluttering over the streets on holidays. The sun sank in the sky, half hidden by clouds, and the King stepped out onto the grass in the reddish light of the dusk. The ravens flapped into the air and gathered around him. All melancholy and all neglect fell from his figure, and he held court once again, sovereign over this urban periphery descending into the wild world of darkness.

That evening I took a wide detour through the streets in the twilight. People stumbled out of the buses with bags of Christmas shopping, and the last workers got on outside the sole remaining factory at the foot of Mount Pleasant Hill. All at once the long section of the street dominated by the factory lay deserted in the light of the

192

street lamps. A mouse-faced boy on a bicycle that was far too small for him rode slowly along beside me whistling as far as the next crossing where children were fooling about with a buckled walking frame, shrieking with laughter as they finally shoved it into the bushes. It began to drizzle. The way back to my flat seemed endless; I had never lost my way before but now felt relieved when I got back to the main road I knew. The evening traffic was thinning and the pedestrians were few. The rain hung in subtly vibrating bell shapes under the street lamps.

The Eastern European grocery store had already shut, but a group of men had gathered and were staring in through the window: the Croat between Kurdish taxi drivers from the rank across the road, a few passers-by, and, at the far end of the row, his body already half turned to go, with his gaze still on the window, Jackie, the only one with an umbrella. Inside, the wobbly shelves had been pushed aside, and a dance group were practising on the cleared floor space. The girls all wore the same traditional costumes, with white blouses, red skirts and flowery scarves; they held hands, danced in a circle, changed direction, clapped their hands, placed hands on their hips, twirled their skirts, linked arms forming groups of four, put their hands on one another's shoulders, threw their heads back, waved the little kerchiefs they wore in their waistbands, picked up their skirts between their fingers, raising them just above their white-stockinged knees and swinging them back and forth. The routines had apparently been agreed on long before, and nobody seemed to be giving instructions or orders, nobody was directing or keeping anyone else in line. The breaks between dances were short, or perhaps it was just one long dance interrupted by a few, choreographed, motionless moments now and again. The neon shone bluish-white on the girls' tired faces, and during the slower dances they mouthed the words of songs. They seemed not to notice their audience and danced as if for dear life to music that was inaudible outside. Only when one sequence ended with the stamping of black high-heeled shoes was something like a brief, muffled thud perceptible to those on the pavement in front of the window. The views of Black Sea coastal resorts, old-town arcades, snow-covered peaks and onion-domed towers on the walls above the shelves, all slightly askew, shimmered a little in a wan bluishness and constituted the mute audience to whom this performance was addressed. They showed places that, by general consensus, represented the lowest common denominators of their yearnings, ciphers of homelands left behind out of hardship, vexation, boredom or for some other woeful reason, and which they were now, during these dismal evenings before Christmas, dancing to shreds on this dingy well-scuffed linoleum floor. The men outside smoked and flicked their dog-ends away into the puddles, immediately lighting the next cigarette. None of them said a word, only the Croat occasionally clicked his tongue. The passing buses spattered their trouser legs with dirty water; the pavement was narrow here, and rain was falling more heavily. When one of the girls stumbled and her group of four was almost dragged down, a murmur went through the row of spectators. Sweaty and flustered, the girls laughed away their wobble, taking pains to get back into the swing, but it wasn't long before another girl got out of step, then another, going over on her ankle, missing a beat. Exhaustion was marked on some of their faces; others exhibited an unflagging, stony radiance, which sat very nicely with the tacky tourist posters on the walls. At length they disengaged and piled into the back room. Someone switched off the light, and all that could be seen in the glow of the street lamps were the outlines of the shelves pushed aside.

XXII. HACKNEY WICK

The Wick lay like a shred of urban tatter in the crook of noisy roads. With only the rear of its crumbling factories backing onto the straightened river Lea canal, it peered through gaps at the thickets edging Hackney Marshes, its abandoned greyhound stadium like a hand shoved in under the overhead road bridges between the two waterways. As an area of town it had little to do with the river. Scarred and pitted by decades of experimenting with the small-scale production of chemicals, by the rise and fall of middle-sized factories with machines so loud they brought down their own works walls, by traces of hastily built and equally hastily demolished post-war housing, dwelling in the shadow of poverty and the twilight hope of prosperity, Hackney Wick was a place apart, an area left behind, bashed and bedraggled by the times and time's passing, a site defined by its own rules of emptiness and wildness between junkyards, garages, warehouses and rubbish dumps, inscribed with its own alphabet of symbols that were crumbling, rusting, skewed and charred, yet still visible through more recent but no less damaged layers of paint, a palimpsest hard to decipher yet everywhere beckoning with glimmers of legibility, with promise of spoors and traces: from peppermint chocolates to Meldola blue, from automatic ticket machines to spare parts for motorbikes and leftovers of raw materials – copper, iron, steel in small quantities, variously bulky, also cables and rubber. Body Parts offered a repair workshop for car bodies, in front of which men wearing oily overalls would stand squinting idly into various categories of dismal weather, inevitably eliciting associations with divers searching for body parts in rubbery-smooth full-body suits, watched from the water's edge by gawkers and waiting policemen on the weed-infested towpath. A slight stench of burning always hung over Hackney Wick. It was a domain of the kind of decay and semi-oblivion that every river to some extent gives rise to, or allows to reside on its banks, or even nurtures by contributing to its accumulation, which the tamer Lea, tranquil, brownish and impassive, did not. Deposits alien to its straightened channel could not expect to stay there long; waterfowl fished them out to line or shelter their nests, built in the reeds close in where the occasional recess in the concrete edge provided a home to forever wary long-beaked waders and fish-eating birds.

Once, after my walk along the tame Lea, I took a bus. A calm winter's day under a white covering of cloud had given way to the sort of rain London was capable of at practically any time of year, with grey-brown, brightly lined clouds and the salty metallic smack of marshland at low tide, when the wind blew in from the estuary and covered everything in a fine film. On the seat in front of me sat two old men. Their jackets exuded every odour known to this part of town: the beer and nicotine smell of pubs, the reek of breakfasts in greasy spoon cafés, the fug of badly ventilated houses, bus exhaust, the rain. The fumes that had permeated their threadbare imitation tweed surrounded the men like a noxious cloud redolent of poverty and constant discomfort, to be borne with a crooked grin and spat out now and again through the gaps in their teeth. The men conversed with a stumpy East London inflection, with severed syllables and cut consonants breaking off, tumbling mute under the seats; the dirty floors of these buses were layered with dropped snippets of words. We ner called it 'ackneywick jus ag'nywick, said one of the men, suddenly half turned to me, and coughed; perhaps the cough was a laugh, or perhaps he had wanted to laugh, but had to cough, and I saw his thin shoulders jerk in time with his hawking rattle. They got out at Homerton Hospital, stumbling off under the bus shelter just as a heavy shower set in, disappearing into the crowd of people who were waiting, or getting in, or getting out, two little old men from Agony Wick, while the usual undependable sun beams stabbed through the January clouds, and, for a few moments, were all encompassing in their piercing, fickle light.

A short distance away from the river the site of the greyhound stadium, where only a few years ago hopes had run so high (money, happiness, a new tomorrow), was now home to a Sunday market, a bazaar for anything and everything, a hub of peddling and hawking on which other hopes were pinned. So empty on weekdays, these dark narrow streets between workshops, goods depots, and shifty dealers in vehicles and vehicle parts were chock-a-block with parked cars, people streaming in their droves to the market: strident, garish, tired and melancholic, wily, grinning and anxious buyers, showy black couples and families in baggy tracksuit bottoms and hooded jackets, and in all their eyes shone the hope of a purchase, the glint of a desire as yet unfixed on any shape, the unattached joy that anticipates taking something home to try out, use or put into action, something to put one in touch with one's own life. There was everything to be had at Hackney Wick market, from the used suits of the deceased to computers with every accessory; there were cables and telephones, toys and car radios, lamps, vases, clocks, things gaily coloured and black, things white, chrome, dirty, clean, and fallen off the backs of lorries, things with no past, just a future and a price, out of sight out of mind, displayed for the customer's convenience, take it or leave it, buy or die. Over all of this lay the air of a tacky fiesta, which may have survived from the days of greyhound racing, a fiesta of Fortune of the kind that pervades any event that can deliver a weighable and measurable windfall, whether by laying a crafty bet on dogs as fleet as the wind or chancing on an object of promise.

Spread out on a piece of oilcloth on the ground were a few treasures that had caught nobody's eye. Lacklustre glass brooches, bright yellow mock-gold necklaces, a string of plastic beads, a handbag worn at the corners, pretending to be crocodile. Half-hidden by the handbag was a photo album, oddly overlooked by the seller, whose wares smelled of petty burglary and hastily rummaged lumber-crammed bedrooms enjoying their first, long-missed breath of fresh air through smashed window-panes. The trader was a small man; he stood there shivering in a grey oversized windcheater, frozen to the skin. His vulpine features peered out from behind a cigarette that was burning too quickly, and a glowing finger of ash threatened to drop onto his wares. Perhaps he was worried, a newcomer who sensed that his side of the display, the vulpine side, where peddlers might quickly get rid of pilfered goods, was not always going to be easy, and that on the other side, where a constant flow of keen customers filed past, somebody who had been relieved of her handbag, jewellery or other things might easily recognize what had once been hers and demand it back. I picked up the photograph album; its cold mock leather felt clammy, and two interlocking rings were embossed on its cover. The album itself was empty, but attached to its inside back cover was a cardboard flap containing an envelope. As I pulled it out, the foxy eyes flashed anxiously, the man's hand shot forward, and glowing ash fell onto the last page of the album and onto the envelope, in which the seller probably suspected banknotes that had escaped his attention. I could feel some photos in the envelope, through which the glowing ash had burnt a hole; a little smoke curled upward, a tiny fire had started, but in the incipient confusion, in which the seller had a hand, the sparks were quickly extinguished. His bony fingers attempted to yank the album over to the vulpine side. How much? I asked him, and he turned up his mouth as if to bite me, as if to plunge his yellow, fox's teeth, now revealed by his tautly drawn upper lip, into my hand to make me release what I was holding. Just this! – holding up the envelope, I let go of the album, whereupon he stumbled backwards a step. To my right and left, people had begun to take notice; an elegant black couple, so finely dressed they looked as if they had come to the Sunday morning market straight from some evening out, turned to me from the highly polished car radio they were studying; the traders on either side of the fox adopted a position that allowed them to keep an eye on their own wares while potentially coming to their colleague's defence. The fox calmed down when I showed him that the envelope did not contain overlooked banknotes but only a few old photographs; for a small sum of money he let me go with a nonchalance that must have cost him an effort to muster, and it was obvious he wanted to return as quickly as he could to the inconspicuousness of his modest display between two stands showing brand new tools and car radios.

Standing on the North London Line platform at Hackney Wick station I took the photographs from their envelope. There were a good dozen, slightly underexposed and turning red, the gloss coating scratched in places: group scenes in the artificial, tone-blind, sunset red of cheap, old, colour photos. Women sitting at outside tables in sleeveless dot-pattern summer dresses, children with smeared, red-tinged mouths: on the women's faces half-smiles produced for a moment of formality, in the children's eyes sheepish self-consciousness, snapped between cake and a telling-off, the leaves of hedges and bushes behind them blurring to a dark mass. Then one of women and children in front of a Victorian terraced house with the number 17. A white cat in a bay window. Nothing in the photos betrayed whether one of these women had owned the jewellery on display, or carried the croco-style handbag, or had kept the wedding photo album under a pile of pastel, washed-thin towels, but had never filled it with the photos it was intended for. On one picture of women posing on green grass without children but with jackets over their dresses and little hats on their heads, the Hackney Marshes electricity pylons seemed to be floating in the blurred background.

The photographs would certainly have been taken over a single summer. Perhaps on the same film. Testaments to a family visit, accessories to a celebration whose occasion remained unrecorded in the photos. They gave no hint of a narrative, revealed no intensity of feeling, no suspense of any kind, no loose thread of some drama to pick up. I found it impossible to attribute anything to these faces and figures, found no way into the scenes portrayed, and the emptiness that presented itself in this bundle of tiny segments of life I had purchased on some off-chance made me feel intrusive. What was I doing here, on this wind-buffeted, elevated station platform with its view over the zone of discontinuities gradually annexing the river Lea and its wild hinter-land, with these snapshots of lives so remote from my own that I had been granted unsolicited access to them solely through some petty burglary or disappointing inheritance or ill-starred coincidence? I could not even think of names to give the two women who turned up in all of the photographs. I asked myself the unanswerable question of what name some other person might give me if they happened upon my photo. The notion that such a stranger, beholding my face, might find no name for me at all filled me with such anxiety that I quickly went through a few names for these randomly encoun-tered women: Liza and Harriet, I thought, Kathleen and Joyce. From Dalston? Homerton? Hackney Wick? But as I tried out the names, not a twinkle did I see in their red-tinged, blurry eyes.

A train going to Woolwich pulled into the opposite platform. A grumpy voice came over the loudspeaker announcing that the next train in the opposite direction was cancelled. A griping and groaning now set in among those who had purchased bulky items at the market and were treating themselves to the more expensive train in-stead of a cramped bus. From the end of the platform where I was standing I could see into a recycling yard. The gate to the yard, which was surrounded by a wall, was closed for the day, and a lone man wearing dirty or-ange overalls was burning rubbish. A fire flickered in a black metal drum, into which he was throwing things. Waiting to go in were cardboard boxes, rubbish bags, a roll of flooring material. He emptied the contents of one cardboard box into the flames and thick billows of black smoke went up, an oily plume of soot that would soon be falling on the surrounding area. As soon as the thick clouds had gone, the man began stuffing the folded cardboard box into the drum. The box was too big; it toppled back out of the drum. Burning at one corner and lifted by the wind, it blew a short distance across the yard, sending up a flurry of sparks. The man ran after it and grabbed it with his thick gloves, stuffing it back into the drum. Selecting a length of skirting board from the objects lined up for the flames, he tried using it to force the cardboard box further into the drum. The box, half of which was now in flames, proved insubordinate and stubborn; it was determined to leave the fire, to get out of the drum, back into the wind. A duel ensued which the man would certainly have lost if the fire had not been on his side. As the box finally submitted, slumping into the flames and smoke, the man set to with the skirting board, laying into the burnt remains and ashes of the box, until the skirting board itself caught fire, imperilling the man's gloves and hands. Turning from the moribund cardboard box, he flung the burning piece of wood or plastic in a high arc across the yard. Caught by a gust of wind, however, the burning slat did not fly far, falling straight into the next cardboard box. At a loss, the rubbish burner gave the box a kick, perhaps to disperse the fire, before stamping on what was left of the burning slat, extinguishing its last little plumes of smoke. Slowly, he began to throw the emptied-out contents of the second cardboard box into the drum. His movements seemed listless and tired as he bent down to retrieve small bits of paper and other objects, photographs perhaps: the sort of stuff that fell out of hastily packed boxes and cartons brought here from cleared out flats and dissolved households. The smoke produced by burning photographs is acrid and pungent. It has a tenacious smell and is difficult to air or wash out. It can provoke a cough that will last for weeks. It is said that when faces on colour photographs slowly crumble to form a stringy, viscid ash, they can impress themselves indelibly on the beholder's mind, taking on new names and a life of their own.

My train arrived at last. I laid the white envelope with its colour photos on the seat beside me. At the next station but one I alighted without the photographs. On the platform I tried to find the small white packet through the carriage window, but the grimy reflections made it impossible to make anything out; all I could see was the sky, the bare trees, shadows of flying birds, and my own face, all a trifle distorted by the slight curvature of the glass.

XXIII. NERETVA

The postcards behind the thin-lipped Croat's counter, with their spurious Mediterranean flair, their lurid, stereotypical idylls in pink, rock-colours and blue, and Serbo-Croatian greetings from here and there, looked to me like red herrings – but who were they supposed to fool? It was, after all, a country that had put war behind it, a country I had sought out despite the wounds it had suffered, or maybe because of them. Post-war was a prefix I had grown up with, despite the war being over for decades. In England it was joined by the phrase inter-war. Here, post-war and inter-war were not just rubble-heavy word-appendages, they also had a knack of wending their way adjectivally through different positions in a sentence, suppler and more expressive than their counterparts in my own mother tongue, and more enterprising. Although in London too, in the battered and seedy eastern quarters and poverty-stunted, urban tracts by the river Lea, the traces of the pre-war era had been razed with dedicated haste, and debris-filled wastelands filled with the sharp-edged fortress-like housing blocks of the new times. And now I was travelling through this hot grey country with its recent history of war, and, trembling, had suddenly come to realize that what I was really looking for on this bus winding its way along a Croatian cliff road was a key, some kind of key to a post-war condition that refuses to be dismissed, even from the green of the grass, leaves and weeds. Looking out of the bus window, I surreptitiously kept my eyes open for vestiges of war, ready to see the entire Croatian coast as a scene of devastation. Shots could be heard in the hinterland behind the crags; people still had weapons to hand, and were not prepared to cast off the mantle of war, enjoying the opportunity to send these shock waves through the air that darkened the sky. Elsewhere I saw old women tending their goats in the rubble of wrecked villages. The bus left the coast and plunged into the green hinterland. Away from the road was a burnt-out building, perhaps an old ware-house. Sheep grazed on the surrounding grass, and a one-legged man sat in the charred entrance. In one hand he held a stick, a shepherd's crook, whose suitability may have extended beyond guarding sheep to guarding against intruders who asked questions or came too near to his stump, or insisted on telling stories about the time they were ensconced in the burnt-out hole behind him. Perhaps the one-legged had a claim to this place that he wanted to defend, because he had lost his leg here, or had found refuge here after losing his leg among the reeds in the nearby marshland. The ground-floor walls of the burnt-out building were sprayed with graffiti, of which I understood only the word for war: *rat*.

The land that spread out in the shadow of the coast-al ridge, a light-flooded plain stretching all the way to the austere, white rock of the mountains in the east, was river country, a broad delta, a wide estuary so saturated with vegetation that nobody heard the river's reluctance in approaching the sea. It was a serene landscape of smaller channels, shellfish-fishers, corn farmers, dis-abled goatherds, old couples punting in straw hats as if in an ink painting of China's distant past, and chang-es of perspective and colour. A panorama of countless still waters traversed by land spits below the high, coast-al road to Dubrovnik, a landscape in green such as one rarely encountered along this coast, from the shady blue-green of broad-stemmed aquatic plants to the pale yellows of the reedy marshes in the distance, between which workers with wide-brimmed straw hats walked along raised paths.

The light was unusual: an inland light so near the sea, almost sharp and bluish where it surrounded the shadows. It was afternoon, the white clouds were high and motionless, there was no wind. I saw a heron standing on the parapet of a walkway above a reed-lined ditch. The rough mountain terrain lay further back from the sea here than it did anywhere else along this coastline between Split and Dubrovnik, but the bluffs, sparsely flecked with brush, were close enough for the light to hone itself on them and cut out such sharp shadows. The countryside here was nonetheless milder than the coast, almost mellow, a gentleness that may have had something to do with the slowness of things moving on the network of waterways, the careful ways of the anglers on the little jetties, and the abundance of waterfowl in the reeds and rushes, whose gulping, chirping, churring and throbbing songs hung over the water and were audible through the half-open bus windows.

I had to change buses for Mostar in a small town at the edge of the delta. Children dallied at the bus stop watching the few alighting passengers, who, aside from myself, were all local and, after exchanging one or two words with the bad-tempered driver, picked up the various bags, sacks and cartons hauled from the luggage compartment and went on their way. The bus to Mostar took its time arriving. It was late afternoon, and the heat was relenting; the air was full of birdsong, not only that of waterfowl, but also of tits and thrushes in the treetops and trimmed willow bushes. Behind the bench where I was sitting was a community centre whose neat herbaceous borders around the entrance were somewhat jaded by the late-summer heat. I heard chairs shifting and women's voices through the open windows, then stillness, then, a moment later, singing. Unaccompanied voices, no instruments, long-drawn-out melancholic melodies. Or perhaps they only seemed so to me, with their unintelligible words and quiveringly dissonant sounds, a choir for this discreet land between the Croatian coast and Bosnian mountains, a place where the river found a thousand excuses for not flowing into the sea. The women were rehearsing: songs were repeated, now and then a voice could be made out giving instructions, then there was singing again. The longer I stood there, the more I felt convinced that the singing was concerned less with unison than with dissonance, with the way each voice, in its own lament, chafed minimally against each of the others. Or this friction itself, this cloud of tiny dissonances, was what gave each of the songs their sorrowful tone.

The street broadened into a square here, at whose centre was a wide strip with trees. Men played cards at stone tables in the shade. In front of a café on the other side of the street small groups of young invalided war veterans with shaved heads stood about drinking beer, jokingly sparring with one another, sticking their feet out when children rushed past, laughing as they stumbled, fell, picked themselves up; one child grabbed a handful of dirt as he hit the ground, threw it in their faces, and ran off. A bus stopped a short distance away from the café. Passengers hauled their luggage from the hold, the driver urging them to hurry; the new arrivals shouldered their bags and left.

The choir rehearsal had come to an end; chairs were moved while women laughed, talking to one another, saying goodbye. Most of the women who came out of the community centre looked like office workers or the upright wives of tradesmen. Their hair looked village-cut, their handbags suggested perfumed hankies, crumbly lipstick and embroidered spectacle cases. There were a few elderly women among them, and two or three girls in high heels, who donned big sunglasses the moment they got outside the door. A peasant woman with an apron settled beside me on the bench at the bus stop. She gave me a friendly nod and placed her hands in her lap. The bus from Mostar arrived; a few people got out and busied themselves with the baggage hold. The peasant woman and I got in, and the bus pulled away with us inside it, along the river, leaving the day behind.

The bus was full. Women dozed over their baskets, men looked out of the window. After a schlager show, a news broadcast came on. The driver turned up the volume; the passengers kept up a running commentary, or talked among themselves, the voices dying down when the schlager hits came back on. The evening turned purple and blue; the rough cragginess of the mountains, softened by the light, retreated into the darkness. By the time we reached the Herzegovinian border, night had fallen. At the edge of the road stood a number of small shacks decorated with garlands of lights, with names like Trocadero, Las Vegas or simply Casino. The view from the bus window showed the makeshift simplicity of their interiors, each with bar and gaming table, but no customers. The only occupants were barmaids in black and dark-red uniforms, whose job was presumably to encourage potential gamblers to gamble away their inexhaustible supplies of banknotes, and who were now sitting around bored, drinking Coke and playing cards, inspecting their long fingernails and staring dismally at the bus.

I had given up trying to understand the borders I

crossed. Borders seemed capable of sprouting up any-where; they could shift and end up in a tangle. Luggage and passports were inspected with varying degrees of curtness and rigour, sometimes by officials sporting significant headwear and weapons who had proudly po-sitioned themselves in front of freshly erected border huts, at other times by drowsy drinkers of lemonade who had little appetite to drag themselves out of their camping chairs in the shade of the pomegranate trees. The border of the bored barmaids in gambling huts belonged to the less serious sort, and half an hour later the bus passed from the glitter of one country into the darkness of the next.

The road beside the Neretva lay in deep darkness. Now and then we passed through a small roadside town; in one we stopped for a while. The passengers stretched their legs, smoked, bought provisions at a neon-lit ki-osk. A wind had sprung up, the sky was starless, the air heavy and fragrant, as before a storm. The wind and the river on the other side of the street sounded like different kinds of breathing. It was late when the bus arrived in Mostar. There were no hotels, and a distant acquaintance called Selma picked me up from the bus station. We walked through empty streets between shapeless, deserted-looking housing blocks. Scrawny cats crossed our path. Finally we turned into an avenue lined by small kiosk-bars. Huge cars were parked along the side of the road. Men with heavy mobile phones crowded the bars pulling business-like faces, their car engines turning over, gold glinting on their wrists, around their necks. Selma lived in one of the older blocks, almost all of whose windows were dark. A bul-let hole, provisionally stuffed with paper, gaped in the wall of her bathroom. The following morning the sky was a dull off-white. The mountains surrounding the town were reminiscent of pleasant Alpine landscapes. I took a walk down the boulevard; the kiosk-bars were open now too, but had next to no business. The waitresses stood around wearily, studying their idle hands. The side streets near the boulevard were full of ruins and rubble; blocks of flats and old-town houses were torn wide open; stray dogs ran around in packs, and cats circled and rubbed up against the legs of the few pedestrians. Mostar was the most wrecked place I had ever seen. Nothing would stay put, and nothing could be put back together. It was like the chaotic set of some disaster movie that had fallen through because the extras had gone on the rampage.

The Neretva formed a flowing border through the town, with no need for border controls; the only people to cross over and satisfy their curiosity were visitors, who would later return through the ruins and blocks of flats to the western side. On the eastern bank the streets were full of pious Muslims. Girls in hijabs streamed out of schools where they were probably learning how to be teachers, nurses, midwives and lawyers; boys poured out of the mosques and houses of learning. There was everything here that was missing in the few streets on the other side: cafés, shops, bustling people on the streets. Yet it all had something demonstrative about it: Muslim life played out against the backdrop of lovely old Mostar, and even the rugged mountains were shown off to their best advantage, with their bubbling brooks and green dabs of conifers. I visited a mosque and kept my eyes steadily fixed on the delicate floral frescos and a shelf of well-thumbed prayer books, so that I wouldn't have to look at the pile of trodden-down shoes that lay by the entrance; I had been seized by an old, forgotten, childhood fear of empty shoes. All was quiet in the mosque courtyard: the only sound was a fountain, and a single bird. Roses grew on the fence in front of the street. Beside the mosque was a new graveyard with shining white steles and the names of young men who had all died in the course of a few weeks.

This is no place for me, I said to Selma that evening. She poured me some green walnut liqueur and put a plate of baklava in front of me that was gleaming with syrup. She agreed with me. We drank our dizzyingly sweet and at the same time slightly bitter liqueur and Selma told me about her childhood village, which was situated upstream by the Neretva not far off the road to Sarajevo, which followed the course of the river. Like all pre-war worlds, the world of Selma's stories was suffused with an unreal light: a world by the bright green Neretva, which, like all rivers, demanded sacrifices – drowned children, lovers, idiots, dare-devil ice-floe hoppers, dreamy moon-gazers who could no longer tell up from down, all of whom had entered the annals as the chosen ones, those whose hearts the river had touched; in the courtyards of the houses the walnut trees rustled, apricot kernels were cracked open, sheep slaughtered, carpets aired and white linen spread out to dry, while fires were stoked under cauldrons in which plum puree bubbled to a thick, black paste and cantankerous goats were dragged in to be milked over troughs.

We talked until it was almost morning; we heard the muezzin calling from the other side of the river, and my anxieties of the previous day fell from me.

On the following day Selma accompanied me to the bus station. The departure times were unreliable; there were no notices with bus timetables. Groups of travellers burdened with luggage wandered from one bus stop to the next, driven by constantly changing rumours. Selma parleyed with a grumpy ticket vendor who eventually pointed to one of the bus stops, and most of the other people waiting now gathered around us, placing their trust in a stroke of good fortune. After some time a rickety bus turned up with space for about twenty passengers. The travellers pushed forward to the bus, negotiating with the driver about where to stow their luggage, their countless, overstuffed synthetic fabric bags, their baskets and boxes. Selma took a plastic bottle from her bag, filled with dark green walnut liqueur. She pressed it into my hand. Be healthy, be well, she said.

Outside the town the bus came to a halt. There had been an accident. Two cars had collided, parts of which, now that they were scattered over the road, betrayed how thin and rusty they had been. The midday light lay still and bright blue on the scene of the recent accident, on the spewed-out baskets and bags, on toys, bread loaves and tomatoes. Jars of preserves had cracked. Pieces of cloth were spread over the casualties. A police car and an ambulance stood at the edge of the road, their flickering lights barely visible in the sunlight. The police signalled wearily to approaching vehicles to slow down and halt; the paramedics stood next to the casualties. The slow approach of another siren was audible in the distance – it made an uncoordinated, fitful impression, as if the driver were alternately pressing differently sounding horns.

The Neretva, its water gushing green over whitish stones, flowed beside the road. The Pure River. The passengers became impatient, children started to cry. Women were praying; the bus driver got out and talked to the policemen. Stray dogs collected at the side of the road, lay down, scratched themselves, their gaze fixed on the scene of the accident. The second ambulance arrived;

its wonky horn went silent. I heard the bus driver and the policemen conferring in low voices. The newly arrived paramedics joined their colleagues, assuming the same attitude with their hands on their hips and their heads down. The bus driver returned to his seat and woke the engine from its dozing idle rumble. A policeman waved the bus through the narrow strip where nothing was lying on the road, only blood creeping in thin trickles across the asphalt to the river. The bus jolted as it went over the stones at the side of the road; the dogs beat a retreat. The river almost touched the road here, giving travellers the optical illusion that road and river were one. Waves on the river gently rippled in the blue of the sky and eddied playfully around the larger stones on the riverbed. The women drew their crying children to the windows and showed them the river. Baby fish, baby fish, they cried, hugging their children and stroking their hair. The bus driver switched on the radio and there was folk music with sprinklings of oriental influence; it was easy to imagine the dancers capering about in traditional costumes. The sun was very hot, and some passengers jammed towels into the windows to create a little shade.

The bus kept on having to stop; the driver set to work with his tools, hammering and turning screws, frowning as he peered under the bonnet. The male passengers gathered around him and offered advice or jibes. At dusk we rolled into Jablanica, our engine stuttering. Everyone had to get out at a large tavern that looked like a caravanserai. We were told there would be another bus later; the driver and his clanking bus vanished into the night.

There were no guests sitting at the long tables under the projecting roof of the caravanserai. Two indifferent waiters with moustaches stood behind a grill on which smouldering chunks of charcoal were turning to ash; small pieces of meat lay shrivelled on the gridiron. Folk music came from inside the tavern, an endlessly looping drone like the music during the bus journey. Some of the travellers ordered drinks; the waiters served them grumpily; the blackened pieces of meat on the gridiron remained untouched. The river could be sensed beside the caravanserai. A fence separated the forecourt from a strip of grass that fell away into the darkness. Water gurgled and swished in the depths, and there was a cool mountain breeze. A gate on the other side of the street opened into a courtyard where men sat under a garland of fairy lights drinking tea. They laughed and talked; the rising wind wafted through the tops of the walnut trees above their heads, shaking something bitter into the air. There were flashes of summer lightening. I could not tell which direction I was looking in.

It was a long night. The weary waiters closed the wooden lattice-work shutters of their veranda and brought out one or two red plastic chairs for the travellers waiting in the cone of light thrown by the street lamp, where we had got out of the bus. There were only a handful of the passengers left; where the others had disappeared to was anybody's guess. Children slept on their mothers' laps; men spoke in low voices, smoked, soon were snoring. Dogs sniffed around the sleepers and thrust their hungry muzzles into various pieces of luggage. One of the men woke up and, letting out a soft hissing whistle, jerked up his arm as if to throw something. The dogs immediately took flight. I remembered what my grandfather used to say, that the fear of thrown stones was so firmly and deeply implanted in dogs that the slightest hint of such an intention caused them to flee.

217

A bus arrived from Mostar in the first grey of dawn, and the stranded travellers found seats between the snoozing passengers. The sun rose over an Alpine landscape and a vigorous mountain river; it was impossible to imagine that the same river would so soon broaden into the flat, irresolute world of the delta.

Below the hillside villages girls washed clothes in the river. They knelt on the riverbank, rubbing their washing on stones or holding it to rinse in the current. Everything they were washing seemed white. At the roadside between dark riverside trees honey was for sale: honey in jars, buckets, tubs. How could this rocky mountainous landscape yield so much honey? Could the inhabitants of a country that had built, as if from a single mould, so many monotonously new, gleaming-white cemeteries in such a short space of time really eat so much honey? It is said that honey heals wounds: sore lips, raw fingertips, red chapped hands. Eyes too then perhaps, burning and full of tears from gazing at the glaring white cemeteries. The river brought purity from the mountains, waters sighing in the service of oblivion.

XXIV. MARKET

London markets, as I realized after only a few months, were border-zones of ambiguity and shady goings-on. To an ordinary frequenter of markets, whose expectations may have been formed and habits acquired in other parts of the world, nothing was quite as it seemed at first glance. Rather than places of commerce, of the to-ing and froing of money and goods, these markets were closed circuits, each of them a ship on a sea of streets ruled by an entirely home-grown set of conventions, and each with its own crew to keep the circuit turning. The skill of the marketeers lay in operating – according to unwritten rules of their own making – a theatre of exchange, turnover and general bustle, which, at least in the minds of some shoppers and bargain hunters, whether hungry, needy or acquisitive, must have created an enduring illusion. For even their repeated discovery that the item they had carried or dragged home had turned out, once separate from the market of its purchase, to be something quite different than they had imagined, something spoiled or lacking in substance, caused few to recognize in this the effects of beguiling showmanship. Even when, on arriving home, all that was left of a freshly butchered leg of lamb, an enormous yellowish-red mango, or a highly practical immersion heater, was a sort of shadow at the bottom of the shopping bag, the shoppers would rarely think to blame the marketeers, putting it down instead to factors outside the market: to the crowded buses or underground, the strong wind, the volatile climate, which, on the way home, had been responsible for several changes of weather, any one of which could have proved calamitous for such a sensitive product. Many market-goers may even have resigned themselves to such losses, to this galloping depletion and depreciation that had overtaken their purchases on their way home, thinking it a fair price, a fee rendered for the inordinate cheapness of the goods in contrast to prices paid elsewhere. No witness to the assembly and dismantling of these markets could harbour the slightest doubt as to the alternative reality evinced by such places: they would pop up in the morning with an alacrity suggesting a complete set of props – half sheep carcasses, crates of mangoes, immersion heaters, balms and remedies, foreign spices and fruits, sales personnel included – had simply emerged ready-made from certain hatches and sheds, the whole caboodle vanishing again in the evening as if, with a single snap of the fingers, it had been returned to the selfsame hatches and sheds. All that remained was a small troop of sweeping and scrubbing stagehands whose task, as the market's daily theatrical epilogue, was to convey the waste left by the performance – fish scales and fins, bones and trampled fruit – into the gutters or large rubbish containers.

Berwick Street, Ridley Road, Chapel Street and Electric Avenue were the names of some of these open-air theatres, where the languages spoken were different from those spoken outside, and the market people, whose aspirations were different from those of people in the surrounding streets and squares, used different gestures to make themselves understood. I frequented the markets more and more often, attracted, as most visitors probably were, by their almost clandestine theatre of gestures and glances. It was like a dance whose sequences and rules remained just beyond one's grasp; watching the dancers – bartering, lending, appropriating with feigned stealth, making things disappear and conjuring things forth, cheating and offering fake assurances

– you might learn the steps and the changes of step, anticipating what was foreseeable, but you still ended up as clueless as ever. It was a spectacle of foreignness in which, thanks to my own foreignness, I felt at home, and it occasionally dawned on me that others must feel the same way, that foreignness was the flywheel at the heart of a machine whose mechanisms these market traders had acquired the resourcefulness and skill to master. I seldom bought anything, but ran my fingers over all I could, hoping they would pick up the traces of things, committing their textures and consistencies to memory. As someone who would frequently show a reluctance to purchase anything, I was not particularly popular with the traders; they needed customers in order to keep their game up and running; they needed payers of sums that were sometimes no more than a pittance to provide their tills with the necessary light-hearted jingle-jangle, while the sham stuff in their customers' shopping bags proceeded to wither and wilt or grew mould at an alarming rate. Sometimes, however, I really was tempted to buy something: a bunch of mint with leaves that seemed especially smooth and aromatic; a rough-skinned apple that awakened a childhood memory; or something practical like an egg-timer or knife, imagining myself using them at home. That kept the sellers satisfied for a while, and they gave up deliberating, in their marketeers' jargon, the best way to send me packing.

During the evenings I would often take a short tour through the small Inverness Street market, which, in contrast to other stages, was something of a rehearsal space, or so it seemed to me. Consisting of only a few barrows – and goods so unattractive one might think their sole purpose, one they had evidently served for some time, must lie in acting as points of choreographic

221

reference for certain sequences of steps – the market was nonetheless fairly lively: there was a lot of pushing and shoving, and a body who had worn herself out all day standing idly at a window gazing wistfully into the distance might pull herself together and take a wander across the market shortly before closing time, venting her frustrations over the futility of such yearning by engaging in some jostling and shoving herself. On my way home I would then be relieved to discover that whatever I had bought – generally a couple of avocados whose fitness for consumption was diminishing by the minute – had, over the short distance I had walked, become considerably lighter.

I traversed, circled, and roamed these markets, their minor and major shows of trade, transition, excitement and propriety providing me with images of the city, whose gigantic configuration – layers, angles, warps and wefts – I was gradually learning to decode. I noticed how the city, constantly and unavoidably rubbing against me as I passed through it, was entering me, while I, by virtue of the same friction, was forfeiting layer by layer of skin and bone, so to speak, to it. One day in an old street into which I had ventured only once in an evening of mild winter wind, and oddly enough in the immediate vicinity of my house, I chanced upon a market I knew practically nothing about, having heard only vague rumours and odd pieces of information. Here the city had stolen a march on the market operators, selecting a particularly decrepit street – one which, as people whispered, was already condemned – to be the site of a refugee market. The street where this market took place was an old, broad crescent that had probably been quite beautiful once, a half-moon at whose outer rim drowsed a neglected green space, strewn with rubbish.

The houses on either side were so dilapidated that the façades were often all that was left; behind them were heaps of stones and debris beside booth-like flats, which had been built by untiring residents around the open spaces whose erstwhile walls they had seen crumbling before their very eyes. Other houses still had one or two floors or rooms, whose back walls, however, were daily going to ruin, while the roofs and attics had long been demolished by storms and other extremes. But defying fate the façades of the former houses had remained, providing a home – partly under the added shelter of wooden lean-tos, partly encamped among the debris of ruined buildings – to individual shops and makeshift kitchens: improvised enterprises run by dealers who made a precarious living from the trifles of daily need. For years now, and through all the phases of its decline, it had been a highly popular street; it had seen and taken part in many things, which the older residents, whistling and wheezing from dust-choked bronchia, were only too glad to talk about. Since the launch of the refugee market the older residents had left their cobbled-together shanties more frequently and also more cheerfully, sampling various goods in memory of richer days, even enjoying an occasional snack, although they must have found the dishes on offer strange. New arrivals from all over the world were now directed to this street, which became their hub. Many of the latter seemed aimless, somnambulant, as if sleep offered protection against realizing how alien were the shores on which they had cast up. Smiling, they touched the items on offer in the shops, breathed in the aromas of the prepared dishes, brushed along façades that were in permanent danger of collapsing, looking out through empty windows and doors at a landscape of ruins that was partly covered by grass and moss. To put this much-loved street to greater use and encourage greater usefulness among the aimless new-comers, the foreigners were granted the opportunity of acquiring a trading license solely for the refugee market, where anyone who had verifiably and permanently left or lost their native country would now be permitted to conduct their business from stands and barrows. Outcasts and expellees applied in large numbers, men and women whose homelands had gone up in smoke or unexpectedly sunk beneath the waves in some faraway region of one of the world's great oceans, but also people who had simply forgotten where they came from. Not everybody received a license, of course, but many did, and they put themselves to work immediately.

It was during this period of optimism that I first came upon the market, which I began to visit regularly; the sight of frenzied activity unfolding and striving to full bloom – to be followed, I suspected, by an equally rapid wilting – gave me a pleasant feeling of giddiness. The licensed refugees went hammer and tongs at the task of creating their market booths, stands and barrows out of street rubbish. They roamed the streets collecting all manner of unused stuff: they fished small gnawed bones out of bins, turning them into small toys and mellow flutes; they caught stray animals, holding them for sale in home-made cages, and netted hundreds of pigeons for slaughter. They scavenged cut hair of various lengths by the sack-load from hairdressers and created amusing wigs; from the scales and fins of fish sold at other markets, they crafted necklaces and hair accessories, whose tang of seaweed or salt awoke happy memories in some of their customers. Plucked pigeons, now a bluish red, hung from rusty meat hooks; their foul-smelling plumage was sold in bags to stuff cosy cushions. Behind the barrows and booths refugee girls in brightly coloured frocks stood in façade door frames – some of which had a new coat of paint but were just as empty as ever – waving solicitously to obligingly strolling men, calling out *lovey-lovey*, leading their sweethearts into the ruins at the back, or up a staircase into some stub of a room, where, under the open sky, they apparently had a great deal to tell each other about lost homelands, a pastime that soon proved highly popular. In less than no time a market had emerged that people commended as cheerful, impressed by how well it was thriving. The short-lived goods on display, possibly precisely because of their ephemerality and fragility, enjoyed a certain city-wide kudos, and people travelled from faraway suburbs to marvel at the refugees and their trading and transforming prowess. Asked where they hailed from by friendly, well-meaning locals, many of the refugees contrived fabulous and highly elaborate tales of their alleged countries of origin. Speaking in jumbled sentences and mixing up their words, they invoked incidents, destinies, heroes, kings and indeed gods whose existence prior to the moment of telling not even their dreams had anticipated, and to crown it all they would finally be moved to tears, which possibly came so eagerly to their eyes because they had run out of anything real to palm off on these locals. The market and the welcome demand it produced turned the refugees of the entire city into collectors of random objects, which they pursued with great dedication: things cloyingly wheedled, scrounged, begged for, valiantly carried off and, with a couple of skilful flicks of their wrist, put to service under new, invented names with equally invented functions. They became professional alienators of objects from their original uses, inventors of new uses, and in time more and more traders and stands found their way to the half-derelict street. A melee of stallholders and customers appeared and, as well as all sorts of new things, there were little spangled dresses, bags, caps, hats, combs and furs of indeterminate provenance. Bands with instruments never seen before paced up and down, or, if there were a crowd, positioned themselves at either end of the street, playing airs, dance tunes and even marches they had thought up themselves, to which young men and women frisked and reeled in time, wearing fantasy costumes, and the lovey-girls sat in the windows with half-closed eyes as if in a dream singing words to tunes they did not know themselves, but which beguiled their half-naked sweethearts on re-purposed mattresses all the more. There was a constant hustle and bustle that went on later and later every night, filling the air, settling over the whole area for miles around like a many-voiced, murmuring cloud.

Could anybody have failed to see that all this would come to an end? Perhaps the jugglers and tradesmen were so caught up in their whirl of refugee marketeering that they did not anticipate what the officially prescribed Festival of Homelessness, a large-scale event that attracted thousands, would do. There was a motley crowd of artistes and performers: counting dogs and ball-playing cats, fire-eaters and sword swallowers, knife throwers, escape artists, contortionists, all kinds of wild animals played by homeless people in magnificent costumes. There were funambulists who walked from façade to façade, magicians and fortune-tellers, and even a genuine trick rider who entered the scene galloping on a white horse. In her pale pink tulle skirt and shimmering sequinned leotard, she performed a number of tricks without so much as interrupting her smile. A closer

226

look, however, revealed she was what people called an old maid, and just as everyone afterwards claimed they had expected, she took a fall while performing her final pirouette, hitting the ground hard from some height, evidently no longer the mistress of an art that was long out of fashion. Deathly pale, she lay on the paving stones with the twisted arms and legs of a discarded rag doll, her black curls, slipping from her bald skull, shown to be a wig. I could not help thinking of the vanished circus rider and his bitter pronouncement that all such riding was a swindle. The casualty was quickly removed, the bystanders wishing her a speedy recovery, and the festival, due to culminate in a fireworks display after it was fully dark, went on as planned. The fireworks were to take place on the raised railway line and be visible from far away. To this purpose the refugees, under their own steam, had succeeded in bringing the entire traffic on the line to a standstill, and they really did manage to put on a tremendous fireworks display, whose multi-coloured sparks showered deep into the night.

The authorities quickly exploited the trick-riding old maid's accident and, to an even greater extent, the so-called *high-handed closure* of the run-down elevated railway line with its clattering and unreliable trains (which had enabled them to produce such an unforgettable fireworks display), to tie the homeless and their market in legal knots, in fact in such a meshwork of knots that the entire trumpet-golden splendour of the market and its traders were swept from the half-moon-shaped street at a single cast of the net, including most of its older residents as by-catch. The very next day the construction vehicles were sent in. The façades were restored to former glory and blind windows filled with glass, behind which delightful interiors were bathed in a warm glow after dark. The rubblescape behind the rows of houses was screened from view and the green space given a clean-up. Pedigree cats were brought in, to be fed mornings and evenings by animal-loving elderly ladies, and selected refugees – so people said – were paid a meagre wage to populate the streets wearing rosy-flush make-up and charmingly pretty clothes, throwing each other casual greetings and pretending to return to their new homes through the artificial doors.

XXV. REKINDLINGS

At the end of January the misty-bleak, shadowless light gave way to a keen sunshine, as if winter had ended early. There were spring smells in Springfield Park; young swans glided in pairs, and the inland gulls, usually seen circling over the street in unruly mobs, roved across the wide marshlands in tighter formations, apparent forerunners of returning migratory flocks.

A wiry young man with short hair and a startled-rodent-like face would often hang about at my end of the street; he had restless, unsettling eyes. In his nervousness he would try to get people to talk to him. Jackie, Greengrocer Katz and his assistant, and the Pakistani owner of the internet café sent him packing by mutely turning their backs on him, but he had more luck with the Croat, who was occasionally game for a natter when in a good mood. The Croat would then join him on the pavement in front of his shop, swirling coffee in his mug and watching the young man, who had no mug and nothing to drink, shifting from one foot to the other, straining to prevent his gaze resting on the Croat's coffee or tea. The young man spoke with the fuzzy accent of the region between Tottenham Hale and Margate, a garbled idiom whose speakers' mouths, perpetually starving for something, would bite off just enough of each word to ensure that only insiders grasped what was said. Whenever I picked up shreds of such conversation in passing, it was about mates, cars and cash; and inserted between the slivers of words came laughs, too, that bore no relation to anything, hissing sounds, whistling between jagged teeth. The Croat nodded condescendingly for a while as the young man spoke, then, nonchalantly raising his hand to hip height to wave goodbye, disappeared into his shop, there doubtless to press the play button again for *Harvest* or 'After the Gold Rush', to attend to his sacks of second-hand clothes, or rummage for treasures in the boxes he had found in front of his shop that morning.

During those mild January days I bought one or two items from the Croat: a sugar caster, a small carafe, and a salt cellar, all in the characteristic ribbed glass – grown dull over the years – that was typically found in cut-price shops. Rough dish scrubbers, and collisions with brassily rasping cutlery in the grey dishwater of large restaurant kitchen sinks, had left scratches; the remains of food, dirt and sweat in the grooves of fumbling fin-gertips had clouded the glass; the aluminium top of the sugar caster with its sprinkling nozzle was dented, as was the perforated lid of the salt cellar. I had noticed the objects lined up on the Croat's counter, who had just re-moved them from a box of junk and had not yet decided on a price. A thin beam of sunlight fell through the back window of the shop and, meeting the glass, was trans-formed into a dim radiance that seemed, while arriving from some distance, to pierce the vessels from within. The Croat took one pound fifty for the items and threw the coins with a careless gesture, and a twinkle in his eye, into the box for takings designated for the needy Bosnian refugees. I left the shop with my purchases, as I did so passing the young man, who, hoping for an opportunity to draw the Croat into a chat, had advanced as far as the shop entrance. With a politeness that seemed almost disingenuous he pressed himself against the door panel to let me pass, and a musty odour reached my nos-trils from his clothes, as if he spent a lot of time in a dank cellar or a room that was never aired.

During the following days I busied myself photo-graphing the items I had purchased in different kinds of light, as if doing so might lead me back to that strange radiance, which, upon my first seeing the objects, had emerged like a kind of absorbed light from their dull, scratched glass ribs. I arranged the sugar caster, carafe and salt cellar in different constellations, exposing them to varying light incidences, in sometimes artificial, sometimes natural lighting, in the morning light of my front room and the dim evening glow of my back room, which looked out on the empty garden and one-windowed brick wall. I photographed each arrangement with different apertures, periods of exposure and distance settings, immediately developing the black-and-white films in my small, lightless bathroom and studying the quadratic negatives, but the vessels, blunted by use, gave no hint of an absorbed light. In the negatives the three objects, standing in the dark cone of an artificial light, formed peculiar landscapes, landscapes of bereavement and implacable homelessness. Exiled from their intended purpose, far from the companionship of their vitreous kind, the three objects placed on the crumpled cloth in the glow of an invisible lamp were a mysterious group of formations in a kind of stone that was both unknown and unreceptive to the rays shining on its worn surface, repulsing them, casting them aside without radiance, without even a glimmer.

I made prints of several of the photos taken in natural light. The objects stood around like some disturbed still life that was not yet – or no longer – given over to a world of its own where the rules apply to nothing but what is depicted: an island deposited in a land with no coastline, lead-footed and dull in the wreath of sunrays falling through my front room window. Or they blurred to silvery shadows in the foreground, while beyond the sharply defined window figures appeared who were out and about in the bright morning light. If I studied the pictures long enough, I thought that in these figures – which, despite their shadowiness, were more clearly delineated than the glass vessels – I could make out the familiar characters of my street, including, in one corner, the nervous young man.

One day I was standing in the queue at the post office when I noticed the young man ahead of me. He was impatient, writhing on the spot, as if he could barely keep from flapping and shaking and swinging his arms and legs. He looked around, his rodent face twitching, his lips forming the silent words of some muted, absent-minded dialogue with himself, curling his upper lip and baring his notched incisors. He went up to the counter and faintly mumbled a request: he wanted to pick up some post, and he gave an address in which I recognized the name of my own street. The woman behind the counter did not understand, and he repeated the address loudly and abrasively, adding: 'the house with the fire'. The customers turned their heads to look. Fires were no rarity in this part of town; in the sublets and smaller flats above shops, nylon dressing-gowns were known to catch fire on the glowing bars of electric radiators, or the flame of a lopsided candle would lick the moth-infested edge of a curtain, or a glowing cigarette eat into a polyester duvet cover, giving rise to a suffocating smouldering fire. There were casualties, there were blackened windows, there were dutifully laid supermarket flowers in thin bunches, joined by cheap soft toys whenever children were among the victims. The fires were soon forgotten, hollow windows boarded-up, buildings sold, gutted, renovated and modernised, and let again for more rent than people in the district could generally spare. The fire the nervous young man had evidently survived or escaped from was still widely remembered, however; simply to hear the nervous young man call out in that edgy manner was to look up and know immediately which fire he meant, which tall narrow building, its blackened remains unaltered, standing cavernous and desolate behind police cordon tape that by now was tattered and torn. It was this area's very own 'house with the fire', and the waiting customers watched on with evident curiosity as the woman behind the counter handed the young man a small pile of letters, which he stuffed into the pocket of his tracksuit top.

The man continued to hang about in the street for a while, his search for someone to talk to increasingly futile. Even the Croat disappeared as soon as he noticed him coming, while the Kurdish taxi drivers waiting for business and sitting on a bench in front of the row of houses at the end of the cemetery wall looked upon him with bafflement and suspicion, as he stood gesticulating agitatedly on the narrow strip of pavement between them and the noisy slow-moving traffic. Once, I thought I recognized him at the front door of the burnt-out house. I was on my way back from my walk, the evening edging over the river Lea close at my heels, whilst in front of me, beyond the cemetery to the west, glowed a sunset veiled in cloud, a promise of brighter days to come. The figure I saw was moving about and bending over to look at something in the front garden, the toe of his shoe pawing at weeds, at debris from the fire and what was left of the flowers in their decay-resistant cellophane. What could he be looking for, months after the fire, after the wind and weather of the frostless winter had raked over the debris, after the forensic investigators and treasure hunters, who were always quick to show up after a fire? Eventually the figure, throwing a glance over his shoulder, disappeared in the dark cavity of the door, whose carelessly nailed-on cross-boards were half torn off. Did he still have a place to sleep there, a bolthole in the crumbling remains of this block of flats? Was the musty room his clothes smelled of here, or some oubliette he climbed down into, its order within and without untouched by fire, where a world of small things, unchallenged, had survived? Perhaps he was simply revisiting a memory, re-enacting a homecoming, rehearsing a long-axed role in this burnt-out theatre of shelter and lodging.

XXVI. STRATFORD MARSH

One day, amidst the vibrating jumble of a dual carriage-way's pillars, I happened upon a desolate piece of land. I had lost sight of the river: perhaps I had left its course, or had it gone underground? Following the wilder branch of the Lea I had become tangled in briar and brushwood along a trail, barely a beaten track, between bushes crowned with rubbish, where tattered plastic bags crackled in the wind and rustled under occasional afternoon showers. The ground was sodden and boggy – which is to be expected where the ground is thin and covers a network of rivers – but it also smelled sour and putrid, as at the edge of rubbish dumps. What was wild here felt like a wound, the scar of a mindlessly delivered laceration, edged by roads that rested on supports and crossed where the piece tapered, passing under and over each other and veering away in divergent directions from north to south-east. This out-of-the-way piece of land was a protrusion of the marshes and meadowland along the Lea, the town-land-river fringes I had extensively walked, where different aspects mixed together, and an urban, rural or riparian character might come to the fore depending on the light, or the time of day or year: it was a twilight domain, overshadowed by roaring expressways, a place that was lost on me until I caught sight of a skewed signpost in the thorny bushes: Cat Cemetery. The path followed the direction indicated by the sign onto a patch of brownish grass, where sticks, boards and bits of plastic had been stuck into the ground. Each carried a name, some had dates, commemorative plaques with scribbled writing, attempted engravings, or burnt in letters. Photos were attached to some of the memorials, battered by the weather despite their plastic covering: bleached cat's faces, wherein death was an entirely credible factor, staring face-to-face at nobody from little round eyes, which, here and there, were the only things that had not blanched. Some pieces of wood were waterlogged or rotten; one half of a bisected plastic bottle, which somebody had placed for protection over a stick with photo and name on a bit of paper, had been pushed upward by sprouting weeds so that it now hung askew over their pallid stalks, while still managing to protect the almost illegible note and oddly unimpaired photograph of a black cat with particularly pointy ears. Who buried their cats here? Who had slogged their way through these hostile bushes with a stiff cat in a sack and dug a hole, most likely stumbling on the bones and skulls of previously buried cats as they did so? Who came here to remember or mourn? Was it a suburban ruse of some kind, a secret address, a whisper passed under pledge of secrecy from mouth to mouth? A few bunches of plastic flowers lay between the memorials; they had been gnawed by winter and were so leached out by the passing seasons that their only remaining colour was an eminently unnatural blue-green. Beyond the cat cemetery, the path led through scrub and under the dual carriageways across a strip of green to a road that seemed deserted and was fenced off on one side from stacked containers that alternated with small, makeshift huts. On the other side of the road were caravans surrounded by low fences. I remembered the island of caravans I had seen in glaring light and shadows from a different perspective along the river, also under dual-carriageways on pillars, but nothing here seemed familiar in the murky half-light under an increasingly thick layer of clouds. Disconcerted, I struggled to remember which directions I had taken, but without the river as orientation I was flummoxed. There was nobody to be seen around the huts between the containers; the gates were barred with padlocks and chains, and a dog snarled and barked behind a fence. I heard a train whistle far away. My path was blocked by a barrier at the end of the street, and I had now lost all sense of the river Lea and its banks. It was as if by coming under the dual carriage-ways and passing through a gateway of scrubland I had set foot in a totally foreign country. Lamps were lit in the caravans, toys lay scattered about; a pink bike with stabilisers stood on the well-trodden artificial grass that covered the passageways between caravans. A barely ankle-height fence surrounded a patch on which stood garden gnomes and pots of artificial flowers. It began to rain, more heavily than I had expected, and I could see nowhere to take shelter. A woman stepped out of a caravan to retrieve the bike; I could feel her suspicions towards me, but could not think how to dispel them. I was in the wrong place. However, she summonsed me almost imperiously to join her and waved me into the caravan. Caravans were unfamiliar territory to me; only once, in an English meadow one cold summer's day, had I sat on the steps of a caravan with its tiny mobile dwelling at my back, and that had been many years ago. In the distance you could see the river Wear between clumps of sparse riverbank brush. You got water for tea from a small stream that poured into the Wear within sight of the caravan. Now the woman set a mug of tea down in front of me, and I wondered where she had got the water for that. From the Lea? There was a smell of food, not any specific dish, but the essence of cooked food itself, albeit of a kind that had possibly been typical decades ago. The woman offered me a seat on a white folding chair. I could sit there until the rain passed over.

A number of photographs stood in a row on a shelf along the wall, mostly black-and-white and, in the front row, a few faux-coloured: the usual prim annual pictures taken by travelling wedding photographers who worked the schools and crèches and made the children look like interchangeable dolls against a background that never changed, children with no past or future, grinning out of nowhere in an eternally trite now.

The woman sat down at the narrow table, which was decorated with a lace-patterned oilcloth, and contemplated me as if I were an extraordinary find. I felt somewhat awkward and barely had the courage to lift the mug to my lips. All of a sudden, the woman threw her hands up in the air – there was no sugar in my tea! She leapt up, took a silvery bowl from the shelf on the wall and, without asking, heaped a spoonful into my mug. Although I found sweet tea disgusting, I made no objection.

As if we were playing a game she now reached across for my hands. Give me a palm and I'll read your future! she said, bending over my hands. From close up, I noticed that her face was much older than I thought. Her fingers were bone-dry, like thin lizard's legs, covered with brown spots. I stretched out both hands; she hummed and hawed, wondering which one to read. What was written in my left, what in my right? I was suddenly eager to know what she might read there and began to study my palms with curiosity; lying there in this strange woman's hands they no longer seemed to belong to me, reminding me instead of two unfortunate tortoises that had flipped over onto their backs. The woman knitted her brow, narrowing her eyes and rocked her head from side to side in thought. She prophesied that I would undertake great journeys. By rivers? I asked. Oh yes, she said, beside rivers: I see great rivers in your palm, in distant lands! She grinned and gave me a wink; one of her lower canines was gold. When is a land distant? I wanted to ask her, but held back. She predicted I would enjoy modest wealth, espied cats in the tiny folds on the heel of my hand, wrinkled her nose because she sensed a life touched by leave-taking, but then her expression brightened as she caught sight of a true king hidden in the crazy patterns drawn by the countless little lines of my palm. But I don't think you'll marry him, she added, almost in warning, as if she wanted to protect me against disappointment. I was quite content: even a brush with a king was quite enough for me. The rain was still drumming on the caravan roof, a soporific sound that made me feel heavy and tired as soon as the woman released my hands. I would have liked to have promptly taken my leave, indeed the more promptly the better; with not a single coin in my pocket, our parting would be embarrassing, and yet the rain dismissed the possibility of an awkwardly precipitous departure into the darkness of the night, when I had no idea where I was or how to get back to the river, which I could follow north, step by step, making my way back through familiar terrain to the bottom of Springfield Park. In my increasing lassitude, I suddenly thought I remembered my grandmother saying that fortunes told, if unremunerated, turn into their opposites. What could be the opposite of a river, or a king? Without being asked, she now set herself up under the shelf of photographs and began to explain them. She spoke in the accent of the broader region, Estuary English, the tongue of the river mouth, open vowels, clipped syllables that nonetheless spilled into one: I found it hard to listen to, as I almost always did with this particular colouring. The words snapped at my ears: malicious fish,

241

whose pursed mouths were probably full of sharp little teeth. The woman broke off for a moment and asked me to sit on the bench against the opposite wall, to have a better view of the photos. I refrained from replying that I was too short-sighted to discern from that distance the little figures and faces in the pictures; I sat down on the designated seat, blinked and listened, trying to remember whether she hadn't spoken with quite a different accent when she was reading my palm. The voice of the commentator of the lives portrayed in the photographs – all of whom, it appeared, had dedicated themselves to the precarious – now seemed different to me than the half-flattering, half-beguiling voice of her prophesies for my future. The fishy sounds gurgled and pattered around my thoughts, and I must eventually have fallen asleep, for I awoke with a start at the jarring sound of a plucked string. My father, the woman said insistently, was the King! As she was speaking she tapped on a small, children's guitar lying beside her on the table, a bright yellow piece that might have come from a funfair. She was sitting across from me at the narrow table with a wry grin on her face, as if she knew something about me I didn't know. She then picked up the guitar and began to strum its clanging strings. In fact her voice was lovely; it was wistful and young. She sang with ardour of a girl on her way to market to meet her sweetheart, who, stopping to slake her thirst from a river, sees his reflection in the water instead of her own and knows he is no longer alive. During the song, I thought of the Lea, of the water puckered by tiny whirlpools I had hoped to encounter that afternoon, of the alder-and-willow-lined crook of the river between Hackney Marshes and Temple Mills, where swans plunged their necks into the semi-exposed roots, the gentle, almost straight line of the Lea along

Walthamstow Marshes, where the swans had rehearsed their return to the wild. It had stopped raining. It was very still, with only a quiet rustling of things that were trying to shake off the wet outside. I was about to ask the way, for a pointer in the right direction, when on the green alarm clock under the photos I saw a time I could not believe – it was far into the night, almost morning. The woman looked at me blankly when I asked for the nearest bus stop, then shrugged her shoulders mutely, stood up and opened the door. With reluctant concern she accompanied me for a short distance through the darkness. Out on the road it was quite still; there was only the dog barking and growling at the sound of our steps from behind the fence that ran along in front of the containers, its bared teeth grinding audibly. In the distance, the rushing and roaring of the town: a dormant beast. The woman did not mention my sleeping, and nor did I. I thanked her and she turned to go. After a few steps she glanced back over her shoulder, and I could see her grin in the lamplight as she waved.

For a long time I stood at the corner of a big arterial road and waited for the night bus. It was not cold, and yet I felt frozen under the orange tinted light of the tall street lamps. Now that the rain had turned to the invisible drizzle of a marshland night, the dim light on the glistening asphalt made the surrounding darkness, for all its flickering lights, neon signs and headlamps, seem a kind of ink, a spilt bluish-black, in which countless lives on every side were now immersed. I tried to remember the story the woman had told me. We never forget what we have heard in our sleep, I was told as a child: a warning not to discuss secret matters within earshot of someone who is sleeping. Perhaps I had absorbed a story – about horses, kings and princesses, the river Lea, a story I would never know but also never forget, a sleeping story that would speak to me only in dreams.

Traffic was sparse but persistent, sometimes a driver would honk in passing, nobody stopped. The direction of the movement alternated like the swell of the sea. Now and again there would be a surge of rushing cars and roaring lorries heading east to the coast and estuary, then a wave of traffic would push townward from outside. The bus arrived. There were two passengers on the upper deck, asleep; impossible to say how many times they had been back and forth on the same route. At some point in the early morning light they would stumble out of the bus, trying to work out where they were, remembering, or more likely struggling to forget, what had happened before their night ride started, and would then begin the possibly rather long walk back to their beds, if they had one. I got out at Lea Bridge Road and walked for a while along the peaceful river. The swans were grouped in faintly luminous formations in the safer places on the water, asleep, motionless. It was completely still. Night birds in the willow thickets on the marshes called hoarsely, a low barking sound; perhaps there were foxes beyond the tracks. I looked over to the island between the rail embankments. A feeble strip of lighter sky loomed in the east. Was the dawn already coming over from the sea? Would there be a first grey reflection on the distant shore mud at low tide? I heard the familiar clattering of a train in the distance. Like a string of pearls pulling the night away, although the sky over the Lea was still utterly dark. The train was a ticking glow-worm leaving the city, creeping across the horizon. In the opposite direction came a second worm, creeping into the city. The Springfield Park gates were closed at this hour; I came in through dark roads along the perimeter of

244

the park. Two foxes crossed my path, a cat darted out of their field of vision. First birds were singing, an earthy smell wafted over from the park. On the road in front of the locked park gate stood an ambulance, its blue light flashing. Across the road, in a ground-floor flat in the red-brick block, the lights were on, the windows open, and two black women were talking assertively to a paramedic. A broken mirror hung on the wall, with only a couple of craggy teeth projecting into a dark field surrounded by fancy gold-coloured mouldings. A large greenish feather, speckled and iridescent, stuck out from behind the frame, its shadow cast on the wall by the glaring of the naked bulb that was dangling from the ceiling. I stopped between ragged bushes at the entrance to the building. The door to a staircase stood open and the lamp above the stairs was flickering. Meanwhile the blue emergency light swept coldly and unremittingly over the bushes, the brick wall, the bare trees on the other side of the street and the park gate. Paramedics appeared from the door of the flat and, balancing a stretcher, came down the three steps to the front entrance of the ground-floor flat. The two black women I had seen through the window appeared behind the medical personnel, one of them following them down the steps to ensure the outer door swung to after they had passed the threshold. A person was strapped to the stretcher, helplessly twitching against the firm belts that held him in place. I recognized the ankles and sinewy legs of the King. For the first time, as he passed in front of my eyes, I noticed the scars that covered his legs: small circular cicatrices wanly shimmering in the blue emergency light, suggestive of pecked stabbings of tips of beaks, although the birds had always circled him gently. The King's magnificent robe had dwindled to a tattered loincloth in which pale gold threads glittered, modest appeals to the memory of his raiment's former splendour. The King's torso was bare and wiry, and a number of scratches and welted scars were visible under the straps that were supposed to restrain him. In this state of nakedness they carried him through the cold, early spring night. For the first time I saw the King's eyes: his semi-upturned pupils sent out tiny golden sparks and the whites of his eyes protruded from his bony face. His head was uncovered.

The paramedics shoved the stretcher into the ambulance and contacted their control centre by radio. A driver emerged from the dark path that led from the red-brick building; they all got in, closed the doors and drove off.

The light was extinguished in the King's flat. I took a quick look through the park gate. I must have been wrong down by the Lea: there was no sign of dawn, and the only bird singing was the one I had heard before, in a tree above the crossing foxes. It called again and again, its voice full and throbbing, as if heralding all the sweetness of spring.

When I got home I picked up a book. It fell open at a page about gypsies.

'I have heard them laugh over their evening fire at the dupes they had made in believing their knowledge in foretelling future events...' was the first sentence to meet my eyes.

XXVII. TISZA

On the banks of the Tisza I met a gold hunter. He was
the first I had ever met, and would remain the only one.
It was on a spring day in northern Hungary, and the
signs of recent flooding were everywhere to be seen.
The riverbank thickets were full of rubbish: equipment
swept away by the flood, smashed furniture and, under
swarms of flies, dead cats. The countryside had been dis-
figured by the excesses of the Tisza and its tributaries,
a picture of desolation, in which one or two people in
waders could be seen stumbling about, yanking ineptly at objects caught in the branches of willow trees still
surrounded by water and cupping their hands around
their mouths to shout out the names of lost dogs, cats,
cows, aunts and uncles. I was on my way somewhere
and anxious to leave these scenes behind me. At a bend
in the river I stopped, because driving across the only
bridge open to traffic for miles around, I had recognized
the place where I had witnessed an unfortunate incident
during the previous summer. The short reach of the river where the accident had occurred was peaceful now,
with not a visitor in sight, and compared to the devastation elsewhere, astonishingly intact. I parked, got out of
the car, and looked over the parapet at the water below,
which, feigning harmlessness, was turning little whirlpools around the pillars.

The river made a bend here, with the landscape rising
to a final hillock before the great plain and forming a
slope down to the riverbank. For no visible reason, such
as a rocky obstacle, the river described a curve, which,
in the course of time, had eroded at the foot of the small
hillside to leave a sandy bay where bathers gathered in
the summer. On hot days the small beach was packed.

Clinging to the slope, which was sparsely covered with trees, makeshift cafés with ramshackle wooden terraces offered visitors a view of the river bend and new car bridge, and there were kiosks selling beer, toys and cheap food on either side of the small road to the bathing spot. Locals had introduced me to this place the previous summer, after a few days spent in their villages listening to stories about the terror rivers big and small, such as the Tisza, Tur, Kraszna and Szamos, spread when they malevolently burst their banks, stealing children, cattle and sweethearts, undermining shelters, causing bridges to collapse and washing from their graves the white bones of poor people – who, unlike the rich, were unable to find their final resting place on some artificial mound – and scattering them so far and wide that it was impossible to tell which bone belonged in which grave. The rivers up in the border region of the north all began to seem to me like gigantic snakes, sluggish and glistening as they slithered their way through the summer days, some of them thicker, some less so, lined by trees and bushes but rarely by villages, as if people were scared or anxious and preferred to keep their distance. In many places there was talk of ravaged villages whose inhabitants, after such floods, had collectively decided to resettle far from the river instead of rebuilding their old village. There were hardly any bridges, few ferries, and their service unreliable. To anyone who was foreign to these parts, crossing a river meant gathering advance intelligence, finding a ferryman, enduring his questions, paying a high price, only to find him generously inviting the locals to take part in the crossing, to enjoy a special outing with the whole family by letting themselves be ferried across the back of this sliding, languidly breathing serpent. The locals seemed to find a mild thrill in brushing with danger, playing with risk. They pointed to things in the harmless eddies at the rope ferry's keel that I neither saw nor understood; raising their hands to shade their eyes they peered upstream and downstream through the tunnel of rank summer growth and read things in the riverbank landscape – which, unpopulated, made a desolate and remote impression – that I could not decipher. I soon tired of the inscrutable tangle of rivers, losing all sense of which bank of which river I was on, or of how far away I was from the nearest crossing place. In my confused state I started to feel afraid of the landscape, sensing a threat for which I found no name. It was then that friendly villagers had brought me to this bridge, via which, travelling south-west, I might safely leave the labyrinth of snakes, enclosed as it was to the east and north by tightly secured state borders. On that occasion my companions proudly wanted to show me this well-behaved river with its bathing beach, which, on that hot and thundery August day, was overrun with visitors. Over the bathing area hung a babble of noise – splashing children screamed, dripping bathers on their way to their towels slapped themselves and each other's wet bodies to drive away or kill the especially large and troublesome local mosquitoes, women pursued or confronted their husbands with shrill outbursts of laughter, men bawled indulgent oaths, wishing upon each other genitals attached to different parts of the body. There was a burning smell of barbecue, also the hoppy, bitter smell of canned beer foaming over and soaking towels and swimming trunks. At the other end of the little bay children had made a mudslide on the slope, down which they whooshed into the water hooting, taking dark-yellow clayey soil with them each time they went down. Clouded with mud, churned by so many bodies, the water no longer radiated an impression of freshness, and the recreation sought by the bathers now seemed to come down to the impact of skin on skin, the intertwining of voices, body parts and smells to make a net that sank over them as the day progressed, and tied them up in a bundle.

I felt ill at ease at the bathing beach. As the storm approached, the air grew ever heavier and the insects more and more meddlesome. The noise of voices gasping for fun buzzed in my ears; every ringing laugh was false, every booming, yelling incivility came as a blow. At the edge of the bay I noticed a woman wearing a bathing suit with a large floral pattern. She had on a straw hat and sunglasses and sat fully upright on her towel, watching the bustle in the water. Beside her lay a bleached beach bag with handles in gold plastic, an article that would certainly have been very modern during my childhood. The frolicking bathers, who seemed to belong to a different time zone than the woman, took no notice of her. The woman took a brightly coloured bundle and bellows from her bag, unrolled the bundle and proceeded to inflate it until by and by she had a kind of kayak beside her that was bright orange and pink and, like a dugout, tapered to a point at each end. This was a highly conspicuous object and made a painfully garish splash alongside the skin and flesh-coloured goings-on. As the woman stowed her bag and rolled towel in the fully inflated dugout and – circumventing the crowd gathered near the mudslide – dragged her craft to the river and set about floating and boarding it, the bathing guests began to view her with curiosity. At the first teenage snigger that came from the area around the slide, the expression on their faces rapidly altered from a hesitant, almost approving wonder to mockery and a

250

resentful spirit of mischief. The woman with the dug-out waded hip-deep into the river, and to the laughter of several spectators, attempted somewhat awkwardly to climb in, on several occasions almost losing her straw hat. She had to keep straightening her large, butter-fly-shaped sunglasses, and was forced more than once to fish her towel and beach bag out of the water. After several attempts, however, she succeeded in getting in; sitting in her boat at last, she floated towards the middle of the river. All this time she had seemed so oblivious to the reactions of the bathers that it was as if their snig-gers and taunts had not reached her ear, and as if she existed, along with her unusual means of transport, in a transparent bubble that was in the process of moving to a different place, borne by a barely perceptible wind devoted to her conveyance alone. To all appearances, the woman was not lying very comfortably in the boat. Her legs stuck up in the air above one of the kayak's pointed ends, while at the other end, her head lay so low down under her skewed hat that she looked as if someone had dumped her there without the least respect for her person. She nevertheless made no attempt to alter her position, merely stretching one arm out to steer the boat further away from the beach. When she reached the cur-rent in the middle of the river, there were caterwauling whoops of applause; people waved, shouted seafaring clichés, and spurred on the youths swimming behind the boat. The brightly coloured little boat was now bob-bling along towards the pillars of the road bridge. The woman was peeping over the edge when there was a sud-den commotion of big waves around the boat, sloshing over the sides and causing it to roll violently and capsize. The woman had lost her straw hat. Rearing up with an incredulous look on her face and waving her hands in the air for help as the boat overturned, she disappeared under the surface. The boat drifted keel up on the departing waves. The beach bag's gold handles glinted for an instant in the dim sunlight, then sank. The straw hat bobbed and circled. It was the bellows that made the fastest getaway; it was already a couple of boat's lengths ahead and had reached the bridge, its tube twisting and turning in the river like a thing alive. Individual spectators clapped and roared their approval, but there was something half-hearted about it, half the heart applauding the practical joke, the other half hardening against the mute chill that beset it. The two youths who, from under the water, had made the boat capsize, now resurfaced. Arms stretched out to them from the mudslide, pulling them ashore and patting them on the shoulder, while the upended inflatable, as light as a child's lost toy, silently and softly spun towards the pillars of the bridge. A few broken sniggers were still heard from the teenager's corner, but otherwise a quietness had fallen on the scene. Thunder growled in the distance, and a wind sprang up. All movements had become angular and leaden; people were pulling shirts and dresses over their heads, rolling up rugs and mats, packing paraphernalia of various kinds, leaving the small beach. In less than no time the youths had disappeared. My companions seemed very embarrassed. They assured me the woman had swum on; she was bound to be somewhere beyond the bridge sitting in her boat again, which had glided between the pillars and could no longer be seen. The storm that afternoon was one of the most violent I had ever witnessed: streams burst their banks, roads disappeared under the deluge, sewers frothed out of the drains, the Black, the White and the Fast Körös, which I crossed further south later in the day, foamed around the pillars

252

of the groaning wooden bridges. Only the Tisza seemed unperturbed by the storm, pushing onward grey-brown under a rainy sky that refused to let up for days: harbinger of an early autumn.

Now, in February, I had come directly from the north, following only the Tisza, shy of venturing further east where I would only be beguiled by other rivers. Along the Tisza the effects of flooding were visible enough. As I stood on the bridge watching the water flowing from the east, I had trouble convincing myself that on my way south I had been travelling upstream; the landscape seemed for a moment to have turned topsy-turvy. A cuckoo, the first of the year, called from the trees on the slope, a spring arrival with its counting rhyme – Cuckoo, cuckoo, tell no lie, how many years until I – and the heart missed a beat if the wayward bird's calls were too few.

At the sight of the slope, its shuttered kiosks and little beach, I felt the same chill run through me as on that August day among the bathers, who, under the first peels of thunder, had flocked to their cars after the mishap as if to escape. I walked down the deserted path to the beach. It looked truncated, as if the floods had torn away some of the riverbank, which now fell sheer to the flow of the murky brown river. Branches, twigs and other bits of wood floated past, and plastic rubbish circled on the surface. A putrid stench hung over the area, although the riverbanks here were not as dirty and marshy as further north. The air was full of tiny insects, although it was so early in the year that hardly any trees had leaves. Near the bridge, where the bank sloped down more gently, I noticed a man. He was wearing a kind of cowboy hat and was busy with a bucket and some other equipment. He looked up and greeted me in a friendly manner, beckoning to me to join him.

He introduced himself as a gold hunter, and without my asking, explained his various utensils to me, which had something toy-like about them. In a blue plastic bucket – blue, he explained, because gold stands out against it quite brightly – he had collected some tiny lumps, leaves and pellets that shined or shimmered in some way. To my mind, none of them looked like gold, more like tin, chipped off bits of paint or varnish, tiny clews or nodes of some bulky wire, in which a ray of sunlight had caught. Actually, I collect glitz, he said. It's the glitz that turns gold into gold, is it not, despite what anyone says? What would gold be without glitz? You might confuse it with a lump of dirt or stone, with any old pebble. No glitz, no glory, no glory, no power. That's it, isn't it? The question wasn't directed at anyone. It hovered in the air, unanswered. The gold hunter was already busy again, leaning out over the river, sweeping his finely-meshed net against the current. As the water ran off his haul, a little shining something appeared between shreds of refuse, swollen plant stems and bits of wood, a small hollow body, open at one end, like a tiny, solidified sack. Aha! said the gold hunter, and lifted it between his fingertips into the sunlight. Look at that then! How can that not be gold? He rubbed it carefully on his sleeve and it was true: the little thing picked up a ray of sunlight and reflected it with such brilliance that for an instant I almost felt blinded. A mysterious something! he continued, as if holding a sermon. An effulgent enigma! A conundrum of radiance! He placed it in the blue bucket beside his other finds, where it looked oddly forlorn and out of place. The gold hunter seemed to be thinking the same thing. Probably a gold tooth, he said, shrugging his shoulders. A gold crown somebody has broken off a tooth. Again he shrugged his shoulders. A lot of dying goes on around here, and people take what they can get. Everyone tries to be first when someone dies, to see what's in their mouth. The floods bring all kinds of things to light, so why not a gold tooth.

He took something out of his pocket that he had found further downstream that morning. It was a pair of sunglasses, of a type fashionable years ago, with a mask-shaped frame: like an accessory for a masquerade ball. The hinged joints were overlaid with a fluted metal in shimmering gold on which tiny multi-coloured platelets shone like the scales of a living animal. I couldn't help thinking of the woman of the previous year, with her dugout-shaped inflatable and old-fashioned beach bag. Of how she had climbed into her boat and the way her sunglasses kept slipping. But her sunglasses had looked different.

I left the gold hunter to his fortune hunting and continued my south-westerly journey until I rejoined the Tisza. The high water had moved on, inundating the alluvial meadows and covering an enormous area that reflected the grey skies. Nothing but the bright white light betrayed it was spring. Groups of herons roamed the drab waterscape edges: their aching screams ripping the air into quivering shreds, pale shadows over water that vibrated to their calls. The tops of bare trees thrust above the floods; the beds and courses of tributaries were no longer discernible in such a huge body of water. The Great Plain between the Danube and the Maros – intersected by the Tisza, which, the further south it flowed, became all the wider and more powerful, whispering more and more stories, generating tragedies in ever greater number, while it was increasingly obvious it would never reach the sea, and that the

Danube would head it off and swallow it – this plain, which, viewed from the slopes falling away to its edge, had the melancholy aspect of an ocean who-knows-what hand had seen fit to drain, had begun, during this dismal spring, to flood once again, creating the illusion of a landscape that existed only in hazy notions, but no longer in anyone's memory. In Szolnok – angular, grey, sad Szolnok, which had placed all its hopes in ways that led out of town, and, in so doing, had looped together the largest rail junction in the country – the trains stood on tracks that were encircled by water, while the passengers stared dolefully at the concrete excesses of the station, at sprouting spring weeds between the sleepers, the rubbish fluttering in the feeble wind in the corners of the platforms, the faces of the passengers in the train on the opposite platform. In the shadow of blocks of flats with views of the Tisza, men sat in a wide street lined by garages that ran along the town-side bottom of a high embankment that uniformed men were elevating and shoring up with sandbags. For garages were a male preserve, and each man had something concealed behind his door, which was seldom a car, but more likely a small workshop, a collection of scrap metal, repaired tools for repairing damaged belongings, or beer. The men drank and smoked, spitting when marching orders flew their way from the embankment, gesticulating with heavy arms and hands, holding short parleys. News of sinking water levels were passed on. The men shuffled their rubber-booted feet until their town was out of harm's way.

Later that year – it was almost summer – I again saw the Tisza at Szeged. It was wide and calm, flowing between thick riverbank bushes which it had entirely covered during the floods; stuff the deluge had coughed up still hung rustling in their branches, which had since turned green with leaves. The plain had been inundated twice in the past two months, and in a little summer colony along a backwater of the Tisza they were airing their stilt houses. The mud left by the floods was slowly drying; rotting upholstery and mattresses lay about in the gardens or stood propped up against front fences; household items destroyed by the water lined the miry paths, and in a kink of the oxbow, behind a riverside wood that stank of refuse, the water surface was quivering with mayflies blooming, the Tisza Flower: after years of larval sleep these insects all hatch at the same time, spreading scaly-looking wings whose surfaces are iridescent with countless, tiny splashes of colour, and for a few minutes, at most for a couple of hours, they unfurl a radiant magnificence we call their 'life'.

XXVIII. RAIN

During my second London spring torrential rains swept over the roofs of the city. An unprecedented rainy season, by all accounts. Pedestrians, blasted by the accompanying wind, floated along barely touching the paving stones under their umbrellas, which, whether by intuition or adherence to time-honoured rules, they manoeuvred adroitly to save themselves a soaking. I could see I would never master the art, so I resorted to taking the bus. Wet and shivering I would wait at the bus stop and board the first bus that came. From the top deck I got to know a different city, providing I kept wiping the steamed-up window. The buses were unreliable and moved slowly through the bumper-to-bumper traffic. The passengers on the upper deck, as I quickly discovered, were generally there for the long haul: people with no homes, or people newly expelled from their homes, or who were on the run, or looking for peace and quiet, travellers whose sole destination in life, once they had got the day out of the way, was the night. There they sat, dozing, reading, or looking out of the window, in full knowledge that the bailiff was knocking on their door, their sweetheart was meeting a different sweetheart in their home, somebody entrusted to their care was vainly whining for warm milk or the daily paper, the rain was coming in through the roof and ceiling, carefully arranged containers had long overflowed and the patterned carpet, like a meadow in springtime, was gurgling with wetness. Some spent the entire day of travel engrossed in the same novel, or pored over last Sunday's inexhaustible newspapers. Others gazed into space, or slept, or, like me, kept wiping the window beside them to get a better view. Apart from the short and noisy invasion of schoolchildren in the mornings and afternoons it was all quite peaceful, the atmosphere soothing. The bus moved off with an almost playfully irritable rumble of its engine, a wiper dragging lethargically across its windscreen; street lamps, neon signs and dark shadows of bridges were hazily visible through the steamed-up window. The buses traversed the entire city, from Clapton to Clapham and Putney to Finchley, certainly longer journeys than the majority of local residents here would ever undertake, especially with the river cutting a line between north and south that was rarely crossed voluntarily. From the upper-deck windows you could see into little flats above shops, into offices and workshops, into the burnt-out upper storeys of small houses in unpopular streets. You could see windows boarded up against rats, pigeons and unauthorized residents in abandoned houses on noisy roads, houses people had left for who-knows-what reason never to be seen again, without leaving a forwarding address – fleeing from debts and their collectors, from deceiving lovers and dreaded visitations. For in this city people came to light and went to ground wearing a different face in every neighbourhood, a different way of walking even: this was the capital of chameleons.

Accustomed to my long walks and habitual routes, which allowed me to cast a glance only through ground floor and basement windows, I had now discovered the world of first floors, where people slept and wrote, combed children's hair, dressed, rocked and fed them, pushed vacuum cleaners about and threw armfuls of clothes into suitcases, where they ironed, hit each other, did turns in front of the mirror, and cried. You could get to know a city far better through its first floors, it now seemed to me, for deeper things happened on these higher floors than on the busy bottom ones, and through my involvement as I glided past in the bus, I began to feel a greater sense of belonging in the city than I had by walking and watching what presented itself to the eye of the pedestrian. Down below, you would see laughing, smiling or grinning, but up on the first floor you became a witness to weeping. Old ladies wept over their broken false teeth, old men as they tried to do up a trouser button, children hugged their father's or mother's legs and cried, young lads wept on the telephone. Crying was not unusual in first-floor offices, either. In fact, wherever the bus went, rolling past windows practically at arm's length, you might feel the urge to pass a handkerchief to some sobbing girl or a big man, whose tears were dropping onto his shirt or braces. Since people at ground level grinned and smiled so much, this insight into the many chambers of different kinds of weeping seemed nothing short of consoling to me; a balance had been redressed, a semblance of justice restored.

Looking down at the pavements you saw a sea of umbrellas, soft black jellyfish drifting past each other with tiny feet, hovering along without banging into each other or getting tangled. Among them were a number of foreigners, conspicuous by their helplessness, wandering bare-headed and clueless through the rain, their hair dripping, their hats, hoods and caps completely sodden. Get into the bus! Come into the dry! Get to know your new home! I would have liked to call to them, but of course, out of consideration for my fellow passengers, I left the windows closed, and my knocking signs caught nobody's attention.

When it was raining I noticed things from the upper deck of the bus that would have remained hidden to me in dry weather at ground level, the small lumps left by scarring, for instance, where different parts of town had collided and then grown together, visible from above in the form of a drawn-out hump, a repeatedly badly repaired rift in the asphalt. These were invisible to the pedestrian, but could cause a bus to lurch. Much as all the signs pointed to a big city, almost every area of town was nonetheless separately attached to a much smaller and older locality, too. Oddly enough, these borderlines were more clearly visible in the poor light of a blurry rainy season than on bus rides through town in brighter light and dry conditions later in the year, just as the features of a face photographed in motion will reveal, precisely because of their lack of definition, all the ages and states that face has passed through or can expect to experience. In the rain – which, despite all rumours to the contrary, fell far less frequently here than in many other places I knew – things had a nakedness they were capable of disguising when it was bright and dry, and perhaps this rather mysterious and unspoken fact was the very reason why rain was considered the city's natural state, so to speak. It seemed to me as if the houses around these scar lines felt unobserved and could let themselves go, leaning away from each other and gravitating towards what they truly belonged to – the richer side or the poorer, blacker or whiter, sweeter-smelling or bitterer, shriller or duller – and that the gaps that opened between them revealed the distinctions between the two sides: the curtains in the bay windows on one side of the gap were different from those on the other; the same was true for the colours of the front doors, for the manner in which the cats slunk between the walls of front gardens, also for the flowers in these little enclosed gardens. I looked in vain for a house that was built on one of the scar lines, a border house, standing precariously, where

262

books fell off the shelves at night, pictures refused to hang straight, and cups and plates could be set clattering by the slightest breath of wind. Again and again I set out with the firm intention of finding such a house, but so many things distracted me that I quickly forgot about it.

By and by the rain subsided; nothing fell for hours at a time. Finally the cloud cover broke, and it stayed dry. Everything was wet through and through: the earth squelched under the paving stones, a steady gurgling was audible from the drains, birds' nests drooped like fringes from the branches, the soaked interiors of buildings dried all too slowly. I continued to travel by bus, exploring the hillsides and summits the town was built on, the grand views from a high ridge over an endless sea of houses that melted in the far distance into a range of low hills or into the milky-grey light announcing an estuary, where it was no longer possible to discern whether the roofs belonged to earth or sky. For the first time I began to see how enormous the city was, and I was much enamoured: such an endless labyrinth, in which one might get lost, hide, or forget oneself, where one could feel most at home and simultaneously most foreign, the end of anything straightforward. These routes with vistas – first the climb towards the whitish sky behind a built-up hilltop, followed by the view down over a solid wave of seemingly clamped-together, initially similar-looking houses with red and grey roofs, then the journey down again to find oneself immersed in a flood of houses and streets – these were the lines with which I established my grid of spring coordinates. These routes taught me how to read the city's light. On other bus routes, less focused on the sky, I got to know the city's timetable, for instance the beggar's hour, which was always on a Sunday evening. The buses were usually full at that time of day, and I would usually avoid them even if I did not always have the choice, for on Sundays schedules could be changed unexpectedly and unwritten rules could apply, with detours and stopovers in outermost suburbs and cigarette breaks for drivers at so-called layovers, where several routes crossed and buses might be parked in a row in some small park or on a patch of green, giving the drivers an opportunity to stand on the narrow strip between the buses and the fence of this random, potentially neglected green area and talk, or offer each other cigarettes and have a smoke together, while the passengers, ignorant of the reason for the interruption or its possible duration, went on sitting in their buses and, at the sight of the gossiping, smoking drivers, would soon begin to wriggle about restlessly on their seats. It was on these Sundays, too, that beggars would board the buses, always in the evening, always in thick, heavy coats, and always cloaked in a damp rainy smell that released the coat's many-layered squalor to the bus's confined air. Ingeniously ducking under the vigilant bus conductor's radar, they would stagger from seat to seat on the upper deck of the bus, holding up a filthy paper cup – picked up who knows where – in front of the passengers' noses in hope of a handout, delivering their requests through the gaps and wreckage of their teeth. Each beggar uttered his story of ill luck, disaster and need with alacrity and few words, wary of the danger of some surly passenger or the beggar behind him dealing such an ungentle blow to the back of his head that he might find himself knocked forward a couple of rows, possibly even past the very row containing that evening's big spender. Of course the Sunday evening beggars' big spender was a myth. Each and every one I felt sorry for and gave a few small coins to, if only because of their sodden, stinking coats. But I never saw anyone give a beggar more than a few coppers, never saw anyone who treated them generously, pouring a gleaming trickle of silver from the hand of plenty into their paper cups, and yet the beggars always had a twinkle in their eye, like the reflection of some distant light phenomenon, which was certainly not to be found in the real world of the upper deck. Perhaps this was their ritual, then, their Sunday evening devotions, which found expression in their supplications, their raising of the cup to the tired passenger, their staggering and bowed head and small steps, and perhaps the knocks they received, the hissing contempt, the arrogant disrespect shown to them by passengers, were a kind of purification, following which they felt affirmed in standing at any corner of any reasonably busy street, the more profitably to pursue their project.

Besides the Sunday evening beggars' hour there were also a number of other, albeit less predictable motifs: knife days, for example, whose sole uniting factor, as far as I could make out, was the strong light of windy days. It was then that dog-faced men would hang about on the back seats, the whites of their eyes glinting shiftily as they ran their fingers over the consummately sharpened blade of the knife in their lap. Occasionally one of them waved his knife about in an apparently jokey manner, or as part of a conversation with himself. People kept away, kept their distance, kept their eyes on the windows, looking at the sky, or into the passing flats and offices, onto the heads of the crowds who had disgorged the knife-flasher onto the bus, and who would soon, at some other bus stop, reabsorb him into their mass. Then there were quiet, grey afternoons that hovered undecided and still between sun and rain, meeting men of prayer at their doors and leading them to the upper deck: pale, pious whisperers, bowed on their seats over little books bound in synthetic black, tracing with grey fingertips, and on pages darkened by turning, the letters of so many different alphabets and scripts, and all the while moving their lips, swaying to their whispered song, an agglomeration of voiceless prayer melodies rubbing up against each other and forming a whirling cloud under the low roof of the vehicle. Carried by buses along the streets of the city, here was a floating temporal order that had nothing to do with days of the week, times of the day or names of the month, a spawn of the sheer mass of different movements grazing, stroking and scraping against each other, who had found no place in the structures of submissiveness, but were nonetheless doing what they could to resist the total chaos and confusion.

One day I noticed the trees were in blossom. In the part of town the bus was passing through, blossoms billowed white and bright pink around twigs that were yet to sprout leaves, and everything in the whitish morning light – trees, blossoms, houses and the softly defined vanishing points of the streets – came together to form an image whose yearning to last was so intense that the few passers-by who were out and about at that hour, even the cats and birds, stopped in their tracks for a moment or two, as if following instructions to be at their most receptive in committing something unforgettable to memory. I got off at the next bus stop, determined not to lose the image, and coming through an unfamiliar area behind the refugee market, soon found my way back to my own street.

One of my neighbours was standing on the pavement, his hand resting heavily on a large box that reached his hips, his eyes staring into the middle distance. His gold spectacle-frames glimmered dimly in the absence of direct sunlight; his finely manicured fingernails gently drummed on the top of the box. The trees are barely blossoming in this street, I said expectantly, for he was blocking the pavement, and nothing in these parts was more conducive to the removal of an obstacle than an unrelated remark. I have bought a new machine, he answered. Taking hold of the large box, he skilfully tilted it at an angle and then proceeded to demonstrate how he used a set of little rollers to enable him to get the box into his house without anybody's help.

XXIX. GOLD

Winter hung on here and there, between the Springfield Park bushes, in the alder grove on the opposite side of the Lea, in the undergrowth along the sloping railway embankment. It stuck to the brick wall with its solitary little window, which had stayed dark at night for several weeks now, and it loitered in chinks of the shutters of shops that had stopped opening from one day to the next, whose leaseholders had absconded, taking the goods with them, or were probably sitting out their accumulated debts in some godforsaken place. Despite everything, the days became longer, the sky brighter, bunches of narcissi sprouted between and on top of the graves in Abney Park Cemetery, blackbirds rehearsed their song in the leafless branches of back garden trees, and multi-coloured clouds were so clearly mirrored scudding along in the puddles that any spectator was bound to get dizzy. One day Sonja-turned-Gabriella crossed my path, the girl with the pinhole camera who had disappeared onto a houseboat. She was pushing an old-fashioned pram, her several-weeks-old child peering quietly out of dark eyes, a tiny bonnet-framed face among the cushions, like a photograph from the good old days when babies knew how to gaze silently and steadfastly into the long exposure of a camera's alien eye. Sonja's name was nothing but the vague outline of her former figure; it clung to her still so that people might recognize her after a long time had passed. By now she was probably a Margaret or a Ruth. She had a wry smile and asked if I would like to accompany her to the Croat's to rummage through his stock of clothes. The Croat had been ill-tempered of late. The clothes donations stood around in sacks he had stopped unpacking.

269

In his disgruntlement he turned away large families who sometimes came to him to be clothed and fitted out, wildly whipping his arm from side to side as if threatening to erase his entire remaining stock before their very eyes. But he gave a warm welcome to the former Sonja, returning her wry smile, emptying a few sacks onto the floor of the shop and allowing her to look for anything she could use. She fished a few items of baby clothing out of the musty pile and stuffed the whole lot into a green imitation crocodile leather bag that had gone unnoticed for months on a shelf next to the till, sagging and eventually losing its shape entirely under an ever-thicker layer of dust. The Croat would not accept her offer of a five-pound note for the clothes she had picked; the welfare of Bosnian refugees was no longer his concern, and he ignored the ringing phone. His cassette recorder stood mutely on its shelf, robbed of its wonted neighbourhood of donated things. With the exception of street sounds from outside, it was quiet in the shop, and perhaps it was the absence of song that made the smell of those towering heaps of clothes – which, during the winter months, had undoubtedly lain crumpled and unwashed in the cold, damp corridor by the shop's back door – seem so very stale and pungent.

The girl stuffed the green bag full of clothes into the pram basket and set off home. I accompanied her through Springfield Park to the Lea, and we walked a short distance upstream, where I did not usually go, passing through an avenue of plane trees occupied by a colony of crows, and emerging onto an undeveloped area, abutted to the west by a ramshackle neighbourhood of terraced streets and a block of flats. The latter, wrapped in arid stillness, looked as if it had been relocated from some provincial spa resort in a distant land, to end up here of all places, opposite the enormous reservoirs on the other side of the river. The boundary line of the stretch that belonged to the swans and wildness lay behind us; here, upstream, leaving town, the river Lea was an abandoned body of water whose past was difficult to imagine, and which seemed to have nothing to do with the future waiting for it not a mile downstream. The girl told me about life on the houseboat, which was moored who-knows-where; her anecdotes could have happened anywhere, small and scattered shreds of a life to which her pinhole camera was no longer relevant, for the former Sonja now placed all her hope in escaping to a different country, as she explained. When the baby started to cry the girl sang a bumbling little song whose words sounded made up, but which had a calming effect on the child. It now gazed as silently and steadfastly as it had from the old photograph in which it had started this walk. We continued through a subway under a big road; weeks of rain had collected in large, stinking puddles on the ground. Industrial buildings stood along the riverside beyond the subway. Bright blue foam curled around a drainage pipe jutting from the embankment. Children were playing with fire in the bare bushes, a yelping dog among them. A white afternoon sun came out, suddenly immersing everything in a bright light, making the outlines of objects stand out so sharply from one another that they lost all their usual cohesion. Searching for something pleasant to say goodbye with, I asked her out of the blue whether she had ever known the King. I realized instantly that it was a pointless question, but when I began to describe his headdress, she knew immediately whom I meant. Yes, that's the King of the Nill, she said. Did she mean the Nile? I thought of crocodiles, cats, Memphis and its high priests. The King of the Nile cast up here beside the tiny Lea, the Bird King of that foreign land. For a brief moment everything I knew about the King came together in my mind and composed a story that would certainly bear telling, including how the King was sadly fastened to a stretcher and carried away. But the former Sonja shrugged her shoulders: No, just Nill. She hadn't seen him for a while. I decided not to mention the paramedics or shimmering scars on the King's legs, or how he had been carried away. I reckon my child would have really taken to him, said the girl in a valedictory tone, and with a certain gravity in her voice, as if her idea of going to another country were a heavy burden she would simply have to shoulder. I watched her trudge away into the green strip along the industrial zone, into the interstices between the sharp-edged objects, among which, between the haphazard, outlying precincts of Tottenham, no coherent image could generate: only a backdrop, deprived of all context, for fragments of a story, which, hacked and sundered, were liable to stick quite painfully in a storyteller's craw.

Instead of returning along the river, I took what was meant to be a shortcut through the streets on the other side of the subway, past boarded-up bay windows, between lurking loiterers, children chasing one another, escaping, laughing, and women panting as they dragged their check-patterned shopping trolleys along cracked pavements, past displays of shrivelling, dusty onions, sweet potatoes and cooking bananas, past limping cats and one-eared dogs, through a world of spring and winter fragrances on this unexpected island between a through road, a decaying river, and the area I thought of as my own. Under the gaze of cats and dogs, idle barbers and fingernail cleaners, youths gliding up and down the streets on their bikes, I was going round in circles, unable to find a way out of this world. On passing the meagre display of vegetables for the third time I asked the owner, who was lingering at the entrance of his empty shop, for directions to Springfield Park. Springfield Park, Springfield Park, he repeated, as if asking himself the question under his breath, then pointed the way with a vague, indecisive wave, and when the sun began to set, I recognized my own area again, where small groups of children, dressed up in costumes, were going up and down the streets and knocking on doors. It was Purim: the children had buzzers and rattles, and were dragging golden veils, undone turbans and loosely slung swords along behind them on the pavement. They knocked on friends' doors, or other doors that were permitted, and were given sweets in return for a song or a saying. In the cool spring twilight, they stood in the cones of light under front garden lamps and presented living, Orient-themed pictures, were applauded for their little pantomimes, stretched out their hands for gifts and went on their way again. Some groups had mothers and fathers in tow, keeping their distance, scrutinizing me with suspicion, an intruder in these streets where their children were temporarily rehearsing the fairy tale past of the Orient, while for the first time since winter, the blackbirds were singing at twilight with that peculiar mellifluence reserved for colder countries, and it was as if their intention was to spread a gleaming cloak of sweetness over the children and their parents, who were walking about the streets in their pantaloons, their veils that glittered like gold, and a jingle-jangle of mica jewellery, attempting to outshine everything else that was here.

It was dark when I got back to my street. Roughly where Greengrocer Katz had his shop, a crowd of people had gathered around the Croat and a Rastafarian whom I had often seen in our street, in fact sometimes talking to the Croat. In Greengrocer Katz's brightly lit shop, his assistant was pressing his nose to the glass door, curious to witness the goings-on, while the greengrocer himself was slowly and deliberately packing boxes in the background as he always did on Thursdays. The Stoller children, attired in moustaches, swords and gold-embroidered turbans, stood looking puzzled, but at the same time excited, beside the door of their parked car, watching their father gesticulating at the edge of the pavement and stretching his arm out towards Jackie, who was hanging about uncertainly at the edge of the crowd. The Kurdish taxi drivers had left the bench where they usually waited in front of the minicab office and had gathered around the Croat. Two elegantly dressed black men, who were possibly on their way to play billiards, were attempting to placate the Rastafarian, who was brandishing a curved knife above his head. Passers-by and residents arrived, left, and came back again. The proprietor of the twenty-four-hour shop stood at his entrance and, in a monotonously querulous tone of voice, accused the Rastafarian of stealing a bottle of rum from his shop. The Croat was holding his own arm; a taxi driver, supporting his elbow, shouted: he bleedy, he bleedy. The Croat removed his elbow and turned away. It was true he had blood on his shirt sleeve, but he dismissed the whole thing – No help! – with a wave of his arm. Tossing a few scraps of Croatian into the ring, he offered the bystanders a few incomprehensible words in explanation and, his head held high, walked to the bus stop, making me realize I had never seen him come or go.

On the following day the Croat was standing on the

pavement blinking into the light. His arm was in a sling, fashioned from a wide, lilac-patterned tie he had probably pulled out of one of the donation sacks. Tomorrow see the things that never come today, sang a distorted, crackling Neil Young from within the shop. The Croat waved me into the shop and showed me what had been the reason for yesterday's argument: the Rastafarian, rummaging through one of the sacks full of donations, had come across a small canister, like the ones used for film, although a little worn and dented. Look, said the Croat, and screwed off the lid. The canister was full of broken-out gold teeth. Lucky, lucky, he grinned. He replaced the lid, shook the canister carefully and pressed it against his cheek. The sun was shining. Greengrocer Katz, letting down the rattling metal shutters of his shop, closed for the day of rest. It would soon be spring.

XXX. BOW

March, already March, with one foot still in the cold, at least wherever the shadows fell. The frostless winter had finally upped and left, however, clearing space for a different kind of light. The sky was constantly troubled, full of birds above the marshlands, flocks flying in from the south-east, with delicate flickering shadows tagging them across the grass, edgy masses, that were indistinguishable from one another in their fluttery blackness against the clouds, and which, thanks to the memory that resided in their wingtips, or a kind of tradition peculiar to birds, still had illusory hopes of finding a resting place in Stratford, Hackney or Walthamstow Marshes. The resident birds flew about beneath the migrating arrivals, preoccupied with the approaching spring and familiar with the cut-back borderland that formed a shrinking island between the variously brick-coloured limbs of the sprawling city. The nearer I came to the Thames, the more the light changed to a wind-sharpened white. South of Hackney Wick, beyond the lake-like stretch of unfrequented, placid water formed by the confluence of the Hertford Union Canal with the tame arm of the Lea, the town came close on both sides of the river, darker from the west, with bricks, stone and broken window-panes facing the river, and grass and weeds breaking up the surfacing of the riverside path. How rare to see a boat emerging from the Hertford Union Canal, the shadow of a barge like some stray mirage! Herons stood motionless on reed-lined brick and stone projections of factory walls, staring into the water, aloof in the surety of their own untouchability in this place where unbridled urban development gaped and split, and small stalks of wild green pushed up

277

through the cracks. The bricks of walls and arches between rusting iron bars had grown porous, returning to their pre-fired state: clay, earth, soil. Deposits of waters long since drained, they crumbled into the temporarily established Lea basin, providing perished hollows for settlements of common grass, couch grasses and moss. In the yards along the west bank, where sparse growths of rubbish-strewn marsh plants stood between the walls and the water, were towering heaps of scrap metal: tin, iron and other metals, dispossessed of any form they had once had and reduced to bare material, rolled, bundled, crushed, and guarded by the dogs whose hoarse barking I sometimes heard. Scrap sidetracked for recycling now reinforced the borders of Bow, which the city had once declared to be its boundary, and where bricks from the clay pits and brickworks of London Fields were loaded and began their journey upstream to Stamford Hill, there to mutate into the new arms, fingers and arteries of the city. To the east of the river had once lain Essex, green and flat, a region of outlying villages that had merged into today's suburbs, former marshes and meadows that had turned less brick-red than grey, disappearing beneath storage sites and industrial zones, beneath through roads, sports stadiums and landfills, and under asphalted sites for the caravans of travellers who had converted to the sedentary life, who had set aside their ponies, put behind them their arts and crafts, their country lore and nomadic ways, keeping what might be folded and stowed away to reappear on feast days only they knew of, when they could be marvelled at and discussed, and when they would whisper to their offspring, their schoolchildren weaned of wanderlust, stories of the wondrous things that somewhere might still be waiting for them.

A mesh fence blocked my way along the river, a hastily erected barrier that looked temporary and had no ostensible reason for existing, but which must have been there for some time: slender climbers hung winter-withered in the mesh, rubbish blown here on the wind had conglomerated in the right-hand corner between the fence and the path wall, where there was no way out, no wind that could take hold of the ball of stuff and shake it apart or shoo it away. The path continuing along the riverbank was visible through the mesh; undisturbed and untrodden; it had succumbed to rank grass and grey-green creepers, which sprang from every crack and fissure. I would have to turn around and go back a short distance to a narrow footbridge that crossed to the west side of the river: to Bow. When I reached the noisy road I realized how quiet it had been by the river, which cut through that part of the city like a valley, forming a boundary that divided its two densely built-up sides – both without riverbanks – more sharply than it did the urban from the wild. From the street I looked down at the water, darkly and indifferently pushing south through its narrow canyon towards the estuary, and over towards a drab, shambolic mess of buildings and grey tin shacks, a crudely wrought lid on marshland.

I was unfamiliar with the district of Bow. I lost my bearings trying to avoid the major thoroughfares, where the traffic hammered its way through between north and south and between east and west, across the Lea on the flyover with its high crash barriers, and from the Blackwall Tunnel under the Thames, concrete arteries along which hectic commerce surged from far and wide, while the rivers crossing their paths flowed invisibly, as if busy people ought not to be distracted, or reminded of rivers' directions running contrary to their own. In Bow I got lost between post-war estates built of dark-brown bricks, and rows of small grey, yellow and red brick houses that had escaped the brunt of post-war redevelopment. Grimed with more than a hundred years of soot and black fumes, these had provided ornate Victorian stabling for poor families: two per house, forever squabbling over the use of yard and toilet, the women sore from the phosphorous and sulphur of the match factory, the men bent by dragging and loading at the river, on building-sites, in the slaughterhouse.

Today black-veiled women, walking in silent groups, carried shopping down these streets, their robes wafting in the breeze and brushing the ground; little black worlds of their own, floating between the rows of houses and buildings of the post-war estates, they seemed to maintain a distance from the area. Did they, under the mantle of their black protective coats, harbour a love – for this light, for a tree, for the river? Did they call the house home where they would set down their bags of shopping on a kitchen table, where they cooked meals for their children, gazed out of the window, and, in the morning, plucked their dreams from between the folds of the bedclothes? The cool, undecided March air blew coloured chocolate wrappers along the pavement; a group of black children were arguing whose turn it was to roll down a little slope in a battered shopping trolley and crash against the dented metal gate of a basement entrance. Men in cement-dust-covered overalls chewed in greasy spoons on fat pies that called themselves after different kinds of meat, and shovelled mashed potatoes into their mouths. In the area through which the main roads roared, the dust, soot and rubbish drifting through the streets quickly and thoroughly erased all traces: everything was grey and now. Only the old church and attendant churchyard, licensed to local residents centuries earlier to allow them to find solace and edification during frequent periods of flooding, towered above the island in the middle of traffic-heavy Bow Road: an unconvincing attempt to position itself as a defiant idyll. The last burnings of heretics had taken place on this island; its peripheral location made it an appropriate place for the stake, whose billowing smoke would drift out on a favourable west wind to the estuary and marshes. There, the tiny particles of fatty soot would probably settle on the plumage of the waders and marsh birds, the herons, bitterns and reed warblers.

The run-down, neglected streets near the Lea revealed in every stone and every brick what this area had once stood for: it had been a buffer, named after a bridge and ford, a transitional space, an intermediary zone between town and country. The Lea was not the only river to mark the boundary beyond which the ground became unstable, changeable, unfit for municipal purpose: there were also the Channelsea River, Three Mills Wall River, City Mill River, and Bow Creek, all of them tidal, all of them capable of changing within hours from a muddy trickle to a swirling river, and vice versa. Placed between a web of streets and a tangle of rivers, Bow became a place for unloading and loading, living off bits and pieces that fell off the backs of carts during the handling and transport of goods. On the east bank, the Essex bank, not part of London town, animals had been slaughtered for centuries to feed the eternally hungry and gluttonous townsfolk, cattle from the marsh meadows, swine from the sties of the abbeys. Blood from the slaughter flowed into the river, red ripples lapping away, turning to streaks before dissolving completely in the serpentine lower reaches that were shared by the Lea and Bow Creek. Perhaps the riverbank soil became coloured where the pinkish-red washed up, particles of blood sinking down and entering material from which bricks would later be made, so that one local brick shade might be traced to Essex-side slaughter blood. The stench would have been foul where the locks are today. Where the gas-holders, surrounded by scrub, still throw their shadows, there once were flood-plains and water-meadows, downstream from the large mills and their machinery of sustenance. Dogs, cats and rats, skulking in holes and recesses, would have kept their eyes peeled, immediately leaping on scraps of offal that fell their way, brawling over sinew and gristle as soon as the opportunity arose, biting, drawing blood, while the rats used shrewd teamwork to make off with the loot. Noisy bragging slaughterers' apprentices would have thrown heavy objects at the strays, fragments of brick hitting dogs hard, or cats, breaking a leg, cracking the delicate bone behind a cat's ear, killing outright or maiming so badly that, defenceless now among the riverbank reeds, they could barely crawl to some bolthole to die.

Crows would have screeched, circling in dark flocks above the east side of the river, their jagged twitching shadows falling on the slaughterers and their apprentices, and on heaps of bones, and the entire lower reaches of the river would have seethed with large eels.

What happened to the bones? Were huge mountains of them sometimes washed into the Lea by floods, were they purloined by wise housewives to boil up a soup for the family, did they bleach in the weak sunshine, or rot and turn green in the frequent periods of rain? Did sea winds encrust them with salt? Were they used for anything at all? Were they carved into flutes that sounded

282

shrill and bitter and were said to bewilder the senses – only whose? The player's, or an involuntary listener's? Were they made into toys, household utensils, small tools? Were they ploughed into the great fields that belonged to the abbeys, were fat ears of grain, fertilized with bone, harvested and milled a few hundred metres upstream from the slaughterers' site on the riverbank? The idea of those mountains of bones haunted me, but I knew, too, that at some time or another a clever man had come upon the idea of turning them into porcelain. Bone porcelain was valuable and famous for its pearly white gleam and hardness. It was said bone porcelain had the lustre and strength of a young, healthy girl's teeth.

What was it like when the formulation for bone porcelain was being devised? Did women, under the supervision of the slaughterer's apprentices, wash the bones in the river before they were taken to the other side? Did they scratch filaments of flesh out of cracks and crooks with their fingernails, fending off the carrion-hungry crows with jabbing elbows and flailing free hands? Or did assistants stand over them waving rags to frighten the voracious birds? Did the women's fingers, as they washed the bones, brush against the slimy mouths and fins of flesh-hungry fish waiting just beneath the surface, quivering to snatch their prey? And when the bones were clean and white, did they drive them through the ford or on swaying carts across the bridge, or were the white heaps of bones shipped in a barge? In Bow, at any rate, in specially designed furnaces with air vents, they were converted into bone ash, a white powder in which apprentices, wise to the lustre of bone porcelain, may have noted a certain sheen and been tempted to divert a handful into their own, hopefully well-sewn pockets. But this radiance of the bone ash was an illusion, as the master porcelain maker repeatedly explained. The gleam in the ash was naught but gossip.

In the years when the master porcelain-maker of Bow was attempting to fire himself a fortune, the bone furnaces were in constant use. They gave off clouds of smoke, and there must have been a stench like burnt horn in the air, a permanent fug that lined the noses and mouths of the residents and covered their tastebuds with a stale film. A thin, slightly greasy layer of greyness settled on surfaces and was difficult to remove, making leaves and tiny birds' feathers stick. In the evenings, if there was a wind from the south, the residents stood in the streets or in their yards, craving relief from the smell of bone ash and gasping like beached fish for the sweet air that wafted over from the sugar refinery on the Thames.

Despite the large quantities of bones, the master porcelain-maker of Bow fell on ill luck. Perhaps the clay they used to mix with the bone ash was not light enough in colour; perhaps this fine, light-grey clay could only be found where slaughter blood had soaked in, giving every batch of porcelain stock a hint of rosiness: pretty maybe, but unable to compete with the white gleam of other famous porcelains. Thus neither fame nor fortune gushed into Bow, and it was the match factory in its magnificent palace between the Lea and Fairfield Road that eventually brought promise, work, and wages back to Bow – in the phosphorous fumes and greenish glow of afflicted jaw bones in the darkness of those little Victorian family stables.

Descending a half-hidden flight of steps near the flyover I rejoined the river and walked down to the locks, where Bow Creek flowed around the big brown-brick site of the old mills and entered the Lea. On their way to the Thames Estuary, trains clattered over the railway bridge above my head. Coots quacked their huffy coos, paddling excitedly between off-colour rushes and the tongue of the sluice. The ground seemed to sway beneath my feet. The large and empty gasholders on the east bank of the river looked as if they were hovering. I walked through the mill area and lost my way between rivers. Some Vietnamese were sitting in a concealed spot behind bushes fishing, next to them a transparent plastic container in which I saw thrashing fish. It was getting chilly: an unusually sharp clearness in the air beneath a cloudless early evening sky, as if we were to be granted a taste of the frost that had stayed away all winter. I walked back to Hackney Wick, on the way passing my fingers over the surfaces of the brick walls at the edge of the river. Clay, mortar, moss. The texture of an edge. In the trees, still bare, blackbirds were singing, swelling their dark throats with sweetness. The water birds held their peace.

XXXI. HOOGHLY RIVER

The bridge over the Hooghly trembled with noise, with
the impact of countless soles on the pavement between
parapet and road, the vibrating of car engines, blowing of horns, shouts, bawling from taxis and vans, the
sounds of people, people who had squeezed into carriages, held on to the outside of doors and windows of a train
that had rolled into Howrah Station, and who were now
streaming across the bridge into the city: flower sellers
pushing their way through the throng with towers of
tagates and chrysanthemums balanced on their heads,
vegetable pedlars with baskets, workers on their way to
factories and brickworks, day labourers. Ferries plied
the river below, broad rusty boats, rattling and creaking, and these too were packed with people, better off
than the pedestrians on the bridge, as betrayed by their
bags, suitcases and shoes. There was a pushing, shoving,
sharp-elbowed jostling for position, a surge overflowing
with ruthlessness and violence, as if crossing the river in
the morning, these people were fleeing from a threat to
their very lives, forcing their way through, clinging to
railings, struts, girders, calling, roaring, grabbing. The
ferries swayed on the water, rolling to one side then the
other, finding their balance, putting in. Released from
the pressure of being wedged in, the torrent of people
exploded onto the jetty and fanned out across the riverbank into the vast city. Ways parted after the bridge – to
the flower market near the river, to the vegetable markets in the centre of town, to factories and workshops
along the riverbank, where bricks and countless small
everyday objects were fashioned in clay, put to use, then
returned broken to the clayey river, a river that spat
things out and swallowed things up, while above it the

sky made such a soft, dense haze that anything garish glowed, relieved of all its harshness. This refinement of light into softness stood in contrast to the water itself, a foul-smelling, polluted, murky flow bearing carcasses and full of detritus, whose eddies were dappled with the circling wreaths of orange flowers that decorated the river burials of children's corpses.

The orange flowers shone out everywhere, on small improvised altars at the edge of the road, on large official shrines on specially constructed galleries, at kiosks and stalls, and most of all at the flower market under the bridge. Here they towered like mountains, whether as single flowers or wreaths, on sprays, arranged as gigantic snakes, overflowing from cotton sacks. Between them were chrysanthemums, white and blood-red, large stiff leaves on thick fleshy stalks. None of it fragrant. Middlemen haggled for sacks of flowers, flat baskets with heaped flower pyramids, endlessly braided flower-chains. Housewives and servants bargained for smaller bunches, rudely, bringing a harshness so clipped and mean-sounding to their exchanges they could have beheaded the flowers, had the blossoms still been attached to their stalks.

After their morning traffic some of the ferries lay at anchor along the riverbank nearest to the town centre, where hordes of loincloth-clad boys were taking their morning dip in the dirty water, romping and shrieking on the strip of mud between an improvised ramp and the river, shining with wet, clambering about on jetties, jostling as they splashed and splattered their way back to the bank, while a little further downstream dying people on bamboo litters were lowered from a jetty and immersed in the waters, that they might at least relinquish their hold on life with one foot in the sanctifying waters of this arm of the Ganges. Not far from the jetty for the dying, young men in white loincloths were adding wood to a funeral pyre; corpses were brought on biers and set down; the sweet, dusty aroma of burning root-wood hung in the air, entering the pores and every fibre of the body.

The whole of Kolkata, including its outermost suburbs, was soaked in a river that was thick with dead things. Ponds, runnels, streams, ditches – the town was swimming in the many-armed Ganges-Hooghly, always on its way to the sea. Wherever I looked there was sprouting, burgeoning, rotting: bananas, mangoes, coconuts, and a heavy, sticky, unsettlingly sweet fruit whose name I did not know. Wherever I went I saw flocks of crows rising, falling, croaking, and everywhere ravenous black kites circling and dropping with piercing cries among crows scavenging carrion and detritus. There were people drawing water from pools where water buffalo stood up to their bellies, catching fish in dark waterholes, conjuring the inevitable snakes, which, in this country of degenerate fecundity, were said to grow to fabulous dimensions, and pampering the dogs that barked at snakes and chased them away. Cats, on the other hand, shy of water, did not do so well; they were even inferior to the rats, which grew smart and fat and had nothing to fear from the dogs. The river with its countless arms and fingers brought food and excrement, growth and putrefaction, poison and health, combining them, blurring them, fusing them to one, a filthy fount of life that devoured the dead.

The sediment of the river, a loam-brown mud, was in constant motion, mutating from river to soil to clay to objects, bricks, domestic utensils and figurine gods, all of which would fall to pieces, decompose and be given back to the river. In the early morning innumerable small teacups, arrayed layer by layer on flat baskets to form towering pyramids, were delivered from potteries to the street cooks. With their slow stride and tall burdens on their heads, the potters' porters moved like giants through the waking city, through herds of pied goats being driven at dawn to a pale excuse for grazing on the Maidan, past children thronging around the cardboard dwellings along the main thoroughfares, and between the concrete piles of Circus Avenue. In the evening the used cups, trodden into small pieces, lay in the gutters, already set on becoming earth the rain would wash into the nearest conduit to the Hooghly, there to be incorporated into its malleable sediment and formed yet again into something fragile and degradable. In Kumartuli, the potters' quarter in the north of Kolkata, long-established artisan families, their skills reputedly passed on since time immemorial, made hundreds of thousands of divine figures for the great festivals: whether thumb-sized, as long as an arm, as tall as children or men, the colour of river mud, whitened or painted in bright colours, simple or grand, all were offered for sale in the days preceding the festivities, bought, decorated and, after the festival, submerged in the river as if to fulfil a promise that all things taken from the river would be returned. The figures intended for the smaller and larger, private or public shrines and altars were crude, stiff, somewhat skewed and distorted in their dimensions. The Saraswati figures that were now – in February – to be seen everywhere, held their instruments in enormous chunky hands: Saraswati, the deific incarnation of flowing, hovering over the waters of origin: a dark pool whose surface resembled the murky ponds in the outer quarters of Kolkata, watery places for fish, buffaloes and snakes. These embodiments in fragile clay, which made the stalls of the street traders sag, and whose assembled head-high company lined the streets, practically brought the traffic to a standstill: cars crept past the displays, the drivers stopping and jumping out every time they saw a figure they liked, discussing, bargaining, finally loading the purchased item into their vehicle, which would wait with its motor running. Saraswati, the goddess of erudition, learning and the arts, installed in yards, verandas, balconies and living-rooms and decorated with garlands of flowers bought in the market by the river, granted a holiday to anybody who was involved with instruction, learning or knowledge.

On the eve of the Saraswati festival in the streets of Baithakkhana, Kolkata's bookshop quarter, preparations for the celebrations were underway. The light was fading; the air smelled of sweet smoke and exhaust fumes, stagnant water and rotting rubbish, at which crows picked undeterred. The larger roads were full of people; the bookshops were almost empty. The shops, kiosks and second-hand book barrows were closing; here and there shutters fell, while boxes and piles were gathered together and everything was cleared away. A tentative holiday atmosphere began to unfold. Candles flickered under the cover of a bulging banyan tree, throwing a restless light on a tiny shrine with ungainly, deformed figurines that looked like a parody of the sumptuous stages on which adorned Saraswati figures were put on display. I found a small shop that was still open, its display chock-a-block with stuff. In front of the shop a row of cardboard boxes containing photographs stood on a rickety shelf; handwritten place names, the majority of which were unfamiliar to me, marked the boxes. The salesman was leaning against the jamb of his open door; he paid no attention to me, and was so absorbed in conversation with a customer that he had probably forgotten to close his shop. He smoked, spoke, illustrated something by waving his hand with the cigarette, laughed, satirized, imitating in different voices, his Bengali sprinkled with scraps of English. The customer, in an effort to drive the smoke away, was fanning himself with a battered, gaudy-coloured paperback he may have been intending to buy, helping himself to the sweets the salesman had hospitably held out in a confectioner's carton. The photographs in the boxes were mostly postcard-sized views of landscapes in artificial colours that were already taking on tinges of red or blue, also a few pictures of flowers, and a glossy print of a snake charmer, whose high definition stood out among the postcards with blurred outlines and fake colouring. The snake's whitish head was visible rising above the edge of the basket. I had never seen a snake's head close up before, and was astonished at the way its mouth broadened downwards and flattened. In the carton marked Kolkata, inserted between pink-tinted photos of temples and tourist attractions, was a small album bound in green artificial leather. Stuck on its black pages under the spider's-web-patterned interleaving paper were brittle photo corners, most of them empty. About a dozen black-and-white photographs were still in the album, most of them out of their corners. They showed waterside scenes, fishing boats and palm trees, a smiling woman proudly displaying a basket of fish, a bleak-looking promenade with European women ambling along holding parasols in what was evidently windy weather, a man with an air of importance sitting in front of a typewriter outside the lavish entrance of a public building. The words Diamond Harbour Telegraph were legible on a building in the background. Diamond Harbour: the name had a certain swagger, and spoken against the background of the broad waterscape and junk-like boats that were in almost every picture, sounded more Far Eastern than Indian. I wanted to take the album with me, and felt the faintly greasy, artificial leather with its scratched surface under my fingertips was as good as mine, but when I asked the salesman what he wanted for it, he shook his head: we're closed, he said almost rudely. No transactions.

Meanwhile it had grown dark, and a dry wind was blowing through the dark streets of the bookshop quarter. There was rustling all about: leathery, grey-green leaves in the trees, paper refuse in the gutters, faded streamers over the shop doors. Murmuring night birds whispered in the tops of trees, dogs barked. The piercing honking of car horns and the thin jingling of the rickshaw wallahs' bells were audible above the roaring hubbub of the traffic from the main road. Without meaning to, I emerged into a web of small streets full of bustle, music and cooking smells. Here, away from the bookshops and main roads and seemingly sealed off by a long brick building that looked in the dark like a displaced bit of England, was the quarter where books were made, where countless typesetters, printers, collators and binders were ending their day's work in tiny workshops, in offices and under raised floors barely high enough for children, and where some had already cleared up and cleaned their workplaces, arranged incense sticks on machinery and other utensils, and were now settling down to their evening meal on the doorsteps outside. I walked through the narrow streets, where there seemed to be hardly anyone who was not a local, and looked in at innumerable theatres of book production, every workshop in these low houses a stage on one, one and a half, or two levels, and where the lower floor housed the printing machine, a large, dark, now silent beast: the focus of all attention. Now it was at rest, had already been groomed, or even decked with various adornments, or workers were in the middle of decorating it for the festivities: revered animals consisting of iron and printer's ink. Various utensils were attached to the walls: brushes, tools, cases, also folding beds, used at night by printers when they slept in proximity to their mechanical beasts. On the upper floors only a segment of the activity was visible: these were sideshows, reserved for the upper body of the typesetters, who were also tidying up their places of work, cleaning, polishing, sorting; beside them were the torsos of collators, who, at great speed, were putting the last sheets in order and arranging them in piles. Here and there, where the broad, low windows were fitted at raised floor height, were only the slightly spread, restless legs of typesetters and collators, or their silhouettes sitting cross-legged, bowed over their work. Each workshop was a world stage of its own, turning on a typeface, its people moved by invisible threads, while the surging life outside on the streets appeared to have nothing to do with them: bare-footed wallahs cutting a path for their rickshaws jangled leaden bells, swerving cyclists jingling theirs, motorized rickshaws moving forward at walking pace honking their horns, porters, groups of unhurried pedestrians deep in conversation, people handing out flyers for restaurants. Here and there narrow alleyways passed between buildings that seemed mysteriously connected: these were larger publishing houses and print works, where the holiday had not yet begun and machines were still running, and where they were stacking print-ed sheets and carrying them to half-lit upper floors to be sorted. Here the sheets were received by mutter-ing women, who, squatting or sitting on their heels, arranged the sheets with expert hands in the correct or-der for the bookbinder. Children hung about in these semi-public alleys that branched off into the printing houses; here too were the back windows of cook-shops, through which food was passed out to the print work-ers. Beggars stepped out of niches, ducking under the head-height rustle of printed paper, the din of printing machines grinding to a stop, the scratch of brush bris-tles on the workshop floor, holding their wiry hands out to passers-by and collecting food leftovers from the window sills. I seemed to recall some old saying that a beggar who has as much as been brushed by the hem of one's dress deserves alms. Did such a saying exist, or had it just been invented, here, in my head, in the theatre of Baithakkhana?

Stages and shrines for Saraswati were under con-struction wherever the streets widened into larger squares. Music blared from the loudspeakers, crafts-men knocked, sawed, hammered, lifted bars and planks, rigged up electric cables around large, brightly coloured figures of the goddess, in front of which people would be coming together on the following day, when all the machines in the quarter stood still and not a rustling leaf of paper was heard: a homage owed to the goddess of ap-prenticeship and teaching. Quiet gradually descended on most of the workshops; now they were islands bathed in yellow light, and I was carried past them by crowds of pedestrians and wallahs, while clanking songs from the loudspeakers and honking horns blown by rickshaws and motorbikes dinned in my ears. By now I had lost my way and seemed to be going in circles, and yet I saw nothing I recognized; the unfamiliarity of the colours and my inability to understand the signs, gestures and events made it all look too similar. The flashing fairy lights on the Saraswati shrines, the soft glow that issued from the half-closed workshops-cum-dormitories, the music from the loudspeakers, the jingling, whistling and honking, the shouting voices and murmured words, the bitter-sweet smoke of incense sticks and the smouldering wood in the street cooks' ovens – all this blended into a resonant, illuminated, smoke-scented river, which, without any action on my part, eventually flushed me into College Street.

On Saraswati's feast day I went for a walk along the Hooghly – among schoolgirls dressed up for the celebrations and giggling as they compared each other's outfits, parents with small children dressed in gold and yellow, the colours of the goddess, to whom they would have been commended for good learning, past the hordes of half-naked boys bathing near the landing stages, past the burial places and piles of wood. The light was smoky blue. The opposite bank of the Hooghly, with the enormous Howrah Station site, swam in the morning mist. The Howrah Bridge floated like a distant dream over the dirty water flowing south with bobbing bundles of orange flowers. I came upon the landing stage for a boat that apparently did river trips, a half-open riverboat, a good deal smaller than the ferries, with folding chairs on its partly roofed-over upper deck. A man lay snoozing on a deckchair on the jetty; next to him a sign advertising cruises to Diamond Harbour.

I stopped and took a look at the boat, the sign, and a row of photos so bleached all that was left of them were patches of colour. I thought of the album I had seen in the antiquarian kiosk the evening before. The man with the typewriter. The woman with the basket of fish. The bleak promenade. Noticing me through his drowsy haze the man rose from his deckchair. He fished out a white sun hat, perhaps to convey an impression of captaincy, setting it straight on his straggly hair. Without a word of warning he suddenly started talking at me and advertising his prices. He painted the river in alluring colours, describing the stunning views to be seen onboard, the beauty of Diamond Harbour with its fish market, remnants of old grandeur, parks. He pulled a file from a battered briefcase picked up from the jetty, where he had apparently carelessly dropped it, and proceeded to show me faded photographs of broadly smiling women in Indian dress on board a ship, which was certainly not the boat moored here, and serious-looking men in white uniform-like suits, as well as blurred sunsets, and finally a lean snake charmer with a basket and snake head: treats that were waiting for anybody who was prepared to embark on the journey to the legendary Diamond Harbour.

When I asked about departure times, he shrugged his shoulders and looked over at the river, as if something was written there. It depended on the number of passengers, the time of day, the weather, the day of the week, he hinted. We agreed on the following Saturday at noon.

He wrote my name down on a sheet in his file and handed me a slip of brown wrapping paper with a diagonal red stripe and, in slightly skewed print, the words 'Diamond Harbour'. Reservation, the boatman stated emphatically.

A small group had gathered on the jetty by midday on Saturday. Three men in light-coloured suits, a young couple, a family with two children, a plump lady in a shimmering sari, who had brought a tiny lapdog with her in an expensive-looking basket. The ferryman and his assistant assumed an air of great importance. One by one they guided the passengers down the wobbly jetty onto the deck of the boat, insisting the parents carried their children. Some distance away a number of street boys were standing up to their waists in water and mud, watching the proceedings. Now and again they laughed and shouted something; nobody paid any attention to them and they carried on fooling about in the water, as if they were performing for the passengers. At the sight of the brown water and indefinable rubbish floating below the landing stage, I was overcome by a sudden fear. Seen from close up the steamer and all its fitments looked even more rickety and unsound than they had from the bank. The plastic chairs on the upper deck were cracked, many of the armrests broken off, and everything was covered with a film of dirt, which, day after day, the heavy, smoky air deposited on every surface. The railings were loose, the life rings made of cracked plastic foam; the surfaces on the decks were blistered with wavy lumps: stumbling bubbles for the heedless, who, deprived of a sure footing, could so easily slip under the railing into the gurgling water.

It was hazy and warm, the sun a small, milky orb in the direction of the estuary and ocean. The ferryman's mate loosened the red chain on the jetty, threw it rattling and clanking onto the deck and leaped after it across the sloshing gap between. He landed so heavily that the boat rolled on its side and the vacant chairs tipped towards the railing. The passengers, apart from the woman with the lapdog, clapped and laughed, and the two children frisked about gleefully, trying to imitate the mate. Although I enjoyed river trips and had always found gliding through the water between riverbanks a special form of travel, I now felt vulnerable, fearful, in – or rather on – surroundings that were utterly unfamiliar. The boat wheeled into the middle of the river and rolled in the wakes of larger ships; I saw water spray over the bow, and could not get rid of the thought of the children's corpses entrusted to the river. I walked over to the railing, though not without difficulty on the bumpy, unsteady deck, and looked over the side. The water was impenetrably dark, and full of swirling, turning objects: rags, straw, branches, rubbish, and things I could not fathom, could not say whether the water was moving them or they were moving in the water. I thought I recognized body parts, which a moment later mutated into tailed reptiles, then stiffened into branches or roots tossing on the waves. I turned my eyes the moment I saw some small bunches of orange flowers. The young couple was leaning against the railing on the other side of the deck. They were taking photographs of each other, also of the boat itself and of whatever interested them on the riverbanks sliding past. But the riverbanks seemed so far away, indistinct in the haze, out of reach. In the blur, the ungainly, web-like shape of the Howrah Bridge dissolved into a pale, insubstantial sketch in the air, while the steamer slid through the dark shadows under the next bridge, beyond which Kidderpore Docks came into view. It was a quiet dock: no cranes hefting loads, no busy tugboats. Long rows of cabin-like sheds enclosed the docks. The sheds were grey to bluish, hovering in the thick, hazy light, vibrating in the stillness; but the ships at anchor hovered, too, with their rust-red seams and scuff marks, as did the heaps of scrap metal between the harbour basins, and also the rigid derricks:

a matt-coloured mirage, a farewell greeting promising nothing to anyone leaving the city on the murky river.

Revolted by the impenetrable brown of the water and bewildered by the tricks of half-living things in the waves, I sat down on a chair in the middle of the deck as far away from the railing as possible under the jutting roof of the shelter. At one time benches were fixed here, but all that was left now was the floor-anchoring. Heat, rain and the noxious fumes of the factories, visible now on the riverbanks, had corroded the small projecting roof and left a delicate lacework pattern, and deceptively milky, burning sunlight fell through the filigree rust-work. I closed my eyes and tried to remember where I had already seen the name that stood in big letters on a passing riverside factory. Berger Paints. A faded, blurring sign, I had read it on a façade in Homerton, near the Lea: a factory within reach of whose noxious emanations nothing grew and where holes appeared in washing hung out in the yards of the little brick houses inhabited by Berger workers. A strange greeting from a different world, whose bricks, streets and bird calls I knew, even if I only knew the hardships of the Berger Paints era from photographs similar to those I had found of the still distant Diamond Harbour.

The corpulent woman in the sumptuous sari sat down next to me and took her little dog out of its embellished basket. The dog had such a tiny face between the strands of its fringe that one might easily have taken it for its hindquarters, had not a miniscule tongue darted forth and fluttering eyelids risen briefly above dark eyes, suggesting a head, eyes, nose and a mouth. The lady introduced herself as Mrs Bose, and gave me a kind of benevolent nod when I told her my own name, as if she were both giving it her approval and explaining that it was of no importance. She fondled her dog and fed it little nibbles spread with pâté, which she picked gingerly out of a plastic box. Mrs Bose made pâté for her dog every second day; her dog lived in Kolkata, while she presided over a hotel near Diamond Harbour. She travelled back and forth for the benefit of the dog, usually by car, but today she had decided on a boat trip with her dog, because her presence was required in the hotel for a whole week. Extensive celebrations were scheduled and important guests were expected, and so she and her dog were travelling 'on the great water body of the Ganges' as she piously put it. Meanwhile her chauffeur, en route with her luggage, would be driving south from Kolkata, taking major thoroughfares and passing through endless suburbs teeming with rickshaws, motorbikes, lorries, buses, cows, goats, pigs and vast numbers of people. Imagining the journey along the congested noisy roads, with the incessant proximity of people and animals and the accidents and traces of accidents one would inevitably witness, the relative stillness of the river now seemed gentle and refreshing, even if the engine of the steamer boomed irregularly, the small children sliding about dangerously close to the railing were shrieking, and gull-like birds occasionally plunged into the foaming waves with harsh, ear-splitting screams. The river broadened out and the town, shrouded in a greyish-golden mist of fine particles, industrial smoke and the humidity of the nearby Ganges delta, slipped into the distance and merged with the horizon. Mrs Bose spoke without interruption in a vaguely sermonizing tone. She spoke of the grandeur of the hotel over which she presided, of the love all animals felt for her, and again and again of the river, of that 'great water body of the Ganges', to which the Hooghly and countless other rivers belonged, all of them bound for the Indian Ocean.

The three men in pale suits were sitting in the covered area of the deck; they had wedged their chairs into what was left of the bench anchoring and were smoking, talking, laughing, taking occasional snapshots of the larger industrial sites on the riverbank, and writing something in thick notebooks. But for their photographic paraphernalia, they might have been sitting on the deck of a chugging Hooghly paddle steamer a hundred years ago, in those days probably buffeted by the wakes of larger ships and cargo vessels and with a view of an estuary that was less densely developed, whose headlands now appeared to be hovering between smaller tributaries and ponds. In those days, too, they would have sat on more comfortable seats, surrounded by servants in slightly greasy yet sumptuous livery, similar to those worn today by the personnel of the more genteel long-distance sleeping cars. The servants would have served refreshments, while the banks of the river, under the increasingly exhausted gaze of the passengers, would soon have been indistinguishable from swampland, whose boundary with firm land would have been as blurred as the thin line of what was probably the horizon rising and falling to the rhythm of the rolling ship. Also, the number of corpses floating in the river would have been greater than today.

Mrs Bose's monotonous chitchat, her dog's miserable whimpering, the rumbling of the ship's engine, the smack of waves and the roll of the boat, in rhythm with which the jabbering voices of the three men rose and fell under a whitish sun that made the damp air heavy and hard to breathe – all of this sent me into a torpid half-sleep where I was beset by a single question: why had I undertaken this boat trip in the first place, and what did I expect to find at Diamond Harbour in the wake of the trio of men in white, the young couple now also dozing on chairs under the roof, the parents silently holding their sleeping children in their arms, their earnest gaze almost sullenly fixed on the disappearing city, and Mrs Bose with her dog? I soon sank into the dreamy vision of a desolate landing stage in the murky evening twilight, for between waking and sleeping it had become clear to me that – with night falling so early and quickly in these parts – I would not be returning to Kolkata that day. Mrs Bose shook my shoulder to liberate me from my discomfort, leaning heavy with sleep over my armrest as I had, and advised me in an unexpectedly commanding tone to follow her to the prow of the steamer. It was late afternoon, and the light had taken on a mellow, grey-blue tinge crossed with pink streaks where the river, now well on its way to the estuary, broadened out in front of us like a funnel. Tiny boats were tacking to and fro in front of the horizon, and along both sides of the river were innumerable little factories, from whose chimneys smoke rose into the air. Those, explained Mrs Bose, were the brick factories, where the silt of the river was turned into bricks not only for the whole of our country, but also for the bordering nations, as she put it; they were exported everywhere, just like our jute, for which, as for the bricks, we must thank the Ganges and the huge delta area through which it flows, bringing to so many people a meagre living. If one believed Mrs Bose, the huts and houses of the world were built with bricks fired beside the Ganges and its tributaries, just as the ropes, cords and sacks of half the world were woven from the local jute. Mrs Bose, it transpired, believed in a kind of benevolent Bengalization of the world via the region's bricks, sacks, strings and ropes, or at least that was the way it sounded to me in the feverish dizziness that had overtaken me during my restless slumber.

Mrs Bose pointed out a reddish promontory in the far distance. That was where she would go ashore: that was her place. My place, she said with a vague, or in fact sweeping, regal gesture of her hand towards the headland. My place! What a refuge, what words – as we pitched and reeled on the river, which increasingly seemed to me a kind of Nowhere from which there could be no escape! What a comfort to be able to say such a thing! – my place! – faced with the river's tremendous maw to the south, which would soon be joined by quite a number of river mouths, each of them gigantic, their combined energies spewing the Ganges into the sea without ever being able to rid themselves of it.

The boat moored at a pier with no name. The sun hung red over the distant outlines of the Kolkata suburbs, which quivered in the pink and orange tinted evening haze, an excrescence of the river: fickle, uncertain, as unsettled as the river itself. Nearer at hand, however, the evening light was suffused with blue, and everything stood out with a balmy clarity: the factories and small settlements along the riverbank, the boats on the river, the coconut palms and banana trees, blood-red thickets and the rust colour of a path by the water, fence posts, and crouched, pale-brown tiled roofs. The pier led to a narrow road between box-like, half-finished houses. Washing hung out to dry in the window holes. Children were playing on heaps of sand and piles of bricks; women balanced loads of building materials on their heads, and men stood up on the walls applying mortar. Here and there smoke rose from behind unfinished walls, where people were beginning to prepare their meals. As in the big cities, families working on building sites lived in the shells of the new buildings, which gradually enclosed them. When the shells were done, the families would move on to the next building site, where the children would play in the sand again, the women carry bricks on their heads, the men apply mortar, while the washing would first hang on the wooden framing, later in the window holes of the rising walls. Time and again the migrant workers would build themselves out of a home, then have to start again under an open sky.

All the travellers left the boat. The boatman and his assistant looked at me encouragingly, and in sudden horror at the idea of having to remain alone on the steamer I ran along behind Mrs Bose, although it seemed barely possible that this was the Diamond Harbour I had seen in the album photographs. There was no sign of a promenade or a harbour; I could see no form of settlement here that had space enough for a fish market, a telegraph office or strolling women. The evening sun made Mrs Bose's gold-threaded robe appear especially resplendent; girded in a glittering sheen she strode in her corpulence and with measured step down the landing stage like an imperturbable goddess, handing her waiting chauffeur the basket with her dog. The passengers, even the cheery trio of men in their white suits, seemed like scurrying dwarfs beside her. Mrs Bose turned around and invited me to get into her car.

Mrs Bose's hotel lay behind a secured gate, manned by a gatekeeper. We were let in, and the car glided through extensive gardens in the dusk, coming to a halt in front of a building set directly beside the river, the latter discernible only as a vast darkness behind some bushes, although I could hear the breathing of the waves, and their faint lapping against the riverbank. Mrs Bose showed me to a small room behind the reception area and ordered me to get some sleep. A small window gave onto the river. Tiny lights glimmered in the distance, on boats perhaps, or headlands jutting into the huge river. I asked Mrs Bose whether there were snakes here. She smiled indulgently. Of course there were snakes. This is the great water body of the Ganges, she intoned again, how could there not be snakes? The snakes slithered ashore at night; during the day they stayed in the river and fed on whatever it provided. But the garden was fenced in, and the servants put down rat poison every evening along the fence by the river. Whereupon Mrs Bose bid me good night, wishing that the great water body of the Ganges might rock me to sleep. I lay in the dark, and knowing how rat poison worked, tried to imagine the snakes lying limply in the water, where they would manage to flee after consuming the poison, and how, surrounded by all the things drifting in the river, they suffered the slow disintegration of their blood vessels.

I listened to the river, and once or twice heard raised angry voices outside my window, servants driving away intruders, whether animal or human, or arguing among themselves. In Kolkata I had become accustomed to a constant background of quarrelling voices. The sounds of night birds blended with the rippling river: throbbing wails, an intermittent shrilling call, a constant churring, that rose and fell like the waves. I fell asleep and dreamed dreams I did not remember, awakening to the puttering noise of an engine. It was still dark over the river. I stepped outside into the garden. Servants dozed on chairs by the fence, their limp arms hanging over their guns. The birds were stirring; above the increasing racket of the crows came the wistfully tender double-note of a koel and the scraping shriek of herons.

The garden lay at the mouth of a smaller river joining the Hooghly. Fishermen came down the small river
on boats with clattering engines and sailed out to fish
in the Hooghly, small lamps swaying under their palm-
leaf canopies. The fishermen called out to each other,
perhaps also to the guards at the end of the garden; the
sound of monotonous singing and children's voices
came from a village taking shape in the crepuscular
light on the other side of the river.

When the sun rose I saw how tidal the river was.
Where I had heard waves rippling against the bank
the evening before, there was now glistening mud; the
feeder river was a narrow channel; at high tide the water came up to the bushes of blossoming four o'clock
flowers along the barbed-wire fence. The fishing boats
were now far out on the water in the first sunlight; the
river was a shimmering blue melting into the horizon,
as if it were already ocean. In the mud, where birds
had left their wispy inscriptions, men and women
waded with hitched-up robes wearing turbans against
the sun; they were searching for shellfish, which they
were collecting in flat covered baskets. By turns they
quarrelled and laughed with one another, their pastel-coloured headgear moving between the gaps in the
red and pink blossoming bushes. I sat by the river all
day, while behind me the servants made arrangements
for the celebrations Mrs Bose had spoken of. White tents
were erected on the lawns, long tables set up, flowers arranged. Now and then Mrs Bose paid me a visit and held
a short lecture about the river, the ocean, the flowers, the
animals, which all adored her. Her dog squeaked in its
cage behind the barred window of the hotel reception.
On the other side of the little tributary, jutting out into
the Hooghly, was the headland Mrs Bose had pointed

out to me on the steamer. Children tended goats in the shade of the palms; cows wandered about. I listened to the children's counting-out rhymes and their canon-like circle songs; they were playing hide-and-seek, but now and again an annoyed woman would rush over and tell them off or issue instructions, which always sounded rough and reproachful. The boats came back with the tide in the afternoon, and the children ran laughing and kicking up a racket along the water's edge to a tiny bay where the fishing boats were dragged ashore and the fishermen heaved large square-shaped baskets from recesses under their palm-leaf canopies. In the bustle surrounding the return of the fishermen, nobody gave any attention to the goats roaming between the huts unchecked, leaving their black droppings on the doorsteps.

Since midday I had been watching the slow approach of an enormous ship, albeit in silhouette, which unexpectedly hove to some distance away in the middle of the river. Soon afterwards, some small boats came into view, all loaded to the gunnels with bricks, making their way towards the gigantic vessel from several places along the riverbank. The bricks were hoisted into the hold of the ship with a lifting device which, in the bluish haze, resembled a shakily sketched gallows; the small boats then returned to their respective brickworks to pick up another load. As the light began to thicken, a number of small lamps lit up around the ship, and thus the vessel lay in the darkening haze, its appearance crudely remodelled by lamplight, suspended in a space that belonged to neither heaven nor earth, while the small boats hurried back to the riverbank, vanishing in the dusk. Heavy with stone-weights of river mud filtered of all flotsam and jetsam, and accompanied by a favourable tide, the huge freighter would sail through the sea-like open estuary into the Indian Ocean, transporting these oblong, uninscribed tidings from the great water body of the Ganges to foreign lands.

That evening Mrs Bose commended me to her driver, whom she was sending to Kolkata to buy fresh ingredients for her dog's pâté, directing him to take me along. On the following day I would be driven across the Howrah Bridge to the station and, boarding a night train for the North, would complete the first stage of my return journey to Europe. Driving through the villages and suburbs proved heavy-going. Wherever we went, crowds thronged on the roads, even after dark, children playing street cricket under flickering street lamps, people dismantling Saraswati shrines. Her countless figures would find their end in their beginning: they would be carried in procession and submerged in the Hooghly to dissolve and be reincorporated by the river, some of them unpainted, others thickly daubed with the crude colours of Berger Paints, whose particles would eat their way into fishes' stomachs, just as paint fumes in the Berger factory in Homerton by the river Lea had burned into the mucous membrane and lungs of workers and local residents a hundred years earlier, depriving them of their sleep, their life's air, their sight.

XXXII. ELEVATED RAILWAY

From the window of the house in London where I stayed the longest, I looked out on bricks: on the yellow brick of the house opposite, which was exactly like my own, and on the brownish brick of a factory where Asian women made various kinds of brushes. Pianos used to be made here, presumably by men, although the more delicate work, not unlike that of brush-making, such as polishing keys and lacquer surfaces, painting the company name in gold leaf or fitting dainty little golden keys in lockable piano lids, may well have been carried out by women, at least in the years when men went to war and came back in smaller numbers, afflicted with wounds and disabilities or the loss of a limb, relieved of any aspirations they once had harboured for precision work. And before the piano makers came, a long time ago, it was mainly women and girls from the overcrowded workers' terraces of the area who were employed here making albumen paper for photographic prints. Women's hands were more suited than men's to carefully cracking open eggs, separating perfect unclouded egg-white from the yolks, and beating it until it was foamy. As a line of work it demanded sobriety and skill, and had much in common with the arts, and although the women and girls may have giggled and sworn as they cleared a way through the hens that flocked in great numbers in the yards and street and supplied the factory with eggs, in the factory itself they were quiet and attentive and posed with serious expressions on their faces for intermittent shop floor portraits in front of the brick wall in the yard, and indeed on one occasion on the flat factory roof, with nothing but the sky behind their heads and wreaths of steam from a passing train swirling around their laced-up ankles.

The bricks continued behind the factory where an elevated railway ran along a viaduct of almost black brick, under whose protrusions huge swarms of pigeons nested, filling the air with their sounds: cooing from countless throats, beaks a-clucking, crops clicking in the dark of the eaves. Delicate feathers fluttered down, and bird droppings splashed on the viaduct walls, continually eating into the brickwork. From my skylight I could see over the viaduct to housing blocks built between the wars, where the windows and balcony balustrades stood out white against the red brick. Hordes of unruly children scurried about on the scrubby wasteland and neglected sports ground between the blocks of flats and the railway line; they hatched plots and harboured secrets in the deserted workshops and warehouses under the viaduct arches, which in better times had housed small businesses. The children competed with dares on the tracks, and I saw them as black shadows against the bottle-green summer evening sky, strutting from sleeper to sleeper, chasing each other, crunching and scuffing the ballast, hooting as they climbed hand over hand from the viaduct onto the factory fire escape, whose black balustrade handrails sliced the sky into narrow strips. As their feet banged on the stairs, the steel pipes produced a muffled echo, and the children's thin voices, sharpened by their wildness, reached all the way to my room, especially when they stood smoking on the top landing of the fire steps, as did the Indian brush-makers in their brightly coloured saris on workdays. In the big factory windows I saw reflections of the sky, trains and viaduct, and of the turrets and bay windows of the disused school at the other end of the short street. The windows of the shop floor were usually open during working hours. There was a muted whirring, shuffling, scraping and grinding in the air that was continuous but lacked any rhythm, and was only interrupted by an occasional cough or knocking sound. I listened for the dread steps of a supervisor, the kind of person who might make such sounds and issue sharp instructions or commands from time to time, but there was nothing to be heard, only the voices of the women, which would suddenly surge up, accompanied by rhythmical clapping and sometimes by ringing laughter. Was it a need to celebrate, argue or pass on some happy news that encouraged them to interrupt the usual hush suffused with whirring, scraping and knocking? I never saw the women at work, only heard these monotonous, measured sounds, and I wondered what tasks they were carrying out, whether they were standing or sitting, walking about or maybe exchanging a little silent banter as they worked. Supply vans delivered goods – boxes of bristles? Large bundles of wire and twine? Brush heads and broom handles? – and the factory porter, who may have doubled as the supervisor on the factory floor, together with the delivery men, heaved and carried and swore, while a woman's face or two appeared at the windows, very briefly, as if flying through the steps of a dance. But whatever the weather, the women would always slip outside in little groups to smoke on the fire landing, as if it were a well-kept secret that they smoked, even though their giggling was audible over quite a distance, and their gaily-coloured figures were highly conspicuous against the sky, bricks and angular frame of the fire escape. The women wore open shoes even when it was cold or raining, the heels of their sandals banging on the open mesh steps of the fire escape, their saris aflutter in front of the brick walls. At the end of the day's work a bald-headed man locked the works' gates behind the women. All the windows were closed and looked like mirrors framed by the wall, which was now little more than a façade on whose bricks weather, time and dirt, each with their own crude writing utensils, had scribbled a script. No two bricks had the same colour.

The women left the factory at five in the afternoon, a throng of clamour and laughter that split up into smaller currents heading for the underground, bus and overground. In bad weather they held up black umbrellas and let out little screams, half in laughter, when strong winds tore at the canopy and turned it inside out, and tangled their long scarves in an umbrella jumble. Sometimes, between the gables of the houses opposite, I caught sight of them, spectral multi-coloured figures surrounded by yellow, red and brown brick, waiting on the station platform for a train that would usually come late.

Depending on the wind and relative purity of the air, the trains might emit a rapid clattering noise, a thumping and chugging, or a groaning accompanied by swishing and whirring. After coming to a halt with a sigh, the trains from the right would set off in an easterly direction, to where the river's exhalations came in tides like the sea's, the broad brown Thames was crossed by a ferry, and the city upstream was protected by the flood barrier, whose gates, above the sugar factory relentlessly discharging clouds of grey-white steam, rose from the water like the petrified heads of giant mythical beasts. The trains from the left were travelling west to suburbs where the Thames was only beginning to cast off its rural charm as a river fringed by the green meadows and gentle slopes of the English interior. The trains described a squiggly semi-circle through the northern hemisphere of the city, at both terminals coming to a screeching halt at the riverbank. On the opposite bank lay a different world, the southern half of the city, where people turned their heads to the right when they looked downstream and trains were operated according to southern-side rules and regulations.

The elevated line was a pendulum swinging unreliably through my days. The trains alternating east and west were often late or cancelled owing to damaged lines, overhead wires or coaches, but it was nonetheless their noise and, in the evenings, when everything bricks could build was swallowed by darkness, their chains of lights floating along behind the roofs of the houses opposite that determined the rhythm of the passing hours. I walked under the overground line almost every day, was familiar with the reverberating rattle of trains going over the tunnel, police sirens echoing from the brick arches, the stench of the piss-spots of the homeless people who hung about in the draughty street-level hall in front of the ticket window, and the pungent reek of pigeon droppings in the less frequented underpasses, the way the birds' ever-cooing throats set everything vibrating, the faintly buzzing rustle of their incessantly trickling veil of befouled feathers. Now and again I took a train in one direction or the other and studied the backs of the terraces, roofs, chimneys, gables and rear gardens in varying light, the strips of waste ground with crows and cats, the whole hinterland of the city that stays hidden from bus-window views of street façades. With my finger on the map I followed the fine line cutting through the green and grey paper surfaces like the jagged outline of a distorted half-moon, wending across the red, brown and black threads of streets, thickening around stations, then trickling through no-man's-land like the hairline strand of a brook. I followed the viaduct, in a westerly direction at first, until I got stuck between branching lines and groped my way back along a crumbling exercise in handwriting, a single letter of endlessly repeated arches in varying shades of brick, which, at upper floor level in the terraced houses that lined the tracks, inscribed something in countless city lives that was possibly indecipherable.

I set off east, working my way through a wasteland of thorn-thickets, fox dens and rusty remains of old railway equipment near the edges of the big train stations. Budding lilac nodded along semi-derelict fencing; battered shopping trolleys were rammed into bare spring bushes. Behind this zone of neglect and devastation, in the shadow of run-down factories and warehouses and within smelling distance of a sewage drain, the viaduct arches were home to goods that had been lost, given away, misappropriated or stolen elsewhere in the city, a loosely pitched series of junk-stall arches selling anything which, for whatever reason, had been rejected, released or purloined from the commodity cycle. Under the rumbling trains trembled coachloads of bicycles, chairs, fridges and tables, half-gutted washing machines, car seats, shelves full of fragile and unbreakable items, jackets, coats and flowery dresses, books and records, all darkened by dust that trickled from the pores of bricks and nipped by pigeon droppings. When the weather was fine the stallholders sat on camp chairs and torn car tyres in front of their open arches. They drank tea from thermos flasks and squinted against the sun. Nobody tried to sell me anything, and indeed I never saw another customer there; here and there a stallholder would busy himself with the stock entrusted to him, re-arranging things, sorting, mending a bicycle. The signs set up here and there to advertise certain commodities – tweed coats or fridges, for example – looked as if they

316

had been written decades earlier and used terms that beckoned from what seemed an incredibly distant era, conjuring up objects no longer in use. The characters who ran the arch-booths were more like keepers than traders, charged with looking after whatever the city discarded: things who-knows-who had collected and carried, dragged or transported here from who-knows-where. A musty, acrid fetor emanated from the arches; something clung to every object, a trace of the handler or owner, and even the traces were infested with fungus or rot, constituting intangible evidence of lives lived in close proximity to objects. The air around these eastern viaduct arches was full of the spore-like offshoots of these lives, blooming from fingerprints, leftovers and sweat stains, all making their own contribution to the immortalization of the city.

Further east the archway stalls became fewer and farther between. Most of the arches were closed, or bricked up, or had been bolted and barred for so many years that their padlocks and bolts had fused into a single, dirt-encrusted, rust-coloured block. By and by briars and scrub barred the lane, which had gradually narrowed to a path and now bent off to the side, away from the viaduct, onto a paving stone road with a narrow rail track, overgrown with couch grass. The tracks made a loop, shortly after which the road stopped and winter-spare, knee-height weeds brushed against the lower bar of a railing, beyond which flowed a river, in which the bridge and a train passing over it were reflected. In front of the viaduct by the riverside railing, separated from me by whispering stalks of thistle, sat a man holding a banjo, his right hand miming the strumming of a banjo player. The wooden doors of three of the arches stood open. They were full of bricks. A black dog lay in a pool of

317

afternoon sunlight. River Lea, River Lea, Lea River, River Lea, sang the man in a nasal voice, banging on his unstrung banjo.

The man was a collector of bricks. He claimed to know where every brick in his warehouse came from. London stock, he said with a sweeping gesture at his store. They were all made of London earth, all fired and stamped here. He knew how to tell the various yellow coloured bricks apart, also the red, brown and mauve-black ones. He knew which ones had been used for churches, which for hospitals and schools, which for houses and which for the boundary walls of cemeteries. There were government office bricks, factory bricks, front garden bricks and backyard bricks, bricks for almshouses, where two families shared three rooms, and bricks for blocks of flats with white stone dressings and mouldings and servants' entrances. He drew the tips of his fingers over the bricks in his arches and showed me the dust that had collected in his skin lines. He gave me a short lecture on London bricks and the reasons for their great variety. Write that down, he added. When you've got a moment.

He showed me the way to the next overground railway station. I stood on the platform and looked down at the river, which I had never heard of. It flowed though a world of bricks towards the Thames.

After a few stations the elevated train suffered a door systems failure. The passengers were asked to alight and wait for the next train: there were not many, some deciding to set off on foot, while the handful who remained spread out along the unusually long platform. It was the first mild and warm evening of spring, in the air a sweet scent of blossoms that were nowhere to be seen. The sun set and the city grew quieter. There was a wait

318

for the train. I gazed over the bare bushes at a big, triangular, brick building surrounded by a high steel fence. The steel bars on the many windows cast a grey sheen on the three dark-mauve brick walls. The brick collector had not told me which bricks were used for prisons, although there were several in London. Men's voices rose from the barred windows, singing in turn: three, four, half a dozen voices, lovely, quavering in the evening air, reflected by the brick wall, echoing here and there, a conversation whose words I did not understand, held in such a way that the short sequences of notes bounced back and forth between the walls, rising, falling, lengthened, shortened, weaving a mesh of tones and unintelligible words.

The light was fading, the song frayed and fell silent, I took out my notebook and wrote, as the brick collector had instructed me to do:

The great city of London is built on a network of countless rivers of varying age. They rise in landscapes characterized by very different kinds of rock and flow to the sea bringing sediment from those rocks. The mud of each underground river has a different colour and is the repository of a different history. That is why London bricks have a greater variety of colours than those of any other city in this world.

XXXIII. STONE

On almost every day of March the sky was white and bright. Sometimes a flimsy sun penetrated the high blanket of clouds. You could have taken hold of that light and let it trickle through your fingers, while objects gently laid down the film of their soft, pale shadows on the pavement, the street, and the walls of houses. The bare tree in my back garden painted a blurred picture of itself on the brick wall, whose perpetually unlit single window had by now taken on the character of a sign. With the various colours and different qualities of its bricks the wall seemed to me increasingly to constitute a text: a system of writing, interpolated by the foreign character of the window and, on days of pale sunlight, an extensive insertion of gentle shadow, in which the story of the past few months, as observed from my observation post, had been recorded. My gaze, hands, fingertips, and even, through my shoes, the soles of my feet had become explorers solely of surfaces, as if, in the course of this long, slow farewell, they needed to retreat from an inwardness of things, at the same time touching and feeling them in order to know that their own traces would remain inscribed in the explored surfaces.

At the beginning of March the Croat gave me a cheap, old camera that took instant photographs. He had found it in a box of junk in front of his shop: possibly left there in perplexity, or out of annoyance, or on an impulse born of remembered kindness. The box was a collection of battered objects, such as can be found on the fringes of any second-hand market: objects far too familiar, too mass produced, too incapable of inspiring in even the most imaginative of finders the vision of a life shared with such things. It was one of those pale sunny days when everything looked lacklustre, even the crates of brightly coloured drinks that Greengrocer Katz's assistant was lugging from the pavement into the shop cellar, while Greengrocer Katz was counting pinkly shimmering grapefruit in their delivery boxes, and recommending his dates, whose slightly wrinkled skin reflected the milky sunlight, to pious housewives. For anything pre-prepared, dried or candied, in which the past summer, autumn or winter still lingered, had to be eaten before the end of the month, or else risk banning at Pesach.

With a mug of coffee in one hand, a cigarette in the other, the Croat inspected the contents of the box with the toe of his worn, barely shiny, patent leather shoe. He no longer wanted donations; he was visibly grumpy and troubled, and he was tired of the shop. He complained to Jackie and the Pakistani who ran the internet café about the number of fusty sacks of clothes and household items piling up in the damp corridor at the back of his shop. These days, his cassette recorder was seldom heard; his preferred repertoire of songs sounded distorted and metallic. He held the camera out to me as I was walking past, a random gift, which I accepted hoping it would still work and prove suited to the false-colour film format familiar to those who take occasional snapshots.

Back in my flat I flipped open the camera and, giving the lens a wipe, tried the shutter release. Groaning and stuttering the camera ejected a photograph; an old film cassette was still inside. The lens had been pointing towards the wall of my front room where boxes of books were stacked. The pale March morning sunlight fell on the brown, slightly tattered cardboard surfaces. The print slowly coloured. It was mainly orangey-red, rust-red, degraded by the increased emulsion viscosity, and only in the bottom right of the photograph, the south-east corner of the picture surface so to speak, did anything show that looked vaguely like a wall: a fuzzily structured area reminiscent of carelessly applied mortar that had gone hard and streaky and from which any gaze would naturally recoil. Only a knowing viewer could recognize the surfaces of cardboard boxes and the milky blur of tiny sunspots.

In a small shop at the corner of Amhurst Park and Stamford Hill – behind a window of faded photos of weddings and other occasions, whose celebrants wore hairdos and fashions that took me back decades to a time when memory seemed entirely immersed in reddish hues – I found a roll of film that matched my camera. The salesman, perhaps the photographer behind the scenes in the window, was a phlegmatic sort who began muttering something in response to my question and set about rummaging in some shelves, continuing to mutter and breathe heavily until he found a box containing the film in question. It was over its sell-by date and he offered me a reduction. Sitting on a bench at Clapton Pond I inserted the film. It had turned cold, and the make-shift snack bar had closed earlier than usual. Children were on their way home, small groups in dark uniforms, pious Jewish girls with skirts down to their calves, pale and prim, whose eyes never strayed as far as a stranger's.

I walked through the late afternoon streets, looking for something to photograph. In the end I decided on the entrance of an inter-war block of flats with several storeys, a brick building with mullion windows, white-washed balconies that were the full length of the narrow street-side façade, smooth pilasters on the right and left of a black-painted front door with an inset vertical window panel. A bluish-green sign above the door read

Rookwood Court Nos 1-9. I looked through the view-finder and saw a blurry entrance, the pilasters, a column of bell-buttons, two narrow flat windows on either side of the pilasters. The release was hard to operate, but the rollers squeaked and out squeezed a photo. Two children were walking back from school, followed by their sheitel-wearing mother pushing a pram. She looked at me warily; the children threw me a furtive, inquisitive glance over their shoulders, and the black door clicked shut behind them.

The picture slowly emerged from the grey surface. The photo was skewed; I must have been holding the camera wrongly; the entrance looked as if the whole building were leaning towards me. The pilasters and lowest balcony parapet were uniformly out of focus, an area of white without recognizable surface features, but the bricks and quadratic concrete slabs between pavement and door showed every detail: every shade of colour from an almost blood-stained red to the dark ashen grey of the bricks, every thumb-smear of the grouting, every unevenness in the thickness and layering of the mortar or in the grey, cracked paving stones, came to the fore, even the tiny blades of grass sprouting from the jagged crack between the pavement and the entrance area. An inexplicable reflection surrounded the door-handle, gleaming on the black paint, and a grey scribble stood out at the bottom of the door, probably recording traces of kicks or accidental collisions with the toes of shoes, whether impatient, bad-tempered, idle or helpless. A hand, which I had not noticed through the viewfinder, appeared from behind the white curtain to the right of the entrance, a scrawny and presumably old hand, a hand that was unsure, reaching for something hidden to me. The picture was an image of my own uncertain future, one I would hold on to and one day pick up, saying: Yes, Stamford Hill, London: that's how the bricks felt under my fingertips, how the cracked paving stones with their sprouting grass and weeds felt under my feet, how the crows perched in the trees, and how their great scattered flocks darkened my field of vision, this and no other lack of shadow was typical of the light there, that was my place, and this scrawny old hand will hang on to a piece of my life forever.

Every few days I took a picture with the Croat's camera. Farewell photos of surfaces, found things, accidental encounters. The same light rested on everything: light grey, shadowless, the light of these March days that almost always, after a morning of tentative sunlight, grew dull but rainless in the afternoon, clearing again towards evening to become almost bright. One Friday afternoon I stepped into a narrow lane I had never noticed before. It was a cul-de-sac, at the end of which a scrap merchant and garage occupied some sheds abutting Stamford Hill backyards. Jewish children were queuing in front of a bakery; young boys wearing kippahs and side-locks were jostling one another, girls with pigtails whispering, and each child left with two white loaves in a rustling plastic bag for Friday evening. Above the queuing children flashed the neon sign of the neighbouring shop: Morris Kosher Milk Restaurant. A crow sat on top of the sign. I lifted my camera to take a picture, but as I pressed the shutter release the crow flew off and all the picture showed was a cloud-covered spring sky between brick façades, a grey smudge like the parting shadow of a bird's wing, and the half-lit sign at the bottom. The last children ran off with their rustling bags, and the way they flew along the pavement made me think of them for a moment as angels hurrying to the houses to arrive with their messages of bread just before sundown.

Returning from my walk one day, I showed the Croat the picture I had taken, but he looked at it blankly. That afternoon's photo showed an object even I had no name for: a peeling, white frame that was rusting and included a semi-circular pole on which hung a brown rag. I had discovered it at the edge of a narrow street where it had been left next to a hydrant on a patch of road where the thin layer of asphalt covering the old paving stones had practically worn through and the bare reddish-grey cobbles were visible underneath. Although I had never seen such an object before, and did not know what to call it, I had immediately found myself thinking of infirmity and a long ruinous decline. Perhaps the Croat had found the same associations disconcerting, although it was more likely that he had simply forgotten giving me the camera. As if to make up for not reacting to the picture, he offered me a coffee, and so we stood in front of the shop while the cassette recorder blared. In my mind I still need a place to go, sang Neil Young's distorted voice, permeated now and then by metallic-sounding vibrations. The Croat waved cheerfully to Greengrocer Katz, who did not return his greeting. I cast a glance inside the shop; it was almost empty. A few small things lay on the counter, and the cassette recorder juddered on the shelf, but all the clothes had gone from the rails, and the boxes of odds and ends, evidently emptied, were tidily stacked one on top of the other. The room looked so small. The walls seemed grey and dirty, the plaster veined with cracks and covered with spots, traces of damp damage that were, in all likelihood, older than the conflicts the Bosnians had fled. Here and there the damp spots had joined up to form map-like outlines I would have liked to have taken a closer look at, and perhaps given a name to. It was a mild, pleasant evening heralding the arrival of spring. On the following day the blanket of cloud tore and the sun shone through. The girls in the Eastern European grocery store wore short-sleeved dresses; the Kurdish taxi drivers sat in shirtsleeves on the bench in front of their minicab desk, cracking jokes and waiting for customers. I went along to Stoller's to buy a yahrzeit candle. It would be the last time I celebrated my father's birthday in London. A corner of the shop had been set aside for Passover products. Kept apart from other products sold throughout the year, these items were waiting for customers on a specially cleaned shelf laid out with paper next to the counter.

I noticed Jackie in the passage leading to the storeroom. It was a long time since I had seen him. He looked a bit the worse for wear, and he gave me a wink, or so it seemed to me. He was standing in the dimly lit passageway between the shop and the storeroom and seemed to have forgotten something; hunched forward slightly, his chin resting pensively in one hand, he looked like someone straining to remember. Meanwhile, Mrs Stoller was speaking loudly into the telephone announcing somebody's arrival at an airport. She shouted the flight number, airline and time in exaggeratedly precise English, presumably through a crackling line across the ocean.

I took my little packed candle in its blue and white box to the counter and paid. Mrs Stoller swept the money into the till; on her hand was a ring with a green stone that matched the bejewelled jacket of her pious reading material. Leaving the shop I glanced into the passage, but Jackie was no longer there. He had remembered what it was he had to do.

That evening I saw him again, standing next to the

Croat. The Croat was shutting his shop; they said good-bye, and Jackie stepped back into the entrance to Stoller's storeroom, which was already shrouded in evening shadow. He lifted his hand and gave a cautious wave. The Croat walked down the street, the cassette recorder in one hand. The sky behind Abney Park Cemetery was red, orange and turquoise from the sunset. At the edge of Stamford Hill the Croat turned and looked back. He was now a black silhouette against the light of the sunset. He raised his left hand and waved again. Whether or not Jackie was still standing at the entrance in the shadows, I could not see.

XXXIV. LEAMOUTH

South of Bow the river disappeared among roads, factories and office buildings. The path stopped abruptly
at the lock, and there I stood on the tip of the tongue
between Lea and Bow Creek, which, as the tide began
to ebb, swirled faster out of the big loop around Three
Mills Island than the Lea flowing down from the north.
The trains passing between town and marshland –
between the Thames of a city robbed of its docks, and
Tilbury Docks in the Thames Estuary – rattled the
old rail bridge above the lock. The top of the tower at
Canary Wharf hung in the sky directly south of where
I stood, a bluish silhouette against a high cloudbank.
The rampant twigs of a small-flowering tree protruded above a wall. The river continued in front of me, but
with no path on either bank: it crept along between walls,
thick scrub and old dilapidated warehouses, then twisted away out of sight. I attempted to pursue it along its
western bank, banging on the steel doors of workshops,
knocking on the rotting windows of grim-looking
office blocks and on hastily erected corrugated iron
gates, shaking flaking rusty bars, always in the hope of
finding a way through the yards and overgrown patches
of no-man's-land to where I supposed the river to be.
The land flanking what passed for the banks of the lower Lea was quite deserted: nobody responded to my
knocking, nobody came to let me through or send me
away; not even a dog barked. I fared no better in the drab
housing estates of Canning Town on the eastern bank.
Children I asked for the way to the river stared at me
blankly, giggling behind my back, perhaps wondering
what they could do to give me a fright. Women coming
home from work could not understand my question,

screwing their fingers at their temples to indicate I was crazy. A weasel-faced girl in a silver-threaded blouse, shivering in the cold of that April day as she ducked into the windy entrance of a station, hissed a few nasty words at me. I began to feel sorry for the Lea: poor forgotten body of water, so close to its mouth and with all those miles and riversides behind it, of which it always brought a little along, letting it sink onto its bed, gifting it to shorelines elsewhere, bringing a small dowry to the Thames. I had followed the course of the river on the map, run my finger along the tentative, elongated S of its final miles as it curled back upon itself before reaching the mouth, encircling a peninsula that was practically cut off from its surroundings by water, thoroughfares and industrial sites, a part of town that had sunk into oblivion, where some of the poorest Londoners had lived until well into the inter-war years, surrounded by iron works, a glass factory and the syrup business, and downwind of the great sugar factories of Silvertown. Such sweetness encircling the quarters of the poorest! But these blind, unwelcoming streets on both sides of the river seemed to know nothing of the network of paths on the map: there was no sign of the Lea, and I did not find it again until I had almost reached the Thames, catching sight of it beneath a through-road that was ill-disposed towards pedestrians, where I barely had room to stand and look over a parapet. The tide was out, and the cold blue sky was mirrored in the narrow channel trickling between two sloping banks of mud – but here too were swans, white against the mud, and in the sparse reeds, hidden behind one of the piles of the bridge, I saw a brooding female on a nest.

The east bank was occupied by factories: smoking chimneys, overgrown fences and walls next to the river, a trail of refuse along the sloping bank. While the view from the west bank had suggested walkable streets, it soon became apparent that the strip along the riverbank was in fact a huge building site: whole areas had been excavated, roads dug up, and great heaps of earth, colonized by tufts of grass and small-leaved weeds, towered over the bulldozed terrain. Skewed site-fencing blocked any view of the river. There were no pedestrians, no workers in sight. The entire scene seemed frozen in this state of primal damage, with no sense of what end its taming and putative improvement served. On a patch of untouched land, screened by a thin bush whose uppermost twigs sported tiny, pale pink flowers, I discovered a snack bar, an ancient caravan with a serving hatch, a peephole to the fare of decades past. The mistress of the snack van was sitting on her front steps: a platinum blonde in a prematurely summery dress and a flowery apron, smoking and squinting her eyes against the sun, which had just broken through a layer of high mist. She greeted me with the kindness of those who have long been fighting a losing battle and who had come to terms with the unlikelihood of her modest hopes ever being fulfilled. I asked her how to get to the river; she frowned and gave me a sceptical look. The boys from the site hadn't been here for weeks, she explained, as if they kept the key to the river hidden somewhere. There was no one there. Standstill. She flicked her cigarette butt onto a pile of earth and climbed into her van. She asked me if there was anything I would like. I saw wrinkly pies, dry sandwiches with solidified mayonnaise, cakes with cracked pink icing. I asked for a cup of coffee, but she only had tea, which tasted old and bitter. To make up for my disappointment over her menu, she showed me a hole in the fence. I could get through

there, she said, and straight down to the river, no prob-
lem. Nobody would stop me. Two sections of the fencing
joined here, and it was easy to move them apart to make
a gap: I noticed a small beaten track leading down the
muddy embankment. Who on earth would go walking
in such a grim wasteland under the enormous flyover?
There was a smell of sewage and chemicals; below the
factories on the other side pipes dribbled onto the embankment. The narrow stream in the riverbed seemed
even smaller here than it had from the road bridge. At
close quarters the swans looked helpless and forlorn; I
saw no sign of brooding swans in the reeds, which now
looked too few and flimsy to hide a nest. I stood on the
bank undecided, searching for the Thames between the
piles of the flyover. I felt uneasy at the thought of teeter-
ing along the miry riverbank towards an impenetrable
industrial zone. The leaving of the Lea would be a sad
affair, probably without my ever reaching its mouth. I
was about to give it a half-hearted try when the woman
from the snack van pushed through the gap in the fence.
She had put on a thick cardigan, and although she could
hardly have been much older than me, for a moment I
saw her standing on a street in Bow or Poplar, an inter-
war girl on her way to the park or river of a Sunday
afternoon, a sailor's sweetheart or a docker's fiancée,
who stitched bits of fabric to percale dresses by the piece
in Commercial Road, and who, for whatever reason,
knew more than other girls.

Striding ahead confidently, she escorted me under
the flyover. Her forceful progress seemed incompati-
ble with her chatter, which was repeatedly shredded by
loud laughter. In fact I understood very little of what she
said for she sent the words out ahead of her, where they
collided with concrete piles, walls, and the slope of the

embankment, and finally fell to the ground. The course of the river was so much lower here than everything else in the surrounding town that I felt in a different world, one that had been shut out or written off, open only to the sections of sky that enclosed the undersides of flyover and rail bridge. The river ran on through an area that was nameless and separate, between walls and fences of industrial facilities, curling around a tongue of wasteland traversed by a narrow-gauge railway, under which rampant bushes provided a secluded habitat for birds. The sight of the naked mudbanks of the Lea glistening in the sunlight briefly reminded me of the dreary landscape of the Gironde estuary, whose embankments fell away more steeply, but had gleamed no less nakedly under the leaden sun, which, during the July following my father's death, had hung day in, day out over the brown water. Neither river nor sea, but a powerful, broad funnel opening to the Atlantic, the murky water had tossed and turned like a never-ending animal whose puckered shell seemed to dissolve in the heat, evaporating in a glare across the surrounding marshland. Locals from nearby villages – women wearing make-up, waved hair and bikinis with big floral patterns, and their moustachioed beaus, whose torsos gleamed with oil or sweat – dosed the sultry afternoons away in tiny sheltered bays, while youths, hooting in vacuous hilarity, slid time and again down a muddy slide on the embankment, slapping into the turbid river water. Children played in shallow pools, screaming, venturing unobserved into the water, pathetically beating their water wings until one of the beaus came to rescue them. Dramas, every one of them, trickled away as quickly as the child's tears, who had been scolded and smacked by its father, and no thunderstorm brought the yearned-for relief; everything was suspended in the combined glare of sky, mud, water and marshy riverside. It had been years since I had thought of that journey, when the perpetually whitish light of the hazy sky had temporarily blinded me, making my eyes incapable of recognizing familiar landscapes and – as I stood on the wan, scrubby grass at the edge of the river looking into the bright haze of the horizon – giving me such bad neuralgia that I was forced to spend several days in a darkened room. Despite the high blanket of mist and white halo still surrounding the sun, here by the Lea I felt safe from bedazzlement as I followed the woman past bands of rubbish and puny lilac bushes, eventually coming to some steps that could have been the worn remnant of an old landing stage from the days when barges and freighters would have moored here. Beyond the steps we came to a narrow path that led between two factory yards and joined a road. The sign said Orchard Place; nothing could have been less like an orchard than this barren spit of land lined by parked delivery vans yet devoid of human life in the midday light.

The road turned a sharp bend, passing some old shipyard buildings and a tiny lighthouse, eventually coming to a derelict and formerly grand house in the sun, which, in the teeth of its newly acquired neighbours in the shape of Canary Wharf's giant towers, gleamed in the light of so much river and sky. Beyond the house lay the mouth of the river. A few ragged bushes leaned over the quay towards the water; seagulls drifted across this river-facing boundary of the city; the Lea whirled brown and green, as if unsure of mixing with the grey-blue Thames. This was the end of my East London way, a place that was unremarkable and practically impossible to find, glanced from afar by the countless eyes that were forever sliding past, forever in motion: gazes of passage at a transitory space. I looked down the Thames, saw how it grew broader with the Lea now on its back, greyer, increasingly indifferent towards its banks, now facing the sea. The woman pulled out a bar of chocolate from the baggy pocket of her cardigan and offered me half. I chewed on it for some time, facing the river, while the woman sat on a wall and smoked. The chocolate was disgustingly sweet and at the same time stale, rubbery and oily: it was the chocolate of memory, plunging me back into the sugar addictions of childhood, to the extent that I felt dizzy and was overcome by the fear that a small pleasure boat might breeze past this strange, half-forgotten East London outpost, from whose railing I, in a child's blue coat, would see myself.

The woman asked me to follow her along the Thames-side bank of the peninsula. We came to a large yard that bordered directly on the riverbank and made a less derelict impression; people were sitting on folding chairs in the sun, behind them a faded, brightly coloured fortress of containers. Pointing to the little lighthouse, the woman began to tell me a story, for which she suddenly adopted a theatrical, declamatory tone. She winked at me almost imperceptibly a couple of times while speaking, as if inviting me to chip in the odd stage direction. The story was about the owner of the grand house's little daughter, who was so in love with the lighthouse that during the night she would creep out into the garden, whose edges were washed by Lea and Thames and swept by damp winds, to watch the nocturnal spectacle of its shining beam. Whether due to cold, dampness or the vile breath of a ship passing too closely, one spring night the girl took ill with a fever, and when she awoke she was blind.

Her spectators, listening on their folding chairs,

began to clap as soon as the woman finished, although they were actually too far way to follow a story that had been spoken towards the river, whereas I, standing with my back to the Thames, was sure I had heard every word and felt nothing less than obliged to applaud, albeit with some delay and concern for the woman herself, who was visibly shivering with cold, indeed had caught such a chill that her teeth were chattering.

XXXV. ESTUARY

In search of a sewing machine I found myself entering a second-hand shop somewhere between Spitalfields and Bethnal Green, an area where sewing tables, seamstresses, pins and bales of cloth would once have been visible at every street corner. The shopkeeper was Italian and proved to be an expert on all manner of old and antique appliances, boasting a whole fleet of Singer machines in polished wooden cases in the back room of his shop, temporarily stored there pending their export to Italy. From the handle of each case dangled a loop of string with a small key for locking and unlocking the wooden lid. I thought of my grandmother and the heart-rending songs she had sung at her sewing machine sitting at the open window, while under her sewing hands and presser foot the most uncomely pieces of cloth would be transformed into the summer dresses we children wore during our travels south. The salesman came from Comacchio, a name he casually dropped into the conversation, and which I seemed to recall, albeit without the slightest visual association. *On the river-mouth*, he added, as if the oddness of that expression might jog my memory, and indeed it threw open a door to long-forgotten days. As he proceeded with studied charm to extol the virtues of various articles in his shop, I recalled the white skies of the Po delta, the brightly shimmering plain melting into the horizon, dilapidated farmhouses by the roadsides, a landscape like a shallow bowl with desolate cornfields rustling in the wind, the dry summer beds of tributaries that had gone astray or refused to meet the sea, a sky that was always hazy, always low and hot, never blue or dabbed with chubby clouds; it was an endlessly flat landscape on a transit route, but one that made a far greater impression on my childhood memory than our actual destinations with their blue skies and rocky beaches. I saw us standing on an old stone bridge in the oppressive afternoon heat, my father pointing to a river that was barely more than a trickle in its blanched bed, a runnel heading for the glistening grey-blue of the Adriatic. In the distance the quivering contours of large factories hovered above the plain, mirages towards which the former inhabitants of the derelict farms must have stumbled across country; the haze will have blinded them with its deceptively bright glare. In times of drought they probably tumbled headlong into the riverbeds, or in watery seasons some may have drowned in the countless streams, food for the fat eels on which Comacchio prided itself. After visiting the river we clambered back into the boiling hot car and continued our journey south, while in front of my light-bruised eyes I saw loops and dancing circles and curlicues, which I took to be a kind of estuarine script that had been revealed for my benefit alone.

I bought a sewing machine from the man from Comacchio and hauled it home. It stood on the table by the window, elegant and gleaming with allure. I tried it out with the window open and red-flowering currant, a shrub found all over London, in full blossom outside, exuding the tangy scent I loved. I refrained, during breaks between trains passing on the elevated railway, from singing out into the peaceful English street; I had become native enough not to imitate my grandmother. As I sewed, humming so quietly that my voice kept below the clatter of the presser foot, Comacchio and the landscape of northern Italy never left my thoughts, nor did the untiring traveller who was my father, with his voracious eyes always hungry for something new, always avid for more, landscapes, towns, rivers, images, a life so full of pictures that he gave up photography.

I went back to the Italian's shop in my first, self-made, London dress and bought the old red car he had offered me in passing while I was purchasing the sewing machine. It had been a while since I had driven, and it took me some time to get used to the melee: to manoeuvring a vehicle in a traffic jam, to the rules for driven rather than walking access to a city. Early one morning I set off east, hoping to find the place where, decades earlier, I had stood with my father beside the Thames Estuary. The sun was rising and Commercial Road, with its street sweepers and swaying drunks returning home, was suffused with a flush of rosy light. Workers were eating breakfast behind the greasy windows of small cafés with Italian names, where the only breakfast was English, with bitter tea poured from large metal teapots. I followed the signs out of town, heading for places whose names I thought I had recognized, mindful that nothing can guide one into the unknown as skilfully as memory. I stopped at various spots along the way to watch the Thames grow gradually broader, while retaining its strange London distinctiveness from the countryside it flowed through. In Gravesend I ate a bag of chips with vinegar and stared across at Tilbury Docks, trying to picture the scene as it had been some decades earlier: what was there then, what could I have seen, or not seen? The rosy dawn had given way to a cloudy day, with a strong wind and good visibility, and I could make out stacks of containers between the modestly employed cranes on the far bank; they looked like small towns, clandestine settlements that had sprung out of nothing at the edges of cities, rivers and oceans. Gulls circled overhead, emitting their piercing shrieks, the tide pushed upstream, on a meadow between factories horses grazed peacefully beside pools of water that mirrored the sky. I walked along the shore of the Isle of Grain, collecting smooth stones and poking my finger at soft clumps of black between mussel shells and indeterminate pieces of flotsam. The black was crude oil waiting to turn back into stone while enormous tankers slid out into the estuary. By evening I was standing on the beach at Sheerness. This was where the Medway flowed into the Thames, which in fact was no longer a river, for it had opened its maw too wide for the sea, as if imagining itself the swallower rather than the swallowed. The borders here were blurred, and only by comparing different tones of grey could one guess where one body of water ended and another began, although even that was probably an illusion. Huge cargo vessels pushed towards the harbour and fishing boats lay far out to sea. The opposite shore appeared as a soft, almost vaporous mass. It was getting dark, and lights flickered on, a series of brightly coloured lamps that seemed to me to be blinking at short intervals and sending signals, although I could make no sense of their message. Perhaps it was here that my father and I had stood all those years ago on our way back to the continent, and perhaps that was what the distant signals were trying to tell me.

Some time later I set out along the north bank of the Thames to search for the lights I had seen from Sheerness. I wanted to stay close to the river, although I would not be able to see very much as I drove along, and ended up on a minor road with sparse scrub on either side, occasional warehouses, and tall cranes along the riverside, motionless, pointing their bony fingers at the sky. There was a clear view of the country to the south; in the distance, across a terrain of dunes and meadowland on which a number of sturdy farm horses grazed as if left behind and forgotten by some past era, I saw a bustling waterfront, a throng of warehouses, ships, and cranes. A wall of shipping containers towered beyond the meadows, stacks of gigantic rusting crates displaying the names of the big haulage companies, the same names that turned up wherever there were docks and harbours, like Hanjin, Maersk and P&O – they were yellow, red, green and grey, unguarded and unattended. Who-knows-who was counting on the delivery of their content, or hoping it would never arrive, whether they were waiting to be loaded or had just been abandoned there, empty shells waiting to be reoccupied, or containers somebody had written off as lost, stuffed with property that had fallen off the back of a ship and had once meant somebody's livelihood.

The countryside as far as Leigh-on-Sea was drab, endless marshland, so flat it barely looked firm enough to support its patchwork agglomeration of undecided, semi-urban settlements, in whose streets hordes of unruly children ran wild, apparently engaged in some pressing quest, already semi-feral, driven by longing for wilderness and challenging terrain.

When I reached Southend, the tide was out. The sunlight, reflected from the huge expanses of wet silt, was blinding. There were people wading through the mud, collecting something. I strolled along the beach until evening, bending down to pick up shells that looked like the remains – coughed up by the deep blue sea – of fabulous animals that had once wandered the ocean beds before finally sloughing off their paws, turning into fish and seeking fresh domains.

When darkness fell I managed to locate the lights I had seen from Sheerness. The amusement park by the waterfront glinted and glittered in different colours, though it barely had any visitors, only a handful enjoying the curves and turns of the dizzying rollercoaster and twisters, screaming in the way you were meant to do when the gondola went racing down on one of its steep descents, or when the spinning cabins stood upside-down in the air – but their voices were drowned out by the background music and piped pizzazz of the ride adverts.

Beside the biggest rollercoaster with the steepest descents, a monstrous serpentine structure festooned with brilliant lights and crowned with a glittering neon sign, stood a small group of children, each with a yellow band around his or her arm. They turned their faces expectantly to where their carer was buying the tickets, then formed a well-behaved queue onto the small platform where the gondolas were waiting.

I wandered out on the long pier that extended into the estuary. It was almost dark, and the further behind me I left the shore, the more beautiful the amusement park became, a brooch of glass pearls on this ultimate stretch of land between river and sea. For a while the shrill yells and screams, accompanied by the rattle of descending gondolas, still reached me out on the pier, and I wondered whether it was the blind children I was listening to, shrieking as they snaked through the twists and loops of the rollercoaster. Would they feel afraid even without seeing the height from which they were rushing downward? Perhaps they were feigning fear, or simply screaming with pleasure, engrossed in the unpredictability of these ups and downs in their bubble of strange sounds and unrecognizable noises, enjoying the sea wind and fairground food smells, the speeds they had never imagined possible.

At the end of the mile-long pier that jutted into the heaving mass of waves and currents, I was practically on my own. The wind gusted across the platform from every angle and waves crashed against the steel girders below. I stood in the estuary between the sea and the river, between the rows of lights that were Sheerness to the south, and the gay blaze of colour that was Southend's lit-up amusement park on the northern shore, between the enormous cupola of unbroken darkness over the sea in the east, and the distant glow of London in the west. Nothing began here, and nothing ended, and maybe that had been the message of the blinking lights I had seen from Sheerness. This place was the centre that never stood still.

XXXVI. TRANSGRESSION

After the Croat's departure, I often saw Jackie hanging around the entrance to Stoller's storeroom. He would be smoking, and his cheeks, somewhat shadowed, had an unshaven look. His kippah was askew, and had I had occasion to approach him, a bitter smell of self-neglect would not have surprised me. Perhaps he was in mourning. But his stubble stayed stubble and did not grow to a beard; he probably scraped his jowls with a blunt blade now and then so as not to upset Mrs Stoller too much. He lolled against the wall of the closed shop, which formed one side of the doorway. And yet there was so much to be done; the week before Pesach was not for lolling and loitering; it was a week of bustling activity. In the houses of the pious it was a time of thorough, top-to-bottom cleaning. Only afterwards was the week's shopping, leaving out anything leavened, brought in: packets of matzo and eggs, fresh foods and bitter herbs, anything that was considered kosher for the holiday. At Stoller's and Greengrocer Katz's, at the butcher and the fish shop, orders stacked up and there were long queues. In the supermarkets, the less well-off women pushed heavily laden trolleys to the cash desk. A young, observant Jewish woman burst into tears of rage because the cashier refused to accept her husband's credit card. On top of her mountain of shopping, around which stood three pale, bespectacled boys, lay three bunches of tulips, and it was on these that the woman defiantly and protectively laid her hand as she swore it was her own husband's credit card she had handed to the cashier. But the cashier knew no pity, compassion was not part of her vocabulary, although her round face was quite aflutter with its stirrings, and she would have liked simply to wave the young woman through with her children, if she had known how. The other observant women in the queue curbed their impatience; those who were not observant grumbled and sneered. Then a rabbi arrived with his disciples, his gangly students, coat tails flapping, side-locks aquiver under black hats: what was a rabbi doing in a supermarket? He recognized the young woman with her shopping trolley full of unredeemed goods as a member of his community. A few Yiddish words were bandied back and forth, and the woman asked the rabbi to vouch for her. The cashier was embarrassed and at a loss. The rabbi paid for her shopping; the three bunches of tulips could now be taken to her household and would do the young woman's heart good, while her three pale, silent boys might be allowed to misbehave for once.

I spent the week repacking the books, maps and clothes I had taken out of my removal boxes between April and August, and taping the torn cardboard. I packed everything I would not need during my last days here, bundling, stacking, putting everything in order for the removals van that had agreed to come after the holiday and drive the whole lot to a different country. I wrote last letters from my London address, and stood in the post-office queue for the last stamps I would buy here and stick on. I didn't listen to music, I didn't read any books, I didn't take any photographs. Towards evening I walked down to Springfield Park, but went no further than the edge of the slope. I looked across the marsh-land, which was gradually turning a pale green, and over to the river, which shimmered between the almost leafless trees and, as always, was carrying the sky and the swans. Crows were perched on the bare branches, the roof of the conservatory and the dark arborvitaes, as if waiting for something. Or they strutted through the grass and pecked, jerking their heads this way and that, then rose in a flock and resettled in a different place, without making a sound.

There was stillness in the streets in the afternoon before the holiday. Greengrocer Katz's shop was closed. Jackie, in clean clothes and cleanly shaved, walked down the street past my house towards Springfield Park, presumably to sit at the table of a relative who knew some pity. The evening was mild and warm – so mellow in fact, it felt as if the sweetest childhood memories of everybody who lived in the street had come together to see in the spring. Later that evening I sat on the steps to the front garden and watched pedestrians pass in the lamplight; they didn't notice me. I looked up and down the street: in the pool club everybody was on their best behaviour. There were hardly any customers hanging about outside the twenty-four-hour shop on the Stamford Hill corner. The taxi drivers sitting on the bench were spending a quiet evening playing a game laying bets with small chips. I saw observant Jews returning home from festive meals where they had been guests: fathers carrying their sleeping children, mothers pushing prams, tired older children dragging their feet. They had all been listening to the story where the angel passed over the doors of those who had painted their lintels with goat's blood, as a token that they were ready to leave. The token is recognized by the angel who brings perdition only upon the other houses, where people are sleeping and dreaming and not wasting much thought on going anywhere soon. With this angel in their heads, who liked passing over and abrupt departures, the children staggered home to their beds.

There was a slight drizzle when the removal van arrived, so fine it was as if the air had condensed into tiny droplets. A Romanian played the role of supervisor; he took no part in the carrying and packing, but stood at the door sticking yellow labels with numbers onto the objects and boxes as they were carried out, entering each of the items, thus registered, into a list. Forty-three: lamp. One hundred and twenty-seven: sewing machine. From time to time he wiped the drizzle from his forehead as if it were sweat. He was from the Danube delta, he told me, when I asked. He was a true man of the Danube, born in Giurgiu with the flat marshes at his back and his face turned toward the chimneys and harbour cranes of Ruse, in Bulgaria, and had grown up in the delta area, where you could never say whether you were at sea or on dry land, and everything swayed like a boat. He had worked for one or two years as a waiter on a Danube steamer that plied the river between Vienna and Constanţa. He had learned many skills there, including good manners and folding napkins into little hats, or writing long lists of items that had to be purchased whenever the steamer put in. The Romanian recited all this as if it were a part he had learned. I imagined him as a diligent waiter, while the crumbling riverside bluffs of Romania and Serbia passed the windows and portholes, then the marshlands of Romania and Bulgaria, and the landing stages for the ferries with their attendant traders, who shuttled to and fro between river and countryside, their vehicles loaded with cheap goods and their heads crammed with profit margins. He was a river boy who had made good, becoming a supervisor over other boys from other rivers. Meanwhile, the packers shuffled in and out, hardly saying a word. In silence, they carried their articles out, stopped briefly while the Romanian stuck on a label, then carried on to the removal van. They conversed quietly with one another in a language I did not understand. When the packers had loaded everything into the van, I had to sign under the list. The Romanian raised his hand to the side of his head as if performing a military salute and clicked his heels. Somewhere between East London and my destination in Eastern Europe, everything would have to be reloaded. The numbers were necessary to prevent anything going astray. No losses, he said, making it sound like one word: nolossos, a new word that seemed inexplicably related to colossus.

The flat was almost completely empty. Removing my things was like taking away the landscape in which my life – shy and watchful – had kept itself to itself in the gaps, fissures and hollows, on knolls and in bottomless pits. What was left in my rooms looked like clumsily distributed props for some merely theatrical affair, a backdrop whose meaning as a landscape was the object of tacit agreement, but which changed according to which play was on, and applied only to the duration of each performance. I had kept my mattress, which I intended to leave in London. My suitcase stood in the middle of my room, my camera bag hung on the door, a cup stood on the window-sill and a book lay on the mattress. The drama that was due to play out between these things remained as yet obscure.

On the mantelpiece I noticed a picture I had never seen before. It was an old sepia photograph printed on thick card, a small postcard: on the back were lines for the address and a dotted outline for the stamp. The postcard format was a little too large for the print, and there was a broad white margin to the left of the picture with half a sepia-brown fingerprint. Could one of the packers have been carrying a photo like this? A photograph that was evidently so old that the figure portrayed in it could not have had anything directly to do with the life of the packer? Could it have fallen out of a book I had bought from a barrow or second-hand shop and never opened? I couldn't make sense of it. The photograph showed a girl of about eleven. Her bright hair was tied at the nape with a broad white ribbon. She wore a dress embellished with dark bands beneath her ribcage and around her sleeves. She was holding a stick diagonally in front of her with both hands. She had a faintly surprised, questioning look, which was nonetheless assertive and not dreamy. Her face was inclined upwards, her mouth, nose and chin clearly recognizable, and yet, for all the expectant alertness of her expression, her eyes seemed closed and unseeing. She was standing in a garden, behind her a wooden table, bushes and a tall, iron, pointed fence. Everything around the girl – leaves, grass, flowers – was flying towards the blurred edges of the picture, as if caught in a maelstrom that left only this still centre intact: the child's face, breast and arms. I placed the photograph back on the mantelpiece. I did not want to forget it.

The night following the drizzly day was unusually pleasant, with a fragrance that was almost summery. A warm breeze wafted past the windows. The trains sighed in the station; they did not sound overburdened. I sat down on the steps at the front of the house. It was late at night and there were few people about. For the first time I noticed a lit window above Greengrocer Katz's shop. I made out a figure standing at the window who seemed to be shading his or her eyes in an effort to see what was going on in the darkness outside. Suddenly I remembered a scene from a story I had read aloud to my father when a condition of the optic nerve had forced him to stay in bed with bandaged eyes. He wanted me to read out the story in Italian and continually corrected my pronunciation. In the scene in question a man in a room watches the belly and feet of a gecko trying to climb up the outside of his window. The spring was cold that year, and when I read out the story, for reasons that I can no longer fathom, I found it unspeakably sad.

I saw the Stoller's car drawing up in front of the Croat's shop; it stopped in front of the entrance to the storerooms and briefly sounded its horn: a short single blast so as not to wake anyone. I stepped up to the low front garden wall and saw Jackie emerge from the entrance; he was carrying two suitcases. He was only a shadowy, faceless shape in the dark; it was his slight stoop I had recognized, at the same time finding it odd I should believe I had recognized him on the basis of something I had never seen in him before, and had never noted as characteristic, a posture that could only be due to the suitcases, which were evidently heavy. I saw him opening the boot of the car and heaving the suitcases into it. Above the top of the seats I made out the restless heads of the Stoller boys, who ought to have been in bed at this time of night, in the glow of the street lamp. Jackie closed the boot and turned around. He fiddled with something, lifted his arms and held something in front of his face. I felt exposed and hoped he would not notice me in the dark. A moment later I was blinded by the bright flash of a camera, and shut my eyes tightly in shock. The startling brightness hurt my eyes, and when I opened them a few minutes later there were shining tops still spinning in front of me, which took a while to twirl out of my field of vision. The Stoller's car had vanished. The street was more empty than I had ever seen it, and the light in the window above Greengrocer Katz's shop was no longer burning.

XXXVII. KING

In the final days before my departure, everything seemed unusually quiet. Not even birds could be heard in the trees behind the house. Once or twice in the early morning a flock of seagulls drifted over, turned a big circle, then flew off again towards the east. Observant Jews were celebrating their holiday week; Greengrocer Katz's shop stayed shut. The Croat's shop was deserted. There was nobody about at the entrance to Stoller's storeroom. I wandered through the streets listening to the holiday noises escaping from open windows, trying to memorize the light of April days, the tiny blossoms of the weeds between paving stones, the way the repeatedly repaired asphalt had left different tones of grey, which had never struck me before as quite so layered and shaped and scuffed to signs and images. The circles my wanderings took me in became ever smaller, and I hesitated to follow my old route to the river Lea. Perhaps I was worried that I might then postpone my departure again and again, forgetting all my worldly goods stored in distant Eastern Europe, where they would need to be collected and given a place in my new life. Instead I would resume my walks, looking out for things I had not yet seen, or had overlooked, left out or neglected, desirous to fill every gap in a map that was always moving, always rolling and flowing, and which carried the price of such restlessness on its back: that nothing remained the same.

In the night before my departure I could not sleep. I sat in the empty flat. The mattress I was leaving behind was thin, and the floor was hard. There was something that annoyed me in every room: the slant of the streetlight, the smell of the floorboards, the emptiness. My remaining cooking utensils were still in the kitchen: I had wanted to give them to the Croat as a donation for the Bosnian refugees, who, anyway, had long since begun to think of themselves as settled in a new place and did not wish to be reminded of flight and the poverty it brought. As the night came to an end I headed off for a final walk, and I finally ended up going east. It was dark, but in the trees along the roadside the first birds were starting to sing. The tops of the trees were thin and had few leaves, only a few tiny ones that had shot out in the pale sunlight of the recent warmer days, but were not yet big enough to rustle. In the streets of the pious all was quiet in the glow of the street lamps. The lamps over the front doors scattered their light on the entrances and concreted strips in the front gardens. Now and then, there was a movement behind a window, a shadow busying itself at a stove or sink: sleepless housewives, wigless in their seclusion, their bowed heads listening now to the breaking waves of sleep of their big families, now to morning noises outside their homes. The buses on the main road were brightly lit, but there was hardly a passenger to be seen. They sailed up and down the streets, hollow vessels, rollicking and rolling along the thin runnels of their routes and timetables. The Springfield Park gate was still locked. Between the bars I could see into the dark greyness behind the shapes of the trees and bushes, into the final moments of the night over the river Lea, the little alder grove and the reservoirs, where a lighter strip was beginning to open up along the horizon. At first pale light streamed through this opening, which then was flooded by a thin film of red, so that the bare trees in the park, which a few moments earlier had been grey shapes in the darkness, suddenly stood out as black silhouettes. The sky grew brighter, the objects darker. Stripes of purple, turquoise and orange formed layers above the deep-blue edge of the Earth. A flock of birds flew up, short croaks issuing from their black throats. In the middle of the round lawn arose a figure that must have been lying there motionless and doubled up all along, a shapeless thing, which, with my eyes focussed on the horizon, I must have taken for a low-lying bush. Against the morning sky the figure appeared gigantic. A personage with a headdress that bounced and splayed in all directions: a many-feathered cap, black and jagged in the rising light. Below his slim, elongated torso hung a shabby, tattered little skirt that flapped about his skinny legs. The King was back. Escaped from the custody of his carers, where he had been taken before my very eyes, he was probably now sleeping rough among the bushes of Springfield Park and within shouting distance of his former accommodation. I imagined him uttering sounds at night, which the two women in the ground-floor flat would be likely to recognize. A voice calling them by name out of the darkness as if from a far and foreign place, or calling to a foreign place from a home-like place, or as a threat that would make them close the window. The King's little skirt had lost the splendour of the robe he wore when I had encountered him on autumn evenings, but it retained a dull gleam that seemed to dwell in individual threads, flecks and feathers, the trappings of a king from a foreign land who was going about his kingly duties here as well as he could. The King raised his arms and curled his fingers to form trembling, twitching, hollow fists. His headdress puffed itself up, ruffled its feathers, a plumed creature standing in as a crown on his regal head, starting to shine in the steadily intensifying light. The King turned in a circle as the sun rose red and orange over the marshlands. He stretched his upper body and arms: the birds flocked around him, a gold thread in the flimsy remnants of his feather-patterned ceremonial dress feebly glimmered. The King paused for a moment, tensed his body, gathered all his strength for a leap, and with his arms flailing lifted from the lawn and joined the flock of circling birds: hovering in the air just above the ground, sunlight streaming between his hovering foot and the pale grass. He was a King among his subjects – the King was flying! Then he fell lengthways on the ground. The sun's rays spread over him, and their radiance made gold sparks glint on his skirt. When the King fell, ending his short flight, the birds took fright and flapped away with a great whirring of wings, and now they returned and circled above him before settling on the lawn and strutting back and forth around him, their heads jerking up and down as they did so. Were they pecking at him with their beaks? Were they trying to wake him? Were they picking the flesh from his bones – this relic of a king, this crashed flying object? Then a great torrent of light poured over the park, the fallen King and the birds, immersing everything in that glaring superabundance of brightness with which days begin that will pass away in rainy gloom, a luminosity that made each object stand out for a brief moment in sharp relief before squandering itself in an exuberant radiance that melted to fool's gold and the sunburst delusions of cold spring days, glimmering, glistening, sparkling, and finally dissolving in a blinding, golden tremor, in which all that had accompanied me in the past months evaporated like a cloud succumbing to sunlight, and this effulgence, which broke over all I could see, transformed the marshland beyond the river Lea and the Lea itself into a shoreline that could barely be distinguished from the sea, and which, as it rose and fell like the surf, let all that was built on it founder.

Acknowledgements

This book could not have been written without the support of my husband, reader, and walking companion of many years, Martin Chalmers (1948 – 2014) who first made me aware of the innumerable echoes of our steps on the streets of London. Chapter XI, 'St Lawrence River', is an amended and slightly extended version of his initial translation.

This book has been selected to receive financial assistance from English PEN's 'PEN Translates' programme, supported by Arts Council England. English PEN exists to promote literature and our understanding of it, to uphold writers' freedoms around the world, to campaign against the persecution and imprisonment of writers for stating their views, and to promote the friendly co-operation of writers and the free exchange of ideas.

www.englishpen.org

Supported using public funding by
ARTS COUNCIL
ENGLAND

Fitzcarraldo Editions
8-12 Creekside
London, SE8 3DX
United Kingdom

Copyright © Matthes & Seitz Berlin, 2014
All rights reserved by and controlled through
MSB Matthes & Seitz Berlin, Verlagsgesellschaft mbH
Translation copyright © Iain Galbraith, 2018
This third edition published in Great Britain
by Fitzcarraldo Editions in 2019

ISBN 978-1-910695-29-6

Design by Ray O'Meara
Typeset in Fitzcarraldo
Printed and bound by TJ International

The translation of this work was supported by
a grant from the Goethe-Institut London

Fitzcarraldo Editions